MW01008671

HOUSE OF BANE AND BLOOD

ALEXIS L. MENARD

Midnight Tide
PUBLISHING

Copyright © 2023 by Alexis L. Menard

All rights reserved.

No part of this book may be reproduced in any form or by any electronic or mechanical means, including information storage and retrieval systems, without written permission from the author, except for the use of brief quotations in a book review.

Developmental and Copy edits: Brittany Corley

Proofreading: Molly Spain

Map Design: Andrés Aguirre

Character Art Illustration: Bella Bergolts

Exterior cover design: Gretchen Cobaugh

CONTENTS

AUTHOR NOTE

Content Warnings:

House of Bane and Blood is a new adult fantasy romance book that contains strong language and content some readers may find distressing including profanity, tobacco and alcohol use, graphic sexual content, mentioned death of a parent and sibling, gaslighting family members, brief breath play, and mentions of suicide. If there is something not included in this list that you as the reader found distressing, please do not hesitate to reach out to the author so it can be added.

For the ones who lost themselves trying to please everyone. You can still be anything you want to be.

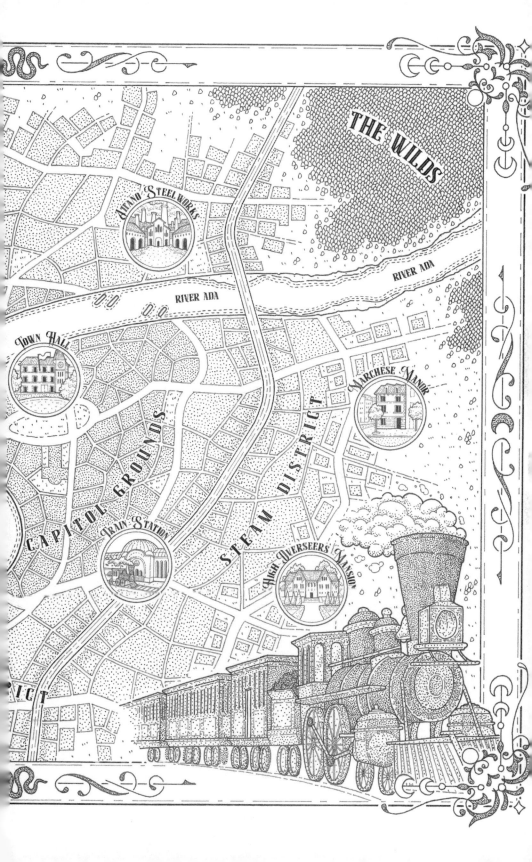

Orders of the Descendents

The classification of the Remni and their descended

Bane

Benders
Darkthieves

Blood

Wearhs
Haelins

Mirth

Scolapa
Mentalus
Shifters

Giver & Greed

All mortals from the original
age of creation

Chaos

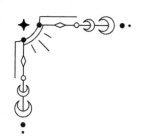
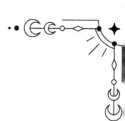

PROLOGUE

The coarse grind of a cell wall caused his eyes to flutter open. He wasn't sleeping. He couldn't sleep here. Not with the noises that relentlessly moaned through the shifting walls. There were no doors, no windows, no light beside the single candle that melted into the floor. No kind sound beyond the screams of his fellow inmates and the wind beating the black cliffs of the island, whistling between the cracks of the exterior fortification. There was nothing here but his broken body, his long-brewed revenge, and the walls that moved and shuffled like a house of cards.

A visitor stood on the other side of the cutout leading beyond his cell, where his enclosure sat at the end of a hall. He pushed off his cot on the floor, the thin pad always cold from the lack of heat source. The man before him wore the wrapped robes of the watchman; the guards who served the Overseer. The golden belt around his waist showed he was of substantial rank, possibly a captain from the assessment of brilliant medals decorating the breast of his uniform.

He always found it amusing that they gave themselves military

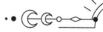

titles. Armies weren't necessary when there were no kingdoms to conquer, no wars to fight. They were merely guards who looked over the cities, enforcing the hands of the Inner Courts and the elite bloodlines that influenced them.

"Get up," the watchman demanded.

"What for?"

The visitor huffed a breath of annoyance. He was a prisoner with no right to question the guards. It didn't matter what they wanted or where they were taking him, he would eventually submit to their demands—by will or by force.

The guard pulled out a metal beater, a not-so-subtle form of encouragement. Had his remnant not been dulled by the glint they stuffed him with, he would have put this guard on his back and shoved that beater somewhere darker than this hole in the world.

But he didn't have his abilities, so he pushed off the porous floor. The textured stone cut into his callouses, bit into his bare feet, making it impossible to feel anything besides those small, gnawing bits of constant discomfort. Without glancing at the lines he scratched on the wall recording his time here, all 1,432 of them, he followed the guard, who didn't even bother using the chains clipped to his belt.

He wondered how the man could move the walls against the clock's schedule, the master of the maze housing the criminals of the Isle. There were no saints that gifted their Remni with the ability to bend the world in such a way, and he would know if there were. The scraping of stone set his teeth grinding. It was a song that played forever here, and yet he had never gotten used to the way the tune rattled the marrow in his bones.

He followed the watchman up several flights of stairs appearing behind another slab of wall, the pattern of their movement so inconsistent it left him too disoriented to remember the path they took.

Not that it truly mattered. There was no escape from Hightower, and his own remnant could not move stone like the man in front of him.

They broke the surface, coming up to the prison's ground level. He knew this because for the first time in 1,432 days, he saw the sky through the oculus above. Grey and sullen, rain spilled over the glass like tears over his fate. As if someone divine cared about the injustice trapped inside this glass cage. It matched the last time he saw it all those years ago, and he wondered if he would ever see the sun again. If he would ever feel *warm* again. Unlikely, seeing as he still had a lifetime left to serve in this place.

This rotting place inside the earth, far from sun and smiles, had pestled his hope into a fine powder of pity.

The top floor was an empty, circular room that he vaguely remembered being dragged through his first day here. The entrance to the prison was just ahead, a beam of glaring light split by the front doors, the last set of many pairs that led to the stormy world beyond. From here, he could smell the salt from the ocean on the draft, something different than the stench of his own filthy body in his cell. Eight corridors sprawled around the perimeter like the legs of an arachnid. The man he followed gestured with his beater toward one of them.

"Third door on the right. If you dare lift your hand in that room, I'll cut it off before you can do anything to harm the inspector," he warned.

The prisoner scoffed. "They fed me three days ago. A ten-year-old could beat me in a fight. Put that stick away before you hurt yourself."

The guard glared at him as he passed, and he met his stare with mutual apathy. His body found a reserve of strength, eager to find out why the inspector, a man only second to the High Overseer himself, requested a visit with him of all prisoners, and followed the watchman's directions to a room off the hall.

Six members of the Watch stood inside, and he took a seat in one of the leather armchairs where their stares pointed. The man he assumed was the inspector sat in a matching one across a rug from him, his station noted by the black suit he wore, tailor cut and fitted like it had been designed for his frame. Pinned to his lapel was the Order of Inner Court's sigil, a golden eagle surrounded by four gemstones of alternating colors, representing and glorifying each of the saints.

For a governing body who cared so much about honoring their saintly origins, they sure treated their descendants like vermin.

"You may leave us," he told his cadre. The men glanced at each other but conceded, shutting the door behind them. The inspector swirled the amber drink in his glass, sipping it as a nearby clock broke the quiet. This was a holding room from the looks of it, with bare walls and another glass ceiling. Lockers lined the back wall behind a table with no chairs around it. This room was not set up for this kind of meeting. This was not protocol.

The inspector finally spoke. "Well, look at you. I didn't recognize you at first. You've grown almost a head taller."

"I was practically a child when your predecessor threw me in here," he spat. "Prison such as this one is not a healthy home for a young man. It changes us. It changed me."

The man nodded, and the smile he wore in welcome gradually faded. "Be that as it may, I don't have much time to speak with you. I'm sure you're wondering why you are here, and by that, I mean this room. You know why you were sent to Hightower."

"Is my family alright? Has something happened?"

The inspector waved a hand, dismissing his questions. "Your

family is fine. I want to make a deal with you, one that will shorten your sentence."

"By how much?"

His smile returned, a cruel thing to witness. "By a lifetime."

A lifetime. That was what the judge had ordered for a false accusation thrown at a boy only sixteen years of age. "Are you saying . . ."

"Yes." He pulled out a piece of paper. A contract. "I have jobs I need done, and I need someone like you to complete them."

He took the paper from the inspector and read over the fine print. It was an acquittal. *His* acquittal. His full name written right there in black ink upon fresh parchment. "What are these jobs?" he asked. Not that it mattered. The inspector knew he'd take it, like dangling a bone in front of a starved dog.

"We cannot speak of them here. But I will be frank: They are dangerous and cutthroat and if you are caught, I will not help you get out of the charges. These jobs cannot, under any circumstances, be traced back to me. Do you understand?"

"You mean for me to kill people." He'd never done such a thing, but the men in his family were well experienced in the area. It was a rite of passage in the kind of life they lived, in their circles of competing pedigrees.

The inspector nodded, staring hard at the prisoner's reaction, possibly recording anything that looked like hesitation. "It is for the good of the Isle. You will be doing your country a service."

But this was not his country. His kind had never been welcomed here, even after the contributions they made to the Isle. "My cousin is here too. I want him out, then you'll have a deal, Inspector."

He sucked a cheek in thought, then finally nodded. "Alright. He goes free as well, but should you break this contract, you both will face the consequences. Is that clear?"

The prisoner agreed.

The inspector signed his acquittal, and the guards brought him the clothes he had worn here, now at least four sizes too small. They gave him a spare uniform, and he followed the man who had given him freedom straight out the front doors.

"And remember, son," the inspector said before they boarded a ship back to the mainland. "If you dare to disobey a single order, I'll make sure you end up right back here." He turned and left him standing on the grassy bank, letting the east wind fill his chest with fresh air.

He still wasn't free. Not entirely. This was just another incarceration dressed in the same colors as freedom. But as his feet hit the bare earth instead of cold obsidian, as the clouds in the grey sky parted and the prodigal sunlight beamed upon his face again, he felt a new hope begin to rise from a shadowed place within his soul.

The chains of this deal had some slack. He could have it all again, even doing the inspector's dirty work. Everything he wanted, it all existed outside of Hightower. His old life, his family, his revenge.

And most importantly, Camilla Marchese.

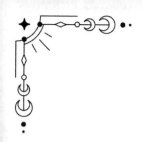
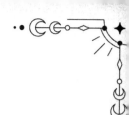

CHAPTER I
CAMILLA

Two Years Later

My driver was late.

I told him the exact hour and minute to meet me near the gate of our driveway, and every second that ticked over that order sent my heart racing faster. If anyone caught me and told my brothers, I'd be an even darker stain on the family tree. Thankfully, the carriage came into view a few minutes later, and I released a foggy breath, jumping into the cabin before the car even came to a stop.

"Where to, Miss Marchese?" the driver asked through the grate.

"The First Sector. Drop me off at the corner of Burnwick and Dellany."

"But ma'am, that's—"

"I know. Which is why I'm paying you so well," I reminded him. He must have been new to our armada, questioning me.

It wasn't my first time sneaking out, nor venturing across the

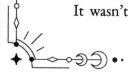
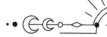

Ada by myself. Giles once told me about a pub near the crossing of those streets that poured ale straight from a tap, and ever since I'd risked the endless scolding of my eldest brother every third Saturday of the month, when Aramis spent his own nights at the Vasilli Hotel downtown playing cards and gambling what little funds we had left.

Tonight, I imagined, could be the last time I had the opportunity to get away. Whatever my betrothed was like, I'm sure he wouldn't take too kindly to letting his bride sneak across the boundary of the river, where our rivals ruled and reigned with their powerful remnants. It was worth the risk, having a last bite of freedom—or, in this case, the last sip of gloriously cold, mind-clearing mead.

It was nearly midnight by the time he dropped me off. I'd only have an hour or two to waste here if I wanted to be home before Aramis, but an hour was all I needed. Tendrils of fog curled around my ankles as I approached, as if they were trying to snatch me and drag me away from the corner establishment glowing against the darkened, sleeping street.

House of Bane.

The pub was packed as usual. I pulled my hood away from my curls but kept my face low until I reached the bar, which—for some reason—was completely open despite two men occupying the far-right barstools. No one knew me on this side of the river. I was just a notorious name here, my face as undistinguished as anyone else in this room.

The barman was hesitant to take my order, glancing at the pair to my right. "Is something wrong?" I asked him. The dynamic was new, so unlike my last visits.

"Of course not," the man a few seats down replied instead. He kept his chin down, his hat pulled low to conceal his eyes, which, by the slight turn of his chin, I guessed to be staring at me as I draped my coat over the back of my chair. Any detail of his face was obscured by the white smoke ribboning from his cigarillo propped on an ashtray.

He nodded to the barman. "Get her an ale, Dom."

I scoffed, glaring at the man who assumed my choice. Even if he wasn't wrong. "What if I don't want an ale?"

"That's what all the natives want who dare this side of the city."

I frowned. "How do you know I'm a native? You don't even know me." There were no discernable features between those who possessed remnants and those who didn't. Just where we lived in the city—unless he *did* know who I was. My right hand slid across the thin material of my dress, where a dipped dagger was sheathed just above the hem.

"Exactly. I don't know you," he said as he pressed out the blaze of his smoke, "and I know every descendant in Lynchaven that comes here. Which means you must be from across the river."

"Frequent patron?" I asked as Dom placed an ale on the polished golden wood in front of me.

He canted his head. "You could say that."

I took a sip of my drink. Cold and crisp, a hint of honeyed sweetness flooded my palate, and I failed to suppress a moan at the delightful taste. His head swiveled slowly back in my direction, as if the sound had called him.

"Enjoying yourself?" he asked, a hint of amusement in his deep voice.

"Immensely." I smiled. I think for the first time all week.

My gaze slipped to the side, glancing at him, and found him still looking my way. He had removed his hat, revealing his eyes. The first glimpse of them reminded me of the grey toning of this city—as if it had sunk itself into his stare. The second time I caught them, I found it difficult to look away. He was strikingly handsome, owning a smirk that was unnaturally mischievous.

"Is there something I can help you with?" I asked when his side glances became obnoxiously obvious.

"May I sit with you?"

My fingers rolled the beaded fringe border of my dress. The idea of sitting closer sent a thrill through my nerves. "It would be rude to abandon your friend, don't you think?" I asked him, testing the waters to see just how eager his current ran as well.

He waved a hand dismissively. "*Ahh*, he was just leaving. Weren't you, cousin?" A not-so-subtle nudge to the ribs had the man jumping out of his seat.

His company sighed, shot back the rest of his brandy, and slid it down the bar to the barman. "That's right, I just realized I need to be anywhere but here. See you in the morning, boss." The second tipped his hat to me to bid farewell. "Goodnight, miss."

And then it was just the two of us at the bar, and far too many stools between us.

He solved that, swapping his seat for the one right next to mine. Dom had begun to take orders at the furthest end of the bar, drawing the patrons away from us.

"What's your name?" he asked before taking a sip of his drink.

"Milla." There were only two people in the world who called me that, and one of them was dead. It felt like the safest option—and not entirely a lie.

"Milla," he repeated, slowly, as if testing it in his mouth.

"And yours?"

"Nico."

I arched my brow. "Just Nico?"

Those perfect lips stretched. "For tonight, just Nico. Perhaps I can get you to come here again to get the rest of it."

Guilt pinched my heart. Not for Felix, but for leading this man into believing I was available. I swallowed a bit of ale to chase the bitterness of it all. "Unfortunately, this will be my last visit."

He cocked his head. "Why is that?"

"I'm getting married tomorrow." I hated how saying the words out loud made it more real. Even more so than the contracted agreement still sitting on my desk.

Nico hummed a thoughtful note. "I don't see a ring."

"That's because it's around my throat." Attached to the proverbial leash my brother pulled me around with.

Without warning, he reached for my neck. Leather-clad fingers pressed against my skin and traced a line across the column of my throat. My breath hitched when they lingered a few seconds too long. "I don't see a collar. You look like you're still free to me."

"Not all cages are built with bars." Some, like mine, were made from the shackles of duty and the chains of domestic obligations.

Those gloved fingertips slipped beneath my jaw, turned my chin to face him with a whisper of pressure. "This marriage was arranged, wasn't it? You don't want to marry this person." It wasn't a question exactly, but an observation. A keen one on his part.

"No," I finally admitted out loud, "but I have to."

He shrugged and leaned back in his seat. "No one's holding a gun to your head. You could always run away."

I laughed at the idea. "I wish, but unfortunately, my family needs this marriage, and I need it to take care of them."

His attention remained inquisitive. "Would you like to run away, just for tonight, then?"

My smile fell. "What are you asking me, Nico?"

He gestured with his chin towards the band playing a smooth beat in the corner of the bar. "Would you like to dance?"

Yes. Hells yes. Absolutely. I'd love to. All the ways I wanted to accept his offer hung just on the end of my tongue, waiting to be released. But the hour grew late, and my carriage was returning soon. As lovely as he was, he wasn't worth the trouble I'd start with my family if I wasn't back in time.

Was he?

I glanced at the flock of bodies between us and the band. "I think the dance floor is full."

"So it is." He motioned for Dom, who leaned forward to catch the words Nico muttered across the bar. Even though he dropped his voice, I could still read three words from his perfect lips.

Shut it down.

I watched in terrified awe as Dom shifted from barman to thug, untying the apron at his waist to reveal a gun sheathed at his side. He started barking orders, shouting at people to *get out* and that they were *closing up*. It took less than three minutes before the bewildered patrons were shuffled out the front doors by the rest of the bar staff.

The band never missed a beat. Nico returned his attention to me. "How about now?"

I let loose a nervous laugh that felt too loud without the noise of the crowd to compete. "Who *are* you?" I asked, more fascinated than ever.

He stood from his chair and offered his hand, still wearing his gloves. "Just a simple businessman."

Before I snatched that waiting hand, I challenged him. "Give me your best sales pitch, then."

His tongue darted between his lips and slid along his teeth. "I plan on seducing you. Simple as that."

I winced. "That is a terrible pitch!"

"It only has to work once." He offered his hand out again.

I laced my fingers between his, convinced by the charm in his smirk. Any concern I had for my brother's opinion was chased away by the palm of his hand. "Well, from one boss to another," I said, following him to the center of the room, "you should know that throwing out your patrons is bad for business."

He pulled me close, slipping his opposite hand around my waist. Something about the way that hand touched me, though its placement was that of a gentleman, was corrupting, tempting my imagination to dream up forbidden images.

"Do you usually flirt by giving out unsolicited business advice?"

"About as often as you clear your pub for random women." My fingers sprawled over his chest, skating over the ripple of muscle to catch his neck. His breath hit me with a sigh, and the gentle guide of his hand on my hip pushed me closer, until there was a sliver of space between our chests.

He cleared his throat; that soft smile never faltered. "Who is this fiancé of yours?"

Just the mention of him made all the heat in my body go cold. "Why do you want to know?"

"So I know whom to curse tonight in my prayers."

"In that case," I drawled, "his name is Felix Firenze."

He slowed to a near stop, just briefly, before picking up the pace again. "The alchemist, eh?"

"You know him?"

"I've met him a few times." Judging by the bitterness in his voice, they weren't fond memories.

"That's a few more than I can claim." I sighed, feeling the weight of those shackles and chains return link by link, until my shoulders drooped. My hand slipped from his neck, smoothed down his shirt and vest—black on black with a silver tie. He dressed well for a bar owner. The band seamlessly transitioned into the next song, maintaining a slow, sultry tempo.

"Let's not talk about the bastard," he said with a lift in his voice. "Tonight is for you, Milla. Tell me more about yourself."

The hand on my back dipped a fraction lower, pushing me toward him until our hips moved together. "What would you like to know?"

His grin returned, threatening to unravel every dirty secret with its lure. "Everything."

I DIDN'T TELL him *everything* for obvious reasons. There just simply wasn't enough moonlight to explain how I was the sole heiress of a multigenerational railway company, and my brothers too discernibly resented me for it. I couldn't tell him it was my fault the family legacy was at risk, or that we owed the Order of Inner Courts over a hundred thousand reoles, and the Firenzes were buying my hand in exchange for a portion of the company.

I couldn't tell him my name was Camilla Marchese because that name held a reputation on this side of the city that could have me killed—or worse—extorted.

Instead, we talked about my childhood, where I grew up, what I would do with my life had I not been betrothed to an alchemist. Somehow, the conversation led to my extensive allergy list.

"How are you allergic to so much? What do you eat?" His face twisted, as if my biology was ridiculous.

I shrugged. "I eat a balanced diet of bread, venison, and whiskey. Apparently, ale is fine as well. I've had three of these so far and I've yet to blow up."

He shook his head, exasperated. "That sounds incredibly tedious."

"About as tedious as your relationship with whoever cuts your hair."

"What's wrong with my hair?"

I smiled. "Nothing. I've just never met a man with your kind of hands look so posh. You must get it trimmed at least once a week to maintain such a harsh undercut."

"Posh," he snorted. "You come in here flaunting around in your Livetan silk dress and Romani heels, and you have the nerve to call *me* posh." When I had finally stopped giggling, he asked me, "What do you mean by my kind of hands?"

I felt my cheeks flame. "Nothing."

"Milla," he murmured. "You're about to walk out of my life forever. You can tell me anything, and it will all cease to matter as soon as the sun rises in a few hours."

A few hours? *Saints*, I had stayed out far past my curfew. But he was right. I'd never see him again after this, and even if by some miracle I did, I wouldn't be his Milla. We would both be a memory by morning. I took one of his gloved hands in both of mine, lacing our fingers together.

"I won't pretend like I have a lot of experience with a man's touch," I admitted, "but you have a strength in your hands, which even in its gentlest form has a possessiveness behind it. Like you know what you want, and you aren't afraid to take it. I've never felt that in a single touch before."

"Strength?" he asked.

I shook my head. "Desire."

His gaze heated, glancing at my lips. "Dom?"

"Yes, sir?"

"Leave."

Dom left without even putting back the glass he was drying.

He brought our intertwined hands to his chest, to the place above his heart. "You think I desire you, princess?"

I was inexperienced, not naïve. The ale was providing the key

17

confidence I had lacked hours earlier. Leaning forward an inch, I shamelessly drew his stare to where my dress fell open at the top and exposed a peek of my breasts.

"Don't you, Nico?"

His answer came out too slow. "Yes."

Oh, *saints.*

He brought my hand to his lips, placed a featherlight kiss on the back of my palm, and I felt it *everywhere.* "Would you like to go upstairs for a bit more privacy? I've got shit I want to forget, but I can't. Maybe we can help each other tonight."

"I've never . . ." I looked at my empty mug. What was I trying to admit to him? "I don't do hookups."

He shrugged. "We can do whatever you want. Talk. Kiss. Sleep. *Not* sleep. I just don't want you to go home yet. And if you give me too much free time tonight, I might find your fiancé and kill him."

Giver and Greed. I think he was being serious.

He was so convincing, and truly, what did I have to lose? I was giving up the rest of my life tomorrow to save my family. Surely I could indulge my own wants for a few hours. It was a once-in-a-lifetime opportunity, the way I saw it.

I *needed* to do something reckless before I was bound to a chemical craver. For myself. For the curiosity that would turn into regret if I turned him down. Besides, I didn't want Felix's blood on my hands.

Yet.

I needed his money.

I finally nodded and reached for my purse tucked into my coat. "Let me pay for these. I'll meet you by the stairs."

His smirk returned with a vengeance. "It's on the house, princess."

Nico snatched my hand and pulled me off the stool.

———————— ❋ ————————

ABOVE THE BAR WAS AN APARTMENT. He mentioned something about owning it. I didn't hear, nor did I care. The minute I tossed my coat across the chaise, his hands were on my hips and my own slipped around his neck, climbing into the short, faded cut of his hair.

"I'll warn you," I murmured into his mouth as he lowered his face an inch from mine. Expensive liquor laced his breath, sandalwood and vanilla cologne followed close behind. "I'm covered in glint-dipped blades you'll never find on your own."

"Is that a challenge?"

"If you need one."

"*Seven hells*," he breathed. "I want to kiss you."

My mouth went dry. All the confidence I used to walk up here had completely drained. I nodded anyway. "Then why haven't you?"

"You haven't asked me." His head dipped lower, passing my lips. The tip of his nose ran a race across the curve of my throat, teasing my skin with a better sensation. In the side of my vision, I noticed a bed pushed against a wall, half made and draped in moonlight from the single window perched above it. The curtains were drawn wide to reveal a view of half the street and a full moon surrounded by stars.

"Should we get more comfortable?"

A coarse sound of agreement trembled his body beneath my palms. His hands slipped from my waist to grab my own, to lead us toward the bed. He sat on the edge, gently tugged me down to sit in his lap. When he saw my hesitance, he said, "We can stop whenever you want, Milla. But I'm begging you, stay with me a little longer."

I smiled, relished in that plea communicated in his eyes, felt the power that came from being wanted. And after a lifetime of having so little of it, it felt good to have control. Especially when it came with the reward of his touch.

I straddled his waist and sat in his lap, my hands finding home on the broad blades of his shoulders. My center naturally pressed against a massive bulge in his tailored pants, too clear now just how much he desired me. It took every ounce of restraint not to rock my hips and chase a mutual need.

"Milla?" he whispered, eyes darting to my arm. "Did your tattoo just move?"

My body stiffened, glancing to the side toward my shoulder. Sure enough, the inky beast was sliding down my arm, inching her way toward the man at the end of my fingertips. I slapped her diamond head, and she retreated up my arm, over the crest of my shoulder, hiding under the fabric of my dress.

"Sorry about that," I said with a breathy laugh. "It's just a familiar. She can't bite you or anything."

"Pity," he murmured, dimples formed in both cheeks. "What's her use?"

"Protection," I said, settling deeper over his hips. Familiars like my serpent were rare, even in the Row where magic was a part of everyday life.

"Protection?" he repeated. "I thought you didn't do hookups."

I slapped him lightly on the shoulder. "Not *that* kind of protection."

He chuckled and smoothed his hands up the outer edges of my thighs. Thankful he had dropped the subject, I placed a palm on either side of his face. I didn't know what I was doing—I certainly didn't do this. I didn't kiss strangers or follow men to their apartments above fancy bars. Certainly, I'd regret this in the morning, but I'd rather be remorseful of him than never know.

He was a mistake—the most gorgeous one I would ever make.

"Take off your gloves," I demanded. I wanted to feel his skin on my skin. The warmth of his hands through the thin material of my dress.

"Alright, just don't . . . panic," he murmured, but obeyed.

"Why would I—*oh*."

Looking between us, I discovered his left hand was completely made of metal. A false hand composed of gold-plated tubes, connecting at a point in his wrist to a solid mesh of pipes that composed his forearm. "Oh, *wow*. How do you . . . how does it work?"

He wiggled the metal fingers in show as I examined it, completely enthralled. "Each tube is hollow, and I bend the air inside them with my remnant to move them. It was difficult to learn at first, but now it's as easy as any other involuntary thought, and I can operate it as effortlessly as my real one."

"That's incredible. You're a bender?" It made sense. Bane was the saint formed from the Creator's hands. His remnant controlled the natural elements, even sound and time if a descendant was fortunate enough to inherit such a rarity.

His proud smirk slowly faded. "Yes."

If he thought that would make me nervous, he was misguided. Descendants didn't intimidate me, nor did their abilities. It could easily be silenced with the blades at my thighs—the ones he currently traced with his pointer finger.

"Where did you get these?" he asked.

"My arsenal?"

"Not the knives, princess." His smile flashed. "These scars."

His touch ran over the thick, pink and white flesh that decorated the back of my thighs, ran all the way up my back to my left shoulder. I shrugged indifferently, as he had. "A fire. I was in a train crash a few years ago. A brave soul pulled me out before I perished."

His hand paused, and he blinked several times before speaking again. "A train crash? That . . . that must have been traumatic."

I nodded. The energy between us died a little. Nico, sensing this as I did, gripped my thighs with a new urgency. He rolled on his back and flipped me to the side, so we lay next to each other, our limbs somehow entangled. My heels had gone missing somewhere between the door and the bed.

"Are you ever going to kiss me, Nico?" I asked.

He smirked, his head resting on a fist. At last, he loomed over me, dipped his head until our lips barely brushed while his false hand cradled my chin to keep it steady. Nothing more than a graze, followed by a soft pinch of my lip between his, and it still somehow stole my breath, left me dizzy.

"Why did you invite me up here?" I blinked the stars away.

"Because," he said and brushed my hair aside, studying the line of my jaw with a finger, "I think you are the most beautiful thing in this city, Milla, and I am an admirer of beautiful things."

The way he said it, I believed every word as truth. My chest ebbed and rose like the tide in a storm, and yet the air felt unsatiating. If I stayed any longer, I'd leave here . . . well, not as inexperienced.

I swallowed. "I should go home, Nico."

He nodded slowly. "I'll drive you."

"I can call a carriage—"

"The cars don't run this late in the Row. Let me drive." He brought my hand to his lips, kissed the inside of my wrist with a convincing peck. "I'd be beside myself if anything happened to you on your way home after I kept you out all night. Grant me more time with you. Please."

He didn't seem the type of man to grovel. Assuming he was my only option at this point, I conceded with a shrug and a hesitant grin.

If he, a descendant, felt safe enough crossing the river to the Districts, then it wasn't necessary to deny him.

Nico had a carriage in the backstreet running behind the business block. There was no driver, but that wasn't exactly abnormal. A bar owner would most likely keep his payroll slim without gratuitous staff.

"You forgot your coat." I noticed as I sat next to him in the driver's seat.

He pushed his cap low over his forehead. "I guess you'll have to keep me warm, Milla. Where to?"

"Bellagio Street. That's—"

"On the east side of town. I knew you were a rich girl." He winked.

Our banter ceased as he drove the horses toward the bridge, yet our bodies seemed to keep up the conversation we had started in his apartment. I was for once thankful for the slamming cold marking the first weeks of winter, chilling the heat this man brewed beneath my skin.

"This isn't a house," he said, assessing where I made him stop.

I smiled at his confusion. "I'll walk from here."

The Main Station for the Iron Saint was just a few blocks from home. It was the safest route to walk alone at night and the easiest way to keep him from following me. I had played a dangerous game, getting close to this descendant tonight. If he had found out my last name, I would've been in grave trouble. As a fellow remnant of Bane, he could turn me over to my family's biggest rival, the Attano Benders. Saints knew they had the money to pay him well for my taking.

I suppressed a shiver at the thought.

He parked the horses, and I turned in the seat to thank him properly for the ride. "It was a pleasure, Nico. Thank you for the lovely evening and the ride back. I hope this won't be the last time our paths cross."

Lifting my hand to his lips, he placed a drawn-out kiss on the back of my palm before letting it slip through his fingers. "Something tells me we'll meet again soon, Milla."

I almost asked how he was so sure, but the clock tower chimed four times, beckoning a more urgent matter. So I stole one last look at him and committed those eyes of steel and sanctuary to memory and gestured him off. Only when his carriage disappeared in the twilight did I start the short walk home, praying to every saint lost in the void Nico's penchant was right.

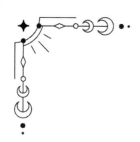
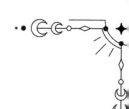

CHAPTER 2
CAMILLA

A long line of white smoke split the distance into city and sky as the steam train whistled its departure. I watched through the rain rolling down the glass window, listening to the hissing demand of my ancestral burden. The combination of burning coal, boiling water, and pumping pistons had become my family's greatest weapons on this smear of land. Remnants had magic, but we had something better—we had science. We had steam.

But soon, we would have war.

My eldest brother, Aramis, stood beside Inspector Gavriel Hawthorn, who currently held an eviction notice. After seven generations of Marcheses had sat in this office, looked out over the city we once owned through the same frosted windows, the entire empire they had built from their blood, sweat, and tears was falling. All thanks to me.

Yet somehow, at the last second of the eleventh hour, there came a way out of this mess. I just had to lose everything first.

"Everything signed then?" the inspector asked.

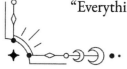
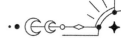

"Almost." My smile slipped over gnashed teeth, and I rolled the contract into the shape of a cigar, wishing I could set the end on fire with my flint box. I tapped it on the desk, thinking over the offer that came in yesterday.

Felix Firenze.

Father would be turning in his grave if the dead could see beyond the veil of Oblivion. The Firenzes were head of the Wet District, one of the four kingdoms dividing the city into unofficial territories. Mixing magic and science, they kept the lights on in this city. More notably, their glint protected natives from the remnant powers of the saints and their descendants. The stuff could be laced on blades, bullets, or taken like a pill to protect oneself from all forms of magic.

Aramis smoothed his large hands down the fitted trousers of his three-piece suit. Solid black besides the silver chain that tucked into a vest pocket and the platinum blonde hair all my siblings shared.

He gestured to Gavriel. "Camilla just needs to sign the license and it will be done, Inspector. We can guarantee the OIC full payment before the end of the quarter. A hundred thousand reoles, to be exact."

The inspector smiled but ultimately seemed unconvinced.

"So what happens next? The OIC gets their money, and I lose my seat in this organization and my place in this syndicate." I shook my head. "I still don't agree with this arrangement. Father left this company to me for a reason. He trusted me, and I don't intend to let him down."

A muscle ticked in my brother's jaw. The whole ordeal was still a sensitive subject. "You'll never lose your place here, nor your profits as a main shareholder," he said. "You might not remember our war with the Attanos years ago, but Father drained the coffers trying to rebuild what we lost. Take the boy's hand in marriage, Milla, and we'll have the advantage again. If we have no money to fund our fights, they'll make us pay with blood."

And I heard the threat laced behind his words, a subtle reminder of what the last war had cost us. It was time to pay back what was due to the OIC and to my family.

The inspector cleared his throat. I'd almost forgotten he was there, acting as a liaison for the family he practically worked for. The Firenzes were big donors to the Society, a specific section of watchmen that specialized in remnant law enforcement—generous with both their money and the glint they provided the force.

"It's no secret, Camilla, that you become the sole owner of the railway when you turn twenty-one. Everything you inherit after you are married becomes dual ownership between you and your spouse. If you marry Felix before your birthday, the Firenzes will inherit the railway as well. Even if something *unfortunate* should happen to you."

"You mean if I die," I said the words he wouldn't.

My brother cut in. "There is a clause that forbids either of you to kill each other, if that's what you're alluding to."

I rolled my eyes. "How convenient."

Aramis shrugged. "I didn't seek this solution on my own, nor am I the only one that believes you should agree to it. That money will help revive our empire. Of course, I don't like the idea of them owning part of the company, but it's an insignificant consequence compared to what will come if we refuse. It's either we play mouse or ruin the family name for good."

"I am not a *mouse*." I tore off the glove covering my left hand and wiggled my fingers. The inky serpent coiled around my forearm hissed in demonstration, showing off a pair of sharp fangs painted across the back of my palm. "I am a Marchese."

"No one is arguing otherwise, Milla," Giles said in an effort to be consoling. His heart was a little softer than the rest, more pliable than Aramis's stone soul. "You'll always be our sister, no matter your last name."

"What do they want with our train, anyway?" I asked, ignoring his sentiments.

"Do you truly not know?" the inspector asked. I looked at him, doubt raising my brow. He explained, "There have been kidnappings in the Row. Civil unrest every day, crime, killings, illicit street fights, the rival families and their remnants causing disturbances day and night. The Firenzes are closer to the OIC than any family on the Isle. Giving them the train would in turn make the government more powerful, giving the Overseer and the governors access to shipping routes and the means to travel through the Wilds and to the mines in the north, along with the ability to regulate the remnants with a tighter fist."

"What do the Firenzes have to do with any of this? Why wouldn't the OIC just buy our company then?" I asked.

He held up the envelope in his hand. "We were. Until Felix approached with a new proposal that would benefit everyone. They need your railway for their glint business. The OIC will always be supported by the Firenzes and thus have influence over the Iron Saint, and your family will keep their legacy."

He stood and crossed his arms, a shadow falling over the side of his face as the glare of the afternoon skimmed his profile. "You're sitting on the Isle's survival, Camilla. This is the right move for all of us."

I paced the worn edge of the ornate carpet, the color washed from previous experiences. Something stunk about this deal. I just needed to sniff out the rotten truth. An idea stalled my strides. "Six weeks."

Aramis sighed. "Milla . . ."

"Six weeks!" I demanded. "Give me six weeks, the day before my birthday, before you turn in the marriage license to the registrar. Give me time to figure out an alternative. Perhaps I can work something else out with Felix."

He sighed and rolled his eyes. "They won't agree to it. They don't have to. If we don't give the bank their due next month, it won't matter who is Father's beneficiary. We'll lose everything."

"Take their cash in installments and in exchange, we give them some of our men to defend their warehouses. They might have money, but we have *loyalty*. We have guns to protect their assets. That's something money can't buy." I stepped towards him, eyes pleading. "This is my *home*, brother. This is where I belong. What is the point of being family if we reduce each other to mere tools?"

"Sign the agreement, Camilla," Aramis said again, "before the Firenzes change their mind. We always knew this could be an option. Honestly, you should be grateful they're offering to help us after everything." There was no kindness left in his voice, nothing left that truly cared about my feelings on the matter. How much he resembled our father in that moment, in his tone.

I read over the binding agreement once more, perplexed at how my brother could have negotiated such a sum for his own blood. One hundred thousand reoles was a small fortune, even more staggering when it was owed. Aramis would have taken anything they dangled in front of his hungry eyes.

Smoothing the contract across my desk, I glanced at the inkpot. My name now the only thing standing in the way of salvation. A simple signature to save us all from certain ruin, buy their freedom at the expense of my own. "Why couldn't one of you marry the idiot?"

He looked me up and down. "Besides the obvious? Giles already offered to go in your place. They refused. The boy wants a bride, and you're the only one we can give them."

"Sorry, Milla. I did try." Giles's lips split in a sad smile.

"His loss," I said with a shrug. "You would've been a better homemaker than me." I stared down at the signature box, losing the fight against my resolve.

I didn't enjoy being used as a pawn, but I could appreciate my brother's long game. Our father had made me heiress in his will for a reason, placed the responsibility of this enterprise in my hands because he had faith in me to do what was right for our business—our family.

I gritted my teeth even as I reached for a quill to sign the damn papers. It was a waste of time trying to get out of this deal at the last minute, but it had been worth a shot. "When will they arrive?"

"They just walked up," Jasper said quietly as he leaned against the hearth. His twin, Jeremiah, was too busy testing how long he could hold his fingers over a flame to worry over his only sister.

"They're here already?" I practically ran to the window, eager to gain a glimpse of the man before the ceremony. Jasper moved the half-opened curtain to the side of the window, so I could see down below where four carriages were parked near the side drive of the Marchese Manor.

A heavy fog clung to the sky, darkening the gloam. What little light broke through the overcast desaturated everything it touched, until the world was mostly variants of grey. The courtyard filled with bodies and faces I didn't recognize, each dressed in navy overcoats that fell to the top of their laced boots.

"Which one is Felix?"

"No idea. He doesn't get out much, but hopefully not that one," he said, pointing to a full bellied gentleman currently hacking into his handkerchief.

"*Giver and Greed*," I cursed the saints. I didn't even know which one I was bound to, not that it truly mattered. I didn't want any of them.

As if in answer, a face turned up among the sea of tweed hats, daring against the light drizzle that pebbled against his pale complexion. His eyes seemed to find me among the wall of windows that lined the east side of the estate, though any quality detail of his face was obscured from my view on the third floor and the shadow of his cap. The man dug into his coat and pulled out a gold watch.

"What time did you say we'd meet them?" I asked Aramis, unable to look away from the attention capturing my interest.

He made a sound of indifference. "We're supposed to meet in the yard at the thirteenth hour."

I shoved away from the foggy window, glancing at the clock on the wall. "It's twenty minutes after that."

"I was enjoying a drag." He held up the cigar he'd been puffing for the last half hour. They'd stuffed themselves into my office all morning, like they were afraid I'd make a run for it. But my name was on that contract now, and I was nothing if not a woman of my word.

"I'll just see myself out," the inspector said. "Good day to all of you, and best of luck. The OIC is optimistic about the future of this city, now that we have combined our influences."

While my brothers muttered their goodbyes, I grabbed my cloak from its rest across a leather armchair and pulled the hood over my curls. "How do I look?" I asked, with a small twirl.

"Like a bride," Jeremiah said dryly, flipping his lighter shut.

"Our big sister, all grown up and getting married," Giles said, wiping invisible tears from his cheeks. "If only Daddy could see you now."

"If Daddy could see me, we wouldn't be in this mess," I muttered beneath my breath. My hand reached for Giles and took his arm as he came to my side, escorting me downstairs where my betrothed waited in the rain. My brother might have allowed them on our property, but no one besides the Marcheses and those who worked for us stepped foot across the threshold. The inspector had been an unwanted exception, one we couldn't refuse.

"Sera will be joining you. Aramis added that late last night," he told me.

"Sera, our tailor?"

Giles nodded once. "They believe she is your attendant—"

"I don't keep servants," I said flatly.

He sucked a placating breath. "The Firenzes don't know that. She'll be our middleman. If you need anything, or if the Firenzes decide to change the rules on us, she'll let us know."

"Can we trust a tailor, Giles?"

"We can trust her. Especially when we can turn that pretty little bourgeois shop of hers into a pile of ash."

I clicked my tongue, descending the final flight of stairs. The footman was ready at the side door with our umbrellas. "Fear is a poor motivator of loyalty."

"Your personality isn't exactly persuasive either, sister. Be nice to Sera. She's risking her neck for us in this case, and we owe her for doing this. She knows it, too." Giles stopped them before they reached the foyer leading to the courtyard.

"Owing people is what got us here. We have too many people on our payroll as it is," I hissed before slipping from his arm.

I stepped away from his side to take in the last sight of my home, unsure when the Firenzes would let me return. The Wet District was on the opposite end of the city, but it might as well have been on the other side of the Isle.

The gas lamps glowed against the dark wainscoting. A brass chandelier scattered the light across the emerald damask carpeting lining the twisting stairwell to the landing over our heads, the arching windows edging the foyer space stained with greens and greys. Our home, our very family name, was immortalized by these colors in Lynchaven.

Just yesterday, I was sitting in my office, only married to a pile of bills and the overbooked registers of the Iron Saint when Aramis introduced me to this arrangement. How quickly had I lost not only my name, but my throne.

"Easy money, Camilla." Aramis stepped between his brothers until he was in front of me. "You can do anything for a hundred thousand reoles."

I pulled out my revolver and checked the round, spinning the cylinder to make sure each bullet was in its rightful place. No. Not *anything*. If he touched me, I'd put a round in him. I made that vow to myself the moment my name stained the parchment. There had been nothing about intimacy in the contract, and I had been careful to scan for any such hidden article. This was a marriage on paper, nothing more.

"Let's just get this over with."

The footman led our group out the side door leading into the courtyard framing the East Wing, where the harrowing conversations of the Firenzes lulled into dull whispers at my appearance. An older gentleman stepped forward from the crowd. The wrinkles layered beneath his spectacles earned him the right to be equivalent in age to my father's father.

"Camilla Marchese," he drawled. "The jewel of Lynchaven." My fists curled into a pallid grip, praying to every saint in the void to get me through this. The bile in my stomach refused to settle, rising in my throat no matter how many controlled breaths I took.

I acknowledged him with a bob of my chin. "I'm afraid reputation does not precede you, Mr. Firenze."

"Lavern Firenze." He bowed, lifting his cap slightly to reveal a balding spot on his crown. "I would introduce the boys, but we'll have time for that later. You've agreed to our terms, then?"

I nodded, too relieved to know this wasn't Felix to say anything else. Aramis stepped forward and displayed my name on the contract. "We'll file this with the registrar after a six-week probation. If this proves to be a relationship we both see lasting long term, we'll make the marriage official."

My knees almost gave out from relief. Aramis had given me a way out.

Lavern's face changed then. His grin twitched into a straight line. "Six weeks? That's not what we discussed earlier."

"Our working arrangements will be honored, but we must look out for our sister, Firenze." Aramis folded the contract and put it back in his cloak. "Remember, you're not just getting access to the train, you're getting our flesh and blood. The jewel of the city, as you say. You can buy our cooperation, but trust around here is earned. Six weeks is a short time to wait for something so important."

Lavern's forced nicety returned with his grin. "Of course, Aramis. Six weeks, then you'll get the agreed-upon payment. I have full confidence you will be more than pleased with Camilla's well-being while in our care."

"Fine."

Something loosened in my heart, hearing Aramis forfeit what he wanted on my behalf. I wasn't entirely sure he cared for my safety, but he had given me a shred of power in the den of my rivals.

A hand clasped over my shoulder, and I winced. Giles's voice rose to a melodic sound as he said, "Lavern, old mate, I don't see the rush. Why don't we bring out a bottle from the winery downstairs and get to know each other. Is this a wedding or a transaction?"

Lavern clapped. His smile touched his eyes. "Yes! Enough talk of politics and money. Today is about the union of our families and new beginnings. Come, Camilla. Allow me the honor of introducing you to my grandson."

The bodies parted, allowing us to cross the courtyard. Giles followed close behind, holding an umbrella over my head to let me lower my hood and keep dry. Standing at the end of the pavement, in front of a sophisticated statue of our father stood another Firenze, a man who appeared to be roughly my age.

Seeing him plucked a new apprehension in my heart. He wasn't attractive in a way that appealed to my taste, with a round nose and oily, ash brown hair. His baby face appeared like it had never required a razor, and the skin of his cheeks was so pale the cold bit them pink.

I closed my eyes briefly and leashed the disappointment in my chest, reminding myself I wasn't perfect either. But his brown eyes glazed over me, rolling a shiver beneath my skin. I swallowed my judgments and hoped there would be something inside this man that I could tolerate.

"Sign the papers first," Aramis said behind me.

Felix's large shoulders jumped an inch before reaching for the outstretched pen in my brother's hand. He finally smiled at me, extending an olive branch.

All I wanted to do was burn it and run.

Three shots from a gun cracked through the courtyard, a whip-like snap that had everyone crouching low to the ground. I had already pulled out my revolver when a carriage skidded to a stop in the gravel behind the stone wall fencing our estate. But looking around, I could tell from first assessment the shots hadn't come from either of our families.

"Are you messing with us, Marchese?" Felix growled at Aramis. "If this is a trap, I swear on my father's grave—"

"It isn't us, Felix. If we wanted to kill your lot, we wouldn't have done it here." Aramis and the rest of my brothers were standing, guns pointed toward the mouth of the gate leading from the courtyard.

Four men appeared from the fog lining the road. Each one dressed in immaculate, steam-pressed, three-piece suits. Their tweed hats pulled low down their foreheads, hiding their eyes but exaggerating the subtle smirks plastered across their smooth faces. The group stopped abruptly when they noticed my brothers and their guns. Throwing their hands up in surrender, their leather gloves were empty of weapons.

"Attano Benders," Felix muttered bitterly beside me, noting the red lining of their coats.

"Hope we aren't late," the one leading the gang spoke. He had an unlit cigarillo in his mouth, and he took it between two fingers to let it hang at his side. "I apologize if we startled you. Didn't want the ceremony to get too far before we made you an offer, Aramis."

"An offer?" he asked, lowering the barrel to point at the ground, hovering a finger over the trigger.

"I heard the Iron Saint was up for sale." The bender turned his head in my direction. A smile stretched his lips, the only discernible part of his face. "I'm interested."

Aramis scoffed. "What are you talking about? You've never shown interest in our company before." Quite the opposite. The Attanos seemed keen on destroying us.

The man gestured with his cigarillo toward me. "We heard the Firenzes were paying to wed your sister. Seeing as they're our local competitors, I couldn't give them such an advantage. I've come to double their bid."

"This is preposterous!" Lavern limped across the pavers, his family awkwardly retreating to the sides of the garden. "Where do you get off in interrupting something that does not concern you, *Bender?*"

"When it affects my own pockets, it does concern me, *Alchemist.*" The man's face turned to Aramis as his free hand reached inside his coat and pulled out an envelope. "I suggest you take a moment and look over my proposal. I think you'll find our arrangement more agreeable."

"And do I not have any say in this?" I asked, finding my voice. "I am not a broodmare!"

The descendant spoke over his shoulder, "Well, princess, if you'd like to say something, we're all listening."

Ass. This man was cold, cunning—apparently rich—and an ass.

I knew plenty of the remnants that had become the family's only competition in Lynchaven in the last twenty years, before the storms made passage between the Isle and the Continent impossible. Claiming the skills to bend various elements in nature, they had offered their abilities to the people here and gained a notable amount of status and wealth. Neither I nor my brothers could figure out how they were able to build such a kingdom north of our railway tracks in such a short time.

I knew less about them individually. The Attanos and their steel factories had become as much a cornerstone in the Isle's infrastructure as the railway. After our feud came to a stalemate nearly seven years ago now, all connection between our families ceased. We found a different supplier for the Districts for our steel, and we hadn't heard from them since. Not until now.

"Lavern, I'm afraid there's been a change of plans." Aramis's voice was dazed as he read the Attanos' offer.

This displeased the grandfather, whose wrinkles only multiplied in his anger. "Turn your back on us now, Marchese, and it will be the last thing you do. I swear you'll live to regret turning us down."

"No, you won't," the bender said. He nodded to one of the men standing behind him, who then handed the old Firenze a different envelope.

Lavern's eyes widened as he read its contents. His chest heaved with quickened breaths, and I worried about the stress on his frail heart. "How did you get this?"

"We all work for the same man, Lavern, just different sides. Get you and your crew out of here before that piece gets the front page of the *Isle Inquirer* tomorrow. And if I hear of you threatening this nice family at any point after this, I'll see to it that your factories fall into the same river you pollute."

Lavern's hands shook, fingers wrinkling the edges of the parchment as if he wanted to rip it apart. Felix came up behind him, reading the words over his shoulder. His face never changed, but he looked at me after, catching my stare. I'd never seen such a quiet rage burn so hot.

Felix growled at the Attano, "This isn't over. The inspector will not be pleased."

"Tell the inspector he can fuck off," the bender replied with an unconcerned shrug of a shoulder.

But my brother didn't even acknowledge any of them, still reading the fine print of the contract. Gravel shifted under my feet, the only sound in the courtyard as I approached my family. "Let me look at it," I said. "If I'm to sign this, then let me see it, Aramis."

A low whistle slipped from Giles. "You know, Camilla Attano has a nice ring to it—"

"Shut it, Giles," I spoke through gritted teeth in the most intimidating voice I could conjure. I snatched the document from his hands, reading it over myself. My jaw dropped at the number, which was in fact, double what the Firenzes had offered. *Two* hundred thousand reoles. Where in Oblivion did the Attanos get this kind of money, and why were they wasting it on *me*?

"You'll find the terms are similar to what the Firenzes demanded. The Attanos will be joint owners of the Iron Saint. As partners we will have access to moving our products across the thirds on your cars. Just like old times."

"The Firenzes agreed to a six-week probation period," I said. Without seeing his eyes he hid beneath the angle of his cap, I felt his glare shift to me.

"Did they now?"

"Camilla . . ." Aramis slipped a warning into his tone.

"Yes." I crossed my arms. "I'd like that added to the contract. Six weeks before any marriage is made official to protect me and my family from being extorted. That's more than fair for crashing my wedding and going about this in such an ill-mannered attempt. You didn't want my train yesterday. It should make no difference if you must wait."

The Attano nodded slowly, sucking his teeth. He took the contract from my possession without warning and handed it to one of the men behind him. "Gideon," he said to one of the men behind him. "Ink."

On command, a similarly dressed bender with wavy black hair and crystal blue eyes reached inside his coat and pulled out an inkpot and stylus, dipping the pen in the ink before taking the contract from his boss. So like an Attano, unable to do simple things for himself like add an addendum or two.

"*Six-week probation,*" Gideon muttered as he wrote, "*until terms are finalized. In which case, payments will be made in quarterly installments. If the union does not proceed after the trial period, all investments will be returned to their benefactors.*"

The boss turned to me, his arms held out wide at his sides. "Anything else you'd like to add while the ink is still wet?"

39

"Yes, actually. My attendant, Sera, will be coming with me. I usually give her the weekends off to be with her family."

"*Sera . . . weekends off,*" Gideon spoke behind him.

He crossed his arms. "Is that all? No trunks of custom dresses or a parure of diamonds?"

I scoffed, wondering if he was always this condescending. "I can buy my own clothes, and I don't wear diamonds."

"Are you pleased with me, then?"

I looked at Aramis. I didn't know why I sought his approval, only that I felt like I needed it. Like every choice I made was a step toward his love, and if I chose wrong and stepped back, I'd fall off that staircase for good.

For once, he seemed at a loss for words. "I'll let you decide, Camilla. If he truly means peace, then it's worth considering."

"I do," the bender said.

My hands wrung together. I glanced between this man whose face I still hadn't seen, to Felix. If I was being entirely honest, my decision bordered on very shallow judgements. I should have thought about what either family could offer the railway, who would be the best fit if I couldn't get out of this arrangement during the six-week probation.

"I have one more request before I sign," I said.

Those lips tipped in a cynical smile he wore like it was part of his uniform. "Well?" Something about him, though impossible, was *memorable.* His voice was a song I'd heard before. This tension in my stomach coiled as it did just this morning.

"Tell me your name."

His demeanor changed entirely, as if my demand was a chisel to his mask. Wordlessly, he handed me the pen and paper, and I thought he'd refuse my last request and make me sign the form without knowing. But he only quietly inched off his glove, finger by finger, loosening the leather from his skin until he slipped one off.

"*Giver and Greed*," I breathed. My heart galloped. Metal and magic replaced flesh and bone, composing a false hand where his last had been cut away for saints knew why. But the contraption of brass tubes and toggles didn't keep my attention for long.

"Nicolai Roman Attano." He lifted my hand with his real one, kissed the velvet lining my knuckle, and I hardly dared to breathe. "But you can call me Nico."

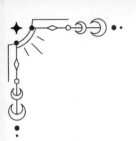
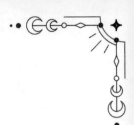

CHAPTER 3
CAMILLA

"Y*ou!*"

Nico's smile stretched impossibly wider. "Me. Isn't this great?"

Was he deranged? Was this why he came onto me last night? I should have known better, grabbing a man's attention that fast. It had to have been staged somehow, though my brain couldn't possibly figure out how he'd known.

"Do you two know each other?" Giles asked, probably recognizing the glare in my eyes. He knew me best out of all my brothers.

"No," I said. At the same time, Nico said, "Yes."

"Don't you dare," I whispered quietly so only he could hear.

He winked. "Then marry me, Milla, before the other guy smells me on your skin."

To his amusement, I turned my head a fraction and sniffed the space beneath my coat. Shitting saints, I *did* still smell like him. Vanilla and sandalwood cologne mixed with leather and cigarillo smoke. When I sneaked back inside this morning, I went straight to

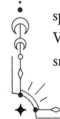

bed, hadn't even considered bathing the night and its scents from my body.

Aramis had given me a choice, but I'm not sure I had a true one. Felix was the safest choice, while Nico was the most logical on paper —and the eyes, to my unfortunate superficial preferences.

I looked to Giles. I didn't trust the man who still held my hand, but I trusted him. If he thought this was the better deal, I should take it. I looked back at Nico, discovering his smile had returned with a vengeance. He knew my choice, even as I struggled to decide it.

"Alright, Attano," I murmured, snatching my hand from his soft grip to sign his contract. "I accept your offer."

He didn't speak again until I was finished signing my name. "You won't regret it, princess."

I looked him in his cold eyes as I said, "No, but you sure will."

Nico looked me up and down, ran his tongue between his teeth. He spoke to someone behind him. "Get her in the carriage, Gideon. Aramis, I'll send a man tonight to pay the first installment. Everyone else can fuck off. I have other things to do today." He spun on a heel and started to walk away.

"What? Wait—" The shorter bender with wavy black hair approached with an uneasy smile, placing an uninvited hand on the small of my back to push me toward the driveway. Nico spoke with the man named Luther, the other Attano, their voices lowered.

"I don't even get to say goodbye?" I asked.

"My apologies, miss, but Nico says—"

"I don't give a damn what Nico says. I'll go on my own time when I bloody feel like it. Get your hands off me—" Twisting to shirk off his grip, Gideon began to look flustered, glancing nervously at his boss like I was about to get him in trouble.

"Please, Miss Camilla," he mumbled quietly.

I looked at my brothers. The twins had already gone inside. Giles watched with a stressed look. Aramis mouthed the words, "*You chose this*," and turned to follow them. The last thing I saw was Lavern approaching him before a gale disturbed the dead leaves carpeting the courtyard.

That strange, isolated wind nearly knocked me off my feet, pushing me in the direction Gideon had motioned before. I whirled on him. "Don't you dare you use your remnant on me!"

"I'm not doing anything," he replied harshly.

My head snapped toward the other benders. Nico was looking over his shoulder at me, too pleased with his performance.

"*Nicolai Attano!*"

"Already using your full name, boss." Luther chuckled.

Another breeze, another shove. If my glare was made of daggers, it would have sliced right through him. "Do *not* use your remnant on me!"

He shrugged a shoulder. "Should have put that in the contract, princess. Get in the carriage or I'll make you."

"You wouldn't dare."

He turned around, facing me fully. And I realized I had just challenged him in a courtyard full of Firenzes, the nosy bastards lingering to watch the finale of this show. This would not end well for me.

A turbulent burst of wind wrapped around my body, spinning my hair around my face, until I was blinded by my own curls and the dead foliage that had fallen from last week's freeze. The force was so disorienting, I didn't even notice my feet moving, not until the wind died and I stood in front of the carriage.

I turned slowly, facing that heinous husband I had just bound myself to standing behind me. "I am going to murder you, Attano."

He only held up our agreement in his hand and tapped it with his middle finger. "Paragraph twelve, line three says you can't." He held open the door and canted his head to the cabin. "I'll ask once more. Get in."

NICO JOINED ME A MOMENT LATER, sitting on the bench across from me as I combed my curls back into form. I refused to acknowledge his presence, my gaze settling on the window instead. Anything was better than those unvarying eyes that unsettled something in my bones. I tried my best to cool my composure, but my chest rose and fell like the treacherous currents in the River Ada, betraying the nerves speeding my breath.

He remained quiet, even as the carriage jolted into motion. Wheels rolled against the cobblestone, worsening the awkward silence. The double bump marking the bridge, crossing into the Row and defining the Attanos' territory, did nothing to help my body relax.

"Why did you do it?" I asked him then.

He propped a heel over his knee. "Do what?"

I peered at him through slits. "You know what. Like my brother said, you've never shown an interest in me, my family, or our business, and suddenly you're concerned with all three. Did you know who I was last night?"

He shrugged and pulled out another dry cigarillo. "Sometimes in our business model, we make moves to get ahead. Other times, we make moves to push others back. This deal killed two birds with one stone. A high price for certain rewards." He gestured to the box in his pocket. "Do you smoke?"

Crinkling my nose, I told him, "No."

"Me either." He lit the end with his false hand, but never took a drag. Instead, he let it burn, let the smoke curl in the air between us and fill the cabin with notes of tobacco, vanilla, and spice. "To answer your second question, no and yes. I didn't know until I felt your scars in my apartment, and you mentioned the train crash. Putting together all I learned about you, I was able to figure it out. When I went home that night, I looked into this deal the Firenzes proposed to your brother."

"Why?"

"That train of yours is very valuable. It can be dangerous to my way of life should it fall in the wrong hands."

My head fell back against the cushioned backing. Saints, I felt like a fool. "Is that why . . ." I bit my lip, unsure if I wanted to revisit last night now that I was sober and aware of *who* it was with. "Is that why you stopped touching me in your apartment?"

His grin reappeared, though it wasn't mocking like the ones before. "It didn't feel right being the only one who knew the truth. Though, now that it's all out in the open, I suppose we could—"

"No," I cut him off before he could suggest it. My hands began to sweat inside my gloves at the thought. "No, last night was a mistake."

He frowned. "A mistake? Why would you say that?"

"Because you're an Attano!" I couldn't help but laugh. The only thing more outlandish than this marriage was being with him in that way. He was my rival, and I didn't sleep with my enemies.

"*Ahh*, yes," he said as a large hand scrubbed his face. "The scum of high society, those Attanos. Made our way up the class hierarchy the dirty remnant way. Well, princess, this lowly bender just saved your posh family from certain ruin *and* the fucking Firenzes. Trust me, I'm a hell of a lot better than Felix."

Silence stretched once again. Judging by his new foul mood, I had offended him. He sat with his arms crossed, staring out of the frosted window. The cigarillo had burned almost a quarter of the way down before I asked, "What did you show Lavern to make him back off so quickly?"

"Evidence of him using children to experiment his new formulas."

"Oh." My stomach turned at the thought. Perhaps he *had* saved me from something worse. I suddenly felt a little better about my choice. "That's awful of them."

He grunted his agreement. "Unfortunately, it happens too often. Children of the Row will do anything for a quick copper, especially when certain sides of the river refuse to hire their remnant parents."

That was a pointed remark aimed to strike at me and my family. The river separated the Row from the Steam District, from remnants and natives. It allowed the descendants to use their magic freely on one side while the rest of us remained safe from their control on the other. After today's little performance, however, I was glad they couldn't use their remnants on our side of the city. I could have had him arrested for what he did but decided to get my own revenge later.

"What do you plan to do with me now?"

"Bring you to my cabin in the woods and lock you in the cellar," he muttered, which earned him another glare. "Honestly, Milla, I'm making this up as I go. I haven't exactly worked out all the little details."

"Are you always this impulsive?"

"*Seven hells*," he groaned. "Do you ever stop asking questions?"

I huffed a breath. I was annoying *him* with my questions? If he thought I'd just shut my mouth and be a good little wife for the next six weeks, then I had hustled him well last night.

My stare slipped, stealing a glance at the bender. His eyes were shut, head leaning back against the cabin. I noticed now he had shadows beneath his eyes, like he'd been up all night. In a few minutes, he might have been able to fall asleep. I stared out the frosted window and felt myself smile as a song came to mind, a hum in the back of my throat.

Nico didn't like my humming.

His eyes snapped open. "Is it truly so difficult for you not to make a sound for a reasonable length of time?"

"Define reasonable."

"Ten bloody minutes?"

I pretended to think about it for a moment. "Yes, that would be difficult for me indeed." A colorful string of curses spilled off his tongue, and I couldn't help the smile that made its way across my cheeks.

"Am I bothering you, *husband*?" I shifted until my feet were flat on the carriage floor, leaning forward slightly. "Let this be a lesson to you about using people to get what you want. I am not a token to trade, and I will make your life miserable as long as that contract exists."

He mirrored my body language, leaning headfirst until our faces were only a bump in the road from smashing together. "Why are the Firenzes so interested in you?"

"Excuse me?" I almost laughed at the question, but his face insisted he was serious.

"Why did Lavern want to wed you to his grandson? He could have just paid you for a portion of the shares and entered a business arrangement that way. Why go through the trouble of a marriage? And why did he look like he wanted to kill me for taking you for myself?"

I shrugged. "It was the only way to bind them to the company by law. If we're married before I inherit the railway, he'll take half ownership just by being my husband. Even if I found a way to divorce him, which the contract is outlandishly strict on, he would remain a shareholder."

"That's it?"

"Why else would they want me, Attano?"

He shook his head and leaned away, gaining some proximity back. "Don't know. But I intend to find out . . . if there is another reason."

I returned my attention back to the window. "Well, I won't tell you how to waste your time. But if you find out, let me know, and perhaps we can use it to get us both out of this mess."

The carriage fell quiet again. The only sound made was the tinkering tubes of his false hand as he tapped his fingers on his knee. "I have a wager for you."

"I'm listening."

"You clearly don't want to be with me."

"Obviously." Which would have been much easier to convince myself if I hadn't been straddling those hips less than twelve hours earlier.

He took a placating breath before replying, "I could use your help with something."

"My help?"

He nodded. "The city is cracking. I've heard rumors of war."

"I've heard the same."

"I want to stop it."

His answer wasn't one I was expecting. Surely men like him, dangerous men with power, would jump at the opportunity to shake this Isle upside down. "How do you plan on doing that?"

His jaw hung for a beat, choosing his words carefully. I noticed a crease in his forehead formed every time he retreated into deeper thoughts.

"I have a . . . meeting with a client at the races. I've been tracking down an underground organization that has been threatening remnants. Come to Newport with me and use your name to get people talking. Help me secure my family's safety, help me stop this threat to our city, and I'll pay you your money with no strings attached."

My jaw hovered for a beat. "You mean you won't ask for anything in return? No marriage, no shares, nothing?"

"Consider it a donation from Attano and Associates Limited."

I crossed my arms, doubt tainting my words as I asked, "What is this organization, and why do you need my help?"

"I'll explain more when we get to the apartment," he tapped the grate behind me, where our conversation could be overheard by the driver. I nodded in understanding. He didn't trust anyone either. "But you're from old money, Camilla. Your name is holy on this Isle —and it's trusted. Descendants in the Row will jump at the chance to gain favor with you because your family makes things happen in this city."

"And if they don't? If I cannot help you stop your little war?"

He pulled out another cigarillo, and I wondered how many it would take to fill the drive to the countryside.

"Then I'll need your train. And I suppose you'll be stuck with me until death parts us."

Over my dead heiress body.

But I bit back the retort, sat back in my seat, and beamed. "You have yourself a deal, Attano."

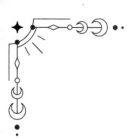
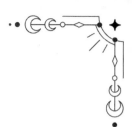

CHAPTER 4

CAMILLA

Two birds, one stone.

This union proved to be a wise investment of my time already. He'd even offered me a way out—and Nico was just as keen on getting rid of me as I was of him. He hardly spoke a word the rest of the way. Our rivalry came to a temporary truce, having similar interests in mind.

I didn't travel outside of Lynchaven often, preferring to remain where my name was the law should I ever need to break or enforce it. And although I was in no rush to visit the Attano residence, my adversary's estate would have provided better company. The flat we were now occupying for the night was a safe house that wasn't regularly used—and we were completely alone.

"The races start in an hour, at dark. We'll sleep here tonight to avoid the city Society." Nico showed me to the parlor, lighting the gas lamps with a simple demand of his remnant, commanding the light inside the glass urns to fill. "I asked our driver to forward your trunk

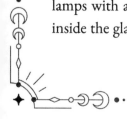

here when he gets back to the manor, but I'm not sure they'll have enough time before midnight."

I nodded, surveying the small flat, thankful I had worn something practical. The sitting room was modestly furnished, with two couches facing each other and a chaise pushed in the corner. A large hearth dominated the outer wall on the left side, facing a wall of books cluttering floating shelves on the right. The flat was vacant, yet clean, as though someone had been here recently.

Nico left to prepare the rest of the rooms, so I helped myself to a dram placed out on the table between the couches, filling my empty stomach with something to numb the hunger pangs. When he returned, he held a plate full of food. Various meats and breads and cheeses scattered around a serving board.

"I didn't know they gave descendants a curfew," I mentioned, disregarding the plate he set out to grab a roll with my fingers. Cheese wasn't kind to me.

He shrugged off his coat and laid it across the armrest. "It's more of an implied rule than a law. The Society technically can't arrest us for being out in the late hours, but they can make our lives more difficult. If there's a crime and we're caught in the area after dark, which is likely, it's easier to blame a descendant."

"Things are still tense between your kind and the Society?" I asked. The group was founded by the previous Overseer of the Mez, the middle third of the Isle. The Society was a branch of the Watch solely created to manage the area's new magic citizens, give them laws specific to their kind to limit how much they exercised their powers.

"Regrettably. Which brings me to our little bargain."

My interest piqued, and I poured a double into the glass. "What can I do for you, husband?"

"For starters, you can stop calling me that."

"Does it bother you?"

"Immensely."

"Hmmm," I said, while taking a sip of the amber drink. A line of fire burned down into my belly. I dropped my voice to mimic his deep, gravely tone. *"Should've put that in the contract, then.* Now get to the point."

Nico's sharp features were even more lethal when he scowled. "My uncle is convinced that the city is sitting on a precipice. That what happened on the Continent is fated to repeat itself here."

I frowned. "Why does he think that?"

He opened his mouth, then shut it again, as if choosing his words carefully. "When descendants immigrated here fifty years ago, the last Overseer offered them protection. Then the storms came. Ships stopped returning, stocks ran low, demand went up, and descendants fulfilled the very need we created in the first place, using our remnant to cover everything from mining to millwork in the Upper Notch to roasting your damn coffee beans in the Lowlands."

A warm breeze stirred the room, settling into the hearth to breathe flames into the logs. Nico hadn't even lifted his gaze to accomplish such a thing. He continued to speak as he tended the fire. "There are many who hate us for it, for taking their jobs, blame us for the storms and all the rest. There have been attacks—"

"The inspector mentioned that. Kidnappings?" I asked.

"Yes, he knows, and he hasn't done a damn thing about them. There are no less than thirty descendants missing over the last four years. There's nothing consistent about the cases. I don't know who is taking them or why, but the Row grows restless anyway. If the Collector isn't stopped soon, I fear there will be an uprising, and the OIC will use any kind of unrest to ban the use of remnants like they did on the Continent."

I shrugged a shoulder, unconvinced. "The government here has no such authority to ban your abilities. We have a democracy, these things are taken to a vote, and I'd like to think the lifestyle is more progressive here than it is on the mainland."

Nico sucked in a cheek, brows raising half an inch. Apparently, he hadn't expected me to be so well educated on the history of the descendants and their immigration to the Isle.

"It's a slow fade, Camilla," he said. "It always starts by targeting small privileges until they've finally taken so much that you have nothing left to fight back with. By the time it's obvious, it's far too late."

"The curfews, you mean?"

"Among other new rules, yes." Nico leaned his shoulder against the hearth, staring down at me as I stuffed my face. "The derby attracts all kinds of people from every level of society. I'm going to get you a ticket to the upper booths, where the socialites are. If by any chance you hear something useful, it could give my family and those who count on us an advantage. If anything, a forewarning of what might be coming."

"Why would I help a bunch of descendants?" I asked. Besides my own motivations to get out of this marriage, I was sticking my neck out for a group of people who quite literally hated my name.

"If there is no war, princess, there is no need for your train. Help me solve this problem, and we can both return to our sides of the city."

My gaze fell across the hearth, thinking over his rationale. Hadn't the inspector said something similar? Could there truly be something going on in the underbelly of the city? If there was, my family's train could make all the difference in who came out victorious.

There were no kings on the Isle, but war gave opportunities for those kinds of things to change. I told him, "I'm not sure I believe in your little conspiracy theory, but I'll keep an ear out tonight."

"Good." He nodded an approval. "Be sure to take some of that glint if you have it. Descendants and natives are mixed here. There are no lines here to protect a Marchese from the wrath of a remnant."

I scoffed at that. "I'm not afraid of descendants just because you have magic."

"Is that so?" he asked with an arched brow.

"Of course not. There are saints, and there is science." With my free hand, I lifted the crystal glass back to my lips. "Your kind uses magic as a crutch, meanwhile I've had to refine my skills over years of practice. I could kill you four different ways right this second."

There was a blur of dark grey and crimson, and suddenly Nico loomed above me. His metal hand wrapped around my throat, the carving knife from the meat spread poised in his other. I swallowed a burning sip as he pressed the cold steel against my throat, skating the tip across my skin and down the middle of my chest, sending a rash of chills sweeping down my spine. But I kept my focus on his face, which was so close now it flashed a warning through my flesh, a threat in those gunmetal eyes that held the danger of a loaded bullet.

"Do you still feel more powerful than me?" His words brushed against my lips, encouraging them to split apart while his false hand snaked up the column of my throat, tightening with a promising pressure. A vow to forbid the breath from escaping my chest, and it made something dangerous dance in my heart.

I smiled despite the risk. "What are you going to do, Attano? Stab me?"

"I've never met anyone who smiles at knifepoint." He dug the tip of the blade into the space above my heart, not enough to break skin but enough to pinch. "You'd probably enjoy it too much if I did."

"I might under the right circumstances," I said, grip tightening on my glass. "You, however, are not one of them. Now get off me before I make you."

I could have sworn his grip locked a little tighter. "Spoiled little heiress."

I scoffed. "More like *broke* little heiress."

His grip tightened, stealing a gasp from my chest. "Not anymore, princess. I'm your daddy now."

Shooting back the remaining sip of drink, I smashed the empty glass against his temple. The crystal shattered, raining glass across my lap and onto the couch while he cried out in surprise. He stumbled back, nearly tripping over the carpet and falling flat on his backside. It took him a few gasps of breath to reorient himself before shooting me a murderous glare.

"Are you *insane?*"

"You're *not* my daddy, Attano," I muttered, dusting the crystal shards from the cushions while failing miserably to hide my grin. "And I warned you. When I say I'll do something, I mean it."

Blood began to slip through his fingers, inching down the jawline I admired with such contempt. "I was *teasing* you, Camilla!"

"Well, *clearly* I misread your intentions." I gestured to my own face, indicating his injury. "That might need stitches. Why don't you go find a kit and I'll fix your face in penance for my misunderstanding."

He stared at me as if I had grown three heads, but eventually, the blood trailing down his face forced him to concede. Nico returned a few minutes later, holding a suture kit and a towel to his wound. His boots thudding across the wood floor offered a warning of his reentry.

"I'm wary of letting you so close to my face with needles, but you made a fine gash."

I took the kit from his hands and gathered the supplies inside, placing them on the table still acting as a barricade between us. We seemed to mark our territories in every space we filled, drawing invisible lines with cutting words and sharp stares. But I relied on these outlines to feel safe in his world, claiming terrain for myself even while standing on enemy soil.

Nico tested this boundary for the second time this evening, sitting at the end of my couch. With a resolving breath, I scooted closer, taking the bloody towel from his hand and accessing my work in the amber light. The laceration was a clean slice down his temple where his hairline started, nearly an inch long and in a highly vascular spot.

"You almost knocked me out cold," he muttered.

"Fortunately for you, you have a very hard head. The edges are well approximated, so it might not even scar." Blood continued to seep through the cut, no matter how much pressure I placed. Only closing the wound with stitches would stop the bleeding. I threaded the sterile needle and turned back to him.

The lighting was poor in the center of the room, where the light from the gas lamps didn't stretch quite as far. My fingers slipped beneath his jaw to angle his face for a better view and wondered how his teeth didn't break from the tension locked in his jaw.

He must have noticed my difficulty finding a good light, because the light in the gas lamps began to collect and converge over the center of the room, draping the corners with thick shadows. Although I'd never admit it out loud, I found his powers fascinating.

Not all remnants of Bane could manipulate multiple elements, nor was any remnant quite like another. There were classes beneath each saint, different specialties marking each remnant. From what I gathered in my very little experience with descendants, the expression of each power was hereditary. Sometimes missing generations entirely, but usually passing the same gift.

"What else do you bend?" I asked him, trying to distract myself from his warmth. Which had become no less alluring since learning his last name.

"Air, light, and time are my best ones. I can mess with shadows, but not as well as a true darkthief."

So he was *polypotentia*. A wielder of multiple kinds of remnants. It wasn't common from what I'd heard.

"Darkthieves are benders?"

"Yes," he tried to nod, but thought better of it. "They have supreme control of shadows. Shape them, stretch them, steal them from the void itself and warp them to create enchanted objects."

"That sounds incredibly fascinating. Do you know anyone with that remnant? I'd love to meet a shadow bender."

Nico squirmed. "I mean sure, I know a few. They're alright I guess, if that sort of thing impresses you."

A cold wind flickered the light in the glass orbs. Too much to be a draft. I smiled to myself. "Oh, it does."

The most magic I owned was the familiar around my arm, which was more ink and science than anything as extraordinary as Nico's talents. It was a gift my father's former alchemist had utilized to win him the seat of the family's supplier—until she passed away shortly after from dappling with one too many chemicals. The Firenzes managed to preserve her formulas, reproducing the same glint stocked on my railcars going all over the Isle.

Nico hardly flinched as I stuck him without warning and threaded the suture through his skin. After losing a hand, there most likely weren't many kinds of pain more unbearable to tolerate. His blood quickly stained the lines of my fingerprints, the site still oozing as I closed the split the best I could.

"Where did you learn to stitch?" he asked when I was finished, rubbing his fingers over the stiff threading sealing the gash.

I wiped the sticky blood from his chin that had dripped down his face. "Four brothers and a house full of winding staircases." And when our father had been unable to keep a mother in our lives, the role inevitably fell into my lap. I tossed the sullied equipment on the table for Nico to pick up later and retreated to the other side of the couch, thankful the lines between us had been reestablished. The silence between the small talk was unnerving enough.

The clock on the wall clicked four times on the hour. In the span of a blink, Nico moved from his seat to his cloak and threw it over his shoulder—a subtle show of his time bending. "I'll have the driver come back to pick you up. Your ticket will be at will call. No one knows about our union yet, and we should keep it that way until gossip spreads the news for us."

"Fine with me," I said. "If I'm with the rich people, where will you be?"

My question pulled a mask over his features, rendering them unreadable. "Busy. Don't worry about me or what I'm doing. Keep your nose out of my business, Milla. I'm serious." He turned to leave, attempting to end the conversation there.

My husband obviously didn't know who he married. My nose had an affinity for trouble, and Nico reeked of it. The door slammed shut, rattling the windows in their panes. I stared at the half full decanter, wondering what in the seven hells I'd just signed myself into.

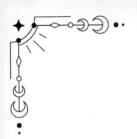
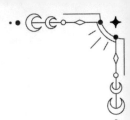

CHAPTER 5
CAMILLA

The races were well underway by the time Nico's car came back for me. The arena was a circular, two-toned wood stadium with mud stains lining the bottom—courtesy of the Isle's hard rains. An overcast sky darkened the evening, obscuring the last rays of the setting sun. Torches lined the edges of the arena like spires of flames, glowing defiant against the grey.

I'd never been to a race. Didn't like profiling myself anywhere other than my home. Out here, beyond the city limits, the descendants were not neatly organized into sectors. They mixed and mingled with the mundane as their neighbors. The divide wasn't needed here as it was in Lynchaven, where the OIC ruled with an iron fist to keep a power balance among the thousands that lived and worked there.

Some people were still afraid of magic, but I believed a bullet was just as fast as Nico's apparition, could cut through a darkthief's shadow. There was nothing about the supernatural that couldn't be challenged with gunpowder, glint, and science. In reminder, I

skimmed a gloved hand over the ivory scales and the gold engraved metal plate of my revolver. Reinforcing that ideal into my heart, I grabbed my ticket from the front desk and ventured through a long tunnel that burrowed into the arena.

There were three levels surrounding the track: A pit where the general public crowded around pub-height tables and watched through the ground-level fence, a theater-style seating forming wings on either side of the track, and the upper booths. A box stood on its own in the center of the track with a glass face to watch the races from their enclosed seating.

I quickly made my way to the booths and found myself searching for Nico, wondering what was so important to bring him here, of all places, outside of either of our fences. But there were too many bodies, a hundred voices mixed to form a dull roar as the racers neared in their lap.

The hard floor of the arena trembled as the crueger, the carnivorous cousins to the horse, pounded onto the track. Their riders were ruthless, wearing clubs should another rider come too close. The rules of the race were watered down into staying on your beast, crossing the finish line first, and keeping all your limbs while you were at it, but the latter was more of an option.

A rider approached his competitor, standing in the saddle as he held a beater in one hand and the reins in the other. But his victim had anticipated his oncoming attack. When the rider lunged to strike him, his opponent dodged, sending his own beater into the rider's face with a backhanded blow that sent the man slipping.

The second rider pulled the reins of his crueger toward the first, smashing the beasts together and knocking the man from the back of it. He fell, screaming out, only to be silenced by the trampling of the crueger coming up behind them. The crowd roared in dark delight as a team came to carry his body off the track.

I pressed on, avoiding the bars overlooking the savage sport, unamused by cheap thrills.

"What in the bloody Oblivion are you doing here?" a voice growled behind me. I knew that voice, and it wasn't friendly.

I whirled to see Inspector Gavriel pushing through stagnant bodies, too absorbed with the race to move out of his way. He was dressed in casual clothes, most likely undercover or possibly even off duty. A charcoal coat fell to his knees, no silver badge pinned to his pressed shirt to note his official rank.

I waved my ticket under his mustache. "I'm enjoying the races. What does it look like?"

"You're supposed to be with the Firenzes!"

"About that," I drawled. "Plans changed. The Attanos gave me a better offer, but don't worry, Inspector. The bank can be assured our loans will be fully paid off by the end of the quarter."

His black eyes widened. "You married—"

"Nicolai Roman Asshole Attano," I replied with a grimace. "Yes, don't remind me."

His head shook slowly, all color suddenly drained from his face. "What have you done?"

He took a step back, so I took a step forward. "Are you alright, Inspector? It's truly not a big deal. The bank and the OIC still get their money—"

The inspector fisted my coat lapels and yanked me hard, pulling me in front of his shaking face. Every word he spat flicked drops of spit across my cheeks. "You think in a time like this I care about *money*, Camilla?"

I shoved my fists between us, pushing him away, but he pulled me tighter, locking me against his chest. The vice raced my pulse into a panicked pace. "Inspector, let me *go*." I'd warn him once, which was once more than he deserved. Only because he could hurt my family hard if wanted to. The deal with the Firenzes had been a mercy we never saw coming.

But he could show us wrath just as easily.

"If you give the Attanos that train, Marchese, I swear to the bleeding saints, it'll be the last thing you do."

"Is that a threat?" I breathed.

"That is a *warning*," he hissed. At last, he let me go, but neither of us took that first step of submission. "Take their money if you must, but get out of this union before your father's will comes to actualization. Anything else will be considered an act of conspiring against the OIC."

I almost laughed in his face. "Trust me, Inspector. I have no plans to stay bound to the bender."

Something shifted in his eyes, a realization brightening the marshy green centers. "He's here, isn't he? He brought you here tonight."

I took a step back then, the hair on my neck rising with unease. "So what if he did?"

Gavriel smirked, but it didn't touch the rest of his face. As if his emotions were blunted by a lack of ability to feel at all. His grin snapped then, lips returning to their usual flatness. "Interesting. Keep an eye on your new husband. If you see anything suspicious, don't hesitate to call on me."

"Why would I see anything suspicious?"

He shrugged. "Perhaps there's no reason at all, or maybe there is. Either way, you would do well to tell me if you catch him doing anything against the OIC. His family has a . . . certain history of causing trouble. Not people you want to align yourself with in the coming days." He tipped his hat. "Enjoy the races, Camilla."

Gavriel stalked off, and I didn't turn away until his backside disappeared in the crowd, leaving me with only his cryptic threats and the chills leftover from his overall creepiness. Why had he cared if Nico was here tonight? And what had he meant by his family's history?

Nico was a stranger in every way except his name, and even that only served to heat my hatred further. Whatever warning the inspector was trying to give me, it served no purpose. In six weeks, I'd be back across the river where I belonged. Owning my train, alone, with our family debt paid at last. Free from inspectors, the OIC, Attanos, and the rest of the leeches of this Isle.

A collision to my right shoulder nearly knocked me off balance, throwing my attention from my thoughts to a man dressed in dark clothes and a cowl.

"Get out of the walkway," he growled, hitting me with the scent of copper and smoke.

A wearh. One that had just come from a feed by the smell of it. A remnant of Blood, more offhandedly known as a bleeder. I opened my mouth just to shut it again. I wasn't afraid of descendants or their magic, but there were exceptions to every rule—and bleeders were mine.

He slipped a low laugh before vanishing through a breezeway, a tunnel escaping the track and leading to the back of the arena. I fixed my coat, readjusting the tailored cut hugging the curve of my shoulder to realize something was off. I patted myself down, dread sinking my heart into the pit of my stomach.

The bleeder had just pickpocketed me. My purse was gone, as was my ticket to the booths. I'd never get upstairs without it.

Shit. Shit. *Shit.*

I bolted to the breezeway, but he was already gone. Nothing but darkness from the fallen night on the opposite end and a gate marking the exit.

I *really* didn't want to follow a bleeder into the shadows, where their gifts were best suited. But more than that, I didn't want him to get away with my money or my ticket, requiring both to get upstairs and win back my freedom. For that reason, I unsheathed my revolver and checked the chambers with a spin of the cylinder.

Satisfied, I shoved it into my inner coat pocket, keeping it concealed and ready in my hand, and followed the trail of the wearh out the back gate.

⁕

THERE WAS NO MOON TONIGHT. The overcast rolled over from the day, sifting over the starlight until the world was blanketed in black. Lanterns dotted the exterior walls, lining a path from the back gate to the building behind the arena—the stables.

I didn't see my thief anywhere; he had most likely used his predatory speed to run far from the scene of the crime. But I was not alone out here. A man led a crueger through the archway of the stable, a short walk from the breezeway. The beast wore a muzzle and the man a thick glove as he pulled it by a chain.

Scanning the scene once more, my eyes strained against the lack of light, but the bleeder was gone. I had lost my ticket and my coppers and could only imagine Nico's annoyance when I told him I'd been jumped, spoiling my one and only job for the night.

From the walkway on the other side of the booth box, another figure emerged, light from the arena silhouetting his figure. He wasn't my mark, but the flash of red in the torchlight distracted my vengeance with immediate curiosity.

Nicolai had claimed he was meeting a client, but what was he doing out here?

An orange blaze hung at his side as he walked casually toward the stable, trailing the route the man with the crueger had taken. I ducked into the darkness lining the path, hiding behind the shrubbery as he turned before he made it to the stables, surveying the grounds one last time before following the man inside.

He shut the rolling doors behind him.

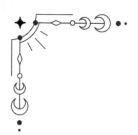
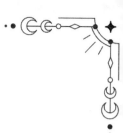

CHAPTER 6
CAMILLA

Finding the living quarters tucked into the back corner of the stables had eaten away some time, but I quickly crawled through the cracked window leading to the stable master's small flat. The rooms at the end of the stable formed the top of a T, and I was able to peek around a corner to scan the aisle.

Nico had the man pinned with his false hand against a stall. Behind the stable worker was a crueger, sniffing his hair through the bars, snarling in a starved way. The races must run them hungry, and the stable workers must feed them afterward, if the trays of raw meat outside the stalls were any indication.

The worker's voice carried down the aisle, too weak to discern anything intelligible. There was a stoop covering the stalls and a ladder just a dash away if I felt bold enough to get closer. And I did feel it, like an underline beneath the word *go,* ordering my feet to move stealthily to the ladder. Nico warned me to stay out of his business, hiding something that roused the inspector's attention.

Power came in many forms. Wealth, status, beauty, but the most

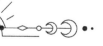
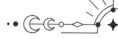

cunning of all forms were secrets. If Nico was up to something he shouldn't be, I could use that against him later. Perhaps to get out of this union with his cash in hand—if his secrets were sinister enough.

I crawled across the gables. Low enough, my body was flush with the stoop, close enough to see the man's face turn an unnatural shade of purple. Nico released him and he collapsed to the straw covered floor. "Mr. Attano, please," he stammered, collecting his breath. "I'm not part of any societies, I swear! I hardly leave Newport—"

"Then what is this, Silas?" Nico dropped something on the floor between them, in front of the begging man. "Is this not yours?"

He swallowed, glancing at what I could now see was a knife with a red blade. Silas had started trembling. "Never seen it before."

Nico sighed, as if that answer disappointed him. He pulled a piece of paper from the inside pocket of his coat and unfolded it, showing the contents to the man as he squatted down to his level. "I might spare your life if you can tell me who ordered the attack on them. Give me a name, and I'll let you walk free."

Silas squinted at the paper, working his jaw.

"Don't lie," Nico warned, his voice almost lyrical. "If you make something up to protect your friends, I'll find out, and I know everything about you, Silas. Where you live, where your mother lives, where your seven children and second wife live—"

"I told you, I'm not involved in such things! I'm a simple stable master! I don't know who those people are—" Silas's mouth gaped open, his voice cut off. Nico pocketed the paper and rose to his feet, lifting the man by his collar with one hand, his opposite on the stall door—sliding the lock free.

"I don't care how many of you I have to kill to get what I want. One of you will talk. You want to make my job harder? You think it's noble to protect your friends? Fine. I'll leave a bloody trail on my path for reprisal with your entrails for my pavers. They might have thought the first death was a tragic accident, the second a strange coincidence, but they'll know with yours, Silas. They'll know I'm coming for them all."

Nico rolled the stall door open and threw the man inside, who barely uttered a sound as the crueger tore into him with jaws of serrated teeth. The bender shut the door and left the lock dangling free, but from my perch on the outcropping, the view was unobstructed as the beast ripped the stable master's throat out first, spraying the walls with a film of blood.

The sounds were appalling, filling the silent stable with the feral grunts of the crueger as it devoured the man's body, tearing open every limb and hollow organ until it reached bare bones. I turned my head, avoiding the sight of it, but the cacophony was enough detail to assist my imagination. Enough to leave me sick and reeling, burying my face into my shoulder, covering my ears with my arms to cease the sounds of consumption.

The crueger finished a few minutes later, minutes that felt twice as long as normal. When I finally looked up, Nico was long gone, and my heart was the only human sound left beating in the stable. Something told me if the bender had only turned around and looked up, he would have thrown me into the same stall for what I'd witnessed.

Before anyone came looking for Silas and found me around, I quickly scurried off the stoop and fled the same way I came in, desperately trying and failing to still the tremors that shook my hands so fiercely. I didn't know what Nico wanted from him, whose faces could be on that paper, nor why he sought vengeance from a stable hand. But I walked away from this night with one truth: Nicolai Attano was a killer, one with purpose, and I was going to find out why.

A wave of cheers burst from the arena, hitting the dark sky and thundering across the wooded area surrounding the derby. Someone must have been devoured on the track or the race had finished, and the medals had been claimed. Either way, I couldn't go back through the gate without a ticket, where a guard now lurked. I wondered if Nico paid him off to take a break so he could slip in and out.

The only thing to do now was head back to the driveway where the carriages waited and hope I didn't bump into my husband before my heart relaxed. If Nico caught on to my suspicions now, it might inspire him to be more careful with his *meetings* in the future.

The sconces lining the wall around the arena were further apart on this side. I didn't even see the group of figures blocking the paved path around the edge until they were only paces away. Their silence forced me to a dead stop, like they had been waiting for me to come near before revealing themselves.

Whoever they were, they moved soundlessly. My slow breath was loud in comparison, pulse nearly deafening in the quiet. Retreating back toward the stables, I kept my front to them, refusing to turn my back to the group blocking the way ahead.

A brush of air rendered my flight impossible. The cold sting of remnant magic followed. Another moved to my left a second later, and the driveway was suddenly blocked from sight as a man and woman stood before me, their features blotted away as the light from the sconces hit their back. Pulling out my weapon for a display of force, I hoped it would be enough to make them back off.

"You're in my way," I said. A warning only because I was in no mood to cause trouble in an area that wasn't mine.

"What do you think?" the man spoke first, addressing someone else.

There was shifting behind me, more of the same of them adding to their numbers, confusing any idea at how many I was up against. More wearhs. The man from earlier had friends. My bullets and blades were laced with glint, but shots could only be fired one at a time, and this was an ambush where I was clearly outnumbered.

The woman canted her head. "She fits the profile, but should we take her with so many potential witnesses around?"

"What are you talking about?" I asked, my pointer finger slipping over the curved trigger guard.

"Well, we have to now, Angel. You just fucking gave us away." The bleeder who grabbed my purse emerged into view.

"Or we could coerce her to forget like the others," she said with a small shrug. "We should drain her first. This one looks like a fighter."

My arm shot up, staring down at my assailants from the barrel of my gun. "You're right. I am a fighter, and I'm also a killer when I need to be. Get out of my way before you give me the proper motivation to make that shift."

I didn't dare let myself so much as blink, but the woman moved at such a speed that by the time her lunge had registered, it was far too late. My gun went off and shot into the void. I didn't even see where the bullet had gone as her hard body crashed into me, mottling my vision as the force switched momentum, shoving me into the wall of the arena.

"How dare you threaten someone like me, *Lesser*? Do you honestly think you're a match for one of us, much less an entire coven?"

"Shouldn't you be hunting the gutters for vermin?" I said. Her hand was at my throat then, squeezing my airway so every word was a challenge to speak. Two others like her held back each of my arms, sprawling me across the wall.

The woman leaned in closer, stealing my scent with a strong suck of her breath. A smile lifted her lips, revealing sharp teeth. "Shouldn't you be safe at home with Daddy? Little girls like you have been disappearing lately. It's not safe to be out here all alone."

"I'm not alone. My husband is waiting for me. I came out for a smoke." A half-truth. "He'll come looking for me too if I don't return soon, and trust me, you don't want to cross him. He's a bender." A complete lie. Nico would most likely let them drain me dry if he saw us now, but they didn't need to know that. If it was one thing any descendant dreaded, it was one of their own.

This sparked no fear in the woman's dark eyes, the color indicating she was starving. A few mouthfuls of my blood and they'd be bright red again. "Well, in that case," she drawled, "we better make this quick."

With a speed only belonging to a natural born predator, the woman clasped her hand over my mouth and sunk her teeth into my flesh without even pulling up my sleeve. My vision went white as pain seared through my veins.

Fucking bleeders.

This bite was not to kill, but to feed. I knew this because of where she drank from me. Hitting the jugular in my neck would have provided an eventual death, but the vein in the upper arm was just as big, easily accessed, and a slower bleed out, giving me a chance. Venom from her fangs spilled into the surrounding skin and burned deep like an internal fire hell-bent on burning me from the inside out.

My scream spilled through her fingers. I struggled against the hands that held me firm against the brick, but the flames scorched through my strength. It was a useless struggle, one I committed to, only because I'd never let anyone steal my choice to fight.

The bleeder on my arm suddenly unlatched and reeled away without warning, sputtering as she choked on my blood. It stained her chin and sprayed her companions' stunned faces as she coughed her throat clear. Her eyes were wide, mirroring my own as I watched her. "What in the void?" she said in a shrill voice after catching her breath. "What kind of glint is in your veins?"

I hadn't taken anything all day, despite Nico's warning.

The man that helped corner me dropped my left arm and sped to her side, worry stiffening his body. "What's wrong, Angel? Does she taste off?"

"Excuse me?" I asked.

"She tastes . . . *wrong*." Angel's hand clutched her chest as her breaths wheezed. I've never been bitten by a bleeder, but I assumed this wasn't the usual reaction. Cold, hungry eyes shifted into a hot glare. "What new glint are the Firenzes pushing now? What in the seven hells is in your blood, Lesser?"

She demanded answers, but I didn't have them. Playing dumb was the most honest act I could rally at this point. "I . . . I don't know. They sold me my usual, just the first-tier stuff."

"They must be trying out a different formula," another bleeder spoke. "I told you we couldn't trust them. They must have given her something special before—"

Angel silenced him with a sharp look. "Someone needs to coerce her. We've been out here too long. Someone will come by sooner or later."

While they debated amongst themselves, I used my free hand to extract the switchblade hiding in my glove just below my wrist and sunk it into the bleeder holding my right side. He shrieked as the glint coating the polished steel hit the storehouse of his remnant, rendering him powerless.

Before he went limp, I yanked it from his chest and launched it at the man near Angel's side. With the momentum of the throw, another knife slipped from my sleeve and into my palm, this one dedicated to another wearh lunging from the shadows to stop me. I reached for my gun but found the sheathe empty. Dismay rolled across my chest when I realized I had dropped it.

I had time to throw two more daggers before the familiar click of my revolver commanded me to still. Angel held it with an extended arm somewhat awkwardly, like she hadn't much experience with a gun. But from this close range, she didn't have to be a good shot to hit her target.

"That's quite enough," she said, glancing at the bleeders clutching their wounds. The glint we laced our blades with stunted their magic, a useful formula against descendants. One that made my father and the Firenzes very wealthy thirty years ago when natives craved protection from those who used their remnant in less-than-desirable ways.

"Do you want to die, Lesser?" she hissed through her teeth. "I could spray the wall with your brains, let the rats lick your remains off the mud." She lowered the gun to my stomach. "Though I've heard natives can survive for hours after a shot to the gut. You'll be in agony, begging for death to take you. A fitting punishment for attacking the Grey Hands."

The world was quiet besides the dull noise from the arena vibrating the brick at my back. My left arm was throbbing from the venom, hanging heavy at my side. Angel nodded her chin. "Fortunately for you, we got a job to finish. Get on your knees. Bind her, Luca. We will take her to him like he requested."

She had made a foolish mistake admitting her plans and her need to keep me alive. One of the remaining bleeders came up behind me with a cord of rope, another shoved me to the ground. After he bound one wrist, I spun on my knee and twisted my free arm out of his grip, and in the next breath, I was behind my captor, pressing the weapon they gave me against his windpipe until his inhale was no more than a whistle. His body became my shield.

"Wearhs can survive gunshot wounds," she hissed. "I'll still shoot."

"My bullets are dipped too, Angel," I said with a baiting smile. "Try it and see what this kind does."

She bared her teeth in a growl and lunged for us, body a blur as she attacked. I saw the gun fall. A shot went off as it hit the ground, damp wood splintering as it struck the wall of the building. Angel ripped the man I held as hostage from my hands with a supernatural strength and tackled me to the ground. Her claws grazed my throat.

"What the hells is going on out here?" A man's voice boomed from the edge of darkness, the sound of his boots insisting he was running. The woman on top of me stiffened, like she recognized it.

He cursed as he neared, assessing the broken wearhs and the one still pinning me to the ground. "I suggest you get off her before I send the bloody hounds on your lot and drag you to Hightower by your ugly teeth. Go on, *bleeder*. Get off and get out!"

Angel took one last opportunity to growl at me, a storm of indecision in her eyes, before shoving off my body, retreating into the darkness with the rest of her bleeding and battered coven.

"You alright, miss? Did they bite you? Scum of the Isle, those Blood remnants." The voice was above me, the light behind him shadowed his face. But his suit was dark blue, like the inspector's.

"I'll be fine." He helped me to my feet, and I swiped my gun that had been abandoned at the edge of the firelight's reach, tucking it back on my hip. The simple movements encouraged lancing pains from the bite, awakened aches from every one of my joints, but I hid the hurt from the guard's critical assessment.

"Are you sure? Sometimes their venom causes hallucinations. I can escort you to the nearest alchemedis, and on the way, I can get a statement from you to charge their coven. They know it's against the law to be feeding off humans." He pulled something out of his pocket. A badge. "I'm an officer with the Society, miss. You can trust I'll bring them to justice."

The Society. It was odd they'd be working this far out of town, unless the inspector dragged them out here intentionally.

"No, sir, that won't be necessary. I've got antivenom back home."

"But miss, I really need to get your statement. This is a crime scene."

I curled and uncurled the fists at my sides, tempering my impatience. Digging into my purse the bleeder had dropped, I pulled out a hundred reoles and handed it to him. He hesitated before taking the money.

"You came out here and found me arguing with a group of friends after too many whiskey sours. A gun went off accidentally. It was my fault, and both parties agreed not to press charges. That is my statement. Good night, Officer."

I made it the rest of the way to the waiting carriages without any more resistance, ignoring the inquiring questions of the Society man I left behind in hopes the shadows would keep my secrets. I'd need to clean off the grime before Nico got home, wash away the evidence of my scramble in the dirt when I was supposed to be in the posh upper booths, rubbing elbows with his enemies. If he found out what I'd seen tonight . . . I hesitated to think of what he might do.

Thank the saints for paragraph twelve, line three.

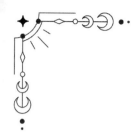
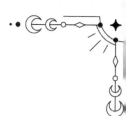

CHAPTER 7
CAMILLA

The flat was still empty when I returned. Night swallowed the home in pitch darkness. I fumbled for the switches, skating my hand across the wallpaper to light the sconces along the foyer that fed into a hall.

My other arm hung useless at my side, sore and heavy. When I found a guest room with an adjoining bath, I made myself at home, stripping my clothes and the night away with each layer. My reflection was not kind to me: my light brown hair matted with mud from the alley and my skin raw from brush burns. The faint lines of the bleeder's claws still marked my neck, and the bite mark on my arm was a vicious red.

I had no antivenom packed, but there was sure to be some somewhere in the flat if Nico was familiar with this area and its rogue remnants. Not all bleeders were bad. There was good and evil, light and dark in each of us, descendant or not. However, their specific class of remnant gave them an advantage in cruelty, and it was difficult to trust someone with all the gifts of an apex predator.

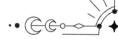

Not only were they impossibly fast and unmatched in their strength, but they had teeth that could cut through steel bars—the old prisons had found that out the hard way. It was rumored they could track someone for miles once they got a taste of their mark's blood, which put me on edge, to say the least. Every creak and moan in the quiet flat threw my heart into a thrill. The sooner we got out of this town, the better. Until then, I kept my gun close.

Once I had washed the filth from the alley from my body and spot-cleaned my clothes, I searched the bedroom for something to wear until they were dry. The guest room was empty, but the adjacent room had plenty of spare clothes neatly tucked into a dresser. I helped myself to a large shirt and some socks, trying not to think of Nico's scent woven inside the buttery fabric. Cigarillo smoke and a fine cologne. An Attano he might be, a cold-blooded killer on top of that, but I could silently admit he smelled delicious. Cheese, strawberries, Nicolai Attano . . . Why did all the good stuff have to be forbidden?

I was about to retreat to my room for the night when a shudder ran through the floor. The front door opened and slammed with such a force, the lights flickered on the wall. Voices followed, one being Nico's and the other, a woman. Out of respect, I should've let them speak in private. But rarely did I let such a virtue order my decisions, so I snuck down the hall and eavesdropped on their conversation in the receiving room.

One of the glass doors had been left cracked, betraying their discussion. Through the clear panes, a tall woman rubbed her shoulders in distress. Her dark hair was curled and set against her head with jeweled pins. She wore a short dress that was snug around her mid-thigh, gold appliques pressed into the ivory fabric, matching her gloves and complimenting her dark complexion. She must have been on her way to a party, dressed so exquisitely.

"You're married!" she seethed. Heels clicked against the wood floor. "How could you not tell me you were promised to someone?"

"Vanya, remember why we started this." Nico cut her off when her voice began to tremble. "I told you when we first met, business always comes first. This union between me and the Marchese is to protect my family."

Her shoulders fell. "It's *always* about the family. You should've at least given me a warning. I told my father you'd come tonight, and now I look like a fool." She dabbed her gloved hands over her cheeks, drying the tears that blurred her thick makeup.

"I would have liked a warning too, trust me." Nico scoffed. "It was . . . a last-minute decision."

"Do you love her?"

Nico's brows rose too far up his head. An audacious laugh burst from a mirthless smile. "Love has nothing to do with this, Vanya. On the contrary, I don't even know her. But like I said"—he stared into the fire warming the room—"it's business. I'll learn to love her if it means keeping my family safe."

My mouth went dry at his confession, wondering why he would admit such a thing. Vanya had finally stopped her pacing to take a long breath. "Love would have at least made this make sense. I just don't understand . . . I thought we had a good thing going."

Nico leaned against the hearth and nodded. "It was fun, but we can't meet anymore. Not without arousing suspicion."

"So that's it, then? You're just going to throw me away now that you have a shiny new toy? After all we've been through, this is a risky move, Nico. Even for you."

"Vanya, it's not like that and you know it," he replied with a leveling look. "Look, there's nothing you can say that I haven't already thought about. This is my choice, and I'll deal with the consequences if they come."

The woman lingered a minute too long, as if waiting for Nico to change his mind. The silence between them was almost as unbearable as the one we shared. She must have started crying again because Nico's face softened. He slowly pushed off the mantle and met her near the parlor doors to embrace her delicate frame, whispering something in her ear I couldn't hear from where I hid.

He pushed her from his chest and said, "Go home, Vanya. Go to your father's promotion party and leave the rest of this business to me."

"I don't think I can go on without you. I'm . . . I'm afraid."

Nico's voice dropped into a tone I remembered from the night we met. Comforting, warm, and vastly different than the way he spoke to me now. "They'll never find out about us, I swear it. I'll always be here for you, Vanya Hartsong. That will never change."

She flung her arms around his neck, and I pulled away from the corner, feeling the heat of their embrace touch my ears. I had officially crossed the line from curious to creepy, and an unfamiliar tightness constricted my ribs. It was hardly a shock Nico had a history, no matter how much his past still persisted to be present. He was strikingly handsome, obnoxiously wealthy, and apparently had a thing for throats. Fortunately for Vanya, I had no plans to keep her Nico forever. With any luck, she could have him back by spring.

I surrendered my search for the antivenom to return to my room, but as I rose from my crouch on the floor, my head hit one of the sconces lining the wall. The orb holding the flame burst, and glass shattered in a hundred pieces over the opulent runner. But I was too mortified to care about the mess or the dull pain spreading across my skull.

"She's *here*?" Vanya shrieked.

I was suddenly face-to-face with her as she rushed to the foyer, her lovely face twisting with resentment when our gazes crossed.

Large green eyes looked me up and down, taking in my bare figure wearing nothing but an oversized shirt that clung to my frame where my skin was still damp from the bath. She must have assumed one too many falsehoods about why I was dressed in such a state, because she shouted an unfriendly farewell at Nico and turned to leave on a dangerously skinny heel. With the slam of a door, I was alone again with a man who now looked like he hated me more than anyone alive in the world.

Nico's glare was icy as he stared at me. Disapproval raising his brows. "It's rude to eavesdrop, you know."

It was also rude to bring his past lovers around his wife, but here we were. "You made quite an entrance. I had to see what all the noise was for." The glass pieces at my feet stirred as a draft of his bender magic blew them into a small pile, clearing the way for me to walk without dicing my toes. It took everything in me to mutter, "*Thanks.*"

Nico scrubbed his face with a hand. "It's for the best. I've been trying to end things gently with her. I feel as though I might have led her on to think we were something more than . . ."

"Fun?" I offered.

He nodded slowly, his eyes assessing my bare skin. "What in the seven hells happened to you? Are those wounds from tonight?"

I glanced down at my legs, where the fabric of his shirt did nothing to hide the red marks across my knees, nor the rest of the cuts and claw marks from his assessment.

He took a step closer. A small one, yet there was a purpose in his stride. A careful approach—almost predatory. "Who did this to you, Milla?"

I swallowed. The name my family gave me sounded pleasant off his tongue. It might have been concern that lowered his voice, a flicker of concern that flashed in his gaze, or perhaps the venom was starting to trick my sanity. "A bleeder stole my purse. I went after him and ran into his coven."

"*Shit*. Are you alright?" Definitely concerned. He took another step closer, and I snatched the bite mark with my hand to hide it. Nico brushed back a thick portion of my wet hair, scanning my neck. The skim of his fingers across my throat sent a blaze where they trailed, spreading heat across my skin.

"They look worse," I muttered.

He grunted, a sound of approval by my translation. "I could have guessed, princess. You fight like my Nonna when we forget to water down her whiskey."

"I don't know what that means, but stop calling me that. I'm not a princess."

His thumb brushed a raised claw mark. "You're saving your kingdom by wedding your enemy. That sounds exactly like what the princess does in all the fairy tales I've been told."

I stepped out of his vice, sensing the discussion shifting into stranger territory. "Well, then I should have ended up with a prince, not the village idiot. But I'll take your word for it, Attano. I'm going to bed."

"Fine. Find some pants while you're at it."

I was thankful I turned my back to him so he couldn't see the blush flaming my cheeks, hoping the thin material of his shirt covered my backside as I left. But I had barely made it three steps from the boundary of the parlor before a wave of nausea knocked me to my knees, doubling me over as my insides folded together with a massive cramp. My hands and feet were drained of all warmth, numb to the world as I reached for something to ground myself in this room that was suddenly spinning.

"Camilla?" My name sounded as if it were spoken underwater. The pain once isolated to my arm bolted straight to my heart, radiating through my chest like a starburst until it consumed every thread of awareness. A hot bead rolled down my arm—blood dripping from the holes in my skin.

"Bite," I gasped through the fever heating my face.

A dark shape stepped in front of me and metal cradled my chin. A calloused hand stroked away the hair sticking to my face. There was compassion in Nico's touch, caressing the rest of my consciousness, completely opposing the ice in his voice as I fell into a merciful sleep.

"You're getting blood on my carpet."

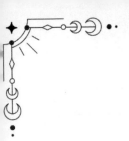

CHAPTER 8
CAMILLA

There used to be this man who worked in our rail yard. He was charming and well-spoken, and unlike the rest of the crew, he gave me attention a thirteen-year-old girl should've never had from someone his age. The papers said he disappeared one day while on the job. The Watch never found his body—and they never would.

I looked down at my arm, the image of a viper painted fresh across my skin, the sight still raw and red from the alchemists' needles. My father chose the animal, insisting this inky creature would protect me from lashing out again. Accident or not, there were consequences for my slip. My father assured me he'd do everything within his power to make sure this never happened again, and Giovanni Marchese was a very powerful man.

So we'd traveled deep into the Lowlands on our family train. The Iron Saint skated across the marshlands covering the southern tip of the Isle, deep into the lowest portion of the land where a strange woman with strange science had worked her craft into my flesh.

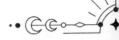

A familiar, she'd called it, and it had *worked*. As soon as the serpent had slithered to life across my arm, the restless tug in my chest had ceased. I could think clearly for the first time, felt no urges or compulsions, my anger was more manageable. My eldest brother, however, believed this entire trip to be a massive waste of time.

"The Attanos could be blowing up our half of the city and you're more worried about your daughter getting a tattoo," Aramis spat at our father, who hardly looked up at him from this week's issue of the *Isle Inquirer*.

"I wasn't aware I needed your approval, son." Father's voice held the danger of a landslide, his tone disturbingly unstable. I never knew if he would speak a kind word or give a lashing.

My brother's jaw hovered for a second; he second-guessed voicing a thought, I assumed. He regained his composure with the slow slide of his glare over my slumped figure sitting on the bench. "I want to know why."

Gio closed the paper and folded it in his lap. "Why what? Why did I drive the family down here just for Milla to see a special doctor? Or why I didn't discuss it with you first?"

"Why does she need that?" he snapped. I held a breath. Aramis was five years older than I was, but he was still a child in my father's eyes. Eighteen and impulsive.

My gaze fell to my lap, wishing he'd just complain behind my back like a normal brother. But Aramis never had a problem with voicing his concerns about me like I wasn't in the same room.

Father replied, "To make sure what happened before never happens again. Do not forget the lengths I've had to go just to keep the OIC from launching a full investigation on our family, thanks to your *illicit* hobbies."

"They aren't illegal—"

"It's a cult, and I won't have you indoctrinated with eccentric ideals. If I ever hear of you or your brothers attending one of those functions, I swear on every beat left in my heart, I will turn you in to the inspector myself."

"At least I didn't kill anyone," he murmured.

My eyes slammed shut, holding back the shameful tears.

Father took a long breath, taming the Marchese hereditary temper. "Your failure to realize your own self-destructive tendencies is exactly why you will never work for me."

I heard Aramis stand, opened my eyes again to see his fists at his sides, face flushing with rage. "You'd cut me from the railway because I disobeyed you *once*?"

"Because you turned your back on me. You've aligned yourself with those lower than our station, and now you will work to fight your way back into this family's esteem. Same for your brothers. You brought them all down with you, Aramis."

"So *she* gets it all, then?"

Father cleared his throat. "For now, yes."

Aramis pulled at his tie, loosening the knot as his breaths picked up the pace. Across the passenger car, I could see his rage tremble his fingers, flare his nostrils, clench his fist so tightly his knuckles turned white.

"You'll regret that." His gaze flickered to me. "She'll ruin us all. She's already tried."

"Watch your mouth, boy." Father placed a consoling arm around my shoulders, a subtle form of his support. I didn't understand why he'd let me off the hook with this. Even I agreed with my brothers that my punishment should have been far worse. Instead, Father covered up my crimes and acted like nothing had happened. Like my innocence hadn't been traded the moment I took that man's life.

Aramis scoffed, blue eyes settling on that arm around me. "Burn in the void, Father."

He left, slamming the door to the train car on his way out.

"I'm sorry," I said, finding my voice at last. As if my brother's presence trapped me somehow, pushing me into a cage of submission. "I'm splitting our family apart."

Father squeezed my shoulder before shifting in his seat, reaching for something in the compartment beneath him. "Don't mind your brothers, Milla. One day, they'll thank me for being hard on them." He handed me a parcel wrapped in twine. "By the way, sweet girl, happy birthday."

I perked a bit at the gift, feeling the euphoric effect of my father's generosity. Unwrapping the twine, I pushed aside the wrappings to discover a train, an exact replica of the one on which we were currently boarded. I faked a smile, feeling a bit old for toys, and assessed the miniature Iron Saint in its glass display box.

The details were exquisite, from the black body to the brass plate in the front, the gilded lettering naming our family's pride written in script on the side. Father leaned close and said, "This train belongs to you, Milla, and you must not let anyone take it from you. Not even your blood. Do you understand?"

Not even a bit. "Yes, Father."

I felt him nod and pat my head. "You are my prize for a life of cruelty, Milla. The Isle knows you as the Princess of Steam, but one day, they will call you queen. When you find your power, no one will be able to stop you. Until then"—he jutted his chin toward my serpent—"you trust no one."

I looked up at him, confused. He only smiled and opened his paper again, like he hadn't spoken such a tall claim over my life. What did he see in me that promised such a future?

A shudder ripped through the car, an explosion booming from the tracks. The last thing I remembered were my father's hazel eyes, the same color as my own, without his usual cold confidence for the first time in my life. Fear brimmed his golden gaze as he pulled me into his chest. An embrace before my entire world went up in flames.

"Camilla." His voice was a punch to the gut, a sound I remembered followed by the crunch of the cab as it derailed.

Camilla. Camilla. Camilla.

"CAMILLA."

My eyes flew open, and I discovered I was lying on my side. A woman gently probed my shoulder. The smell of rose petals from her perfume replaced the smoke from my dream. She was beautiful with an old charm. Fine lines pinched the corners of her eyes, years of smiles forever recorded in the creases of her face. She had short copper hair and skin warmed by a sun that never shined on this city.

"I'm Fran, Nicky's aunt."

My head still felt dense as she attempted to make conversation. "Nicky?" I asked.

"Nicolai." Her Continent accent was thick, one of the richest I'd ever heard out of all the descendants I'd come across. She said his name with an exotic twist, gave it extra syllables that made it sound even better.

"Where am I?" I asked, pushing off my sore arm to sit up. My own assessment put me in a four-poster bed almost as large as my own back home. The sheets were a deep crimson with swirls of gold satin that stole the firelight in their threads from the hearth across the room. The walls were decorated with thin striped wallpaper and dark wainscoting. Ornate frames bordered the painted faces of strangers.

She stood from a chair placed near the head of my bed and began tinkering with a water pitcher and glass cup. "Nicky brought you home after you received that nasty bite. We were worried when he arrived in the dead of night, but when we saw the state you were in, we understood why he risked the curfew to get you back. I always told him he needed to keep antivenom in his apartment."

She handed me the cup, and I gratefully accepted, tasting the gravel in my voice. She continued as I drank. "You were so pale I thought you had been drained at first. And burning hot, almost difficult to touch. Venom doesn't usually affect natives so harshly."

"I wouldn't know," I said. "I've never been bitten before. How long was I sleeping?"

She sat on the edge of the bed and smoothed the wrinkles that formed with my rousing. "You slept two full days away. I was just about to go downstairs for the morning and wanted to check on you before breakfast."

I'd been sleeping that long? It had been three days since I signed the contract. For a moment, before I woke, I could have passed it all off as a bad dream. But this was not my room or my sheets, and it was not my family at my bedside, but one I'd been sold to. This woman, Fran, might appear kind on first impression, but she was one of them and just as part of orchestrating this deal as Aramis or *Nicky*.

"I'll have something sent up. You must be starving," she said. Realizing then I had been staring at her, lost in my animosity, I could only nod and take another sip of water.

"I'd like that. Thank you."

When she left me alone, I checked the bite. Black lines inked the surrounding vessels like venomous cobwebs across my skin. It was still tender to the touch and to move, but I figured whatever medication the Attanos' healers had given me had denied it the ability to kill me. A little soreness was preferable to the initial symptoms.

Testing the strength in my legs, I gradually crawled out of bed and searched for my trunk, which had been already unpacked and the contents neatly folded inside an immaculate wardrobe of polished mahogany. Eager to replace Nico's shirt I still wore, I snatched a linen blouse that fell off the shoulders, fitted breeches, and a quilted vest that hugged all the curves beneath my leather jacket.

A knock came at the door then.

"Come in," I called to the visitor.

The door cracked open slightly, and through the slit of the opening, a head popped through. Our tailor, Sera, who owned a shop in Seville Square, a profitable business strip my family owned in the Steam District. Giles oversaw most of the books on our tenants there, but it had proved to be a decent stream of income to fund the railway repairs after the war with the Attanos.

Sera slipped inside as I gave her an encouraging smile. We had only met on a few occasions when she visited the manor to take my measurements. She couldn't have been much older than me, though her brown hair was already streaked with grey. Nimble hands smoothed nervously across her threadbare skirt before folding in front of her.

"Miss Camilla, I am pleased to see you looking so well. How are you feeling?"

"Please, call me Milla," I said before gesturing to the pile of clothes in my hands. "And I'm ready to get out of this room. Why don't you help me get dressed for the day?" My eyes darted toward the door linking to the adjacent bathroom. I didn't need assistance putting one foot in my pants at a time, but I wanted to know if I had missed anything interesting while I'd been unconscious, and it was far from any listening ears lingering outside the bedroom door.

Sera nodded and began to head in the direction I suggested when the door burst open without warning.

"Why—" Nico paused, looked me up and down, then frowned. "Why are you still not wearing pants?"

"Why don't you *knock*?" I countered, feeling suddenly very exposed under his inspection. Nico was dressed well as usual, wearing a crimson vest over a black shirt that clung to all the hard planes of his chest and shoulders. Fresh wax pulled his hair to the side from a hard part, but my gaze caught on his false hand, the same that had squeezed the life out of a man only days ago.

My intrigue concerning his hands might end up becoming the death of me as well.

Nothing about my appearance seemed to impress him, though his gaze was slow to snap from my bare legs. A familiar rage animated his face once more. "Why didn't you tell me right away, at the races, that you were bit? You could have died, Milla! There are lives depending on this union of ours. Nowhere in that contract did it protect my family from the consequences of your reckless and inconsiderate behavior."

"Inconsiderate?" I dropped the clothes into a pile on the floor and stomped across the room to meet him where he stood. "That's rich, considering I wouldn't have gotten bit if I hadn't been trying to help you. You were the one who brought me to that awful place to navigate *alone*. Nowhere in our contract does it protect me from your poor choices."

His nostrils flared, a hot breath fumed against my face as he looked down at me. "Who were they?"

"Can the interrogation wait until after I get dressed? I still have a pounding headache." I turned from his glare and started to walk away, but he snatched me by my good arm and yanked me back.

For once, he wasn't wearing gloves, and his bare touch sent a rash of chills sweeping down my back despite the heat lingering beneath his skin. He pulled me close. So close, I could smell spiked coffee lacing his breath as he spoke in my ear. "I've waited long enough for you to wake up from your nap, princess. I need answers, and I needed them yesterday."

"I'll come back later, Milla," Sera squeaked somewhere behind the man that towered over me, consuming my sight.

"*No*," I hissed. "One of us will need a witness in case we kill the other." And I wanted her to hear every word, so I didn't have to repeat myself later, so she could tell my brothers.

The way he held me, somewhere between gentle and bruising, I sensed the urgency in his touch, in that slight tug in his voice. I closed my eyes and thought back to that night, replaying the scene in my head until I could recall some identifying detail. Perhaps if I gave him this, he would give me something back. And I didn't think he'd let me go until I spilled my truth.

"They called themselves the Grey Hands. They planned on taking me to someone, but they didn't mention who exactly."

He thankfully released me, and yet the ghost of his touch lingered, haunting my skin. It was the first time he touched me since the night at the pub. "The Grey Hands? Are you sure?"

"Positive. Why? Have you heard of them before?"

"No, that's the problem. If there's a new bleeder syndicate running around, we haven't heard of them yet." He shoved his hands in his pockets and began to pace the plush rug in front of the bed.

"Could they be working with the Collector?" I pondered.

He winced. "I haven't heard of anyone being taken outside of the Row, and the Collector has been exclusively targeting remnants. What would his hands be doing at the derby, and what would they want with *you?*" Shaking his head, he paused. "No, this had to be an isolated assault, one with their own motivations. Did they know who you were?"

"No, she kept referring to me as a *Lesser*." I grimaced at the way the memory stung. "Whatever that means."

He turned completely to face me, heaving a placating breath, and my eyes traced the lines of his shirt as they edged the defined cords of his chest. "That's an old, derogatory term descendants used to call those without remnants. It's foul and degrading, and you shouldn't let anyone call you that ever again."

A shiver rolled down my spine, thinking of facing the coven again. "Could this have anything to do with why you were at the derby in the first place?" I cast a line, hoping he'd take the bait.

A flash of irritation rippled in his stormy eyes. "I don't control bleeders. Blood remnants are the Salt Queen's problem. I told you to stay out of my business—"

"I'm afraid it's far too late for that." I held up my arm. The sleeve of his shirt fell to my shoulder, giving him a flattering view of the horrid bite. "That bleeder tasted me, and it was clear they wanted to take me back to whoever they work for. I would bet money she'll be tracking me, and when she does, she'll find me *here*. Keeping secrets from me only puts all of us in danger."

A muscle clenched from his jaw to his temple. He knew I was right, but I doubted those words would ever leave his lips. "I need to go down to the factory today. Do not leave the house until I find you decent escorts."

"That's not necessary—"

"You *need* protection, Milla," he said, his voice the steadiest it had been this entire time, a wall of sureness. "We might have been rivals in our past, but we are together now. You are *mine*, and long as you are bound to me, I will do everything in my power to keep you safe."

His. Like I was his property because he had paid a wealthy sum to stamp his name behind my own. I scoffed, brushing off the way his admission made my heart skip. "You must really need my help if you care that much."

He stared at me, his mask that rendered him unreadable now fitted back into place. "I do."

Nico left, shutting the door with a swift breeze behind him. The sparks of his magic tingled my skin as it brushed my cheeks, and I fought the urge to lift my hand and study the unique touch of his remnant.

Sera came up from behind and sighed. "Do you think he's lying about not knowing who these Grey Hands are?" she asked.

Doubtful. Nico had a look about him, those creases splitting his forehead betraying his concern. "I don't think so, but he's hiding something."

"What do you mean?" she asked.

"When you go back to the Districts," I said, dropping my voice to barely a whisper, "I need you to look into a murder."

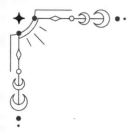
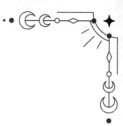

CHAPTER 9
CAMILLA

"*Shitting saints*, you've got an arm," I gasped as Sera combed down my bed head. I had never employed a personal servant before, had never seen the need to hire someone to do things I could easily do myself. But it was a nice change to have someone to talk to, even if they only listened because I was paying them. True friends were difficult to come by in my line of work.

"You shouldn't curse the divines like that, Milla," she said with a raised brow, as if to warn me of saying sacrilegious words out loud.

I shrugged indifferently. "They died after they split themselves into fragments and scattered their power to their Remni. I doubt they can hear me in the void."

"My father used to say the veil between our realm and the void is thinner than we think. There's no telling what they hear in the passing place between this life and the afterworld."

My father educated us lightly concerning the history of the realm. The Creator formed the Continent, the Isle, the Outer

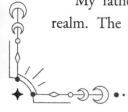
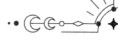

Reaches, and everything in between. From his body, the saints were born.

From his heart, Giver and Greed, a two-faced deity that decided the new world needed beings to worship them, made from their image. They created the first mortals, sharing the balance they were given from their opposing sides until the life they made was full of contradictions, forming and instilling a humanity to all who breathed that first breath.

From his mind, Mirth. From his hands, Bane. From his body, Blood. And then, another Saint came to fruition, though this one from a more complicated part of the Creator's self. From his soul, Chaos was born.

Chaos discovered the world had a certain order, and she despised it, deciding to create her own beings to challenge the balance humanity had known for ages. With her power of creation, Chaos created monsters with a heinous purpose, to cause disorder in a once peaceful world. The first demon hordes hit the skies and thus marked the beginning of the First War.

The saints knew they could not defeat Chaos's monsters themselves, and humanity was too powerless on their own. To save creation, the divines split themselves into fragments, passing down their unique gifts to multiply their power, remnants of themselves to help humanity fight the demon hordes and restore the natural order. The original recipients of their gifts were known as the Remni, and all those who descend from them hold the same power used to fight the hordes that rose and fell centuries ago.

Shattering themselves into so many fragments, the saints withered away, leaving behind their power in a world that was no longer plagued by monsters. Chaos retreated to Oblivion, the darkest, bloodiest hell in the void. Some say she waits to return, when the descendants have weakened and scattered like fallen rice to the corners of the map.

I never put stock into legends and fables. Some people had magic in their blood, and some did not. That was a measurable truth, and only that which was certain was worth the time of a considerable thought.

"Giles mentioned you had family in the row," I said, changing the subject. "Which saint do they descend from?"

Sera slipped my hair around a hot iron rod, curling the ends, insisting the look would soften the sharp angles of my face—whatever that meant. "My father is a descendant of Mirth. I didn't receive his remnant, however, inheriting my mother's side. She's a native."

"Mirth? That's one you don't hear of very often."

She grabbed another thick strand of light brown hair and looped it around the rod. "Not many of them attempted the exodus from the Continent, the few that exist. It's a rare remnant, as Mirth apparently didn't give his gifts to many to fight the hordes. It wasn't as necessary being a less physical power."

Curious, I asked, "What does his power entail then?"

She cleared her throat and glanced at my reflection in the mirror. "Mirth created the Scolapa, thought controllers, the Amov, which are shifters, and the Mentalus, thought readers. My father is the latter, though I have a distant cousin whose a shifter. Our abilities keep us ostracized for obvious reasons, so we don't discuss them much."

My skin prickled with unease. I'd never met a Mirth remnant, and I wasn't sure I wanted to. Protecting my flesh was one thing, protecting my mind was another battle entirely. "That must have been difficult, growing up with a father who could read your mind."

Her brows rose half an inch as she nodded. "It was . . . until he disappeared."

"Disappeared?"

She sighed, gaze falling beyond her task to look at a deeper thought. She didn't reply until my hair had begun to smoke. Patting it cool, she said, "Technically, they can't call him dead since they haven't found his body."

I murmured something like a condolence, not knowing quite what to say. I knew what she felt, a relentless desire to return to that very thought that had taken the spotlight in her mind. A hope sometimes confused with denial, that it was all a dream and they would walk through the door at any moment, meanwhile possessing the right-mindedness to know the odds were never that generous. Even in a world blessed with such extraordinary powers and wonders, some things were still impossible.

Magic might exist, but miracles did not.

"What happened?" I asked, pulling my knees to my chest. The topic pulled my own grief and guilt to the stage, and my misery longed for some company.

"An accident. At least, that's what they told me. The Overseer's watchmen weren't particularly forthcoming with information. The Society didn't want to involve the Watch, and they swept the incident under the rug like they do most remnant *accidents.*"

Her hands roughly pulled at my hair, yanking my head back as she spoke, offering an apologetic smile when she realized my pursed lips translated an uncomfortable experience. "Sorry, I still get a little worked up about it."

"Don't be sorry. I have a tough head." I watched her as the last strands fell from her fingers, and she gathered my hair in front of my shoulders, showing off her work. The wispy, natural curls I regularly wore were smooth tendrils of golden-brown hair. I had to admit, it looked much better this way. A little attention to my appearance went a long way.

Turning to face her, I asked, "What was your father's name? I have a few connections with the watchmen. Maybe they can get me some intel."

She shook her head and set down the hot rod on the vanity counter. "Marco Gallo. But you have enough on your plate as it is. Don't worry about me, I'll be fine."

"Then after this is finished," I suggested. "At least let me try. You're doing so much for my family, and I want to do something for you in return."

She swallowed hard as her bony hands wrung themselves in front of her waist. "You'd do that for me?"

"Of course." I stood and turned from her reflection, looking straight into her jewel-green eyes. "Have my brothers sent any word yet?"

She nodded. "I was just about to get to that. Aramis is expecting dirt on the Attanos. While you're here, he wants you to learn their secrets, get into the factories, get close to Nico to discover his weaknesses. Should anything go wrong in the next six weeks, they want something to use against him."

I bit the inside of my cheek in thought. "You can report back that I'm way ahead of them. What I told you before, about the murder, needs to be passed along to Aramis as well." I explained to her in hushed tones about the stable, the man named Silas. Her eyes widened when I got to the gory part.

Her cheeks paled from their usual rosiness. "Nicolai Attano is dangerous, Milla. I've heard rumors of his ruthless business model from my patrons. We need to be careful in this house."

"Trust me, I had a front-row seat to his *business model*. If there's anyone who can outplay him strategically, it's my family." I motioned for her to follow me from the bathing room and back into the main area of my bedroom suite. "I'm eager to stretch my legs. Would you take me on a tour of the estate?"

The delicate features of her face sharpened with a wince. "Of course, but I'll warn you. The rest of the Attanos are home, and I'm afraid there's no avoiding them."

"Are they difficult?"

"The grandmother is a piece of work."

This would be an experience then. I didn't grow up with aunts, uncles, grandparents, or cousins. Technically, since this contract would be shredded as soon as I turned twenty-one, I still had none of those. I certainly wouldn't find them in the den of my rivals.

"Can I ask you something?" she said. "What's the reason for the bad blood between your families?"

My gaze fell across the luxuries of my new accommodations. The vaulted ceiling, the marble lining the hearth, the windows framed by gossamer curtains so light, they appeared to float on the air. The Attanos had done well for themselves, even after our feud.

"I was a child when it was going on, so I didn't understand at the time." My feet drifted to the window to gaze upon the sprawling green yard on the west side of the massive house. This must have been the old Overseer's estate, before there was a need to split the city into sides. No one in Lynchaven had this much yard. "One of Nico's predecessors had a deal with my father to move materials from the mines up north to their steel factories, a more efficient process than the ships that come down the Ada.

"But something happened. Something terrible, and the Attanos wrongfully blamed us for being a part of it. My brothers were part of a cult, or so my father said. I think they were involved with something that ruined the working relationship between our families."

I faced her, turning my back on their nauseating display of wealth. "When I was thirteen, we took a trip south. They found out we'd be out of town, and the Attanos used the opportunity to bomb the tracks and derail our car. My father died in the crash, and our feud settled into a stalemate, seeing as neither side would win. We couldn't afford to keep up the fight after that, and the Attanos went silent."

Until two days ago.

"Do you think they felt bad?" she asked. "For killing him, I mean."

"Families like ours don't get remorseful," I said, gesturing to the room around us. "We get even."

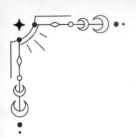

CHAPTER 10
CAMILLA

I once vowed after the death of my father that if I ever met an Attano, I'd kill them. Instead, I married one. I slept in their bed and strolled their halls without a blade in sight. I surveyed the family portraits large enough to fill the walls with their grandeur, listening to Sera list off all the things she'd learned about each of them while I slept.

"There are three aunts, one uncle, and a grandmother. Fran and Solomon are married, their children being Esme, Adler, and Gideon. The only couple remaining are Lucinda and Ianthe. They have an adopted son, Luther."

"Luther is adopted?" I asked. It made sense now that I thought about it. He didn't have the dark complexion his cousins claimed, having paler skin, reddish hair, his frame a bit more gangly than his boss's. Who, to my unfortunate discovery, was neither bulky nor skinny. A rare collection of lean muscle beneath tan skin and skillful hands that could wrap the hollow of my throat.

Sera moved onto the next portrait, displaying the youngest gener-

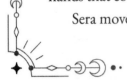

ation of Attanos. Nico stood in the center. The cousins I met posed beside him. A young girl who could have been his twin sat in a chair with a child on her lap.

"Yes, but he is still a remnant of Bane. I believe he dabbles with sound, but I've heard from the staff that he hasn't used his remnant in years. Nico seems to be the only bender I've known who can claim so many variations."

"Do they all bend something different?" I asked.

She canted her head in thought. "Adler"—she pointed to the youngest male cousin, a shorter man with Nico's haircut and eyes the color of coal—"he controls heat. I've heard he can suck the warmth from any living creature and use it to feed the flames in his hearth. Gideon, however, is only an air bender, and a very adept one at that."

She gestured to the only male cousin who smiled in the portrait. His face was composed of softer features, or perhaps it was because I was familiar with his gentle touch and apologetic demeanor.

"And what of her?" I asked about the gorgeous cousin sitting in the chair.

Another voice joined us in the large hall. "Esmerelsa is the oddball of the family."

I turned to find the living version of the picture sauntering towards us. She was dressed in a welder's smock, rubber boots, and goggles hanging around her neck. Ash dusted the edges of her cheekbones. Patches of clean skin surrounded her eyes where the goggles once sat. "You must be Camilla. My name is Esme, Nicky's favorite cousin." She thrust her hand out and snatched mine in a firm grip, shaking it once before releasing.

"Please, call me Milla. It's nice to meet you," I said, trying my best to return her polite smile.

"I doubt you truly mean that, but I appreciate the attempt at courtliness." She winked. "I cannot express how excited I am to have another girl in the house. It's no secret our families have been at odds for some years, but I think this union between you and Nico will be beneficial in more ways than one. At least, I *hope*."

I cocked my head. "What do you mean?"

Esme gestured to her uniform. "I'm a metal bender. Unfortunately, most of the refineries are owned by the Firenzes in the Wet District. Nico offered me a job, but I really don't want to bend steel for the rest of my life. I'm an innovator, you see."

"Are there no other metal benders who can help you?" I asked.

She shook her head. "Metal wasn't in high demand when the saints gifted us their fragments, just a few Remni were made to craft weapons and defenses. It's a rare remnant, but I've been practicing on my own. Even crafted that nice contraption for Nicky."

My eyes widened. "*You* made his hand?"

Her smile broadened into a prideful grin. "Yes, I did." She stepped closer, dropping her voice. "By the way, should you need me to *add* anything for yourself in there, I'm way ahead of you, sister."

It took me a moment to realize what she suggested. My mouth hung open for a beat before replying, "That won't be necessary. Ever. But thanks for the offer."

She stepped back and shrugged. "Never say never. Nicolai has a way of growing on people."

"Yes, like a wart."

Esme released the most obnoxious laugh I'd ever heard before, echoing down the main hall. She grabbed my hand again, this time holding it affectionately. "I like you. You're pretty, but I can tell you don't bend for anyone. Tough and unbreakable"—her gaze leveled on mine—"like cast iron."

Before I could resist, Esme pulled me down the hall. "Come with me. I'll introduce you to everyone. Are you coming, Sera?"

My tailor smiled hesitantly before shaking her head, and I

wondered if it had anything to do with this grandmother she spoke of earlier. "Thank you for the invitation, but I'll pass. I'll be in my quarters if you need me, Milla."

I shot her a look before she turned and left me stranded with the sprightly Attano.

"Esme?"

"Yes?"

"Who's the girl you're holding in the picture?" She'd mentioned there were no other girls in the house, but the evidence was painted in living color on the wall.

The cousin stopped, the joy in her eyes leaking slightly from the hole made from my prodding. "That's Anna. She's . . . no longer with us." She tugged my arm gently, pulling me away.

I followed but stole one last look at the portrait. The soft face of the child smiled at the painter, who had somehow captured a pinch of mischief in her eyes and a honey sweetness spreading her smile.

That mischief, I noticed, was steel grey and familiar.

Esme brought us to the kitchen, where she claimed her Nonna was preparing dinner. "But it's barely noon," I said, glancing at a nearby wall clock.

"Nonna is making a special dinner, since we have an important guest tonight." She wiggled her thin shoulders beneath the weight of her thick clothes. "It usually takes her all day, and she doesn't let us forget it."

The bender pushed the door to the kitchen wide, where we were greeted first by the heat. Gas stoves warmed a kitchen so large, it appeared to be built for a full staff, separated into stations. A T-shaped island spanned the width of the room, lined with the chopped remains of root vegetables and raw meats. The scraping sound of metal utensils against a pot competed with the gossiping voices of those who sat around the island.

Several women, I recognized from the portraits as Nico's aunts, sat on barstools across from one another while a much older woman had her back turned toward the stove.

"Look who I found wandering the halls," Esme chimed. All conversations ceased abruptly as I entered, absorbing the weight of their combined attention like fresh bread in a pan of melted butter. *Saints*, I was hungry.

"Camilla!" It was Fran who stood first to greet me, wrapping me in another embrace I wasn't sure how to return. Besides Giles, my brothers rarely expressed their affections through physical touch— not that they had much affection to give.

I just gave her a soft pat on her shoulder and hoped it would be over soon.

She released me, motioning to each of the other aunts in a quick introduction, though I'd already memorized each of their names. Ianthe was in the chair beside her, a book open in her hands. Lucinda sat across from her on the other side of the butcher block, Luther's other mother.

The last relative cleared her throat and crossed her arms, clearly not impressed with being saved for last. Esmerelsa said with a sigh, "And this is my Nonna, Edith, the leader of the Attano clan."

"I thought Nico was in charge of things around here?" I asked, challenging the old woman's poor manner.

She frowned, a wooden spoon protruding from a white knuckled grip like a weapon. "Well, he certainly acts like it. I let him play the big man when I get tired of dealing with these stubborn children of mine."

"He's also her favorite grandchild," Esme murmured beneath her breath.

Nonna rolled her eyes. "For the last time, Esme, I don't have favorites. But he deserves a bit of favor after spending his inheritance on this little Marchese harlot."

"I am not a harlot!" I said, voice sharper than intended.

"You trapped my grandson," she spat.

I scoffed. "Your grandson offered himself up as bait. Not my fault he got himself caught up in my problems."

Her frown only deepened, muttering something in another language. *Un cancidamus orbitur.* "Do you know what that means, Camilla?"

If she was trying to make me feel dumb, it wasn't working. I shrugged and muttered, "How should I know? I don't speak old dog." The room seemed to take a collective breath, waiting for Nonna's response, and I wondered if I'd just sealed my death. Nonna hadn't signed an agreement not to harm me after all.

And then, slowly, she nodded. A faint smile pulling one side of her wrinkled cheek. "It means *where we fall, we rise.* An old Attano saying. Keep that spirit, Camilla. If you want to survive life in the Row, you'll need it."

Or it would get me killed. Either way, I wouldn't be taken down by a four-and-a-half-foot tall elderly woman who spoke in tongues.

"Esme, wash your hands and help me with this caper sauce for the roasted boar."

"But Nonna, I was working—"

Her grandmother quickly cut her off with a single stare. "You've been in that shed for days, Esme. How do you expect to find a husband if you spend all your time molding and meddling?"

"Very simple," she replied. "I don't want a husband. In fact, I don't wish to be married at all."

Nonna's stare slid to me. "Maybe you can change her mind while we cook. Wash up. You're on sides."

"Actually," I interjected, daring to defy her, "if I'm to be dragged into this, I'd rather take on the meat. It's kind of my specialty."

Nonna set her bony shoulders back like she'd just been challenged to a duel. "*Your* specialty?"

I angled my chin a little higher, despite the height difference. "Yes. *My* specialty."

Her small eyes nearly disappeared into slits. "Fine. But it better be half decent, *Belladonna*, because Nicky loves my cooking. I'd hate to see you disappoint him so soon in your marriage."

I wanted to tell her that I didn't give a damn what *Nicky* thought about my cooking, but there was a sudden urge to prove myself in this house, and if that was accomplished with tenderloin and caper sauce and her grandson's approval, then so be it.

My smile had the old woman inching back. "Don't worry about me, Nonna. Worry about your sides."

⁂

THE DAY PASSED QUICKLY as we prepared the seven-course dinner feast. Esme hadn't been exaggerating when she said Nonna took all day to cook. She made everything from scratch, from the breads to the post-dinner pastry filling, without the help of a single staff member that passed through to take up the dirty dishes and clean behind us.

The aunts popped open a rare bottle of wine and portioned it between us all, even offering me a glass to my surprise and gratitude. I sipped it savoringly slow, letting the bright aromas of raspberries, vanilla, and pomegranates numb some of the soreness still gnawing down my arm. It was a treat to try, as there were no vineyards on the Isle to make such a dram. The Attanos had brought this over from the *old country,* as they called it, and I understood why they bothered packing a cask all the way across the sea—even if my stomach twisted with every satiated sip. One more thing to add to the list of forbidden fruits.

By the time Nico and his cousins came home from the factory, the afternoon glare spilling through the skylight had been purged by night. A small window over the sink overlooked the courtyard behind the house, where his horses were being returned to their stable.

They announced themselves with the slam of the double doors leading into the kitchen. I spun toward the sound after checking my capers a final time.

"What are you doing in here?" he asked with a pointed glare.

Conversations fell quiet. His cousins followed behind him as he stepped further into the kitchen, Gideon heading first to the arrangement of cheeses sitting on the island. Nonna slapped his hand with the reach of her cane before he could steal a bite.

"What does it look like I'm doing?" I waved the spoon in my hand.

His lips flattened. "You were bit by a wearh two nights ago. You should be resting." He looked at his grandmother. "Shame on you, Nonna. Milla's barely been here a day and you're already putting her to work."

"I believe as the only senior in this room, I can do whatever the hells I want," she replied, glancing at me with her beady eyes. "Now come here and give me and your wife a proper hello. I didn't brave the Narrow Sea with your grandfather to let my descendants boss me around."

Nico pushed up his sleeves and sighed. His broad shoulders had fallen slack. Just when I thought he'd refuse, he rounded the island and took his Nonna's hand, kissing it once before placing another on her cheek. "My apologies, Nonna."

I couldn't help the surprise that showed itself on my face. One minute he'd thrown a stableman into the stalls of a man-eating horse, the next he bowed to an old woman. Ruthless and cold-blooded, then submissive and affectionate. He switched sides so seamlessly, and I didn't understand how he could play both roles with such flawless execution.

He turned to me, but before he could greet me in such a way, I dipped the spoon in the creamy sauce and held it in front of his face. "Try it."

Grey eyes narrowed on the spoon. "What?"

"Nonna and I would like to know which version of the caper sauce you prefer. Hers or mine."

A dark brow arched. "Aren't you allergic to half of the ingredients for that?"

"I endured for the challenge. Now taste it."

He conceded, taking the end of the spoon in his mouth and licking it clean. I was all too aware of the shape of his mouth and the roll of his tongue across the silver as I slipped it from his lips. Nico leaned his hip against the counter in thought.

"Well?" I asked. "How is it?"

He winced, looking uncomfortable. "Fucking *hot*."

"Mmmm." I glanced at the steam rising from the pot—hadn't even thought about turning down the heat. "Sorry about that."

He smacked his lips a few times and canted his head, swallowing at last.

"Well?" Luther said as the rest of the room waited on bated breath.

Nico fought a smile, but the deep dimples in his cheeks betrayed him. "I think . . . I have a new favorite caper sauce."

"*Nicolai*!" Nonna's enraged voice filled the kitchen, drowning out my cry of victory.

He held up both hands in surrender as she lifted her cane. "I'm sorry, Nonna, but you've finally met your match. Serves you right for putting her to work on the first bloody day she's here."

I couldn't help but roll my eyes. "I'm not made of glass, Nico."

"*Someone* has to look out for you, Milla." His comment was careless, thrown back at me as he reached for a bread roll. I noticed Nonna didn't strike his hands for trying to sneak food early.

"What in the void is that supposed to mean?"

"Exactly what I said." He shrugged, indifferent. Didn't even look at me as he kept shooting and hitting a vulnerable target in my heart. My defenses slammed around it.

"I have plenty of people who look out for me." I didn't know why it bothered me so much that he thought I'd been on my own until—what? He came and *saved* me from my cruel family like I was some princess in need of protection.

"Like whom? Your brothers?" He snorted. "Or the men who work for you? If you have to pay them, Milla, it doesn't count."

"My brothers have always looked out for me," I spat.

He turned to face me too slowly, and I knew I had said something that crossed a line between us. The ease in his shoulders suddenly filled with tension. "Your brothers sold you to the highest bidder. I don't believe for a second they were concerned about your best interest when I showed up in your courtyard and waved a few coppers in their face."

"I don't care what you believe. You know nothing about them."

"I know enough, and they certainly don't care about you as they should."

I flinched and hated myself for it. I hated that I let this man see how his words whipped me. I hated that they affected me to begin with.

And I hated that he was right.

"Nico. *Cousin*," Luther spoke quietly behind him.

Nico pretended not to hear him. "I sent word to them that you were hurt. Gravely hurt. Do you know what Aramis replied, Milla?"

The kitchen fell so quiet, I could hear each wrathful breath as it escaped me. Knowing my eldest brother, my health would be the last thing he concerned himself over. "I don't need to know."

"There's nothing *to* know. Because he didn't even write back."

Somehow, it didn't shock me. But the weight of the room's attention settled on my chest, making it difficult to breathe. I swallowed the gravel in my throat and smiled like my heart was still intact, like my hands weren't shaking from embarrassment and rage. "Are you quite done?"

His jaw locked, and he nodded once.

"Well, your point of view has been very insightful, but I'm afraid it has ruined my appetite, so I'm just going to go to bed."

I practically ran out of the kitchen, my strides devouring the length of the hall as I searched for the staircase of solid mahogany leading to the bedrooms. It hadn't been enough for him to put down my family. No, he had to shame me in front of his own on top of it. In hindsight, I shouldn't have even started that conversation. It was obvious where it would lead. What I didn't anticipate was just how accurate his shots would hit their mark, and how much they'd rattle me in the crossfire.

"Camilla!" Nico's voice followed me. I despised that I didn't know this place better so that I could lose him. But the Attano estate was a sprawling mansion, with multiple wings and levels, each more inconspicuous than the last and easy to lose one's way.

112

"Milla, stop!"

Screw that. He'd lost the little respect that remained for him in my heart, and I continued to stomp off in the direction of my room, taking the stairs two at a time. Somehow, he caught up to me, which was probably due to the fact his strides were twice the length of my own. I raced him back to my room, anyway.

His hand wrapped around my arm just as I made it past the threshold and pulled me to a forced stop. I whirled around, glaring at him. "What do you want, Nico? Did you forget to say something down there?"

"Milla, I'm—"

My smile returned, and I must have looked mad to him, the way he startled. "Maybe next dinner, we can dissect my father. Then at breakfast, we can discuss all the potential reasons my mother left when I was an infant. There's just so *much* to unpack when it comes to my family. We'll never run out of fresh material."

"I'm sorry, Milla," he growled. Nothing in his expression made me feel that it was even close to sincere. His grandmother must have put him up to this.

I twisted my arm out of his grip. "You had no right to speak about my family that way, to me like that, in front of everyone."

His face softened. Sharp edges smoothed into someone safer. "I know. I don't know where that came from. I just . . ."

I crossed my arms. "You just . . . what?"

His glare slid down my body as I stood there, fists clenching at his sides. "Nothing. It's nothing. I've just been stressed lately, and I've taken it out on you."

That hardly made me feel better, especially after witnessing him kill someone. The look on my face must have told him so. He added, "Can we start this night over? My family apparently really enjoyed you today, and they'd like you to come downstairs."

"*They* would like me to come downstairs?"

He frowned, forced to slide the words through his teeth. "*I* would like for you to come downstairs."

It made me smile, watching the notorious Nicolai Attano grovel at my bedroom door. I thought I might pick more fights with him, just to replay the experience. "That's benevolent of you, Nico. But my answer is still no."

"Are you always this unforgiving?"

"Yes. Remember that the next time you feel like pissing me off."

I took a step backwards, leaving enough space for the door to slam shut in his face.

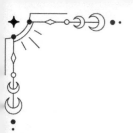
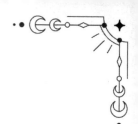

CHAPTER 11
NICOLAI

"Don't. Say. *Anything*."

My entire family eyed me as I entered the dining room empty-handed, the path to my chair at the head of the table feeling similar to a walk of shame. To my surprise, they remained wordless, though my aunts' eyebrows threatened to fly off their faces, the way they arched in disapproval. Thankfully, my Uncle Solomon was late from the office and had missed the entire fiasco.

I didn't know why I felt the need to prove to Milla her brothers were shit. She probably already knew. They'd set her up with Felix Firenze, for saint's sake, just to save their own skins. Milla would've been miserable bound to that man. Lucky for the heiress, the only family richer than the Firenzes was my own, and I could make her much less miserable if she'd just stop being so captious.

But the Marchese sons . . . I didn't trust them. The arrangement between her family, the OIC, and the Firenzes was too convenient not to have been orchestrated by a knowing hand—and I needed to find out why.

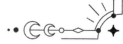

Nonna sat with her hands in her lap, staring across the table at me. When I inadvertently caught her stare, she said, "You should bring her up a plate. She must be starving."

"She made her choice. The stubborn woman can go to bed hungry."

"Nicolai . . ."

"*Nonna.*"

More silence interrupted by the teeth-grating sounds of forks across porcelain plates. Esme was the next to speak up. "I'll bring it to her if you'd like."

"*No*," I hissed the word. What was it with my family today and getting on my last nerve? "She can get her own plate if she's hungry. Which, apparently, from the way she slammed the door in my face, she is not."

I stared at the caper sauce. I didn't even *like* capers.

"You need to be patient with her, Nicky," Fran said softly, trying to appeal to a side of me that had gone cold a long time ago. "If what you said is true, can you imagine what she must be feeling?"

No, I couldn't understand what someone as entitled and spoiled as Camilla felt like being torn from her life of luxury. A life where everything had been handed to her, inheriting status, protection, security like all the rest in her father's will. Everything I needed to know about her was summed up in the way she looked at me differently when she learned my last name. If her heart could change so quickly, her feelings weren't worth understanding.

Perhaps that's why they'd tried their best to include Milla today, to make her feel too at home. I told them to keep the peace I paid for, and they'd done a better job than I expected. I resented Camilla, but I respected her. I related to her unwavering faith in her brothers, despite their trespasses. The family in front of me, the ones having full conversations with their side-eyes alone, were my life and my world. Like Milla, I'd do anything for them, including bind myself to a pampered heiress and her even less-than-desirable bloodline.

However, I also related to her relentless pursuit to free us both from this marriage before our six-week timeline came to an end. That much we could agree upon at least.

Ignoring the looks from my aunts, I lifted my spoon to eat and bit air instead. On the way to my mouth, the silver utensil had bent in half, the contents in the scoop fell back onto the plate. "*Esme.*"

"You don't eat until she does," she said flatly. I lifted my gaze to glare at my cousin. The rest of the table seemed to be in agreement.

I flung the broken spoon across the table, where it clattered against the polished ebony. "Fine. I can see I'm outnumbered here. Grimm?"

Our family attendant stepped from his station near the door. "Yes, Mr. Attano?"

Standing from my seat, I rolled my glare across the lot of them. "Get me a fucking plate and a tray. I'll have my meal upstairs as well."

⁂

GRIMM FOLLOWED ME, holding a tray with both our dinners. It wouldn't be the first time I took my meal in my room, and knowing my family, it wouldn't be the last.

The floor was quiet as I stepped across the landing. Her door was shut. The light beneath the door had gone dark beside the fading glow that must've come from the dying fire in the hearth. I knocked three times, softly, in case she had gone to bed. No need to wake the beast if she was already asleep.

There was no answer. I shrugged to Grimm, was about to tell

him to leave her plate by the door, when a crash sounded in her bedroom.

The hair on my neck stood on end. "Milla?" I spoke her name urgently. When silence met me again, I jiggled the door handle—locked as expected. Manipulating the tubes in my false hand, I pulled out a skeleton key and threaded it through the lock while my opposite unsheathed my gun.

"Grimm? Get my cousins."

He dropped the tray with little care for the contents, breaking the shallow bowls to disappear back down the stairs.

"I'm coming in," I warned, before throwing the door open.

The room was empty.

And destroyed.

My heart slammed against my ribs as I pieced together what had happened from the evidence. The furniture was tossed on its side. The bedding shredded and spilled down across the scratched hardwood. A freezing wind from a broken window tossed about white feathers, floating like flurries in the moonlight behind the painted glass.

There had been a struggle here. That was clear. But against whom? And how did they get in? The trail of blood at least told me how they escaped.

The window.

I crossed the room to the open window, the curtains half-ripped, the rod bent like Milla had held fast to the canvas while someone dragged her away. Looking down to the patch of green space below her bedroom, I found the next victims on my kill list.

"Nico, what happened?" Luther spoke at the door, assessing the scene.

I didn't even turn to look at him, to break eye contact with the four trespassers that held the limp figure of my wife in their grips.

"We've got company in the east courtyard. Be mindful of your shots."

I tossed myself through the window, letting the resistance of a force of wind slow my descent, but swiftly redirected my remnant to the trespassers, hitting them with the gust of a hundred storms. They dropped her body as they flew across the lawn, and I shot two down before they could find their feet.

Milla rolled to her knees, something shining against the moonlight in her hand as she crouched, swiped it over the man who'd fallen beside her to lash his neck open. She'd been faking unconscious, waiting for the right time to attack.

Hells, she was fast. Milla fought dirty, something I really wish I hadn't learned.

One of the bodies I knew for a fact I hit suddenly popped up, like it hadn't been given a new hole. In a blur, it was behind her, throwing an arm around her neck and a gun pointed at her head. Dread ate at the ends of my ribs, slipped its cold tendrils around my frenzied heart.

What in the seven hells were bleeders doing with my wife?

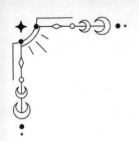

CHAPTER 12
CAMILLA

Angel held me against her chest, crushing my airway with her predator strength. "Come any closer, bender, and I'll kill her."

Nico didn't move, her threats too uncertain to chance. His eyes slid over me, grey gaze in the moonlight darkening into a cloudy storm. I didn't know Nico well enough to know his thoughts by a single look, but there was something possessive in the way his anger washed the world in wrath. He said before we were rivals in memory but allies on paper. I wondered how far he'd be willing to stick his neck out for me, and this certainly was as good a test as any.

"Let go of my wife, or *you* will die tonight."

His words held the weight of a steam train, slamming into me with a startling force. It pushed the fear in my heart aside, replacing it with something stronger. A feeling molded in steel, forging something permanent where sand once sifted.

Trust. At this moment, he was my salvation. I'd never fight off the two surviving bleeders without him.

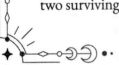
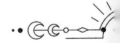

"You're not really in the position to make demands." Angel pressed the double barrel harder into my skull, making me flinch. The cousins spilled out the east wing, running towards us until Angel gave them the same warning she gave Nico. She had all the leverage she needed in her left arm, and by their reaction, she knew it.

Nico looked directly at me then, lending me his reassurance with a simple look. Here at the door of death, I should have begged for my life. I should have been ravaged with fear, barren of hope. But there was a greater power in those eyes of storm and smoke, and I clung to it, growing more certain with every second that passed that I would find a way out of her arms.

"What do you want with her?" he asked.

She hissed in my ear. "As if you don't know. Why else would you stick a Lesser in a home with the Attano Benders, if not because you want to use her as well?"

"What in the void are you talking about?" he rasped, voice coarse as rough stone.

A breathy laugh brushed the shell of my ear. Her grip on me loosened slightly. "You really don't know, do you?"

Nico's body jerked once, as if fighting his own instincts to attack. That gun in his hand was almost irrelevant compared to the sheer power of his remnant. Angel laughed. "It's alright, Attano. I'm going to find out her secrets for the both of us."

"Angel, quit playing with your food and let's go!" the second bleeder shouted from their getaway car.

One. I mouthed the number. Nico's jaw clenched. The smooth fabric of his shirt clung to the tidal waves of his breath, the fall and rise of his chest the only movement in his disturbingly still body.

Two. A whimper escaped me, feigning fear as the bleeder dragged me across the grass with a fist rooted in my hair. The gun was still pointed at my brain, but Angel was too focused on getting me into the carriage. I swallowed hard against the parch of my throat, wide eyes locked on Nico. He nodded, giving me the extra boost I needed.

Three.

I sunk the glass shard I'd been hiding in my palm into her thigh. She howled, her arm slipping around me enough that I could push the barrel from my head and toward the sky. Angel, in her suffering rage, clicked off three shots, but in the next moment, Nico raised his hand and there was a distortion of his image as he commanded the time around us to stop with a single lifted finger. Still intertwined with the bleeder, I was caught in his corruption.

It was like a single second hadn't even passed, and yet I nearly fell backward when the weight that had been holding me up suddenly vanished. I rolled to discover Nico had the bleeder pinned against the ground. His metal hand wrapped around her throat, anchored to the lawn as Angel squirmed and thrashed beneath his hold.

Alright . . . perhaps controlling the time *was* more impressive than the shadows.

"It looks like your Grey Hands will have to crawl back to whatever master you serve empty-handed. You, however, will not be joining them." His voice was crude, hardly recognizable in the monster slipping into his form.

"But I let her go," Angel said, trembling. "You said you would only end me if I harmed her, and there she is without a scratch—"

He held her at an arm's length, motionless as he watched her struggle for breath as he stole the very air from her chest. He asked, "Was this the one who bit you, princess?"

It took several seconds to realize he was speaking to me. "Yes," I said, despising how weak I must have sounded. "There were others, but she was the one who poisoned me."

Nico's tongue clicked in disapproval, shaking his head. Angel's

---

eyes fluttered, her struggle weakened to a pleading grasp around his arm. Her pale lips mouthed the word, "Please."

He leaned closer, and in a growl so low I almost didn't hear him over the wailing breeze, "Anyone who puts a gun to my girl's head will lose their hand." The fingers of his false hand were replaced with golden claws, a sharp sound marking the slide of daggers from their tips.

Angel screamed as they dug into her wrist, slipping through the framework of ligaments and tearing it from her body, tossing it somewhere behind him. Her shrieks called out to the city, a solemn warning to all that stood beyond the iron fence what happened when enemies crossed their boundary.

"And then," he spoke above her sobs, "they will lose their head. Burn in the void, bleeder."

Nico ripped out her throat. The scene was so shocking, my eyes forced themselves shut. But it was impossible to avoid the squelching sound of shredded flesh or the smell of iron as blood splattered the manicured grass.

I've shot men down before, men who wanted to hurt me or my brothers, people who threatened our syndicate with their lives, and never once have I looked away from the death I delivered. Not even the bleeder I tore into a moment ago.

But this was different. This was *messy*. It took a greater fury to paint a portrait of destruction so vivid as the one Nico bled across the floor.

"He's getting away!" Luther shouted as the carriage that had waited for me bolted toward the broken back gate, leaving the estate.

"Let him," Nico muttered. "Whatever retaliation that follows might lead us to the one who ordered this."

I didn't open my eyes again until I felt his touch, steady and light over the curve of my shoulder. Blood dripped from the false hand at his side, and I listened to the rasp of his breathing as he snapped from a trance of rage, his anger finally releasing the Nico I was acquainted with as I met his gaze again.

"Are you alright?" he asked, kneeling beside me in the grass.

I nodded, feeling numb all over. "I think so."

He ran his own assessment anyway, scooping my right hand in his bloody ones. "*Saints*, Milla. Your hand is shredded!"

"It doesn't hurt," I admitted, following his gaze to find my right hand was completely torn apart. The skin peeled back over bone, bleeding profusely.

"It will." He cradled my wounded fingers, clipping out his next words. "What happened?"

I suppressed a shiver, recalling the details. "They were waiting in my room. When you left, they grabbed me. I fought as hard as I could, not because I thought I had a chance, but just to try to make noise so someone might hear me. Thankfully, you came back upstairs, so I smashed the window with my hand before they pushed me through the open one. I was able to grab a piece of glass to fend myself with."

"Your resourcefulness never fails to impress me," he murmured.

I almost laughed. There was nothing impressive about throwing around a piece of glass while he quite literally stopped the second and ripped out a woman's throat with metal claws. My familiar slithered down my arm where Nico still held my hand.

"Curious thing, isn't he?" he pressed a thumb on its inky head, stroking the length of my forearm. The serpent flicked its tail, looking pleased at the attention.

"Only when it comes to you." I cleared my throat, unsure why I'd said such a thing. The blood loss must've been lowering my reserves.

Nico's lips cracked into a subtle smile. His lips parted to say something, but he was silenced by the approach of his cousins.

"Are you both alright?" Adler was the first to reach us.

"Milla needs a haelen. Immediately. Send Esme or one of the aunts. The rest of you"—he gestured to the lawn and the bodies surrounding us—"clean up this mess." With that covered, he gathered me into his chest and lifted my beaten body from the grass, bringing us back inside.

As soon as I was in his arms, safe again, the feeling in my body unfortunately returned as he promised.

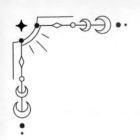
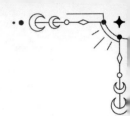

CHAPTER 13

CAMILLA

White hot pain seared up my arm, and I bit back a scream as Nico cleaned my hand while waiting for the haelen, the remnant healer. He was mercifully quick, pouring the cool water over the various cuts and gouges until the edges of the wounds were easily distinguished. The sight of my own mangled hand made me ill, and I shut my eyes to avoid it altogether as I sat on the counter near the sink.

"What's taking her so damn long?" Nico shouted from the bathroom, one of many on the first floor, the one near the family lounge.

"Nico, calm down. I'm fine," I gasped. I tried to breathe through the agony, but my chest sputtered for air. It took all my concentration to hold back the tears pricking my eyes.

"You're shaking like a hairless cat in a snowstorm. You are not *fine.*" He spat the words like it was my fault. I wanted to tell him he had the bedside manner of a mountain troll, but his temper was already hot enough as it was, and I didn't feel like wasting my very limited breaths on him.

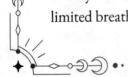

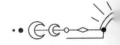

A cool breeze hit my cheeks, lifting the stray hair around my face. So soft and subtle, I thought I was imagining it at first. I forced my eyes open to glance at Nico. "Are you . . . *fanning* me?"

"You're sweating." Like it was an obvious use of his remnant—making me more comfortable. Had he not worn such a scowl, I thought he might have been being kind. Perhaps this was his way of it.

"Thanks." Because it did help. The small distraction it was.

"Margery is here," Esme said as she appeared in the doorway with an older woman roughly the same age as the aunts. Nico left so she could enter, but not before muttering his distaste with her timeliness.

"I'm sorry for him," I said as they all left, offering the healer my hand. "I'm afraid I've put him in a foul mood."

She smiled. Her grey-streaked hair was bound in a braided bun on top of her head. "I'm quite used to Mr. Attano's conduct, being one of the haelens on rotation for the family. From my observation, he only acts this way over the ones he cares about."

I scoffed. That was hardly the case here. "You don't have to be nice about him. He's out of hearing range."

A laugh burst from her lips. "I'm well aware, but I've known the Attanos for several years now. You'll never find a more generous, devoted family, including Nicolai."

As she spoke, she worked her remnant over my wounds, sealing the gaps, mending the scraped flesh, and closing each edge until my hand appeared like it had never been introduced with a broken window. The pain leaked from my body like she pulled a plug, dripping fast, drop by drop until it was gone entirely.

"*Saints*, that feels so much better. Thank you, Margery." I wiggled my fingers, thankful—and not for the first time tonight—for descendants and their magic.

ALEXIS L. MENARD

"You're very welcome." She bobbed her head in goodbye and started to leave. "Tell Nicolai I'll send my bill later this week."

"Charge him double for being rude," I advised, hopping off the sink.

I followed her out, and we split in the hallway. Backtracking where Nico had brought me, I found my way back to the lounge where he argued with his Nonna and another man. One I faintly recognized.

"What have you done now, Nick?" Solomon Attano, an older gentleman that must have taught Nico how to dress, given his taste in suits. We had business with him a few times when the Attanos still supplied our steel. He was mostly grey with an undercoat of black hair and a matching beard shaved close to his face. Solomon carried a gun in his left hand, one he sheathed in his waistband beneath a knee-length coat.

"It was unavoidable. I did what I had to do." Some of Nico's authority shrank in the presence of his uncle, similar to my brother's reactions whenever my father was about to scold them.

"Just like spending your inheritance on the heiress?"

Inheritance? That money had been given to him by his dead relatives—and he had the nerve to call *me* a spoiled heiress?

Nico's hands made fists. "I told you: I have a plan to get it all back and then some. Don't worry about the Marchese."

But Solomon began pacing the room, shaking his head. "What have I always taught you? Killing is *always* avoidable. Negotiations can be made; agreements can be reached. Death is too final and carries too many consequences to be the best option. Every time you pull the trigger, you are giving someone else more to use against you. Don't feed the beast, Nico."

Perhaps it was the way Nico avoided his uncle's glare in that moment, the way his eyes fell to the dark blood still staining his hands, or how his once strong shoulders fell an inch. It might've been because this was my fault, leading the bleeder here, and the fact Nico had killed to save *me*. Any of those reasons could have been why I felt the urge to defend him.

"This isn't on Nico," I said. Solomon and Nico both snapped their heads toward me, finally realizing I was there. "It's my fault. Angel bit me a few days ago and tracked me here. She was trying to take me—"

"She had a gun to Milla's head," Nico interrupted. "If someone did that to Fran, I don't think you'd be any more forgiving."

Solomon's icy stare slid back to him. "Do not compare our marriages. When Sabina finds out you killed one of her wearhs, there will be a penalty to pay. You know the sacred laws, son."

"Don't call me son." Nico's false hand tinkered as he opened and shut his fist. He jerked his head toward the door. "Pack a bag, Milla. I need to get you out of here for a few days in case her friends come looking."

"But—" I looked at Nonna, who shook her head quickly.

"*Now*, Camilla."

I returned to the remains of my room and quickly put some things together. When I had finished stuffing a bag with spare clothes and returned my revolver to my side, I found Nico waiting for me in the hallway.

He didn't look back at me to see if I followed or slow to bid me the ability to walk beside him. His strides were long, devouring the halls as we took the side entrance where the carriages were parked near the stables. The midnight chill slammed into us on a strong breeze, cooling the sweat that had pooled down my spine and my neck. But my clothes were thin, and my coat was stuffed in my case. I wrapped my arms around my middle just as two horses pulling a carriage flew up the gravel driveway.

It stopped short and let out Adler and Luther, seeing us standing at the mouth of the side gate. I recognized the driver as Gideon, the kind one. His reputation preceded him when he removed his coat and offered it to me, noting my shivers.

"I'll be fine, Gideon, but thank you."

"Are you sure, Milla?"

"She said she's fine," Nico spat. "Did you take care of the bodies?"

Luther answered as he removed his gloves. "Flushed down the Ada, off to clog the pipes."

"Good. I'm taking us to the house on East End, so I'll need you to send a squad to watch the flat for a few days. Her tracker is dead, so she should be fine, but if the Grey Hands come looking—"

"Say no more, boss. We got it from here. Just get you and the lady to a safe place."

"Thank you, Luther. Keep your eyes out for Sabina and her men while we lie low for a few days. I'll see you all at work."

The rest murmured their agreement and brushed past us to go inside, leaving us alone once more. A stable hand approached to take the horse, but Nico batted him away. He snapped once at me and pointed at the carriage. "Get in."

The crash of adrenaline left my body and spirit both threadbare of strength, and I ignored the rude commission, if only to save myself a headache as well. I grabbed my suitcase in one hand and started toward the car, my joints already sore from the fight and the chill sinking into my bones.

Nico held the door open for me, his stare on something far away, hidden behind the frozen smog.

"I'm sorry, Nico." It was all I could give him for the trouble I caused tonight. Too much damage had been done. I grabbed the handrail and was about to step inside the carriage when he grabbed me by the arm. There was no urgency this time, nothing to warrant his reach for me.

"Why are you apologizing?" His voice was made of iron, hard and cold.

"Because you finally understand why my brother sold me off to the highest bidder," I said, trying to laugh off the way the admission made me crack inside. "Aramis told me once he thought I was cursed, the way death seemed to trail me like a shadow. He said I was more trouble than I'm worth. You must realize by now you wasted your inheritance on a terrible investment." My grip tightened on the suitcase. I didn't know why I was telling him this. The flat affect of his features was enough to project his indifference.

But he saved my life when he didn't have to, and there was a bond between us that had been cast in gold, a gilded thread that tied my soul to his whether we liked it or not. He sighed, shutting his eyes briefly, as if this whole night had been a massive waste of time and resources.

"Do me a favor, Milla."

"What?"

"Don't ever listen to your idiot brother ever again. Now get in the car."

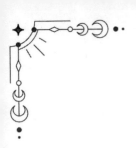
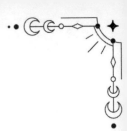

CHAPTER 14
CAMILLA

Nicolai Roman Attano was wealthier than I could've ever predicted, but the number of apartments he owned felt somewhat excessive.

East End composed the middle class of Remnant Row, where apartments were stacked against one another, utilizing as much space as practically possible. Nico parked the carriage down the street, where a man in street clothes had been waiting to bring it back to the estate.

"See you in the morning, Mr. Attano," the man had said before leading the horses back to the heart of the sectors. Nico picked up my suitcase and started down a pothole ridden street where the apartments were painted black. The night collaborated with the streetlights to stretch shadows across the cobbles, blending with the brick. We stopped in front of a unit in the center of them all, unmarked and unremarkable.

He looked left and right before unlocking the door and ushered me inside. The foyer opened to a small sitting room with elegant

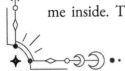

furniture that appeared like it had never been used. The curtains were drawn shut, their embroidered gossamer filtering the grey light and any unwanted attention from the street side.

"There's a kitchen straight back that usually has something edible stocked and some tea. There's also a bathroom next to the kitchen, but it's the only one in the flat. The bedroom is upstairs." Nico spoke quickly, as if ready to rid himself of my company.

Bedroom. Singular, as in we'd have to share the same room for several days.

He sat my case down and released a long sigh, staring at the dust floating on a stream of light escaping the curtain. "Did you need the bath?" he asked.

"I had one this morning after I woke," I muttered. Though, Angel's smell still clung to my hair, and I would have loved to wash her from my thoughts and my skin.

"It has a shower, but the plumbing here is fickle during the winter months. There's only enough hot water for one, so if you need it, have it now. Otherwise, I'll claim it." He ducked his head, sniffing his shoulder with a grimace.

"It's all yours then," I said. "I'll just be upstairs if you need me."

The quiet was too heavy to reside under any longer, and I snatched my luggage quickly to escape the awkward silence. I started up the carpeted stairs when Nico stopped me.

"Milla?"

I braced a hand on the railing and looked down at him. "Yes?"

He passed a hand through his hair. It was becoming a regular habit of his. A nervous tic? "You aren't my worst investment, but you are certainly the most surprising."

"In a good or a bad way?" I asked skeptically.

That face of steel finally cracked a smile, one that had me gripping the handrail a little tighter, if only to keep myself upright. "That's the question I toggle with frequently these days."

Toggling was becoming more habitual in my pastime as well. "You have a very nice family, Nico. I was pleasantly surprised by that as well."

"Even Nonna?" he asked, a thick brow raising.

I scoffed. "Despite Nonna. She's a bit rough around the edges, though I think she's the abrasive that smooths out the rest of them."

His smile widened. "She's difficult, I'll admit. But she's fierce for those she loves. Loyal to a fault. I don't think there's anything my family could do to make her stop caring for us. You remind me of her a lot, actually."

Heat flushed my cheeks despite being compared to an old woman. Something told me he meant it as a form of high praise. "Two compliments in one night. Are you feeling alright, Attano?"

A breathy laugh escaped him. Not a true one, but good enough it made something in my chest shift. "Don't get used to them."

THE BEDROOM HELD a double bed with a plush comforter and an empty dresser. But other than a few other pieces of staged furniture, it was completely bare, nothing personal on the walls or folded in the drawers. I set my suitcase on top of the dresser and drifted to the lone window looking down to the street below. Pushing aside the thick drapery, I noted a man clad in all black, lighting a cigarillo as he stared up at the unit.

Having the flat watched and my tracker slain made me feel safer, even tucked behind these naked walls that seemed to close in on me the longer I focused on them. The plaster groaned as Nico turned on the tap downstairs, and I could hear everything through the hollow floor that echoed every step I took. His annoying whistle, the stream of his piss, the rush of water through the rattling pipes as he started the shower. A reminder that neither of us would have any measure of privacy in this small space, and I collapsed on the bed, shoving a pillow over my head to gain some quiet.

I must've fallen asleep, smothering myself. For when a knock sounded at the front door, I woke to daylight glaring across the room. Through the paper-thin walls, the sound of the door opened, low murmurs of two men filled the gap in the time until it shut again.

I intended on ignoring Nico while we were both trapped here. Three days we'd been married, and he'd started to give backhanded compliments like we were friends. My curiosity, however, ultimately won the duel against my stubborn vow of isolation, and I rolled out of the bed to see the reason for the visitor.

The foyer was empty by the time I made my way down the steep stairwell, each step groaning as I descended. The only light came from the back of the house from a set of gas lamps. Nico sat at a round wood table with the chair pushed back, his legs spread wide as he contemplated a gold bottle in front of him. Bloody rags piled on the side of him, possibly from cleaning the rest of Angel from his false hand. From the frame of the doorway, I took a moment to watch him in the warm light.

He had forgone a shirt after his shower. There was a single tattoo drawn over his heart, three overlapping circles with a shaded center. On his other pectoral, a date in numeric letters. But the ink didn't catch my interest for long as the dim glow of the wall light painted his skin a dark, golden shade. Shadows caught in the deep striations of the muscles molding his chest and slid deeper with each soft breath. A thin dusting of dark hair trailed the center of his abdominals, leading below his belt, where it took every ounce of willpower to look away.

"Is sneaking around a frequent pastime for you?"

The only move I made was with my eyes as they finally shifted back to his, their steel grey now narrowed on me instead of the bottle. His black hair was more like spilled ink when it was wet, the length slicked back like he'd just made a pass with his hand.

"Well?" he spoke again, a smirk afflicting his cheek.

"I didn't know you had so many tattoos," I said, hoping the poor lighting would hide the heat that crept up my neck. Accompanying the ones on his chest was a sleeve of them from his shoulder to the elbow of his false arm, an intricate design filled with vague symbols that meant nothing to me at first glance.

"Well, none of them can move, so I didn't think it worth mentioning." His gaze slid to my forearm, where my familiar slipped across my flesh at the attention. Normally, the serpent hid from others, receding beneath my sleeve whenever my brothers stepped into the room. But with Nico, it came to life, almost like it delighted his company.

Inky traitor.

"Good to know," I said, leaning on the door frame. I gestured with my chin down the hall. "Who was at the door?"

"One of Solomon's runners." He stood then and paced across the kitchen to open a cabinet, retrieving a tall glass. "My uncle insists on interrogating you."

"Me?" I almost laughed. "Was it not *you* who swooped in and bartered for my hand? I knew I was marrying into this family approximately three minutes before the paper was signed. Why would you need to question me?"

"Because he believes the Firenzes and your family have something else going on." He placed the glass on the table with a sharp sound next to the bottle. It was then I realized what was happening here.

"So he sends you a bottle of Vex Veritas to spill the dirty truth from me?" I crossed my arms, my anger a boiling pot, a degree of heat away from spilling over.

He placed the glass on the table, hard enough the bottom of the flute smacked the wood with a sharp sound. "We could use knives, Milla. Would you rather we question you with more traditional methods?"

"I'd rather you not use magic alcohol or methods of torture at all. I told you I wasn't hiding anything from you concerning who I am or why the Firenzes were interested in uniting our families. It was for the train, nothing more. A simple business endeavor."

He pulled the cork from the bottle with his teeth, spitting it at my feet across the kitchen. "If you have nothing to hide, then this should be painless for you." He poured a generous amount into the glass. "You don't have to answer anything you don't want to, but this will at least appease my uncle, and we can move on. I have to admit, what the bleeder said is causing me to have my doubts as well. The Collector has been taking descendants, not natives. Why should I believe you aren't hiding something from us all?"

"Fine." I forced a bitter smile across my lips before crossing the kitchen to retrieve a second glass, slamming it on the wooden table-top. "But I never drink alone."

His glare could have cleared the fog over the Ada, but I refused to bend on this. He returned a strained smile and sat down again. "Okay, princess. Whatever you want."

I sat down across from him, my grin more sincere. "You'll find your life will be much easier if you keep replying to me in such a way. *Yes, Milla. Whatever you want, Milla. Do you like milk or cream in your coffee, Milla?*"

"Do you ever shut your mouth, *Milla*?"

"It's neither in case you were wondering. I forgot to mention dairy is high on my allergy list despite my love affair with cheese."

"*Shitting saints,* this is not what I need right now," he mumbled, eyes shutting briefly in exasperation.

Good. I had officially irritated him to the point of muttering to himself. It was less than half of what he deserved for making me drink this insulting dram.

"Let's just get this over with so you can run back to your uncle and tell him how obtuse he's being." I filled his glass with an equally substantial amount of gold drink, a heavy shimmer sunk to the bottom. I'd only had one experience with Vex Veritas in my lifetime, seven years ago when my father suspected me and Giles of harassing the boys that worked at the rail yard. Apparently, the alcohol lowers the inhibition to lie, but if one does manage to tell a falsehood, the drink makes you violently sick.

I glanced at the kitchen sink in search of the closest empty vessel —just in case I needed it.

"Take a sip." Nico leaned forward, resting his thick forearms on the table. Against my better judgment, I lifted the glass to my lips and forced down a small swallow. The bubbles burned the back of my throat as it went down, tasting like a sour champagne.

"What would you like to know?" I asked, folding my hands in my lap.

"Let's start with something easy," he said. The smile growing on his lips made me rightfully nervous. "Did you like what you saw?"

My nails dug into my palms as I curled my fists. "Do be more specific, Attano."

"When you were staring at me a few minutes ago. Do you find me attractive?"

"I wasn't staring at—" My stomach gurgled, and I stopped short.

Damn him to the void. There was no way I'd admit my appreciation of his body. Absolutely not. I'd rather wear my lunch, which was likely going to happen.

"Are you feeling alright, Milla?" he asked, sarcasm dripping from his grin. "The sink's over there if you need it."

"I'm fine."

Another lie. Another wave. Fuck this stuff.

"Then answer my question."

"Saints, I hate you." I squeezed my eyes shut and braced myself for what was about to come. "I was not enjoying myself—" A wave of nausea slammed into my chest. Here went nothing. . .

"*Ithinkyouareabsoutleyhideous*," I spilled the words before I choked on them, gagging just as my stomach squeezed itself empty. By the time I reached the sink, I was aggressively vomiting gold drink and Nico *laughed*. Deep and pillar-shaking, it bubbled out of him from a hidden place in his chest that would've been more charming had it not been aimed at my misery.

Wiping away the tears in my eyes, I joined him back at the table with my head still high. He said, "You really can't just admit you think I'm attractive?"

"I'd rather show you what I ate for breakfast yesterday." Thankfully, I hadn't eaten since yesterday, so there wasn't much left in my stomach to hurl.

"To be fair, you can ask me the same." The bender took a sip of his drink with candor.

I canted my head in thought. I already knew he thought I was beautiful. He'd said so that night we met. "Fine. What exactly do you think is attractive about me?"

His eyes squinted into slits. "That's not fair."

I shrugged. "The sink is over there if you need it."

Nico sucked a long breath through his nose before nodding.

"Alright." Grey eyes studied my face, swept down my neck and over my chest. It was impossible not to squirm under his inspection. To ignore the heat that dipped low, coiled low in my hips.

"You have a face that looks constantly pissed off, making you fundamentally unapproachable, and it's highly arousing to me. When you sat at the bar and Dom didn't serve you, I thought you might've burned down my pub with your glare. The only thing more beautiful than your smile is that *look*. The one you're giving me. Right now."

How was I looking at him? And why did he have to describe it as *arousing?* It made that coil twirl tighter, beg to be unraveled. "Is that all? You like my face?"

A slow smile wandered across his lips. "I like how your hair curls more when it's damp outside. I like how your hips look in a silk dress. I particularly like the way you say my name when you're frustrated, as it gives me a hint of how you'd say it in my bed."

"*Nicolai!*"

"That's right. Keep practicing." His grin was enigmatic now. Was he messing with me? Couldn't be, not with the Veritas in his system. Perhaps speaking the truth was worse than leaving it unsaid. I started to wish I'd never asked him.

"You're awful," I said without a hint of sickness because he was absolutely torturing me. My hands dug into the tabletop, leaving indents in the soft wood with my nails.

"At least I'm not a liar," he chided.

I took a sip of Veritas, shooting him my *look* above the rim of my glass. "Can we proceed?"

"First things first then," he said, changing the subject curtly. "Do you or your brothers have a remnant?"

A slip of a scoff broke through my teeth. "Definitely not. I'm as plain and ordinary as any other native on the Isle. The Marcheses have lived here since the mortals who weren't given remnants immigrated here two hundred years ago, when they fled from the demon hordes in the First War."

"Yes, I understand your ancestors were essentially one of the founding families, which is why everyone regards your name as something holy around here. But that doesn't mean none of them broke from the line and reproduced with a descendant, and therefore, introduced a remnant to your family line. What about your mother?"

Dread rolled in my stomach. "What about her?"

"Where did she come from? What was her family name—"

"I have no idea."

His mouth shut tight, thankfully. I looked toward the kitchen window hovering over the sink, avoiding the look in his eyes when I explained. "She left after I was born. I have no idea who or where she is now. My father refused to speak much about her."

"Oh . . ." He appeared lost for words. "That's unfortunate. I'm sorry."

His condolences were unnecessary. I couldn't miss someone I didn't remember. "It doesn't matter who she is, anyway. Angel told me I didn't taste like any remnant she's ever sampled before, so I can't be a descendant. Besides, I have no magic, nor do my brothers. Jeremiah set the house on fire twice when we were young, but that's as close as any of us has gotten concerning dappling with the elements."

Nico rested his head on a fist in thought, realizing my truth was too sound to dismantle with logic alone. He took a sip from his own cup.

"Your turn."

I slanted my head in thought. There were so many things I wanted to know about Nicolai Attano. Starting with that intriguing contraption of Esme's design. "What happened to your arm?" The question I finally settled on.

Metal fingers opened and closed, delaying his response. "I did something foolish and got sent to Hightower when I was sixteen."

"Hightower?" I whispered. It was unfathomable, thinking of a boy his age going to the island prison, where only the worst of descendants were sent to inhibit their magic. I'd heard rumors of the atrocities there. The shifting walls and glint treatments to dull their power, the pitch darkness they kept prisoners in for weeks, sometimes months without light.

He nodded, surveying his false hand as if it reflected the horrible memories of that place upon the polished brass. "I was wounded before I was arrested, and my arm got severely infected to the point that my flesh had begun to rot away. The alchemedis there gave me a choice—cut it off, or let the infection kill me. I chose the latter, but as I would come to learn, Hightower will do the exact opposite of what you wish for."

"*Saints* . . ." I could imagine it, Nico thrown into a dark cell after being dismembered, bleeding, cold, starved, and suffering. How he survived such an experience was a question I didn't think he could even answer.

Nico took another sip as I wondered and continued. "I spent five years there. Luther was one of my accomplices, so he was there with me. I never saw him, of course, but even after two years of being out, he's still not free of that place. After prison, I followed in my uncle's footsteps and took over the steel factories. He's too weak to oversee them all now due to a degenerative condition, but that doesn't stop him from giving his opinion on everything."

I nodded mechanically, taking a matching sip from my own glass, the contents starting to taste better with every mouthful. "Why were you sent to Hightower?"

But he shook his head, a lazy smirk returning. "A question for a question. No doubling up." He leaned back in his seat, giving me an expanded view of his perfectly proportioned chest. "Why are you so afraid of your brothers?"

His question prompted my eyes to roll. Not this again. "I'm not afraid of them."

"Then why do you let them treat you so terribly? Especially when you have no trouble putting me in my place at all hours of the day."

I leveled a look at him. "They don't treat me terribly. Why do you even care about my relationship with my brothers?"

"I don't know what's sadder, Milla. That you truly believe that" —he leaned forward, bracing his arms on top of the table as if to scrutinize me—"or that you don't have anyone to show you just how much better you deserve."

I didn't know whether to be enraged or flattered by the back-handed inquiry. I was suddenly very thirsty, gulping down the Veritas in place of replying.

"As for the answer to your own question," Nico murmured, "you wouldn't understand because you still see me as your rival."

"I will always see you as my rival, Nico, because that's what you are. No contract can change the past."

"I'm not," he repeated, "and I never was, Milla. My . . . my father set the bombs on those tracks because he thought your family did something horrible to mine. I've done nothing against you or your name. Just because our predecessors were rivals, doesn't mean we have to be. Times change."

Somehow, I doubted that very much. My scars itched even now, thinking about that day the Attanos had set their bomb in just the right place, detonating my entire world with a single explosive. The bad blood between our families ran too deep in this city to forget— another reason I had to get out of this marriage. How he could say

145

such a thing without a hint of sickness, however, left me uneasy. Planted those seeds of doubt.

"Milla?" he spoke my name, snapping my thoughts back to the present.

"They are all I have."

His brows pinched in confusion. "What do you mean?"

"My brothers." I looked him in his stormy eyes. "They're all the family I have left. I don't have nonnas or uncles or cousins. My brothers can treat me however they want because they know they are all I have, and being used feels close enough to being wanted. I don't understand why that's so difficult for you to understand, seeing as you're using me as well."

I let him hear it, knowing it was the fullest truth I'd spoken since we arrived. He barely flinched. Not a muscle moved in his body.

"I think they are afraid of you, Camilla. I think they know how capable you are, and they are making sure you never realize it for yourself." He stood quickly, sending a harsh sound from his chair across the tile. Rounding the table, he leaned low to look me in the eye, his hand braced on the back of my chair.

"As for comparing me to them, how fucking dare you. Because I wanted you the second you rolled your eyes at me in my pub, and you didn't offer me a thing then."

"You wanted a different person, Nico. That girl was only a piece of who I am. When you found out the rest, you jumped at your chance to make your life easier using my name, just like *everyone* else." I stood, forcing him to back off or risk smacking faces.

He shook his head. "I think the girl in front of me right now is just a piece of you. And I'd bet I met the real you that night when you shed your last name, the worries over your family's judgements and expectations, and just lived in the moment. This you"—he

146

clasped my chin—"is a lie. It is controlled by too many outside influences to be genuine."

I blinked away the tears fighting to collect and spill over, pulling out of his grasp. "Don't assume you know everything about me after a few hours together over drinks. You have no idea what I've been through and what I've done. You want there to be something more dramatic about who I am, but I was raised to be an heiress, and that is exactly what I am. Nothing more."

"Another lie," he hissed. "The Grey Hands wouldn't be hunting you down if that were true."

"It must be!" I was shouting now. "I'm not throwing up, am I?"

"That stuff only works on what we believe is true, not the truth itself, Camilla." His voice softened on my name. Like he thought I could be swooned by his tongue now that the champagne had loosened the rusted gates to my heart.

He hadn't made a move to step back to put any distance between us. We were chest to chest in the empty apartment. For a moment he reminded me of the Nico I'd met in the pub, when I was similarly inebriated, every bit as lust filled as a consequence of his proximity. I silently wished I could reach out and touch him as freely as I did when he wasn't mine. "Do you . . . still want me, then?"

He hesitated but shook his head. "No. You were right before. It was a *mistake*."

His answer shouldn't have stung quite as much as it did. He was a killer, my rival, and had too many secrets to ever trust him completely. I'd have to be clinically depraved to want anything more than just his body. It was good to know those feelings were a one-night, onetime thrill on his end as well. I didn't want him, either.

Thankfully, the Veritas didn't work against lying to myself.

I nodded, stepping out of the enchantment of his personal space.

"Good. Now that we settled everything, I'm going to sleep off the rest of this crap."

He didn't stop me, didn't say another word, and I envied that aura of indifference his quiet carried. Wished that I could be so uncaring too. Retreating to the bedroom upstairs, I shut him from my thoughts with the close of a hollow door.

The only noise in the flat was the sound of Nico's retching.

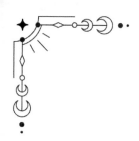
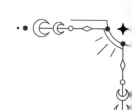

CHAPTER 15
CAMILLA

"You're not coming?"

Nico assessed my undressed state from the bottom of the stairs, his arms crossed in a crimson-lined coat. Where he'd gotten another pressed suit overnight, I had no idea—until Gideon sauntered down the hall from the kitchen and waved at me in greeting. I gave him a warm smile just to irritate Nico further.

"No," I replied. "I'll stay here for the day. Lots of plotting against you to do and all. Might want to bring home another bottle of that liquid truth of yours. I'm a Marchese after all. You can't trust us."

Gideon murmured at Nico's side, "I take it she didn't appreciate Uncle Sol's request."

"No, she didn't," Nico spoke through his teeth. His eyes narrowed back at me. "You're acting like a child, Milla. But if you insist on sitting here all day by yourself, so be it. I'll warn you, though, if you have any ideas of trying to sneak out, one of my men will tackle you before you can even reach the sidewalk."

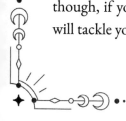
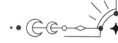

"That sounds quite stimulating, actually," I said. "Is that blonde one with the neck tattoo still out front?"

"Camilla . . ." Nico seethed.

"Oh relax, I'm not going to go anywhere. Being far away from you is good enough for me." Before he could respond, I shut the bedroom door, which conveniently had become my own private sanctuary. The bender had remained downstairs all night, smart enough to know where he wasn't welcome.

And my bed was certainly one of those places.

Nico's curse cut through the quiet house and his cousin muttered something about *having his hands full.* Their exchange made me smile at the back of the door, but that fleeting satisfaction dissolved as soon as they left. I was alone with nothing to do but count the ceiling tiles and rearrange the furniture.

Nico didn't bother me that night when he came home, nor the next morning before he left for work again. He was pointedly ignoring me, which was easy for him when I isolated myself to the second floor. I didn't know what I was supposed to do here in this drafty apartment, all by myself with nothing but the Attanos' men to keep me company outside. They were stationed in the front of the building, the alley stretching behind it, and sometimes I heard footsteps on the roof when the sun fell.

They changed every ninth hour, rotating between schedules. I had nothing better to do than watch their movements, noting the pattern and timing and how they switched seamlessly between each other; the way they changed clothes throughout the shift to appear as different men, hoping to throw off clever onlookers.

Sometime around noon, a knock tapped on the door, opening just enough to catch the chain lock.

"Who's there?" I called out from the chaise in the sitting room. Through the foyer, I could see a blue eye staring at me.

"You know it's me."

"What do you want, Gideon?" I asked, looking back down at the book in my hand.

"I brought food."

I promptly shut the story mid-chapter to let him inside. He carried four brown bags to the kitchen, full of what were certainly food-like *items*, but my appetite quickly disappeared after reviewing the commodities.

"Why are there so many cans?" I asked, looking around the table at the contents he pulled from the sacks.

Gideon shrugged under a coat that resembled Nico's, black threading with a red, silky interior. He removed his tweed hat and passed a hand through a mess of curls long on top of his head. "Nico told me to go to the store during my lunch hour, along with your *very* specific allergy list. We haven't heard anything from Sabina, and until we do, you both need to stay away from the estate." He gestured to the stack of aluminum. "This was the best I could do."

"This was not the best you could do," I murmured, picking up a can of noodles soaking in red sauce. "Let me make you a deal, Gideon."

"What?" he moaned, like he was already dreading my offer.

"Go back to the store with a list I provide you, and tomorrow night I will make dinner." He stared blankly until I added, "And you can join."

He squinted his icy eyes. "You can really cook?"

"Why is that so surprising?"

At that, he shrugged and handed me a pen from the inside of his coat. "Make your list, then."

As I scribbled down a proper grocery list, settling on a meal my brothers used to devour when I made their dinner every night, the

Attano waiting impatiently cleared his throat. "Oh," he said, "I almost forgot to tell you: Nico will not be coming home tonight."

"What?" I asked, ceasing my writing. "Why?"

He looked unsure of himself, rubbing the back of his neck. "I can't say. Personal stuff."

Oh. But his stubborn silence told me enough, and a fresh anger shook my hands until I could hardly write the word *cream* without it appearing more like something epically inappropriate.

"Interesting. He cares so much for my safety and yet feels it fine to leave me all night by myself." I wished I hadn't said the thought out loud, because as soon as I did, Gideon grinned.

"It's not like that, Milla. I promise."

"Don't placate me, Attano. I wasn't born yesterday. I know what men do at night when they don't go home to their wives."

He said nothing else on the matter; instead, he waited for me to finish my list. He met me with a stiff smile as I handed it to him. "If you'd like, I can come over tonight and keep an eye on the place. If it makes you feel safer."

"I can take care of myself," I snapped, regretting my tone immediately. It wasn't his fault his boss was an ass. "But thank you anyway. I wanted to ask, is there a way I could get some information about the missing descendants? If I'm going to be stuck here all day, I might as well try to do some digging."

He nodded with a bob of his chin. "Nico has some files at the office. Why don't you come by and give them a look? I'm sure he wouldn't mind."

Because Nico was there, and I wanted some distance. Perhaps a night off from him would benefit us both. We had at least a month left to deal with each other, and we still needed to figure out who this Collector was and put a stop to the disturbance in the city. If I could temper my irritation with him for a few weeks and fulfill my end of the bargain, I'd come out with more freedom than I did going into this.

"I'd love to get out of here, but I just . . . don't feel like seeing him right now." I despised how much it bothered me, his nightly activities. I only wished I could get back at him—but how could I do such a thing without leaving the flat? "Is there a way you could bring them here?"

He frowned. "I don't see why not. I'll ask Nico and drop them off this evening if he's alright with it."

I scoffed. "It's the least he could do after everything." Gideon bounced on his heels nervously, like he didn't know what else to say. Stuck between me and his boss. An idea struck me. "So you're going back to the office, Gideon?"

"Of course. Did you need me to tell Nico something?"

"No," I sighed, trying my best to appear downcast. "I'll just *deal with it* myself, I suppose."

As expected, the softhearted bender came close and braced an arm over my shoulder. "It'll be alright, Milla. I promise Nico would never—"

The words were knocked from his chest as I embraced him, hoping to leave my scent on his clothes with a long hug. My unwitting accomplice patted my shoulder. "He would never betray your contract, Milla. Whatever he's doing, it's for a good reason."

I slipped from his arms and smiled sweetly. "For his sake, Gideon, you'd better hope you're right."

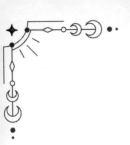
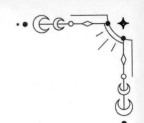

CHAPTER 16
NICOLAI

G ideon returned shortly after lunch, thankfully still in one piece after visiting Camilla. He stepped into my office, immediately filling it with her scent, somehow always succulent and sweet even after using my soap. It started to stick to everything I owned, making it impossible to escape her. Even now it had followed me here, as if she were chasing me, never giving my senses a second of peace.

"Why do you smell like her?"

My cousin arched a brow and slowly sat in an armchair positioned in front of my desk. "Why do you look like you're going to blow my head off for it?" When he realized I was serious, he said, "Relax, Nico. I only gave her a hug because she was upset you were leaving her tonight."

"Upset?" Unlikely. Camilla Marchese would never cry over my absence.

"Murderous is a better word. She thinks your business tonight involves a lady friend."

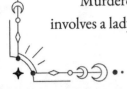

That made more sense. "She was jealous?" I asked him.

"It appeared that way, boss." Gideon leaned back in the chair, staring at me strangely. "Why are you grinning like that?"

"I'm not grinning." I smoothed my face free of whatever he thought he saw there. I didn't care if she was jealous. Even if she was, it didn't stem from a place of attraction on her part. She said she hated me while still on the Vex Veritas and hadn't stifled a single gag.

Though she definitely didn't find me hideous.

His smile was too wide to suggest he believed me. "Oh, you've got it bad, boss."

"On second thought, maybe I do want to blow your head off," I murmured, trying to distract myself with the latest safety report.

He waved a hand, dispersing my warning. "There's no shame, Nico. She's Camilla Marchese. Half of Lynchaven would give their family fortune for a night with her, and the other half are liars."

I slammed the folder shut, the ink rolling together as his words painted a provocative picture in my head. An irritation I'd never felt before dipped claws into my concentration. "Camilla and I will never be, Gideon. No matter what a piece of paper claims."

"And why not?" he asked. "You married her, for saint's sake. Why can't you like her?"

"Our marriage was one of convenience. She needed money, and I needed to keep her train out of my rival's already incredibly powerful hands. You forget the war between our families ended in the death of her father. How could she possibly stop seeing me as her enemy when we were responsible for that?"

"If you told her the whole story, she would understand," Gideon said quietly. "If she hated us, she wouldn't have mingled with your aunts or tolerated your grandmother. Esme wouldn't have tried to befriend her if Milla had been cruel and off-putting. It seems the only rivalry between our families is the one between the two of you."

I rolled my eyes and tossed the folder onto a stack of waiting documents. "Do you think Milla will be particularly happy if this marriage continues through her birthday and I take her company? Do you think she will fall in love with me after I steal something the past four generations of Marcheses have built out from beneath her? Don't be ridiculous, Gideon. We are opposites in every way, and she will resent me even more than she already does if we don't figure out a way to stop the Collector."

And that was a big *if*. That license might bind us together for the rest of our lives if I didn't find a way out of it. I owed her that, at least, the ability to leave me before I destroy her life.

"Actually, about that," he drawled. "Camilla wanted me to ask if she could view the files on the missing descendants."

I gestured to the boxes stacked in the corner of the room. "Be my guest. If she thinks she can find anything significant in these cases, I'd love to know."

"Oh yeah?" he asked with the cock of a brow. "You haven't looked at those files all week. Something tells me you're not so interested in finding the Collector anymore."

I shot him a glare before standing from my chair, searching for my coat, prompting the end of this conversation and all his insinuations.

"Boss, I didn't mean anything by it. Just having a bit of fun," Gideon said quietly.

I shook my head. "It's fine. I'm going out now. Might as well get an early start."

My cousin's face darkened, a shadow veiling the mirth in his eyes. "And you still won't tell me where you're going?"

"The less you know, the better," I said, turning from his disappointment. "Would you mind keeping an eye on East End tonight? I trust the eyes, but I'd rather have one of you there, just in case."

"I'll keep her safe," he replied, hearing all the words I didn't say. "Watch yourself tonight, cousin."

———— ✳ ————

SOME CALLED it extortion to pay an undertaker who worked for the OIC with coins and threats. I saw it as a trade of interest. It was in my client's best interest to learn the old man who would die tonight would pass from natural causes, and it was in the medical examiner's best interest to keep his livelihood. When I paid him off on the first job, the rest had been easier to convince. Once I involved him in my crimes, he was less likely to snitch with every false report. And he'd made plenty of those on my behalf to lock him in the native prison for the rest of his life.

Once I wrapped up my final preparations, going to my private flat on Decatur where I kept my equipment for jobs such as these, the sun had already sunk far beneath the world. My cowl and mask concealed my skin, the black leather and wrappings blended my form with the shadows. The stars shining over the skyline were both witness and accomplice to the night and every dark deed I committed under their watch, winking down at me like shrewd companions.

The undefined border of the Capital Square was where most of my marks lived and reigned under a false pretense. Everyone in power in Lynchaven was simply a puppet of the master above them, and I served the head jester, ready to cut strings where new acts were required to be introduced.

When the Summoner had given me the name, I knew it immediately. Isaac Branwick was one of the city politicians and current owner of a red blade, marking him as a member of the underground organization, the Nine Crowns. The inspector had tried to weed them out for years. Their obsession with restoring the streets and the city leadership with purely natives was the reason some remnants with less influence paid for penalties that didn't belong to them.

I'd always wondered if the Marcheses had been part of the club, and that was how they got me life in Hightower without a trial. I hadn't even been able to say goodbye to my family, to beg my Nonna for forgiveness before I was thrown at the feet of General Grisham, the former watchman superior, before they'd tossed me still burnt and bloody in the back of a carriage for the island.

Some errands for the inspector kept me awake at night, but I'd sleep just fine tonight knowing the world had one less Isaac Branwick.

The clock tower chimed twice, signaling the second hour of the morning. His home had been charmed against magic, so no one could use a remnant once inside. The glint the Firenzes founded fifty years ago when the descendants immigrated here had evolved into more sophisticated uses beyond the physical body; now, it could also lace the air or paint thresholds, so anyone who passed through a window or door was powerless when they crossed it.

I slowed the time until I couldn't, slipping past the handful of guards posted in the general's courtyard and careful to be quick enough they wouldn't feel the rebound hit them too harshly and raise the alarm. Once in the inner gates, I dropped my remnant and entered the house through a back door I had to pick open, feeling it go cold and quiet inside the space of my bones almost instantly.

My false hand went dead beneath its glove, no longer able to control the air inside the tubes to manipulate the contraption. I concealed it anyway, in case someone caught me lurking. A metal hand was a distinct characteristic not many people in Lynchaven could claim.

The upper windows were dark from my view of the outside, the house asleep beside the occasional servant roaming the hall and the ticking of a clock from a nearby room. I climbed the stairs, searching the three-story home for Isaac's bedroom. From the profile the Summoner gave me, he had an estranged wife and three daughters who were all wedded and gone, which meant he had no one to care about him until the servants woke him in the morning. Less staff to worry about as well. This was an easy job, in and out, especially once I found his bedroom on the third floor.

With any luck, I'd be back before Camilla could burn down my flat.

Resorting to picking the lock the old-fashioned way, it was increasingly difficult to manage with one hand—and even more so to do it quietly. A groan rumbled on the other side of the stained mahogany, and I paused my fingers, glancing down the hall to make sure no one would come to investigate, but the house remained silent and still.

The lock clicked loose, and with the silent twist of the brass handle, I nudged the door open an inch. Darkness hung thick on the other side beside a lone candle burning near his bedside, shining a low glare on a lumpy shape beneath a quilt. The hinges hardly squeaked as I pressed it open, slinking further into the room and shutting it behind me—locking it for good measure.

The old man was already on his back, as if anticipating his reaper. The most convenient position for the death I planned to deal, one that would make him appear to have passed in his sleep. At least, that's what the undertaker would record on his papers in the morning.

But first, I had some questions.

As soon as my hand snapped around his throat, Branwick's eyes flew open, widening impossibly more when he realized who I was.

"Good morning, Isaac." I didn't loosen my grip enough to grant him air to answer. "I'm going to make this quick. My name is Nicolai Attano and ten years ago my mother and little sister were murdered in broad daylight by a member of the Crowns. Would you happen to know anything about that? Blink twice for yes."

His mouth gaped, but his eyes remained wide.

I cursed his tenacity. Another one who thought their silence made them a hero. How many would I have to go through until one of them finally talked?

"Is that your final answer, Branwick?"

His face purpled, the tiny blood vessels in his eye began to burst, bleeding into the white. After years of practice, one would think this would come more naturally, leave less of a stain on my soul with every life I claimed with my hand around their throat. But it was appalling, the way his pulse raced beneath my fingers, the way his eyes bulged, awakening from a dream to find a nightmare looming over him. Their fingers clawed into the leather, trying to peel it from my arms. I preferred it when I could use my remnant and just take their breath. The more hands-on jobs left me ill.

The pulse beneath my fingers slowed to stillness, and the fear in his eyes dissolved into an unfocused stare. Gone. Like all the others I'd introduced to death, a willing courtier to protect my family and my freedom, at the expense of being a pawn in a political game of power. Whatever the inspector wanted out of his ending, he had it now, and I was free from the island for another day, from the prison that motivated me to commit such horrendous acts, and the worry of bringing my family down with me.

But the guilt remained, as did the useless wish that life could be different.

I slipped from Isaac's corpse, covering his chest with the sheets and closing his eyelids so no one could witness how he looked at me in his final seconds. I had just opened the window to climb my way down the south wall when a noise drained my heart of blood. A door opened, and then came a bloodcurdling screech only a woman could master. I realized then why his wife was estranged.

Isaac had a *mistress.*

"Thief!" she shouted, pointing at me from the bathing room door. "Help! Someone help!"

"*Shitting saints,*" I groaned, gripping the windowsill, and calculated my next potential moves. I could kill her, but it would've made it even more obvious the general's death wasn't natural. No, killing her wouldn't change the outcome of anything. I snatched my gun from its holster and aimed it at her half-dressed figure, silencing her wretched screams so I could think straight.

"Listen to me carefully," I said in a low voice. "You're going to tell everyone who comes running in here that you went to the bathroom and came out to find him dead. Do you want to know why?"

Her lower jaw trembled, but she said, "Why would I do that?"

"Because as his mistress, you're the first person they'll look at when they can't find the killer. And believe me, sweetheart, they'll never see me leaving, which will make you look like a liar."

She whimpered, her full chest rising and falling with heaving breaths. Her eyes glanced at the bed. "Killer? He's dead?"

"Yes," I spat. "Now I'm going to leave, and you will wait until I am out of this window to call for help again. Got it?"

The poor woman trembled all over, reaching her arms around herself to embrace her shaking form. "I . . . Okay."

"Good," I breathed. I turned my back on the mistress for a second too long, hadn't even had time to duck beneath the windowpane before a shot sounded—and a pain hot as dry lightning jolted down my arm.

A bullet. The force of it knocked the wind from my chest, drained the strength from my legs, and my knee hit the carpet, lunging to brace against the pain stealing my control over my body. I turned my head to find the woman with a gun in her shaky hands. It had been a miracle she hit me at all with that grip, and somehow didn't hurt herself in the process.

A thin line of white smoke curled from the barrel. "Now they'll know it wasn't me. You'll stay where you are until the guards come."

Definitely not. I couldn't be sent back to Hightower. I couldn't leave my family without securing our place in the fluctuating political chessboard.

I couldn't leave Milla, who still waited at home, most likely with a revolver in her lap ready to put more rounds in me for thinking I betrayed both her fickle friendship and our union. If I could get out of this, get back to her, I'd happily take another bullet to the back if it were by her hand.

"Burn in the void," I hissed and heaved myself out of the window with little finesse. As soon as I crossed the boundary of the building, my remnant began to refill my marrow with power, and I bent the wind to form a cradle beneath my fall, gently lowering myself to the earth on two feet.

"Stop him!" the mistress shrieked from the window to the guards lining the perimeter, but it was no use. I was formless in the shadows, bending the light to form a glare, pausing and restarting the clock as the guards ran to the places they last saw me. By the time I reached the street, the well of my power had begun to trickle, leaving my remnant weakened and faint.

Calling on so many various forms of bending at once was draining. No magic was bottomless, certainly not mine after years of it being suppressed in prison and using it throughout the day to power my false hand. Even Adler, who was two years younger than me, had better stamina. But I was thankful to have just enough to escort me to safety. If I didn't . . . Well, getting caught would have been the least of my problems. Bottoming out wasn't an option to consider.

I fled the scene before the watchmen showed up, cursing myself for being sloppy. The Summoner would be furious. Most likely wouldn't even compensate me for now exposing his death as a murder. The rest of his friends would be on high alert, and we'd have to hit more infrequently for the next few weeks to hide the association.

Sticking to the back alleys that dipped low into the slums of Lynchaven, I crawled into an abandoned flat to lie low and tend to my injury. The bullet buried itself just above my shoulder blade in the soft flesh that moved the ball and socket joint, my good arm in even worse shape than my left one.

To make matters worse, there was no exit wound. The mistress had done a fine job of missing anything important while simultaneously finding the path of most resistance. I'd have to see Lilian soon to get it fixed before it had the opportunity to get infected. If they laced the house with glint, the bullets might be poisoned.

Once I'd crudely wrapped my chest and stopped the bleeding, I sank against the peeling wallpaper of the forsaken apartment. A fire was most likely the cause of the derelict home, apparent by the dusting of ash that covered the burnt edges of forgotten furniture and the holes in the charred ceiling that provided a comforting view of the stars above.

To Lilian's, and then I could go home. Milla was a strange comfort tonight, beckoning me to push through the exhaustion in my bones and venture the side streets on foot back to Decatur, to change these clothes, this identity, and return to the man I wish I could remain.

—·—✧—·—

"Nicolai Attano," Lilian Green purred as I rang her doorbell three hours later. "What brings you to my home at such a dark and dreary hour?" The Blood descendant had a remnant for healing and a mind not to ask too many questions. We'd first met in the hospital where she'd worked as a nurse over a year ago, when Nonna had taken frequent trips to receive emergency care before we hired someone to treat her at home.

"Same as always, Lilian. I've got a bullet in my shoulder that needs your attention," I said. She cracked the door open a little more, standing to the side to let me in. "Sorry about the time, but this couldn't wait."

She shut the door to her flat and gestured to the kitchen in the back of the long room. It was completely dark besides a few gas lanterns that lit the hall splitting the home, but I knew the layout well. Had been here frequently over the last year for both business and pleasure.

"You're welcome to my side of town anytime, Nicolai. Now, you know the drill. Sit and take off your shirt before you ruin it with your blood." Lilian patted my back gently to nudge me into a dining chair, gathering her supplies while I removed the shirt I had changed into just minutes before. While she was turned, I noticed she wore a silky night shift with lace lining the bottom. It lifted alluringly high, showing off her slim legs as she reached for something on the top shelf, and I shifted my eyes to look at literally anything else in the small kitchen.

She returned with a warm washcloth, a magnet, a bottle of disinfectant that counteracted anything the bullet might be laced with, and a glass of strong whiskey. Her hands were always warm as they fingered the edges of my wound, gentle as she cleaned the site at a pace that was slow, paying the kind of attention only a caregiver could provide.

"Take your draught now, love," she said. Her nimble hand grabbed the drink before I could reach it, bringing the glass to my lips while caressing the back of my head with the other.

In the past, I'd always let her serve me. She liked it, and I liked making her happy. But now as she watched me swallow each sip, the hand at my nape stroked my skin with a feathery touch, I felt uneasy at the intimacy. I shot the alcohol back quickly, feeling the burn scorch my throat on the way down and warm my middle.

"More?" she asked, wiping a drop from my lip and licking it from her thumb.

"No." The word came out croaked.

"Maybe after, then."

"I'm afraid I'm in a hurry, Lilian."

She scoffed, returning to my back. Cold disinfectant leaked over my skin, running down my back as she cleaned the hole. "Where could you be in such a rush to run off to at this hour?" Her hands returned to my skin, and I flinched, fighting this strange instinct to jerk away. "Are you alright, Nico? Did I do something wrong?"

I grimaced, knowing she couldn't see me. "You're fine. The spot is just tender, I suppose."

"I'll be very careful then, love."

Lilian was many things, but most of all, she was a fantastic healer. She had the bullet out and my skin sealed shut with her remnant in less than a minute. Pain lingered like a sore muscle, but other than a few aching rolls of my arm, it felt like I hadn't been shot at all.

"*Saints*," I groaned, working my arm, "incredible as always. Thank you."

She smoothed her palm over the curve of my shoulder,

commanding me silently to still. "Of course, anything for my favorite bender." She rounded the chair, keeping a hand on my chest as if to keep me in the seat. "Is there anything else I can do for you, Nicolai?"

I swallowed, realizing she most likely assumed we'd continue where we left off the last time I'd come in here bleeding and bruised. "Lilian . . ." She stepped between my legs, pushing them wider with her hips before she leaned forward and let her shift fall open, exposing her bralette. I cleared my throat and felt the heat surge from my chest to my face.

"Lilian, I can't do this anymore," I grunted, trying to scoot the chair away. But she climbed on top of me, straddling my hips.

"Don't tease me like that." She spoke the words into my neck. It had been months since I'd been touched so affectionately, but I was already crossing a line I promised myself I wouldn't go near. Even if Milla hated me, I wouldn't treat her like Isaac had treated his own wife. Even if she never touched me like this, or seated her wide hips on top of mine, or if she refused to let those perfect pouty lips suck my neck. The jewel of Lynchaven, the Princess of Steam, the very bane of my ambition. Why did her last name have to be Marchese?

"I can't do this, Lilian."

"Nicolai," she whispered in my ear. "Touch me, love."

The whiskey had already taken its toll, blurring this reality and my wildest fantasies. And then those hands that would never touch me were suddenly stroking my chest, her foul mouth kissing the column of my throat. Golden hazel eyes blinked down at me, soft with lust and desire.

"Nico," she moaned.

"Milla . . ."

"Milla?"

Lilian pushed off me with a start, looking down from her seat in my lap. Her gentle features were sharp with disdain. "Who in the void is Milla?"

I swallowed, sobering quickly. "My wife."

That was not the answer she was expecting. Dodging no less than three shot glasses, I quickly darted from Lilian's apartment to avoid receiving a worse injury. When I was out the door, she threw my shirt at my face, so naturally it landed in a puddle at my feet instead.

"Don't you ever come back here, Attano *scum,* or I'll shoot you myself!" Lilian shouted at me before slamming her door shut. The streets were starting to awaken with activity as morning commuters left for work, and I was thankful the dawn was still dark enough to hide the heat lingering in my face. I tossed my wet shirt over my shoulder and started the long walk back to East End.

Something about seeing Camilla Marchese at the end of this long night made the sun rise a little faster and my strides a foot longer. She'd give me hell for being out all night, and I couldn't wait to hear it. Thank the saints she was safe at home, and I had one less thing to worry about.

"Nicolai Attano?"

I was getting really tired of my name tonight. The voice spoke behind me as soon as I stepped onto Belfar, the main street that stretched through Sector Three all the way back to the flat.

"Who wants to know?" I turned to find myself face-to-face with no less than four Society bastards. Two of them jumped on either side of me and snatched my arms while a third stuck a needle into the bend of my neck, pumping me with glint. "What the *hells* are you doing?" I shouted, drawing attention from the carriages driving down the street, slowing to watch the scene.

"You are under arrest, by order of the Society of the High Overseer," the last one spoke.

My heart slammed against my ribs. There was no way they

could've found evidence of Isaac's death and followed it back to me this quickly. I hadn't botched the job *that* badly.

"On what charges?"

"Three counts of murder."

"*Three*? That's ridiculous—"

"Not to Sabina Bianchi." He gestured with his chin toward a waiting carriage. "Get him to the loading docks. You'll go to the island to await your trial—"

I didn't hear the rest—I didn't need to. They bound my hands and shoved me in the cabin of the car, a windowless space that reminded me of a cell, like the one on an island not far from here, awaiting my return.

I didn't panic until they closed the door. When I was alone, I let the walls close in and strangle my mind first.

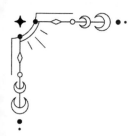
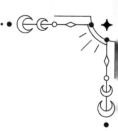

CHAPTER 17
CAMILLA

Nico didn't come home last night, hadn't even concerned himself with checking on me this morning. I didn't know why it bothered me. I should've been happy to be rid of his presence for the evening, enjoy my books and canned peaches in peace. But that bastard left me bitter, and I couldn't wait to give him a piece of my mind as soon as he decided to return to our flat.

I'd just settled on the settee with another can of fruit for lunch when the door banged open, breaking the chain lock from the drywall.

"Gideon, what the hells?" I jumped from my lounge on the chaise in the living room.

He removed his cap, ran a hand through his damp hair. His skin glistened with a sheen of sweat despite the cold outside. "Milla, we've got to go back to the estate right now. Grab your coat."

"Why? Is something wrong?" He was already up the stairs, grabbing my things. "Gideon!"

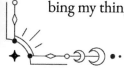
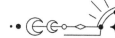

I chased after him, and he explained as I followed him on the way out of the apartment. A carriage waited. "Nico was arrested this morning," he said. "Sabina pressed charges for killing those bleeders."

I stopped, the shock of his statement freezing me into place. "Arrested?"

He held open the cabin door, shoulders slacking when he saw me still on the steps. "Milla, please, we need to get home. I'll explain on the way."

I nodded numbly, worry stealing some of my stubbornness. Luther sat on the bench across from mine as I slipped inside. Adler drove, and Gideon slammed the door shut just as the horses broke into a trot.

Gideon explained in a few words that there was a sacred law, a life for a life should another be taken. When Nico killed that bleeder for me and let the witness flee, it gave Sabina enough leverage to press charges. And while it was never legal to murder someone on the Isle, it was different for descendants. A balance must be maintained and taking a wearh's life had tipped a very sensitive scale.

"They'll take him to Hightower to wait for a trial, which could be in a few months at the earliest," Gideon explained, "but the penalty is always a death sentence."

"So that's it?" I snapped. "You aren't going to do anything but go home and *wait*?"

"Milla . . ." Gideon murmured. "We can't do anything until the trial is won or lost. Only then can we wage an official war on the bleeders and take action."

"I don't care about war, Attano, I care about Nico! You need to do something *now*, before he gets sent back to that awful place."

Those words came out of my mouth, and no one was more shocked than I was.

"I'm with Camilla," Luther mumbled. He'd gone pale. His hair was messy without the wax to style it back. "You don't understand what Hightower is like, Gideon. We can't let him go back, no matter how short a time."

My heart broke for him, watching his throat constrict, how his hand slid back and forth down a bouncing knee. Nico wasn't exaggerating when he said Luther hadn't healed from his time there.

Gideon shook his head. "We'll go to Uncle Sol. He's next in rank. We get orders from him."

"We go to the Meat Market, and we demand to speak to Sabina," I corrected him.

"Milla . . ."

"Nico is your boss, is he not?"

"Yes, but—"

"And I'm married to your boss, correct?"

He sighed, understanding where this was leading. "Yes, you are."

"Then the power shifts to me in his absence. If you are too cowardly to face the bleeder, I'll go myself, but you will bring me to the Meat Market this instant." I set my glare on him, but he didn't budge. His jaw locked, refusing to make the call.

I crossed the width of the car and snatched the gun bolstered to Luther's side.

"Milla!"

Pointing the barrel toward his balls, I said, "If you ever want to have children, Gideon, I suggest you let me do what I want."

That had him moving. "*Shit*, Camilla, fine!" He pushed the grate to the side and gave the order to Adler, changing our course. I sat back a little but kept the gun in my lap.

His eyes remained on my hands as he crossed his legs. "Nico was right. You're a handful."

I would've smiled if my nerves hadn't stolen all satisfaction from my heart. "No, Gideon, I'm a boss, and I'm about to negotiate to get yours back."

The ride was quiet for the next fifteen minutes as we drove into Sabina's domain. But as I glanced at Luther, who still stared out the window, I could see the beginnings of a smile ease some of the trouble in his face.

⁕

SABINA'S DEN was in the center of a covered market, where glass panes framed a latticework of steel beams shielding the long bazaar from Lynchaven's daily rainfall. Outdoor shops lined each side, with a center building running in the middle of them all. The black lettering painted on the side defined the bleeder queen's territory.

The Salt Exchange.

From my limited understanding of the workings of the Row, she ran the markets and the meat trades, the only sector the Attanos *didn't* own. Those who were in her favor dubbed her the Salt Queen, called her Madame, the overly cliché demands of someone trying too hard to compete for power against a family like Nico's.

The car came to a stop, and I let myself out.

"Milla, wait." Gideon was a step behind, following me into the muddy street.

"I can do this alone," I said. "Go home and be with your family. This is my mess, and I'll take care of it."

He followed me out anyway. "You'll have to shoot my kneecaps to keep me from coming with you. Nico would never forgive me if I let you go in there alone."

I smiled at him and waved off a hesitant Adler, who appeared like he was very uncomfortable with the situation. "Well, by all means, come along. But don't hover. I won't give Sabina any reason to find me weak."

Turning on my heel, his boots sloshed in the mud a few paces behind, keeping up with my pace. "With your charm, Camilla, no one would make that mistake."

Two wearhs stood in front of the central building entrance, where I assumed the queen reigned over her salt streets. "Business?" one of them blurted.

"I'm here to see Sabina."

His red eyes scanned the crimson lining of my coat. A smile curled his lips. "She's been expecting you, Attano. Take off your coats. We'll need to confiscate your weapons."

"Don't touch her," Gideon growled behind us. "You will grant this woman her meeting with the Salt Queen for the grief the Madame has caused her. I'll remind you that the sacred law requires a descendant to hear first the side of the accused before passing judgment. Sabina has broken the law herself, and we demand to be seen —and protected."

The man smirked, shrugged, and looked to his companion, who told him, "Let them go, Damion. Not like their bullets can do much, and they're vastly outnumbered down there."

Down there?

I steeled my expression into something more determined and followed the wearhs into their den, reviewing silently what I knew about Sabina if I were to negotiate with her successfully.

Her legitimate business oversaw the meat markets and the hunters who brought her stock from the Wilds in the Upper Notch. Other Blood remnants didn't bow to her, but the bleeders remained loyal to her laws and demands. Partly because her legal industry made good money for those who worked for her, but mostly because of the Pits.

I'd never been to the fights, but their brutality was notorious throughout Lynchaven. Every other night in the underbelly of the Row Market, three fights took place. Descendants took their chance against the beasts of the Isle in a completely barbaric brawl to the death. If there was more than one winner, the Salt Queen would choose her champion, who was apparently paid lavishly for their performance.

Some descendants had made a career out of fighting, living in the Pits at night to earn their wages. The real trophy, however, was achieving the title alone. To kill a beast of such macabre association was a fast track to fame and respect. Some descendants, even with their remnant abilities, never made it out alive. Their bodies were quickly disposed of, and their names forgotten.

This reputation carved itself into the hind places of my thoughts as the bleeder escorted us through a descending hall. Music from a brass band built in volume as we treaded deeper into the den. It led into a large room with a dome-shaped ceiling, dark and furnished with high-top tables and a bar that wrapped the right wall.

"Where are we?" I asked. I'd never been to Sabina's den, preferring the meat from our butcher in the Square who didn't also run illegal fighting halls—to my knowledge.

"Beneath the markets," he growled.

Our destination was a club. The lighting was low, the music disorienting and loud; obscure light from crystal chandeliers hung from the rafters above. I tried to remember the way in, but between the darkness and the drums, the brass horns wailing into the fog of cigar smoke, it was all I could do just to follow the bleeder leading us to the Salt Queen. He came to an abrupt stop when the number of bodies thinned.

"Madame." Damion bowed at my side. In front of us was a platform overlooking the entire den, and a bleeder sat upon the slab of obsidian she must've used as a throne. Her skin was dark, slightly darker than Nico's, reminding me of polished bronze the way it glimmered in the candlelight. Snowy white hair curtained her sides all the way down to her waist.

"What have you brought me now, Damion?" she asked, sounding bored. Her black eyes flickered between me and Gideon, who had maintained a distance behind me as I requested.

"The Attanos have come crawling, as you anticipated."

Sabina snapped her fingers, and the band stopped playing, draping the room in quiet. I neither smiled nor shriveled under her inspection, being face-to-face with another woman of power.

"State your name and business."

"Camilla Mercy Marchese-Attano, and my name is my business." I was mindful for the first time at how well our family names complimented each other, saying it out loud at last.

Sabina's eyes widened. A slow smile crept across her flawless face. "My, my," she drawled. "Have the fires of Oblivion frozen over or do my ears deceive me? A Marchese and Attano union?"

"A union you have rudely disturbed, Sabina. You have filed charges against my husband, and I've come to negotiate with you."

Her lips split apart to let loose a barking laugh. "What could you possibly offer me that I don't have? You think I care about Nicolai? Good riddance. One less Attano running through the streets. He got what was coming by murdering my wearhs."

Her crowd murmured their agreement, but I spoke above their dull roar. "Your bleeder held a gun to my head. A wearh group calling themselves the Grey Hands snuck into my room on the Attano property and tried to kidnap me, but not before biting and poisoning me. How do you think a man like Nico would react to such acts of cruelty against his wife?"

"That is a nice story, Attano, but there's one problem," she replied. "The sacred law states that a descendant cannot kill another remnant, that such things are sacrilegious to the old line of saints and to the survival of our remnants. If we killed without consequence, no matter the reason, what would stop remnant from conquering remnant? What would stop the powerful and rich Attano Benders from killing off each of my numbered bleeders, one by one?"

"This was not an attack, Madame—"

"Silence yourself," she hissed. Her hands wrapped themselves around the arms of her throne, black claws scraping the black stone. "The death of a wearh is an attack on our kind. The sacred law has a price that must be paid—a remnant for a remnant. A life for a life."

I understood then why Solomon had been so cross with Nico. The cost of killing Angel was far more than I'd considered at face value. I looked at Gideon, whose jaw was set firm. My voice hardly shook when I said, "Then let me pay it."

Sabina's smile widened. "You Marcheses were always the most wretched creatures on the Isle. But why would I take the life of a powerless native in payment for a remnant? Just because the law says so, doesn't make us equals."

I swallowed down a knot in my throat, thinking quickly about how to increase my value to the queen. I thought of my own steam empire, what would be appreciated in my line of work beyond tangible resources. The room maintained a heavy silence. This trial was just another form of entertainment in this underground world of deadly debauchery.

And then I came up with an offer.

"The Pits," I said.

Sabina arched her brow. "What about them?"

"Have you ever had a native compete in your fights?"

Her wild laugh returned. "Of course not. Letting a native fight one of these creatures from the Wilds would be a death sentence. None have ever volunteered."

"Then consider me the first."

"Camilla, what are you—"

Gideon started to speak, but his words were smothered by my own. "I'm the reason Angel is dead. I'm the one who should be punished. If my life isn't good enough on its own, then I'll let you have the satisfaction of watching your beasts tear me limb from limb. I'm sure my name will draw a big enough crowd to pay back the loss of your wearhs. And if by some miracle I survive, then I will have earned my right to walk free from this place."

It was a chance slimmer than the page of a book, but it gave me a hope just as thin—a fighting chance.

Sabina's smile fell slowly, thinking over my proposal. "One fight to the finish in the Pit." She looked up at her audience and waved a dismissive hand. "Place your bets while you can."

"*And*," I said, knowing I already had the Madame hooked, "you'll drop Nico's charges. You will send a letter to the Society right now. I will not fight until he is free."

"Deal." The single word was a falling knife. She beckoned to the recorder. "Draw me up a letter and I'll sign it immediately. Boys, take the other Attano back to his family."

She nodded and waved once more, having received more than what she demanded. The bleeders holding Gideon began to take him away, and I looked at him then, only to see his anger replaced with true fear. Fear for *me*. His family's rival. The woman who nearly ruined his cousin's life. I didn't deserve an ounce of it.

"Camilla, don't do this," he warned, even as they dragged him away. "Nico wouldn't want this!"

"I'll fix this, Gideon. I promise." I let that vow swell the tears brimming on the ledge of my gaze, letting my own fear catch up with me, processing what just transpired and what was about to happen.

Gideon fought back in a futile effort until I could no longer see him through the bodies of descendants standing around the makeshift dais. I saw his mother in those wide blue eyes and knew I'd made the right decision, making sure Nico returned to his family. He had people to miss him. My brothers would mourn me for a moment. I wondered if the company would fall to Aramis then, if I had no one but my next of kin to pass it onto.

"Are you ready to meet your maker, Camilla?" Sabina's words slid into me like a cold breeze, and I suppressed a shiver.

"No," I sighed, looking at her. "But I'm ready to meet my beast. What will you make me fight?"

A wheeldevil? A gildedback? Mostly everything in the Wilds had at least one horn and four pairs of claws. It didn't quite matter what I was up against, but the unknown made the anxiety clutching my gut squeeze a little firmer, until I was moments away from showing the den my peaches.

The bleeder queen's smirk did nothing to improve my apprehension. She leaned to the side of her throne and whispered something in her servant's ear, who quickly took off to complete whatever she requested.

"To be honest," she said with a small laugh, "I have no idea. We caught this creature near the foothills of the Falling Mountains. Not one of my hunters have ever seen such a beast roam the area before, so we have no idea how to classify it, but we have decided to title it a voidwalker."

I shifted on my feet. "Why do you call it that?"

Something darkened in her eyes, the kind of shadows that hid behind stars. "You're about to find out."

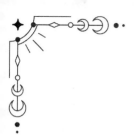
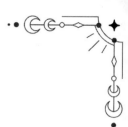

CHAPTER 18
NICOLAI

Inspector Gavriel stood in front of my holding cell. Here to gloat, no doubt, but I was too drowsy to shoot him the glare he deserved. My head, my bones, my blood were filled with glint, drowning away any memory of my remnant, a feeling I remembered well from the prison.

"After all I did to get you out. You're going right back in."

I shrugged. "At least this time they'll just kill me." Death was preferable to a sentence in Hightower any day of the week.

He crossed his arms and stared at me through the bars. "It's truly pathetic how unmotivated you descendants can be. Death is the end of it all, the moment everything we worked for in this life becomes pointless. Dying is merely the failure of living, and you would rather lose than do whatever it takes to succeed."

"It's only a failure if you leave behind unfinished business." I slurred the word. "*Regrets.*"

The inspector crossed his arms, staring at me through the bars. "And what about you, Nico? Did you leave anything behind?"

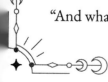
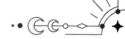

I shut my eyes, my failures flashing in the shadows behind my eyes. "Yes."

He sighed, then a scraping sound of metal on metal. Hinges groaning with the sway of a door. "Fortunately for you, there's still time left to wrap things up."

My eyes flew open, and I stared at the open door. "What is this about?" I asked, carefully standing on my feet. It took all my focus just to stand upright.

"Sabina sent a letter. She's dropped all her charges."

"What?" I asked, shocked. "Why?"

"Why do you think?" He stepped inside the cell, snatched my hair between his fingers to shove his face in front of mine. "I've always admired you, Nicolai, how you always seem to find the best deals in this city. But you get rid of the heiress before her birthday. I don't need to tell you why."

Milla's face was a blur in front of the inspector's scowl. What did he care about our deal? "If I give her up now, the Firenzes will take her—"

Her picture cleared as Gavriel rammed his forehead into my nose, where it cracked just as pain spread across my skull. I stumbled away, but he yanked me back by the top of my hair, holding me in place. "Know your place, Attano. The Row might look at you like you're a king, but you're nothing here. I put you on top. I made you who you are, and if you step out of line again, I'll bury you under that prison."

He left with the door still open. Any hope that fleeted in my chest was stomped out just as quickly.

"Milla," I groaned to the walls, "what did you do?"

I CAUGHT a carriage in the Square, practically dragging myself out of the station. The glint wore off gradually, but I needed to get home as soon as possible, to figure out why the Salt Queen would change her mind on something so consecrated. This strange development had Milla's name written all over it, and that terrified me more than facing the island again.

The sun set behind the cover of clouds by the time the car pulled into the driveway, and I snapped at the footman to pay the man well for his troubles.

"Nicolai!" My Aunt Fran was the first to meet me at the door. I hugged her briefly before pushing out of her arms, scanning the foyer. When she wasn't there, I entered the parlor, where the rest of the family stood, speaking amongst themselves.

"Where is she?" I asked the room. Their conversation silenced abruptly, an answer all by itself.

It was Adler who stepped forward, his throat convulsing with a swallow. "She went to negotiate with Sabina. Gideon escorted her."

"And why would he let her go to the Meat Market? He knows we have no sway there!"

"She quite literally had him by the balls, cousin," Luther spoke from the chair. "She held a gun to his crotch and threatened to shoot them off if he didn't take her to see Sabina."

"She *what*?"

But just when I thought my wife couldn't get any more reckless, a carriage rolled outside the parlor. Gunshots—three of them. Everyone inside ran for cover, but I stalked to the window inside, peering past the frosted panes. The shots weren't aimed at the house, but at the sky. A warning.

From my view and the waning light marking dusk, I couldn't tell who drove the car. The passenger door was already open, two men standing outside, one with a smoking gun. A body was shoved from the cabin, where the form of my cousin fell into the gravel. The men proceeded to load back into the carriage and drove off as quickly as they'd arrived.

"Gideon!" My palms pressed against the window. When I saw the blood on his neck, I shouted, "Someone send for a haelen!"

I was the first to get to him outside, discovering his hands bound and his right sleeve wet from a wound on his shoulder. His neck had been bitten into, just enough for someone to get a hit off his blood. But he was alive and mumbling, which was enough to give me hope that Milla still was as well, even if she was still missing. With help from Adler, we quickly ushered him into the parlor where it was warm, his body having little strength to do anything more than sit up straight.

"Gideon." I knelt in front of him, my hands on his shoulders as his head rolled from side to side.

"Nico?"

"Yes, cousin. What happened? Where's Milla?"

His eyes widened, like he'd just had a sudden realization. "Nico, you've got to get to the Salt Exchange immediately."

Solomon was at his side then, a true worry that satisfied my own filled his voice. "Sabina negotiated with her?"

He nodded lazily. "She offered to fight in the Pits in exchange for your freedom"—his eyes shut—"and Sabina agreed."

"She . . . *Fuck!*" My fingers went cold, ice seeping from a black place in my soul to chill my body into a cold-blooded rage. I glanced at the clock. "What time do the fights start?"

"Ten minutes ago," Adler barely whispered.

Groaning in frustration, I stood quickly to look at the rest of my cousins. "Get every gun you own and meet in the yard in two minutes."

"Nico," Solomon drawled.

I shoved a finger in his face, too. "Don't even challenge me on this, Sol. I swear to the bloodiest hell in the void, if Milla does not walk out of that pit alive, I will kill every bleeder on this side of the city and fill her beloved Pit with their mangled corpses."

"I was only going to say that I'm coming." He pushed his coat aside to reveal his revolver already sheathed. "She saved you from going back to that wretched island. If we have to bleed every wearh in that market to get her out, so be it."

I hadn't expected him to be so encouraging, nor recognized him with such a carnal anger in his eyes. In all my twenty-three years of life, I'd seen my uncle shoot his gun twice. Neither had ever been a choice, both calculated in a thoughtful decision. It had been barely over a week and Camilla had sunk her teeth into us all, it seemed.

"I'm coming, too! I want to test out a new skill I taught myself," Esme chimed. Four throwing daggers slowly lifted from enclosed pockets, hovering in the air around her as she displayed her newly crafted weapons. "If Sabina has her usual guards posted for the fights, then you'll need all the hands you can get to bust in there."

The clock ticked another minute, and my bones felt like hot rods, branding my flesh with impatience. "Alright, then." I nodded to Luther. "Get some men and meet us on Salt Street."

He nodded, that same thirst for retribution rimming his gaze. Of all my cousins, I knew he understood the significance of Milla's actions the most.

Grimm met us at the door, handing me my coat and my shotgun. I threw them both over my shoulder as Adler and Esme brought the carriage around with Luther hanging off the back.

His grin was wild, the look in his eyes just as savage. Ready for a bloody fight. "Let's get your lady, boss."

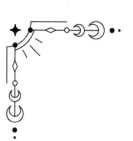
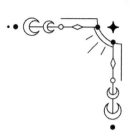

CHAPTER 19
CAMILLA

My father warned me about pissing off the wrong people. He cautioned me about looking for trouble, how curiosity wasn't an admirable trait but a fatal one. I should've taken his counsel more seriously before spying on Nico and running into bleeders in the process, but like Aramis always said, I was cursed with a shadow of misfortune. At least this time, no one would pay for my mistakes but me.

They gave me blades and whiskey. Not even good whiskey, but the stuff on the bottom shelf you only brought out once everyone's too drunk to know the difference between that and the real stuff. But no matter the quality, it helped settle some of the nerves in my chest. One shot to numb the nerves, two for good luck, and a third so that I wouldn't feel the ending when this creature inevitably killed me.

A man opened the door to my cell and announced, "It's time."

I was taken into a tunnel dug deeper than the club or the markets. There was a light at the end, where an iron gate parted on rollers to let us through. Beyond was a place I could only describe as a

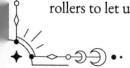

small arena, with raised seating surrounding a flat stage no bigger than the holding hall, all of which were separated by metal bars enclosing the lower floor.

I still wore the skimpy knee length dress and sheer tights, feeling more exposed than ever beneath the dim glow of the lanterns and the inspection of the crowd. They gave me a belt for the dagger and a few throwing knives, not for the purpose of assisting me but to help draw this out as long as possible. The people came here for a show, and I was to give them one.

On the opposite side of the stage was a second gate. Chains rattled behind the bars as the bleeders drew my beast toward the mouth of the tunnel, leading it towards the pit. My fist closed around the dagger, if only to hide the shake of my hand from Sabina and the onlookers. She watched, just above the second gate, drinking a large goblet of a deep red drink. Catching my stare, she smiled. Her white teeth smeared with blood.

"Tonight," she shouted to her patrons, "we will introduce a new creature into the Pit. A demon who could only be born from the hellish hole of Oblivion. Championing this fight for her freedom is the one and only Camilla Marchese. The *Princess of Steam* is now bait in my pit. A bet for you to profit, just as her family has profited off us since remnants came to this Isle."

The room filled with cheers and slanderous words aimed at my body, my family, my intelligence. They harassed me from the safety of their seats, spitting through the bars, defamation fueled by alcohol and the anticipation of watching me meet my death. They were excited, punishing, the very worst side of humanity on display to me from the stage, just as I was on display to them.

And I swore to the saints, if prayers could reach them in the void, that if I survived this, I'd rid the world of that side of creation. I'd purge their cruelty with a bullet and a vow.

"Open the damn gate, Sabina," I demanded. From one knockoff royalty to another, she listened, nodding her chin at the pair of men overseeing the pulley.

The metal gate groaned, splitting apart just as dark tendrils of a black mist slipped from the obscured tunnel beyond. They curled like fog over the river, ribbons of shadow spreading across the blood-stained floor as the quiet steps of the creature approached. Its head emerged, skimming the circle of light illuminating the stage just to the edges of the Pit, and I lost my breath, staring into the void of which it was named after.

It crawled out on all fours, but as soon as it noticed me on the other side of the arena, it *stood* on its hind legs, showing its full height, which almost scraped the dome of the arena—at least twice my average stature. Two horns curled ribbons of grey and red from the top of its head, matching the spikes jutting out its back all the way down to its tail. More spikes lined its arms, sharp as the claws on each hand that were unnervingly humanlike.

I stepped back, feeling the smooth boundary of the arena wall prevent my retreat. It stepped with me, slipping a long, bloodred tongue between the gap in its skull as if it was sampling my scent. Its towering frame was covered in scales, smooth rows reflecting the torchlight like thousands of woven onyx stones. I couldn't find a gap in its body to penetrate it anywhere, nothing to reveal a weak spot.

Like most beasts from the Wilds, its feet were decorated with claws, six on each. The tail whipped from behind its body, a pincher at the end like a poisonous scorpion Giles had been stung with once. It snapped twice in my direction, and I had to swallow the bile rising in my throat, shoving down the fear that would only make me easier prey.

But it wasn't its form or the clicking sound coming from a deep place in its thick chest that struck a terror like no other in my heart. It was the darkness that clung to it, darker than any abyss that existed in this world. The creature walked amongst them, neither friend nor foe of the shadows, but a part of them. Voidwalker was an appropriate title.

It crouched low again, pincher arching above its head. Three sharp hooks snapped, mucus stretching in the space between. Somewhere, worlds away now, I heard Sabina's voice.

"Good luck, *Lesser*. Let the fight begin!"

The creature flinched as the crowd roared. Irritated by the noise, the way it thrashed its head back and forth, as if wounded by the sound. It rasped a snarl in fury, a roar that was sharp like a hiss, before turning its pale gaze back to me.

I returned a far-from-vicious squeak, hiking up my dress with one hand as my other clung to a suddenly unimpressive dagger. It caught the movement, must have tasted something in my decision. As soon as I pressed my weight into my toes, it charged.

There was no time to think, only react, as I flung myself to the side and out of its path in a clumsy escape. I staggered, slipping on the tights around my feet as it smashed into the wall of the arena, sending a shudder through the stone. I was *not* a hunter. Father made sure I was trained well enough to fight back. I knew how to use a switchblade and every kind of gun, but beyond my skill as a sharpshooter, I lacked in more creative ways to defend myself from something this large—this supernatural. This blade in my hand might as well have been a dinner knife, seeing as I'd never get close enough to the beast to even use it.

It charged again, leaving me barely time to gather my momentum and change direction. A swipe of its tail hit me in the side, throwing me across the arena where I landed hard on the floor, rolling to a stop. My dress was pushed high over my hips, leaving the audience little to the imagination as my lace undergarments were on full display. But I could hardly care about propriety in a situation like this, when the voidwalker was slowly creeping on all fours towards me, almost like it was curious.

I clenched my teeth to still the rattle of my skull, blinking its figure into focus. Running was pointless, would waste precious energy. I'd need a distraction to buy me some time, to even have the opportunity to wound this thing. Fear like this, fear desperate for a miracle, always awakened the dormant religious side of me. My gaze fell above the cage, pleading with the saints beyond the void to help me, to send a quake in the earth or to maybe nudge one of these drunk descendants over the barricade and into the cage.

Instead, I noticed a chandelier holding several flames in its extended arms just above the Pit. Without looking for another option, I slipped a hand into the belt and pulled out a throwing knife. Taking one glance at the voidwalker, only a few lunges away, I shifted the point between two fingers and flung it at the string tying the flames to the rafters.

It hit, by some divine mercy I didn't think existed, but the suspension didn't snap completely. I quickly dug into my pocket and pulled out another. My next shot missed, then another went flying into the crowd—who, by their *boos* and slurred curses, didn't appreciate my creative approach. The first throw must have been beginner's luck.

The rumble of a breaking mountain groaned from the creature's chest. It crawled over me, obstructing my view of the ceiling, blocking out the light and the sounds of the crowd. I couldn't breathe, make a thought, look at anything besides the ghoulish face of what could only be a demon from the darkest corner of Oblivion.

I scooted away on my backside, crawling even as my thoughts paralyzed with fear. It prevented my retreat with its tail, planting it behind my back, cornering me with its whole body. The trembling of my bones beneath my skin only worsened as it dipped its head low, looking me eye to eye in some wordless conversation. It was . . . *studying* me. Just as thoroughly as I'd done it.

That red tongue slipped from its gaping mouth, and from this close, I could see four rows of serrated teeth in the hollow of its head. Like a snake, it curled on a hiss, briefly skating the skin of my throat where my familiar wrapped my neck in an analogous fear. I didn't dare move, could only squeeze my eyes shut and suppress the sickness twisting my stomach.

A snap of its tail whipped behind me, the only warning I was given before one of the pinchers shot into my back, straight into my spine. The pain was immeasurable, consuming every piece of my being, swallowing me whole until my vision blacked out. There was a scream, possibly my own, as I descended into a deeper agony. The blood in my body was replaced with molten metal, burning my soul until nothing left to connect me to this body or this place. This world was stripped away by the woes of death.

And then it stopped.

ALL SUFFERING CEASED AS QUICKLY as it came on. But when I opened my eyes, I was no longer in the pit. Burning plains stretched as far as I could see. A lone figure wandered amongst the flames at a distance, walking through the fire unscathed. I stood on shaky legs, surrounded by a charred circle of grain.

The figure neared, draped in black robes that snuffed out the flames as it covered them. Leaving behind a trail of ash in his path, he stepped in the circle, silently staring from a dark cowl.

"Where am I?" I asked. "Who are you?" This place was nothing like the void in the stories my father had told me, in the religious tomes he'd forced me and my siblings to read when we were children.

"A monster," he said in a deep voice that echoed across the plains. "But today, I'm a messenger."

"For whom?"

"The Forgotten One." The figure pulled its hood back, revealing the bone bleached face of a man whose skin and flesh had long withered away. "There is a threat that has returned, set to change the order of the world if it is not stopped. She needs you to find her. She needs you both to stop the faces of order."

I blinked, wondering if this was just a strange fever dream, my subconscious coping with the pull of death, or something in between. Because nothing this mangled messenger said made sense. "What are you talking about?" I asked. "Who am I to find?"

"I cannot speak her name here. It will call them, but the answers to all your questions are etched into your soul. She left them there, for you."

"My soul?" I echoed him. He nodded, returning the cowl back over his skull.

"Patience, daughter. We have been looking for you for a long time, but so have the others. Be careful who you keep close. Order hates what it can't control." He turned to leave, taking the bare path through the field of fire from whence he came.

I started after him, wanting to demand a better explanation, but the path was quickly set ablaze once more. The fire followed him on the way back and blocked my way. "Wait!" I shouted after him. "Are you a demon? A true demon from Oblivion?"

He paused for a moment. A voice slid into my head, washed a cool feeling down my spine, between my legs. "Demons were once angels until they feared us. Don't let them turn you into a monster as well, daughter."

"Daughter?" I mumbled, suddenly feeling very tired. Smoke layered itself in thick sheets until I was wrapped in a net of night. *Order hates what it can't control.*

———— ✹ ————

SHOTS. Gunfire. Screams.

My eyes flew open, finding the demon still over me, his tail behind him and pincher thankfully now out of my back. I tried to scramble away from the beast, but my legs were heavy with lead, weighed down by an unseen force. The lack of sensation sent a panic through my chest, thrilling my heart.

The voidwalker hissed, baring its teeth in a subtle warning of what would come next. It seemed not to have remembered our last conversation. Quite rude of it, piercing me, dragging me to Oblivion, now threatening to eat me on top of it all. I swung my dagger, grateful I still had control of my arms. It opened the gape of its mouth, jaw hyperextending as rows of teeth jutted out to claim me at last. It took everything inside me not to squeeze my eyes shut, and instead, fling my dagger straight into its throat.

The demon wailed, swallowing the blade as it sunk into the thick membranes lining its throat. It choked, coughing up a dark fluid I could only assume was blood and spraying me in the process. I rolled to my front and began to crawl, using the strength left in my arms to distance myself far from the wounded voidwalker. My attack might kill it, but it would do so too slowly, giving it the opportunity to seek vengeance before it perished.

"Camilla!" My name came from the crowd above, and I lifted my head weakly to see Nico standing there, a gun in his right hand. The bodies in the stands had scattered, and I noticed the rest of the

Attanos running down the steps of the arena to meet him. Nico beckoned for me to run to the wall he stood on top of so he could pull me up through the cage top. "Hurry!"

I tried to stand a second time and failed miserably. My legs were completely numb, unfeeling the scratches marring my knees as I dragged my body across the coarse floor. "I can't!" My voice was a whimper, a plea for help. "I can't walk!"

Just as I spoke, the creature whipped its tail again, and I looked back at the sound to see it creeping toward me, giant talons scraping the stone. I was a rat who snuck into the wrong house, legs snapped from a trap. With nowhere to go, no more knives in my arsenal, I could do nothing but crawl. Crawl to those steel-grey eyes that held a fear in them I'd never seen, so raw for me.

The demon shrieked as more shots were fired off. Nico railed the demon with bullets as he crossed the width of the floor to where I inched toward him. He'd dropped inside this hellish hole willingly, even seeing what he'd be up against. The creature retreated to the far wall, neither weakened by the bullets, but not quite enjoying them either. It replied with a groan, a deep rattle humming through its chest.

"Milla, what's wrong? You can't move your legs at all?" he asked, dropping to his knees beside me. I let him pull me into his arms and sit me up, unapologetically wrapped my hands around his bare chest. I didn't think I'd ever feel a kind touch again, and I craved it. I craved him and his hands, both solid and soft, as they held me firm around my waist.

"Its pincher stabbed me in the spine," I said quickly.

He whispered a curse. "Any idea how to kill it?"

"I was working on that." I looked up at him, but the glare of the torchlight blurred his image.

"The light!" I pointed above us, where the chandelier hung

crooked from a half-shaved string. "Cut the rest of it down. I think it dislikes fire."

Nico's hand left my side to draw his gun. In two perfectly aimed shots, the lights fell, candles falling from their iron posts to scatter across the arena floor. The demon lurched, but Nico waved his hand, squeezing me firm against him as he focused on an invisible force.

As he knocked the beast against the wall, he shouted, "Adler!"

I didn't even see the cousin, but the flames from the candles suddenly grew to a hot blaze, forming a line across the stage floor to separate us. Nico bent the breeze with the underground draft to feed the flames until we were separated by a wall of fire. The voidwalker made no move to transcend it. Instead, it cowered against the side of the wall, shrieking as if in great pain just from the breath of its heat.

Nico grunted beside me, as if mentally pushing through a physical boundary with his remnant. The wall of fire shot forward, consuming the beast as it writhed. It let out one last howl before disintegrating into vapor. The flames disappeared, having nothing left to feed their appetite. The floor where the demon once cowered was covered in red ash.

"What the *fuck* was that thing?" he said between pants.

"A messenger," I murmured. His pulse slammed erratically against my fingertips, his body still in fight mode. I reached for his jaw, smoothed the stubble that had already grown from missing his morning shave. "It's over, Nico. It's gone."

His hands trembled slightly as they dug into the bend of my waist. "Are you . . . are you hurt anywhere else?"

I shook my head. "Just a few bumps and scrapes. Nothing I won't survive."

"*Saints*, I'm so pissed at you, Milla. Don't you ever do something this fucking stupid ever again." His words shook. I'd never seen Nico truly upset, his negative emotions usually manifesting through his rage and temper tantrums. But in those eyes usually framed with cold steel, I saw something different. The desaturation of all that anger, leaving only sadness to fill the monotone centers.

My smile was as shaky as my hands. "Are you going to punish me, husband?"

"On the contrary. I'm going to punish the ones who did this to you, and if your injury is permanent . . ." Nico reached his metallic hand beneath my knees and scooped me from the floor. "I will make sure Sabina and her wearhs never walk again, either."

My breath caught at his threat. "We promised to stop a war, Nico, not start one."

He stopped in his tracks to look at me, a snarl running across his lips. "If you would have died like Sabina wanted, I would've filled this pit with the blood of those who bet on your body. I wouldn't have started a war, Milla. There wouldn't have been any bleeders left to fight."

I gulped, feeling the promise in every word sink into my heart like stones in deep water. "Where is Sabina now?"

"She's gone, as well as everyone else. It's just the family and our men," he said, bringing me to the side where Solomon and Luther were reaching down, ready to pull us both up.

They put me with Esme on the highest bench, leaning against her shoulder. It took all my focus just to stay awake, to ignore the tremble in my bones still trying to fight for their life. Nico's famous scent, cigarillo smoke and my favorite cologne, filled my head as I pulled his coat tighter around my body. Esme smoothed her hand over my shoulder, her silence more comforting than she'd ever know.

"I'm so glad you're alright, Milla," she muttered.

It mended something cracked inside me, knowing she cared at all. And perhaps it was because of a train or the contract, but I think Nico did as well. That look in his eyes when he saw me in the Pit. It wasn't for the risk of losing money, his investment, or a war. It was for *me*. No one had ever looked at me like that since the crash. Not since my father.

I pulled the lapels of his coat tighter across my chest, where the thin strap of my dress hung on by threads.

When the gang had finished trashing the bleeder den, Nico approached us and gathered me into his arms once more, since my legs were useless for the time being.

"Where are we going now?" I asked. Another safe house? Maybe this time we could go back to the bar. I could use a pint—or six.

"We're going back to the estate."

"Has my room been fixed then?" I muttered, losing the fight against my exhaustion. "I'd really like to sleep in my old bed again."

His breath hitched as I rested my head in the curve of his shoulder. *Saints*, I was tired. The crash of adrenaline left me shaking, weak, and limp against his hard chest.

"Whatever you want, Milla."

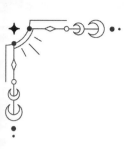
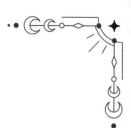

CHAPTER 20
CAMILLA

"You don't have to do this."

I sat in the vanity chair, watching through the mirror as Nico prepared the bathtub while I wiped a layer of demon blood off my skin. He acted as if he didn't hear me. "Where's Sera?"

"It's the weekend."

Oh.

That's right. Of all the days she had off, it just so happened to fall on the same day I was numb from the legs down. Nico had put himself in charge of my care, not even acknowledging his aunt's offers. It was slightly mortifying, knowing they all knew what was happening up here.

When a proper amount of water filled the copper basin, Nico came to me and knelt beside my chair. I turned in my seat with a question on my brow. "What are you doing?"

He tapped the side of my knee. "Do you usually bathe fully dressed?"

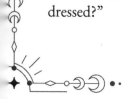

I swallowed, some of the nerves returning from the fight. "No. That would be a bit ridiculous."

"I thought the same," he said dryly. "May I then?"

I nodded and hiked up the scraps of dress still hanging together over the tops of my tights. Though I couldn't feel his touch, his fingers were gentle and quick, slipping beneath the clasps to smooth the tattered remains of sheer fabric down the length of my leg.

"Can you feel any of that?" he asked.

"No." Thankfully, I couldn't. Just the sight of Nico's false hand gliding over my bare skin was delicious enough on its own. On his knees before me, his broad shoulders filled my view, the soft material of his shirt clung to cords of rippling muscles as he slipped the end off my toes and flung it behind him. If I could feel those cold fingers digging into my thighs, my heart would certainly be in trouble. For now, it remained blissfully ignorant of those sensations.

He moved to the next leg, this time taking a second longer. I knew because I counted, concentrating on the time instead of this intimate exchange. He sat back on his heels then, eyes swept over my crossed arms, the pile of silk around my body. "I never thought I'd get the chance to tell you this, but take off your dress, Milla."

A nervous laugh slipped as I looped the tiny straps down my arms. My fingers curled around the hem of the dress, lingering a moment. He caught my hesitation and said, "I'll go get Fran or Esme if it makes you more comfortable. I just wanted to take care of you after what you had to go through to get my charges dropped."

"It's fine." I forced myself to nod and mechanically pulled the wilted fabric up my chest and over my head. My muscles ached with soreness from the fight, feeling a hundred bruises line my bones every time I roused them. Tossing it to the side next to my tights, I was almost glad to be free of the dirty thing. *Almost.* Doing so in front of Nicolai Attano was painfully intimidating.

"Well, hello to you too," Nico said sweetly. His fingers stroked my forearm where my familiar had slid to meet his touch.

I poked her on the tail, forcing her to skurry off. "Stop talking to my tattoo."

"She likes me."

My brows raised at the pride it brought him. "She's made of ink. Don't get so cocky."

Instead of replying, his insufferable smile only stretched. He stood quickly and rounded my chair, his breath inserted sharply at whatever he saw. "That's not good."

"What? What's wrong?" I looked at him through the mirror, trying to twist to see for myself.

"Wait," he commanded, before lifting me by my waist with surprising ease. My hands fell across his shoulders as he held me against his chest, wearing nothing but a bralette and matching undergarments in front of the vanity mirror. His hands were fixed around the small of my waist as we locked eyes in the reflection. I quickly looked away, to the spot on my back that demanded more attention.

A black symbol marked the area I was stung. Inky lines followed the length of my spine just above the small of my back and dipped below the lace elastic. A crescent shape surrounded the initial puncture site with disordered lines piercing the half-moon, while a jagged line ran from the center of the symbol and through the mouth of the hooked symbol.

My hand slipped from Nico's chest to touch it. The skin had already sealed over the wound, but the black lines were somewhere deep beneath my skin, haunting the space between my skin and my flesh.

"Not good at all," I murmured. "What is that?" Our eyes found each other again, and he cleared his throat before setting me down. He leaned against the rim of the tub and crossed his arms.

"I have no idea, but until we know something, it might be best to keep that mark covered. I was going to send for the haelen when you were cleaned up. Does it hurt?"

My fingers grazed the spot absentmindedly. "Not really. I'm just sore from being tossed around that arena."

"Good." He nodded in approval. Grey eyes skated over me like an assessment. "Will you . . . be taking the rest off?"

The brashness of his question snapped my arms over my chest like a reflex. "Absolutely not. You're not seeing me naked that easily, Attano."

"*Ahh*, so there's a chance then?" he said with the tip of a smirk—which did nothing to dissolve the tension coiling in my stomach. "Relax. It's nothing I haven't seen before."

I wanted to kick him where he stood but couldn't, for obvious reasons. "That may be true, but it's nothing I've ever *shown* before."

I almost crawled out of the bathroom on my elbows when his brows raised half an inch in surprise, realizing I had just confessed my incompetence to a man who was most likely well adept in all forms of intimacy. "You've never—"

"I have," I said quickly. "Once. But it was a quick thing, and I didn't take off my dress. I just wanted to get it over with."

"What's the fun in that?" he asked, his smile drifting into unnerving territory.

"Some of us don't fuck for fun, Attano." I leveled a look at him. "And that's by choice, just so you know. I've had plenty of opportunities."

Saints, Milla. Why couldn't I just shut my mouth?

My skin pebbled as his stare dropped to where my arms had fallen away. "I have no doubts about that, princess."

"Then what do you doubt, Nico?"

"That it was *your* choice," he said, grin fading slightly. "I don't think you've made a single selfish decision in your life."

He truly believed that, and it broke my heart. The admiration in his voice was so greatly misplaced. "I've made plenty of them." Raising my right hand, the serpent inked across my skin writhed awake. "Why do you think Daddy gave me this guy?"

"I figured it was to protect you from remnants."

I shook my head. "There's a medication in the ink but it's not glint. It doesn't protect me from a remnant being used against me, as you probably know from experience."

He shook his head. "I don't understand then."

I sighed and glanced at the bath, yearning to feel the water scald my skin and remove the film of blood. "You promise not to judge me?"

He frowned. "Do you forget who you're talking to, Milla? Whatever you're thinking, I've probably done it at least twice."

He had a sound argument. If anyone would understand, it would be Nico. He was starting to feel more relatable than my own reflection. My eyes fell to my empty hands in my lap, avoiding his gaze.

"I accidentally killed a man when I was thirteen, and before you ask for details, I don't have any. My father had the memories wiped away by a Mirth remnant—but he left the guilt. It was the reason we got on that train, so we could go see the alchemedis, a kind of healer who treats with science. She gave me the familiar." I clenched my fists, wishing I could crush the memory between my palms, gone with the rest of them. "It was the same train your family derailed, the crash that killed my father."

A silence stretched between us. My confession left me feeling more exposed than the absence of my clothes. I glanced up at him, but his face was unchanged, listening to what I confessed with the indifference of a casual conversation. I explained, "I've killed men since then, but it was different after that. Like the bleeder in the courtyard, it was always a firm decision, a black and white choice. The circumstances surrounding my first time are . . . foggy."

"Is that why you blame yourself for your father's death, Milla?" he asked.

I shrugged. "We wouldn't have been on that train if it weren't for me. My father would still be alive."

He stood. I thought he might leave, but instead a warm hand wrapped around my chin, lifting it gently to look at his face. "Is this also why you bartered your life to Sabina in exchange for my freedom? Did you think you were responsible for my crimes?"

A rash of chills spread across my skin as he stood over my half-dressed, seated posture. I was completely aware his belt was only a reach away, and by the bulge pressing against the fabric of his pants, I didn't think he'd mind if I acted on the impulse. I craned my neck further to expose my throat, longing to feel that hand clasp around it and steal the breath from my chest. "Among other reasons."

Thank the saints his remnant was that of Bane and not Mirth. The thoughts that were spurning from this position were traitorous to my ambitions. But he seemed to read the desire coded in the part of my lips, the way his closeness manipulated my breaths to shallow, needy shards.

"They've tamed you too well, princess." For a moment, his hand traced along my jaw, almost a caress, before slipping it behind my neck. "Let's get you cleaned up before the water gets cold." His body heat lined my side as he lifted me in his arms again, slowly dropping my numb legs into the hot water before letting me sink into the tub.

"Good?" he asked.

"Perfect." I eyed him warily as he took a seat in my vanity chair. "You don't have to stay. I can bathe myself."

He shrugged. "I don't have anywhere else to be."

I leveled my gaze at him. "I'm not a form of entertainment, Nico."

"I disagree. I've seen enough of you to keep me very busy tonight." His infamous smirk explained too much.

I sunk an inch deeper into the tub, which drew a laugh from him, a bright one that deepened the dimples in both his cheeks. He said, "Sometimes I forget how sweet you are, Milla."

Sweet? That was a word no one's ever used to describe me before. "You are aware I almost castrated your cousin, right?"

"He mentioned that, yes. I'm quite jealous."

"*Why?*"

He leaned forward, bracing his forearms on the edge of the tub. "You've never threatened my balls before."

I raked my teeth over my bottom lip. "Maybe I have other plans for them."

He held my gaze for a second before letting it drop to my thin bralette, now wet and revealing the peaks of my breasts beginning to harden from this conversation. My attention caught his hands hanging over the rim of the tub, and silently wished I could remember what they felt like running over my bare skin.

His brow arched. "Are these plans for good or evil?"

Fire filled my belly. "Wicked purposes, of course."

"Don't start with me, princess," he warned. "You are in no shape to handle everything I would do to you." The muscles of his neck went taut.

I smiled, satisfied at his distress. Taking the soap on the small table next to the bath, I gently rubbed my raw skin clean. I dragged the bar across my chest, shoulder to shoulder. He followed the movement. "I can handle more than you think, Nicolai."

"Is that a challenge?"

My grin slowly fell. Were we still teasing? Was I?

203

"If you need one."

Suddenly, the soap was no longer in my hand. The chair beside the tub was vacant, replaced with the cold brush of his remnant as it settled in the air. I almost jumped when soft lips brushed the shell of my ear.

"I have my own plans for you as well. Would you like to hear them?"

My throat closed on a dry swallow. What the hells had I started? I gripped the sides of the tub, occupying my hands. "I'm *mildly* curious."

A snide laugh tickled my ear. "Firstly, I'd take these damn things off." His metal hand slipped over my opposite shoulder, tugged at the lace. "Then I would take this soap"—he edged the slippery bar down the slope of my shoulder—"and rub it over *every* inch of your skin. I'd work away the pain from this evening with my hands, giving precious attention to one muscle at a time. I'd count every scratch, every bruise, and replace it with a kiss. I'd wash away the memory of that creature and replace it with my touch, my reverence, my undying gratitude. Only once I had paid you back for every wound you received on my account would I pull you out of this tub and bring you straight to bed."

Seven hells, his plans were far more thought-out than my own. Nicolai Attano once again proved he was always one step ahead, a better schemer than his reputation had made known. "What . . ." My lungs burned. Had I been holding my breath? "What would you do then?"

His false hand slipped around my throat, tipped my chin with a metallic forefinger to look straight up at him. "I'd thank you for fighting a demon to save me from hell."

From the shadows darkening his eyes into silver, I assumed his thanks went beyond those two words. My skin became littered with chills despite the heat of the water, knowing only that cold metal circling my neck.

"It's a good thing you don't want me then," I whispered, reminding him of his lie.

He slipped away. "A good thing for you." The soap returned to my hand, and Nico took his time returning to the vanity chair.

Slow breaths tamed the sparks his words ignited. In the bastard's defense, he'd warned me. Now I was left with an ache between my legs that challenged even the most swollen joint in my body. If I wasn't trying so damn hard to get away from him, I might've wished he'd commit more to his plans. Might have made more of my own.

It was a tedious job, washing away the layers of filth from the Pit. The bender watched me from his seat, his gaze locked on my hands as they kneaded my muscles, and I might've made a show of it. He sighed as I took a cup from the table full of water and poured it over my hair.

"That was for drinking," he replied, sounding hoarse.

I shrugged. It was easier to wash my scalp with the help of a cup. "Tell me something no one knows about you," I said.

His dark brows furrowed. "Why?"

The quiet was terribly imaginative, and I needed a distraction from all the problems I caused. "Must there be a secret motivation to get to know you, husband?"

Grey eyes squinted at me, but he sighed, taking a few seconds to think over my request. Finally, he blurted, "Well, for starters, I can't read."

I almost dropped the soap. "You can't?" The words came out wrong. Leashing some of the surprise in my voice, I tried again not to sound like an utter prick. "I mean, you seem proficient enough to me, especially given you were incarcerated instead of in school."

He tilted his head, shrugging. "Technically, I *can* read, but it's difficult. I can't do it fluently, nor can I remember what the hells I read a second after I read it. The letters jump off the page, they mix up, they don't look complete. It's why I hire a secretary to go over all the contracts at the factories. Also why I was up all night after you left the pub, trying to scrape together something that sounded professional enough to convince you to marry me."

My lips fought a smile, picturing Nico slumped over a desk, scribbling something down only to crumble it up and start again. "You thought your fancy words could sway me?"

He shrugged sheepishly. "It worked, didn't it?"

I wrung the water out of my hair. "And you gave me grief about my allergies."

"We're a pathetic pair, for sure." His fingers dipped into the edge of the water, stirring the foam from the salts. "I think we'd make a good team, though."

I nodded. Despite the rivalry between our families for saints knew how many generations, we seemed to complement each other's strengths and pitfalls. "Perhaps," I said, twirling a wet lock around my finger, "we can form a different kind of union after this. An alliance between our families. Think of it, we'd be unstoppable."

"I've thought about it often," he admitted to my shock. "But your brothers will never agree to it."

"My brothers will work for me in a few weeks," I reminded him. "If they have a problem with it, they can leave."

"The proper way to say it is *fuck off*." He winked. "You'll get there."

I rolled my eyes. The word was so versatile to him. "We act as if we have options, but we're still no closer to figuring out who the Collector is or why the Grey Hands targeted me."

"We've got a few more weeks. The important thing right now is to get the haelen here to see you. Let's get you better, then we can get back on the streets."

"In that case"—I draped my arms over the sides of the tub in a regal position—"I'd like to get out now."

He frowned at my exaggerated posture. "Where would you like me to bring you next, princess?"

My smile returned. "Straight to bed."

Nico laughed darkly, and the sound was a salve to all the pain lacing my every move. "*Evil* little heiress."

THE ATTANOS WAITED in my bedroom when the healer arrived.

Haelens were remnants of Blood. Not the kind that used it to feed, but to heal. It was said they could manipulate the components of blood, using a person's own fluid to heal their wounds and ease their pain, among other types of disease prevention. Her name was Ruth, a woman dressed in the white robes of a hospitalist and the feathery touch of a skilled healer.

I laid on my stomach as she pressed her palms against the mark. Her remnant slipped beneath my skin like a cube of ice melting across my back. It wove deeper, poking my flesh, pulling at other spots.

She finally stepped away from the bed, covering her hands with gloves. Esme had remained beside me since she arrived and helped me sit up.

"Well?" Nico spoke first, breaking the heavy silence. "What is it?"

The haelen folded her hands in front of her waist. "It is merely a mark, like the ink in your own flesh. I'd remove it, but that might cause more damage to the area and the design of it covers many nerve endings that I would be uncomfortable getting close to. There is no actual damage to the spine, but there is a fair amount of swelling from the injury that will take a few weeks to subside. I can come by every few days and work it out gradually to speed up the process."

"So, you're saying I'll walk again?" I asked to clarify.

She nodded. "Absolutely. Until then, you should stay in bed. The more rest you get, the quicker the swelling will go down and the sooner you'll be able to get back to your normal activities."

Esme squeezed my hand at the good news, and I smiled, feeling a weight lift from my chest. I looked to Nico, who hadn't left my side since he called for the haelen. The update hadn't apparently affected him, but I noticed he had snuffed out the cigarillo he'd been burning. He murmured something to Luther that made the cousin laugh.

Aunt Fran came to my side and gave me a tight embrace. I was still getting used to this family's persistent show of physical affection. "Thank the saints, Camilla. We were so worried."

Gideon approached next, and I was pleased to see him standing on his own feet after being dragged away by a threesome of bleeders. His blue eyes were clear as sea glass as he tapped his hand on my knee and gave it a squeeze through the covers. "I've been ordered to let you take my balls next time, just in case you feel like using them against me in whatever situation you drag me into."

"Noted, Gideon. I'll find some other indispensable body part to threaten next time."

"Indispensable? I—"

"Gideon," Nico called from across the room, sounding annoyed. "Downstairs. And you, Ruth"—he looked at the haelen—"do not leave until you've sealed every wound and healed every bruise on her body."

"Does he ever say, *please*?" I asked Esme loud enough for him to hear.

She smiled and leaned into my space to whisper, "He does when he's not too busy being territorial."

I glanced at her questioningly. "I don't know what you mean."

"Sure you don't." She rolled off the other side of the bed and stood at the end. "I'll let you get some rest since I'm sure you're exhausted. Sera sent word that she's coming back early. Apparently, it's all over town that a Marchese fought in the Pits and came out alive."

"Wonderful," I groaned. "I can't wait for the lecture next time I see Aramis."

She cocked her head, squinting her almond eyes. "Why do you say that?"

I shook my head. "Nothing. He just doesn't appreciate it when I do stupid things that risk my life."

"You mean a brave thing. I would've lost another cousin yesterday if you hadn't." She followed her family out, her mother waiting at the bedroom door. "Sleep well, Milla. I need you better so we can keep these Attano men in line."

I realized I smiled even after she shut the door behind her. I'd always wanted a sister. I just wished I hadn't found her here, in the one family I couldn't have. Maybe all I could do was enjoy it before it would all be ripped away.

Her last words hung in the air, a haunting reminder of our previous conversation in the hallway. My mind was forced to wander.

Another cousin?

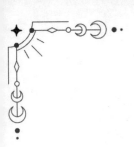
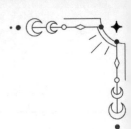

CHAPTER 21
NICOLAI

"**S**abina is waiting in the parlor," Solomon said to me while the haelen examined Milla. I almost hadn't heard the healer, the world covered in a bloody filter knowing she was just below my feet. Whatever the bleeder's reasons for visiting, she'd better be on her knees in my house, begging for forgiveness. I had killed one Blood remnant already. I'd happily do it again to avenge Milla's pain.

Seeing her body, bare and beaten, the swipe of claws, the force it must have taken to leave bruises that large, it sent me into a quiet rage that could challenge the wrath of a thunderstorm. Saints, I had almost let the truth slip when those big hazel eyes batted their innocence, had almost abandoned three years of work and five years of isolation for a moment on her lips. The black lace hadn't helped the urges.

Then I remembered what the inspector demanded. Taking a risk on something as precious as her heart wasn't just cruel, it was forbidden.

But if I couldn't have her, Gideon sure as hell couldn't either.

"What's going on, boss?" he asked as he joined me, Luther, Adler, and Sol in the hall.

"Sabina's downstairs. You would've heard Uncle if you weren't too busy fondling Camilla's knee." I regretted the words as soon as they left my mouth, watching Luther and Adler's knowing exchange between each other. "What's with you two?" I asked.

"Nothing, Nicky," Adler said, even as he wrestled a smirk.

"We're just surprised, is all," said Luther, my ever-honest cousin, who never refrained from speaking his mind. "It's just, for a woman you despise, you've broken the sacred law, nearly started a war—"

"And he came out soaking wet after giving Camilla a bath," Esme muttered as she walked by. All three of my cousins only stared at me with raised brows. My uncle never looked more uncomfortable in his life.

"It's not like that," I said before any of them could come to conclusions. "I was just helping her after she threw herself in the Pits to get me out of my charges."

Luther crossed his arms. "I've done lots for this family too, but you've never given me a bath."

"*Seven hells*," I growled, tearing my fingers through the gel in my hair. "This conversation is over. Get downstairs. All of you."

They finally descended the stairs, but not before Luther slapped me on the back like I'd accomplished something monumental. *Saints,* if he wasn't my flesh and blood . . .

Sabina sat on a velvet couch, a leg draped over her knee. Two guards stood behind her, dressed in plain suits and tall hats. I glanced at the clock, nearly the same hour and minute they shoved Gideon out of the car yesterday. Incredible how one day can shift the game board, reroute the power dynamic.

A body sat hunched over in a chair near the window, identity covered with a sack over his head.

I stopped short of where she sat, letting my cousins fill in behind me. Solomon stood in the space between us, ready to intervene if he must. "You have nerve, Madame, showing up here so soon," I said.

She shifted in her seat, placing her heels on the carpet. "I came to give the Marchese her winnings, though I redacted some to pay for the damages. You all left so soon after rampaging my club. Fortunately, she made the house a lot of money last night."

"It is fortunate that the creature didn't kill Milla in the Pit, or you would have more than just a ruined club on your hands, Sabina."

She flicked her wrist like it was water under the bridge. "How could I have denied such a sweet sacrifice? And honestly, it all worked out in the end."

My false hand clicked as I primed the tubes with air, stretching the fingers one by one. "Why are you here?"

"I brought you someone in consolation for our little misunderstanding." She motioned to the body. "A peace offering."

"Throwing me in prison and then nearly killing my wife is hardly a little misunderstanding."

She shrugged a shoulder and gestured to the window again. "I'll take him back then."

I aimed my attention at the limp figure starting to wiggle against his bindings. Removing the cowl over his head, his face was faintly recognizable.

She explained, "He's the man who sold you out to me and testified for your arrest. I believe he was the wearh driving the getaway car."

"Interesting." This was good. We could work with this bleeder, get some information out of him. I turned to Sabina. "Coerce him and see what he knows."

She arched her brow. "You don't want to do it yourself?"

"I don't have time." I pushed a chair with a sharp breeze behind the fold of my knees, sitting in front of him. His throat convulsed with a hard swallow. "Coerce him *now*."

Sabina sighed, as if I'd asked too much of her, but finally stood and rounded the seated bleeder, whose hands were tied behind the chair. His eyes rolled lazily in wide sockets, like he was under a spell and yet knew exactly what was happening to him. She took a fistful of his hair and snapped his head back to look him in the eyes.

"What would you like me to ask him?" she asked.

"Who are the Grey Hands and who are they working for?" She repeated my questions, using her remnant to force the man to spill his truths. He resisted at first, evident by the way his body trembled like he was having a fit, fighting against an invisible dredge that would only hurt worse the longer he fought.

"The Grey Hands are just a mercenary group," he said between gasps. "People hire us to take care of private business. Following unfaithful spouses, interrogate scheming business partners, kidnap certain pretty girls out of their beds . . ." His eyes rolled to me. "That sort of stuff."

"How do people hire you?" Sabina asked.

He shrugged. "Our clients know how to find us."

"Who hired you to take Camilla?" I asked. That question made him hesitate. Sabina pulled his head back to further his discomfort, compelling him with my same query.

He finally broke. "I . . . He didn't say! Our clients don't always give us their names."

I shook my head. He knew how to avoid directly answering questions, even coerced. "Just because he didn't say, doesn't mean you don't know him. A client that could pay enough for you to risk breaking into my home must be somewhat established around here."

The bleeder squirmed, whimpered as Sabina dug her claws into his scalp. "Tell him the bloody name," she hissed.

"He'll kill me!"

I leaned forward in my seat, so he'd understand every word with crystal clarity. "Here's how I see it. This client might kill you if you tell me his name. I will definitely kill you if you do not. It's up to you if you want to wager dying now or risk doing so later."

The slump of his shoulders told me he'd bet against the latter. "Felix Firenze."

His name turned my blood hot until it was simmering in my veins. "What were the rest of your orders from Felix?" I asked.

"To bring her to him. That is all I know. I swear it."

"Could he be the Collector?" Luther asked behind me. It was possible, now that we knew he had the means. But what was his motive? What would an alchemist need with a bunch of descendants?

The bleeder shrugged. "Felix? It wouldn't be out of the question. Not sure where he'd hide all the people he's taken, though. Have you been to the Wet District? It's mostly greenhouses and laboratories next to their chemical plants."

"Did he say why he wanted Milla?"

He scoffed, and I wanted to knock the sneer off the leech's face. "He doesn't *want* the girl. She'd be safer if he did."

I didn't appreciate his tone very much. "What the hells is that supposed to mean?"

He got serious again, looking me dead in the eye as he said, "My clients don't share their business. They give us the job, we get it done, no questions asked. But I will say that Felix contacted us way before the derby races. He's had his sights on Milla for a while now. The original plan was to hang around the Wet District until she tried to leave their estate. But when you two got married instead, he sent us chasing after you." He leaned forward despite Sabina's hold on him. "And he offered to pay us triple for the trouble. My guess is

214

Felix wants your girl dead, Attano. You might want to figure out why."

I had a few theories, all of them involving a certain company. But why would her brother orchestrate a deal with the Firenzes if they were going to kill her? Surely the two families had discussed this ahead of time. Felix wouldn't have claimed his shares until Milla's birthday, but I couldn't even begin to get into their heads. The contemplation was making me sick.

"I will also give you some advice, Mr. Attano," he said to me. "Your wife needs to be more careful. She was too easy to grab that night when we saw her leaving the stables."

My heart twisted, dread gnawed at my ribs. "What did you say?"

He opened his mouth to explain, but the window behind him exploded. Sharp-edged glass sprayed my face as I ducked away from the blast. The broken cry almost covered the sound of a gun, and I looked up to see the descendant slumped in his chair, blood leaking from the back of his head and rolled around his skull, dripping into his lap.

By the time I could aim my own gun to the window, the trespasser was gone, slipping into the shadows of the evening fog.

Shit.

"Luther? We still have a few darkthieves that owe us favors. Get their names from Fran and have them watch the Wet District until further notice. And get some men around the perimeter, at least for the next few weeks."

He murmured a confirmation of my orders before leaving the room. I glanced at Sabina, who plucked a window shard out of her forearm, grimacing in distaste. "Well, someone is certainly watching you, Nicolai. Pity about the rug. It's lovely."

"It's replaceable." I glanced at the carpet, wondering how many times we'd ripped up the damn thing. "I wanted to ask you, how did you get such a hellish creature into Lynchaven without the Society noticing?" Her creatures could be useful in the coming weeks, and if she had alternate routes into the city, it would be helpful to know about them.

Sabina crossed her arms. "The poachers on my payroll wouldn't appreciate me giving away their tricks. Would you like to explain how this little union came to be between you and the Marchese? It was quite sudden, hearing Nico Attano was off the market."

I shook my head. It was none of her business how I won over my wife. "No."

"Then ask your next question. I can hear your heart racing from here."

I glanced at Solomon, then her men. "I need to speak with you privately, Madame. Just the two of us."

"Nicolai . . ." Solomon warned. But he'd given up his privilege to order anyone in this room the day he lost his temper, when he made his first decision out of rage, out of vengeance, and started the war with the Marcheses. He vowed to never make a choice for this family again, and then had allowed me to take that burden. Even knowing the weight of it.

I loved my uncle, but my father was the strongest man I'd ever known, right until the very end.

"It wasn't a request, Uncle." Never taking my eyes off Sabina, she nodded, and I listened to the sound of their footsteps leaving the parlor. Waited until the door had shut completely before standing from my seat and walking to a crystal decanter my Nonna must have left out. I poured two glasses, handing one to Sabina.

"I happen to know from a reputable source that the High Over-seer will fall in a few weeks' time. The power in this city will be up for grabs, and I would like to have the support of the Salt Queen should there be a war. We have similar interest—"

"Similar territories," she finished, "and enough to lose should things not go our way."

"Precisely."

Sabina stepped closer until I could smell the copper on her breath. "My family left the Continent to protect our remnant and our freedom. The day I let a Firenze take over is the day I join my radical mother in the grave."

"Good." I stepped back, getting some distance from the bloody scent. "On a lighter note, I have a question about blood sampling."

Her brows rose. "Go on."

"The bleeder that drank from Milla, she said she tasted different. Not like a native, but not like any remnant. What does that mean?"

She sipped the shot and licked her lips, letting the robust notes cover her tongue before answering. "That would be hard to say without having a taste myself. Could it be a kind of glint?"

"Not likely," I said, leaning against the marble hearth. "I haven't seen any glint on her, though I might request she start taking it again, seeing as she made a lot of remnants lose their reoles last night."

She slipped a low chuckle. "What is the saying? Out of the frying pan and into the fire. How is she?"

"Healing," I spat, not encouraged to give her anything more.

Noises stirred in the floor above us, drawing her gaze to the ceiling. "Would you mind if I visited your newly beloved? You have me curious about this taste of hers. Do you think she'd let me have a bite?"

I swallowed back the remaining sip and slid the glass across the mantle. "Honestly, I'd love to see you try. Come, I'll bring you upstairs."

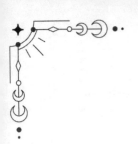
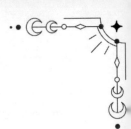

CHAPTER 22

CAMILLA

"Why did you lie to him?"

The haelen's hands paused over my knee, where torn flesh held together by bloody scabbing wove into a seamless new patch of skin. "What do you mean?"

"You felt something during your assessment. I felt it. This is not just another mark on my body. Why didn't you tell him?" When her remnant pushed against the black stain, it pushed back. Whatever the voidwalker pierced me with, it was alive and reacting, shriveling away from the healer's touch like a shadow against the light.

"A haelen's purpose is to care for the individual. It is *your* body and your decision to share what is going on inside it. Not everyone wants to share their diagnosis, and that's just fine." Moving to my other leg, she looked up at me and smiled. "Your body, your secrets, your choice. I'm just here to heal."

I didn't know what to make of her confidentiality, only that I appreciated it. I didn't want to give the Attanos any more reason to

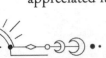
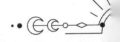

be concerned about me. "You'd risk Nico finding out you lied to him? Most are afraid to get on his bad side."

"I've been one of the family healers for years. Ms. Edith wouldn't let him harm me, nor do I think Mr. Attano would try. He isn't a cruel man. I think he'd understand, however I would appreciate it if you kept my withholding information to the two of us."

"I will if you tell me more," I offered. "Have you ever seen this before?"

"Never. I honestly have no idea what it could be, only that I have no desire to remove it. Whatever it is, it has made itself a home in you. It's like you're a host, but it has no parasitic tendencies." Glancing at my face, she quickly added, "And hopefully it never will."

"Hopefully," I said dryly. The haelen wrapped up her work, erasing the evidence of the fight one bruise at a time. When she was finished, it was like it had never happened. The only thing left was the numbness lingering in my legs and the mark on my back. As she gathered her supplies to leave, I asked, "Do you know anyone who would have an idea about this? Are there other haelens who have encountered anything similar?"

She sighed and bit her bottom lip. "Not a haelen, no. But perhaps an Acolyte."

"An Acolyte?"

"They are keepers of the remnant history. If anyone knows about what attacked you and the mark it left, it will be them."

"Great," I said, feeling more optimistic. "Where do I find them?"

"You don't." She shut her case and stood at the foot of the bed, ready to leave. "They live on the Continent. None of them immigrated to the Isle, refusing to abandon their towers and the knowledge inside."

My chest deflated with a scoff. "That does put a damper on my plans, I suppose."

She offered me a kind smile, one that exaggerated the lines around her eyes. "Get lots of rest, Milla. Do not hesitate to call on me if you are in any pain. I'll come see you in a few days when I make my weekly rounds on Ms. Edith."

As soon as she opened the door to leave, I saw another person waiting on the other side to come in. When I recognized Nico, I fell back onto a feathered pillow, wondering if perhaps he might disappear if I pretended to be asleep.

"Is that anyway to greet your husband?" he asked.

Apparently, he would not. My eyes flew open to find him standing above me, looking down with a bemused look on his perfect face. "Go away, Attano," I told him, before snatching the pillow beside mine to cover my face. I was exhausted, and I fully intended to follow the haelen's orders as soon as possible.

"You have a visitor."

"Take them with you."

"Come on, princess. I promise I'll let you sleep after this." He gradually pulled the silky pillow from my face, and for some reason, I let him.

"Would ten thousand reoles wake you up, Camilla?"

The voice belonged to a woman, one too memorable, and I sat up quickly, discovering three more wearhs in my bedroom. I would've punched Nico in the throat if he hadn't retreated to the chaise. I settled on glaring at him.

"What are you doing here, Sabina?" I asked.

"Nico offered me a taste."

"We agreed it would be up to you," Nico clarified. "I told her what Angel said regarding the taste of your blood, which made her curious. Perhaps she can offer some insight."

I glanced at her warily. "Can you?"

Sabina lifted her chin as she said, "I'm not a Madame for nothing. I have certain experiences that bleeders like Angel do not. I was a young girl when we fled from the Continent, but I still have memories of the old country."

"I didn't realize you were so old," I said. Her only wrinkles were the ones lining her lips as she frowned at my retort.

"My age is irrelevant. Now, will you let me sample your blood or not? I'm a very busy woman."

I shrugged and held out a wrist in offering. Sabina smiled and waved two fingers at one of her bodyguards, who procured a shot glass and a thin knife from his jacket. As he came to the side of my bed, I noticed Nico had moved from the chaise to my side, watching the bleeder as he pricked a vein in my wrist and let the blood dribble into the shot glass.

Satisfied with the amount, he walked back to Sabina and handed her the sample while Nico grabbed a towel for me to hold against my oozing puncture wound. She swirled the blood, sniffed it, put a small amount on her tongue and rolled it around her mouth like my essence was a fine wine. She finally threw the rest back in a single gulp and handed the dirty glass to her guard.

"Well?" I asked.

Her brows pinched, lips still smacking around the taste. "That is strange," she murmured. "It is not pleasant to drink, burns when it goes down. I've never tasted anyone like this." She licked her lips. "But I can tell you what it tastes *like*."

"What?" Nico asked, returning to my bedside.

Sabina's red lips tightened into a line. "It's hot and smoky. A remnant usually has a marker. For example, benders like the Attanos taste sweet while a darkthief is more tart. But this is like . . . the burning of blessed water when it touches something unconsecrated." She looked directly at me. "Like fire from Oblivion."

That was oddly specific.

Her words left me hollow inside. First the bond with the void-walker, then the mark. Now my blood apparently tasted like I was born from the darkest hell in the void. "That sounds ridiculous," I said, holding my bound wrist to my chest.

"Do you truly believe it was a demon you captured?" Nico asked, promptly changing the subject.

The mark on my back began to throb, haunted by the possibility. I said, "Wouldn't that be impossible? History says demons of Chaos were either killed off or driven into Oblivion. Why would there be one here?"

Sabina dragged a sharp canine over her bottom lip in thought. "Not everyone believes the written history is entirely accurate. Some believe Chaos never left. Some say she still hides in the disorder, that Oblivion is *empty*."

Empty.

Something about the word made the shadows in the room stretch a little longer, their darkness requiring a second glance. If the darkest hole in the void was empty, did that mean all the demons were still here? One thing was certain: whatever I'd faced in that pit, there was one less in the world to worry about.

The bleeder clicked her tongue and stood. "I will let you know if my hunters see anything in the Wilds going forward, but I should be going." She looked to me instead of Nico, as if I had the higher authority in this room. "You know where to find me should you need my services again. I do hope to see you both at my ball in a few weeks. It would be a perfect opportunity to enter society under your new union."

"Yes, because being around a bunch of bleeders worked out so well the first few times," Nico hissed. "We'll pass."

Her smile was forced. "The invitation stands." Red eyes flickered back to me. "Get well soon."

They left, and Nico shouted for one of his cousins in the hall to follow them out. He returned to me. "That was strange."

I could only nod, looking down at the smudge of blood already clotting over the hole in my wrist. "What do you think it means?"

"I don't know, Milla. But we have more pressing problems on the horizon."

"What do you mean?"

He explained in minimal words what had transpired downstairs. The parlor was on the north side of the house, and I didn't even hear the shot due to the sprawling layout of the estate. It explained the splatters on his throat, though seeing Nico covered in someone else's blood wasn't such a rare sight these days.

It was—unfortunately—horrifically flattering on him.

"Felix is hunting me, then?" I summed up his story, my voice shook to my annoyance.

"The Firenzes have a bigger plan, like I assumed before, and you are a means to an end for them. But trust me on this, Camilla"—he stopped his pacing around the room and came to my bedside—"I will keep you safe. As long as you are within these walls, nothing will touch you again."

He spoke with such certainty, I couldn't help but believe him. To trust him.

"If Felix is the Collector, we need to find out what he's planning." I frowned, collapsing back onto the pillow. "And now I've lost the ability to walk for saints know how long. What if my recovery eats up all the time we have left and we end up being stuck together?"

Nico pulled the covers higher over my shoulder, moved a lock of hair out of my face in a way that felt affectionate. "There are worse fates, I suppose. Get some rest, Milla."

Letting those words warm my heart, I slept.

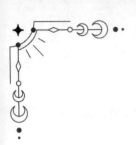
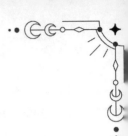

CHAPTER 23
CAMILLA

"Is she ready, Sera?" Nico asked from the bedroom.

"Just about," she replied, waiting on the other side of the lavatory door. It had been nearly a week since the Pit, and I still couldn't walk on my own. Nico decided to temporarily move his office at the factory to the library just down the hall, insisting he couldn't depend on his aunts to mobilize me.

Whatever wall that had been between us had become a paper-thin structure, an unavoidable consequence when he was forced to bring me to the bathroom six times a day.

"I cannot wait until I can piss by myself. This is humiliating," I groaned through the door.

"In sickness and in health," Nico chimed back, reciting hallowed vows we never promised each other.

Every day that passed, I could move an inch more. Sensation returned first through my toes, then I could roll my ankles. Up until yesterday, all I could do was bend my knees and swing my legs.

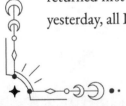

But at dinner on that eighth night, I finally turned a corner. Nico sat across the long dining table from me, Esme on my right and Fran on my left. When the conversation over a roasted duck and potatoes finally waned, I cleared my throat, drawing the Attanos' attention.

"I have some good news I'd like to share with everyone," I announced.

"We could use a little good news these days, Camilla. What is it?" Solomon asked from the head of the table.

Throwing my napkin from my lap to the table, I edged the chair back a few inches. Fran and Esme held out their hands for me, knowing my surprise. I'd been working with the aunts and Sera while Nico was busy, eager to get my strength back.

With a bracing breath, I squeezed their hands and slowly shifted my weight off the chair and onto my feet. It was an invisible battle, the hardest thing I'd ever done, demanding my legs to straighten and stand. The muscles I hadn't used in over a week ached from being stretched awake. My bones trembled from the onset of body weight, but my legs were as stubborn as the rest of me, refusing to give up.

My eyes shut tight, the work demanding all my focus until the sound of clapping broke through the wall of my concentration. I opened my eyes to find myself standing over the table, still clutching their hands, and Nico's small smile growing larger by the second.

It made my own lips tip into a matching one, the terrifying beauty of it. I'd earned his amusement, his mockery, his disdain, and all the smirks that came from them. But only a few times had I seen such a genuine joy touch his face, and only the first I'd ever seen him look at me like that. That pride in his eyes. It summoned a brand-new desire inside me, more than pleasing my father ever had, even greater than appeasing my family now.

I wanted him to look at me like that all the time.

"Well done, Milla," he said. His voice quieter than before, meant only for me.

"Thank you." The words came out on a breath. It was arduous work, doing something so simple I too often took for granted. The women helped ease me back into the chair when the shakes had reached my arms. "There's still a way to go, but Ruth said in a few days I should be able to walk without assistance."

"Never doubted you for a moment, Belladonna," Nonna said down the table. "And what good news this is indeed. Just in time!"

"In time for what, Nonna?" Esme asked.

"The Salt Ball is just a week away. Milla will be ready for dancing in no time."

Nico rolled his eyes. "We're not going to the Salt Ball."

I asked, "Why not?"

"Nico doesn't trust Sabina's events," Esme explained beside me.

"Every remnant in the city is going to be there. I'm not bringing my wife, who seems hell-bent on attracting trouble, to the bleeder event of the year," Nico said, decided. His cousins murmured their agreement, but Esme sighed in disappointment.

"Then stay home." Grabbing her hand, I said, "Me and Esme will go together, and we'll dance to every song and drink our weight in champagne. Perhaps we'll get lost in the sprawling gardens or hide in a darkened alcove with a mysterious stranger . . ."

"Enough, Milla," Nico growled. Gone was his pride, returned was his irritation.

"I'm kidding. Sort of. I'm going and anyone else that wants to come can join me. That's final."

"The lady boss has spoken," Adler murmured. Muffled laughs filled the spacious dining room, but I refused to look at the family and witness their reaction to my rise in station. Nico's lethal stare was satisfying enough. A few weeks ago, that look would have haunted me. Now, it made me grin.

I arched my brow to twist the knife a little deeper. What did he have to say about that? The screech of his chair as he pushed from the table told me I was about to find out.

"Sit down, Nico, you haven't been excused," his grandmother chided him.

"Sorry, Nonna, me and the missus need to discuss something of importance."

"What are you doing?" I asked, feeling him jerk my chair back. "Nicolai Roman Asshole Attano, you will not—" My protests turned out to be futile as he lifted me by the hips and tossed me over his shoulder.

"Put me down or I swear I *will* murder you! Damn the contract!"

Nico's strides never faltered. "Say goodnight, Camilla."

"I know where you sleep, Attano!" My voice echoed down the hall as we turned out of the dining room, where the servants waiting outside shot us curious looks. I looked at each of them and grumbled, "Don't ever get married!"

"You know, if you wanted to sneak into my bed, princess, all you had to do was ask nicely. These threats aren't necessary."

"They are until you carry me normally!" I pounded my fists into his lower back, trying to grind down his patience. But he only smacked my ass in a crass response. I gasped, tried to twist my body to look at the back of his head. "Did you just—"

"Fair is fair. Hit me one more time and I'll do it again. Go ahead, I enjoyed it."

The noise that slipped out of my mouth could only be described as a growl. We came to the staircase, and I finally conceded, deciding it was best not to throw off his balance while ascending.

He brought me back to my room and tossed me in a leather

armchair. Sera, who was changing my bed sheets, quickly found something to do in the bathroom. Nico flicked two fingers, and a wild breeze slammed the door shut. The lock slid itself across the threshold.

"How do I get rid of you?" he asked, caging me with his hands braced on the armrests.

His question was more than that, though. He wanted to know where we went from here, what we were doing to ensure neither of us had to remain in this arrangement. Nicolai Attano didn't enjoy the idea of sharing his power, the thought of a queen sitting next to his throne over the Row.

"Polys," I said.

His brows kissed. "What are you talking about?"

"Every descendant taken so far has been a poly. When I looked at the files you gave me, I categorized each remnant and the saint they descended from. They're all different."

His face contorted. "How the hells did I miss that?"

Pride stung my cheeks as he stepped away from the chair to pace in front of the fire. "Probably because you're around remnants so much, it's not as significant to you. But to someone mundane and ordinary, the similarity was easy to spot."

His steps stopped, and his gaze slid sideways at me. "You know you are anything but mundane or ordinary, Milla."

His remark didn't help the heat in my cheeks. I fought to hide a tiny smile, too pleased with it despite being manhandled up the stairs. "Maybe it's time I found out for sure."

"And how would we do that?"

"My birth certificate," I said. Nico's face betrayed no thought, hiding whatever he thought about the matter. "I want to visit the House of Records. What you said about my mother, maybe there's something about her that makes me different. My past feels like a breadcrumb, and maybe it can help us understand why Felix is so keen on snatching me."

He took a long breath and finally released the chair, shoving his hands in his pockets. "Alright. That sounds like at least the start of a plan." He looked me up and down. "Do you really intend to go to that ball?"

I nodded. "Absolutely."

He muttered a curse, looking off into the fire. "I can't protect you there, Milla."

I couldn't prevent the smile creeping over my cheeks. "Are you *worried* about me?"

He glowered. "You're trouble. I've lost ten years of my life these last three weeks looking after you."

"Quality over quantity, Nicky. Speaking of numbers, I looked over those receipts you gave me." I gestured to my nightstand, where a stack of the factory's stocks and payoffs were neatly organized according to his request. Not having his assistant to double-check his accounts, he actually asked *me* to assist him.

Having nothing better to do, I obliged. It also gave me a unique insight into the financial status of his company. While his family's steel company made a generous wealth, it was still not enough to explain how he could afford to pay off my family's debt, inheritance or not. He had to be getting money elsewhere.

"How did they look?" he asked, standing to retrieve them.

"I found a few discrepancies, which I placed on top, that you'll want to investigate. It appears someone may be embezzling small amounts every pay period. They started a few months ago, very abruptly. I almost missed it."

I'd never seen him snatch something so quickly, reading over the portions I circled and annotated. He grabbed the rest of the documents and started toward the door, hesitating before he reached it to look at me. "I need to go take care of this. Would you like to go to bed or . . ."

I waved a hand. "Sera is here. Go do your boss things."

"Appreciate it, *lady* boss." His voice was low, sweetly seductive.

I smiled and relaxed in the chair, shut my eyes so I wouldn't see his reaction when I said, "I could get used to that."

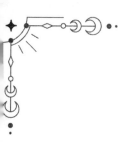
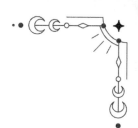

CHAPTER 24
CAMILLA

The House of Records was at the crossing of Billings Street and Newton, nestled in the heart of Capital Ground, the district that contained most of the government buildings and the men and women who served in leadership over the Mez. Nico had the carriage drop us off three blocks from our destination after finally giving into my pleas to walk. I'd been stuck inside for so long, even the sodden sky was refreshing to walk beneath on this misty afternoon in the Districts.

I pulled my hood high to shield my wavy curls from the dewy breeze, wearing a matching coat to Nico's. The crimson lining marked me as one of them officially. I wasn't sure how I felt about that, other than I liked myself in the color—and not necessarily because it flattered my complexion. My coat was cut differently than Nico's, hitting higher above my knee, trimmed with golden embroidery and a high collar that skimmed my chin. The inside was lined with convenient pockets to hide all my favorite blades.

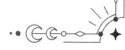

I fiddled with one, flipping it nervously between my fingers. My husband adeptly snatched it from my hand.

"Would you stop? You're going to cut yourself," he said in a hushed voice. He was dressed in his usual attire, with a flat hat pulled low down his forehead. A cigarillo with an orange blaze leaked a trail of silver fumes behind us as we walked.

"Why do you always light your cigarillo but never smoke it?" I asked.

He glanced at the burning stick, as if surprised he held it. "My father smoked them all the time. I hate the taste, but the smell reminds me of him. It grounds me when I feel anxious."

I didn't realize he was anxious so often. He always held himself in such a quiet confidence, a stone mask constantly worn over his worry. "I'm nervous too."

"Knives aren't safe stress relievers," he said, handing the blade back to me. I slipped it inside my glove. "Why are you nervous?"

I wasn't entirely sure, but as the House of Records came into view, an ancient building chiseled in the architectural style marking the founding years of Lynchaven, my heart challenged itself to a race. Part of me wanted to know everything about my birth mother, while another never wanted to think about her again. The two warring sides of my soul that were once at a stalemate had now taken up arms again.

"If I don't find out the truth, I can pretend she's anyone I want," I admitted. "Almost as if I can control the past myself. Facing the facts will destroy that veneer, and I'll lose control of the one thing I could always count on—who I am."

Nico was quiet for another block until we made it to the stone steps leading to a polished pair of brass doors. He stopped short of the first step and turned to me. "Our last names, our families, the legacies written before us, they don't determine who we are, Camilla.

You'll be the same troublemaking, hellish, loudmouthed, spoiled little heiress when we walk out those doors. I promise."

His demeanor was still cold, but not as withdrawn as before. I smiled anyway. "You forgot beautiful, charming, incredibly smart, looks surprisingly stunning in Attano red—"

But Nico had already begun to walk away. "I didn't forget any of those things. Let's go, Milla."

"WHAT DO YOU MEAN, they're *sealed*?"

The woman peered over her half-moon spectacles at me, as if my problems were hardly something she was paid to care about. She grabbed the book she'd been reading before I walked up to her desk and smoothed out the fold marking her page. She was the only worker on this floor. The only sounds were the patter of rain against the looming windows, worsening the damp draft inside the walls.

"It is as I said, Camilla Mercy Marchese, born in the month of the Giver, 24th day, year 278, has a court ordered and approved motion to have their records sealed until birth date of year 299 at the request of a Giovanni Marchese." She looked at me. "Your legal guardian at the time."

"I can't access my records until my twenty-first birthday?" My voice echoed through the department of certificates, a wide room filled with bookcases that contained the files of all who were born and had died on this Isle.

She shrugged, her attention already shifting back to the book in her hands. "Return in a two weeks. Until then, I can't help you."

I slapped the cherry-stained desk in frustration with both hands, my chest deflating in disappointment. Unable to think of a single way to sway the woman to break a government ordained order, I turned from the record keeper and stalked from the wing. Nico trailed close behind.

"I can't believe he'd seal my own information!" I said when we finally emerged from the building.

"I can't believe your middle name is *Mercy*."

"Not now, Nico." I breathed, rubbing my temples.

"Calm down, Milla. If we can't get something the legal way, we'll just have to get creative."

I spun to look at him. "What do you mean?"

Nico winked. "I own half this city, princess. Surely someone I know has a key to the House of Records. I'll get your information, Camilla."

I answered with an approving nod. It would've been a kind sentiment, him going out his way for me, if I hadn't reminded myself he most likely wanted to know my history even more than I did. He still hadn't fully explained his motives for marrying me. If he knew my secrets, he could use them against me, just as I planned to do to him.

Distracting my focus from my wondering, an intuitive part of my brain noticed two men donned in all black leaning casually against a storefront. Guns on their hips flashed as their coats caught a breeze. As we passed, they shifted to a more active position on their feet. In the reflection of the glass, they turned to follow us once we passed.

"Nico," I murmured. "Don't look now, but I think those two men are following us."

He said nothing in reply, hadn't let my arm go even after we made it to the street. Instead, he pulled me closer. I glanced up at him, his eyes taking in our surroundings in a cold calculation. "Where's the carriage?"

"It dropped us off in front of that bakery." I remembered because my stomach did a dance when I scented the pastries on display in the window. The curb was vacant now.

"Keep walking. Don't break stride."

"Where are we going?"

"I don't know. Let's see if they are truly following us."

We made hard turns down random streets, each one turning out more barren than the last. The industrial turned residential as we skimmed the borders of the Grounds. The two figures maintained a healthy distance behind us.

"Definitely following us."

"Shit," Nico cursed. "We're too far from the Row. I can't raise my remnant here without trouble. But if it comes to it, I will."

"Excuse me, sir," one of the men called behind us. "We'd like to have a word with you."

"I'll talk them down. Take the next alley, go through the Steam District, and get back to the Row."

The thick tension settling over us was shattered by two long laments from a steam engine. An idea struck me.

"I have a better idea, if you trust me." I said, nudging him with my elbow. He dropped my arm, sliding his hand into mine, squeezing it gently in agreement. That was one perk about marriage. Despite being tethered to someone for eternity, it was convenient to have someone there when you were being trailed by two ominous men.

"We warned you nicely once, don't make us ask again," the second man shouted. Twin clicks of their revolvers insisted his threat.

"Milla . . ."

"I'm not leaving you."

I looked over my shoulder for a moment, taking their bait. I didn't know if I was strong enough to outrun two grown men, but I definitely wasn't faster than their bullets. A stir of cold wind unsettled the curls resting across my shoulder, the faint whisper of Nico's remnant priming. I'd been in its presence so often, I could recognize it anywhere.

"We said *stop*!" The command was followed by a shot, and Nico shoved me in front of him, still holding my hand, his arm wrapping around my waist like the part of a dance before he'd send me spinning. I gasped, hitting his hard chest, bracing myself for the whirr of bullets. But none came. The world around us fell silent, unmoving. Even the swirl of fog hovered in place, frozen in time and movement.

I looked around Nico. The spark of gunpowder still floated from the barrel of the first man's gun. The bullet hung suspended in the air at the midpoint between us and the gun. Nico slipped his arms around me and tugged me into motion. "Run, Milla! I can't hold the second for long!"

We took off, sprinting up the cobbles while Nico held the time so we could distance ourselves from the men. I led him deeper toward the boundary of the Grounds, further from the Capital and deeper into a part of the district. The line of steam ahead was so close, I could taste the burning coal in my throat as I gasped for air.

My legs burned, slowing despite my demand to keep their pace. Nico's enchantment eventually dropped after we made a few blocks, but the magic he left behind stained the air like a perfume. A trail they could follow straight to us. It wouldn't take long for them to catch up with my stamina at its worst.

But I knew the time and the train schedules. I knew we were close to the freight depot and that the train returning north to collect cargo would be leaving as we ran for it. The apartments began to fall away, buildings turned to slums. The streets no longer paved with cobbles, now instead padded dirt that pressed moisture into my flats as we fled.

A crack split the world behind us, the sound of a gun and its bullet ricocheting off the train cars as we neared the tracks.

"Milla, watch out!" Nico shouted above the hissing of the wheels, the scream of the air pump, remaining behind me no matter how much I slowed us both down.

I spared a look behind me to shout back, "Jump!" I gestured toward the empty cars. Nico nodded, passing me with ease to leap gracefully into a car with the loading door ajar. Once he was settled, he reached for me, knowing I'd never make the jump on my own. My legs were giving out, my heart demanded to quit. My breath came out in hungry gulps that burned my chest as I shoved them down.

Three more iron bullets hit the rusted railcar, and sparks bit at my face.

"Camilla, jump! I've got you!"

His eyes were as desperate as the urge in my bones. That hand was so close and yet felt like an entire world away. I had one chance to make it. The train built speed, even as I weakened with every step. But I didn't think about the sharp pain shooting down my legs or the flames filling my chest as I gasped. I focused on Nico's steel-grey gaze, that outstretched hand. Reached for it, for him, and with one bracing breath, I jumped.

His hand gripped mine in a connection that promised to never let go.

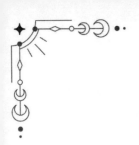
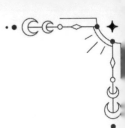

CHAPTER 25
CAMILLA

I thought maybe Nico had slowed the time again. That this stop-motion pace was the result not of my fear but his remnant. I felt everything with such clarity. The feel of my glove sliding into his. My body pushed and yanked into free air. The way his hand gripped mine with the wrap of a serpent, welding us in an inseparable bond.

The eventual crash brought everything back to speed as we both fell against the floor of the car, a mess of tangled limbs and panting breaths. His heartbeat knocked wildly against my temple as I rested on top of him, too exhausted to move, to do anything but let sweet relief wash away the fragments of fear cutting sharp inside my chest.

We remained like that for several minutes until the bullets striking the steel walls outside finally ceased. The only sound was the rhythmic chug of air pistons as the train rolled further from Lynchaven, and the song of Nico's heartbeat slowing to a regular rate. I didn't realize his arms were around my waist until they peeled from my body.

I pushed off his chest to sit up, gracelessly rolling off to let him do the same. "Are you alright?" I asked once I collected my breath.

He manipulated the arrangement of his metallic hand, gold fingers stretched and flexed. "Physically, yes, but my remnant is drained. Thankfully, the train wasn't far. I'm too weak to hold the time for long, and I don't like getting close to the bottom of my power."

"Weak? Stopping time is no small feat, Attano." I had to laugh. "What do you mean the bottom? Can you drain your remnant dry?"

"Draining a remnant is more difficult than you'd think," he replied. "Most of the time, the wielder would pass out before they reached the bottom, but it's possible if you unleash too much, too quick. Doing so can cause permanent damage not only to one's remnant, but to the user as well."

"What kind of damage?"

He didn't answer at first, a pause stretched. "Some say you go insane. Though, I'm not quite inclined to find out for myself."

My gaze lifted from the floor to his face, finding him resting his arms on his knees, staring back at me. His eyes were bright, matching the overcast. Like sunlight behind a cloud, their monotonous centers always hiding something beautiful behind them.

I looked away before I gained a glimpse of it. "Well, we made it. That's all that matters now. That, and getting back. Who were those men?"

He shrugged. "Lavern's men. I didn't recognize them at first. He must be getting desperate, since it's obviously not a secret anymore that they're after you."

"How did they know we'd be in the Capitol?"

"Could have been chance. The Firenzes probably have people posted everywhere outside the Row. We'll have to tread more carefully if we leave." He looked around the car, empty besides a few cargo boxes. "This is the freight train?" he asked.

I nodded. We only had one for cargo, utilized to ship resources from the North and South to the cities across the Isle, the other for passengers and travel. This one was empty, most likely on its way to the mines just north of the Wilds. The day and the hour confirmed my guess, remembering the schedules from years of staring at the calendar.

"Which means we'll have to catch the Iron Saint going home, as this car will be full of coal and ore. It won't be far behind, but we may have to stay the night in Mordun."

"That's just bloody perfect," he hissed, scrubbing his face with his hands. "I had something very important to do tonight and—" He growled instead of finishing his sentence, holding his head between his hands as his focus disappeared, deep in thought.

I rolled my eyes, like getting stuck with him on a train was the first thing on my to-do list. "Something or someone?"

He lifted his head to shoot me a violent look. "*What*?"

"Are these plans of yours the same ones that pulled you away a few weeks ago? The night before you were arrested." I asked him, hoping my casual tone hid some of the jealousy behind my question.

He pinched the bridge of his nose and took a large breath. Judging by the exasperation locking his jaw, I hadn't been subtle enough. "*Giver and Greed*, Milla, please tell me you're not insinuating that I'm sneaking around behind your back. How would I have the energy at the end of the day for another woman?"

"You've disappeared several times since we've gotten married. I saw you just a few nights ago, leaving at the midnight hour down the driveway, just to come home in different clothes right before everyone woke up."

"You waited for me to come home?" he asked, brow arched.

"I couldn't follow you, so I had to settle on the bedroom window." My stare fell to the open door, watching the landscape roll by. The blur of farmland surrounded the city, stretching miles of uninterrupted land as far as the eye could see. "You can just tell me. I won't be upset. It's not like this is a real marriage, anyway."

His face softened with a sigh, and he shifted to sit closer. "It's real to me, Milla. I made a vow to you, on paper and in word. I would never betray you in that way."

I wrestled with a stupid grin trying to form itself on my face. "Then why can't you be more specific?"

He sighed again, stalling his reply. "I have my own private job on the side, one not even my flesh and blood know about. The less they know, the less *you* know, the safer you all will be should anything bad happen."

His own private work. . . . So he *was* a mercenary. That night in the stables wasn't just a one-time thing. But for whom? The newspaper that next morning had the general's death on the front page, and after what I saw in Newport, I had a feeling Nico had been involved in some way. The man in front of me betrayed no further information.

"You saw me in Newport," he said then, as if reading my thoughts.

The claim startled me so much, I lost my composure. He knew? "I . . . What?"

He dug into an inside pocket, tossed two pictures on the floor between us. I picked them up, opening the folded photographs to discover the same faces from the hall of portraits at the Attano estate. One picture was of the small child that sat in Esme's lap and the other a woman who had stood with the rest of the aunts, next to a man that looked exactly like Nico.

"I'm looking for their killer."

I knew his parents had died, that much was obvious from the introduction of his inheritance. It put a new perspective on things, however, realizing it might've happened under sinister circumstances. "Who are they? What happened?"

"I should probably start from the beginning." He shifted in his seat, scooting closer so he could see the faces in my palms while he spoke directly into my ear. The sounds of the train picking up velocity filled the empty car with a grating noise.

"My father was in the process of buying the factories from the Clemonte family, who had owned the assembly lines for decades before the descendants showed up. We could replace their workers and use our remnants to produce twice as much product in half the time, which not only led to more profits for the factory, but for the OIC as well, who tax everything from when it's bought to where it's sold.

"Anyway, he was able to scrounge up the money to buy out their investors, thus owning the majority of the shares and firing the Clemontes from the company. What he didn't know, however, is that they were heavily involved with the Nine Crowns."

"The Nine Crowns?" I asked. "Why does that sound familiar?"

"They're an underground syndicate whose goal is to oppress the inclusion of descendants in society. So when my father stole their empire, well, that didn't go over well." His gaze fell. "I had a little sister, Anna."

I looked at him directly then, sensing this story was about to take a dark turn. He only nodded, confirming my worst assumptions. "She went with my mother down to the Riverwalk, because it was a sunny day for once and Anna loved watching the train. They were attacked by assassins in broad daylight with blades specially formulated for Niners. It killed Anna instantly since she was so small. My mother suffered for weeks."

"*Hells*, Nico." My hand covered a gasp. "That's horrible. Who would attack a woman and an innocent child?"

Grey eyes narrowed. "There are true devils in this world, Milla. There are consequences for crossing the wrong people, and my father had pissed off the worst of them all. These blades of theirs are only harmful to a remnant. It drains them of power immediately before replacing it with a poison that kills slowly. It's like a deadly glint. There is no remedy for it."

I stared again at the pictures, connecting every line and crease in their faces to that of his, matching every shared feature until it was impossible not to see them when I looked at Nico. "And your father? What happened to him?"

He licked his lips, hesitating before sharing the rest. I slipped my hand in his false one, holding it in my lap to offer silent support.

Nico squeezed my hand and continued. "My father died later. When my mother was struggling to survive the wound made by the blade, I went searching for a cure. I heard of a special doctor that could heal people with something called arcane science. To find them, I did something very illegal and was caught by the Society. Luther supported my endeavor and went with me, was caught by association, and they threw us both in prison. My father became riddled with guilt, knowing I was suffering and he'd done nothing to stop me.

"He shot himself on the bridge and let the Ada consume his body. Solomon tried to talk him down, but it was too late. He was too decided. He had enough grief to fill a lifetime, losing both his children and his love, and he needed a way out."

Nico's gaze fell to where our hands lingered together, a connection I couldn't quite explain. "I relate to you, feeling responsible for your father's death. Like my arrest had sent him over the edge, that I'd given him one more burden too much to bear."

Despite the cold sureness that hardened the sharp planes of his face into stone, a thin tear rolled down the side of his face, and I caught it with my thumb, wiping it away as easily as he had dried my own. "It was as much your fault as my father's death was mine."

He heard all the words I didn't say. A small smile flashed across his lips. "Exactly. Thank you, Milla."

I once believed he had too much to understand what my brothers meant to me, what their approval meant to me. Now, I realized he'd lost just as much, perhaps more, and that grief was not a chain of duty or a responsibility to bear, but a part of life.

"Have you found anything out about your family's killer?" I asked.

He shook his head. "The Clemontes disappeared after losing their empire. I've tried to track down the family, but there's none left alive to question. No one else in the organization feels like talking."

"Clemonte is an old name," I recalled. Almost as old as Marchese. I didn't recall my father working with anyone from that family, however. I knew nothing to help him.

Nico nodded. "I'm hunting ghosts at this point, but I can't . . . I just can't let it go."

"I understand," I murmured. His face hovered above my own, a solid body shielding me from the slap of cold wind threading through the car. His cheeks and the tip of his nose were red from the bite of winter's teeth. But I'd bet his lips were still warm, the way they breathed his scent along my skin. Spiked coffee and cigarillo smoke and . . .

"Are you cold?" he asked.

"No, I'm fine. We should close the doors, though, to keep the wind out."

He stood, exposing my side to the whip of wind and lack of him, to shut the doors as I requested. He slunk against the furthest wall, face relaxed like we hadn't just bonded over his plans of vengeance. "I guess we should get comfortable, seeing as we're stuck here for a few hours."

"Giver, grant me patience."

—————————— ✦ ——————————

"MILLA, WAKE UP! WE'VE STOPPED."

I woke to Nico shaking my arm, my coat folded beneath my head like an expensive pillow. When the silence between us had stretched too long to tolerate, I'd settled on sleeping away the passing hours, if only to ignore the hunger pangs and dry mouth that couldn't be helped while we were stuck in this car.

Night had fallen, the darkness filling the car matched the kind behind my eyes. Once they adjusted to the dark, I stood with Nico's help. His image was an outline, features barely traceable.

"Where are we?" I asked him, peering outside.

The first stop should have been Mordun, the mining village settled on the edge of the Falling Mountains. There was a checkpoint the train had to complete before entering the valley. But there was a taste to the air that wasn't common this far north. A spray in the breeze as it slipped through the rolling door.

It smelled of salt.

"Is that . . ." I whispered.

"The sea." Nico's voice was behind me as I peeked through the gap. A beam of moonlight skimmed the choppy waters as small waves quietly lapped the shore. Several miles off the coast, the edge of the storm that filled the inlet flashed dry lightning behind a dark cloud wall.

This route hadn't been used in decades, not since the storms voided the use of the Isle's main harbor. The tracks led straight through the center of the old shipyard, where the wooden skeletons of schooners and ancient ships slowly decomposed in their mooring to the docks. Shreds of their sails caught the gust, whipping the faded flags of a neglected regime.

"I take it this isn't a usual stop?" he asked.

"I don't understand," I murmured. "This wasn't on the books when I was approving the routes a few months ago. What are we doing here?"

"It sounds like something is being unloaded."

Tremors ran through the length of the train from where stock was being transferred. A harsh, grating echo filled the quiet night. Raised voices carried down the dock, too incoherent to catch their words. I peered around the car door, disregarding Nico's warnings to catch a glimpse of what was happening.

By the light of the full moonbeam, I discovered a ship—a working ship—was docked at the very end of the loading bay, where a group of men were directing a cart of something large, some kind of piece of machinery. Another cart pulled up to the car next to ours, too close for comfort. I slipped back behind the concealment of the door before the drivers spotted me.

Just as the doors slid along their rusted track in the neighboring railcar, one of the men unloading called out to his colleague, "Check that one for parts, Fritz. The old man said to make sure every car was emptied."

"We need to hide!" I whispered to the bender hovering behind me like a shadow. A quick search of the nearly empty car led to the shipping box pushed into the corner. I popped open the top, taking care not to let the corroded hinges squeal too loud.

"I'm not going in there," Nico hissed behind me.

I paused, turning my head to look at him. "Yes, you are. We can't be caught here, Attano." If my brother had taken the trouble to hide this from me, I wanted to know why and what he was conveying on this impossible ship. I also wasn't keen to find out how far these men would go to keep such a secret.

His jaw locked, and he shook his head, retreating from the box with a single step. "We both can't fit in there."

The cart rolled just outside the train car; shadows of the men stretched across the walls. I hoisted myself over the grimy edge and reached out for him, asking with my eyes why he was being so stubborn. Could he have been that reluctant to be near me? I wanted to scold him for being so childish, for risking our lives over something so frivolous.

"Nico!" I whispered as the door to the car was beginning to roll open. He looked back at the widening gap, whispered a curse, then finally gripped the edge of the box and flung himself over. I closed the top behind him to seal us inside.

Crouching low, we listened to the men outside open the door the rest of the way and work in quiet collaboration. There was a space in the fold of the top where the hinges made a gap, spilling silver light inside our hiding place. The shipping box was just big enough we could both stoop inside without feeling cramped. I balled into myself, letting the bender have most of the room since he was so averse to being close to me.

But he wasn't making use of the space, pulling his legs into his chest and bracing his arms atop his knees. His breathing turned ragged and gasping, threatening the quiet and our concealment. I reached for his hand and prodded it gently, but there was no awareness of my touch. A slight tremble shook his fingers. An unnatural breeze tore through the box, scattering chills across my skin.

"Nico," I whispered, his name as loud as a breath from my lips. He moaned something in reply, his tongue suddenly leashed, fighting an invisible battle within himself. If I didn't find a way to help him, the men outside would surely hear his gasping and groaning. And for some reason, it bothered me to see him struggling so much. A man like Nicolai Attano, so sure of himself all the time, solid as steel in every harrowing situation, be brought to his wit's end by a box.

I pushed myself between his legs to touch his face, to tip his chin from his chest up to look at me. "Nico," I said his name once more, and grey eyes finally focused on me for a heartbeat before squeezing shut again.

His lips moved. "I'm going to be sick."

That would be incredibly inconvenient. I needed to think of something and fast, to distract him some way from his struggle. But what could be enough to pull him out of this trance?

"Don't overthink this," I muttered, before taking his strong jaw in both my hands. The stubble of a beard he always kept groomed to a bare chin brushed the pads of my fingers, and I reveled for a sweet second in the coarse connection. Before I lost my nerve, I tipped his face to meet my lips—and I just did it.

I kissed him.

The moment our lips crashed together, the wind wrapping the box suddenly ceased as he took a deep breath at last. It was almost amusing, the way my kiss had been so unexpected that it confused him enough to stop shaking and fall still again. But I had no chance to laugh, no opportunity to second guess my methods of distraction when I realized . . . he kissed me *back*.

His hands shifted from his knees to smooth down the bend of my spine, pressing me closer to eliminate any space between our chests. They stopped just above my hips, hesitating to go any lower, gripping them with a kind of pressure that demanded I stay. And *saints*, his lips were so soft and convincing. His taste an expensive gin inviting me to get drunk, to lose myself in his caress.

248

After years of being careful, of calculated choices and suppressed needs, I was ready to get lost. Ready for someone to find me.

The confines of the box forbade any advanced exploration, but Nico slipped his bruising fingers around my hips, cupping the slope of my backside to pull me higher onto his lap. I quietly helped him straddle my legs around his waist, drowning in sensation after sensation. His heat. His hands. His hardness. My stomach tightened as his perusing touch pinched down my thighs, as if the leather pants I wore offended his pursuits.

My plan to distract him had turned against me, and soon my hands had made their way behind his neck, molding themselves with the bend of his body. I suppressed a sound of distress with a shuddering breath as every perception of his touch converged into one consuming plunge into my center. A rumble shook his chest as my lips parted, and I let him sweep my mouth, matched each frenzied stroke for stroke, fed this want in my heart that was starved for his attention the moment that cocky grin of his appeared across the bar.

The hands nestled on my hips slowly dragged up my waist, following my curves. His thumbs skimmed the bottom of my breasts, teasing his interest, and I sent a roll of my hips to appeal my own. His hands seized around my sides before exploding across my back, pulling me down against his length, encouraging me to repeat my request.

I thought I was stronger than this. That I had built steel walls around an iron heart. But a part of me, the place housing that heart, had suddenly shattered. Nico's kiss was a stone thrown at a glass house, and every last fortification fell to reveal a white flag in place of my stubborn resistance.

The door to the train car slammed shut, jarring us both enough to split apart. A silence followed, and I didn't know what to say to fill it. We only stared, breaths hot and heavy, waiting for the other to say something first. Nico, thankfully, decided to spare me the obligation.

"I don't like confined spaces," he blurted.

A mirthless laugh slipped from my chest. "I suppose we should get out of this one, then." Still seated on his hips, I quickly readjusted, shifting to my knees to stand. Before I could, those persuasive hands pulled me down again.

"Wait, Milla." He squeezed my waist in a silent plea. Murmuring in a voice silky as sin, "I'm sorry."

His apology was disheartening. What was he sorry for? For kissing me? For letting a simple distraction get out of hand? All the potential reasons crafted by my imagination left me similarly disappointed.

I shook my head. "I'm the one who should apologize for practically attacking you. I just didn't have time to think of something less invasive."

"Well, I definitely prefer that assault to your last one." He pointed to his temple, smirking.

I smiled. "I don't know what you're complaining about. You don't even have a scar."

"You sound disappointed."

"I would have liked to have left my mark on you," I admitted, bringing my hand to the side of his face to trace the spot with my pointer finger.

"You've got time, princess. There's no chance I'll walk away from this unscathed. Not anymore." His stare fell to my mouth as he licked his lips. I wondered if they also tingled like my own, if they felt heavy and unsatisfied, the pull to reforge our connection.

I didn't quite know what to make of his confession, hadn't much experience with men, nor concerned myself with the ones in my family's social circle. Perhaps I shouldn't entertain this feeling he spurned inside me, like every inch of my skin was an accelerant and his touch a flame threatening to set me on fire. I definitely shouldn't be kissing him. If Aramis saw us now. . . My family would be so disappointed in me. The thought alone sobered the thrill in my heart.

I was here to ruin him, not claim him. This moment we shared would have to remain in this box, along with all my other feelings beginning to take root.

"Is everything okay?" he asked, brows kissing in the sliver of light.

I nodded, grateful for a silhouette that shaded my face. Darkness hid the tear rolling down my cheek. "Of course." I stood to push open the top of the shipping box, and this time, he let his hands slip free of my hips. "We should find out what they're unloading."

"Right," he said. "Good idea."

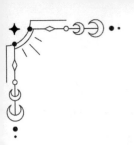
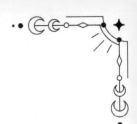

CHAPTER 26
NICOLAI

M y life had been damned long ago by fate, but if ever I was destined for the deepest hellhole in the void, it was after that kiss.

I sat for a moment inside the shipping box, trying to compose myself and shake the blood back to my brain so I could make intelligent decisions again. I'd let myself slip, gave in to something so selfish, knowing what it could cost us both in the end. The inspector had demanded I end this, and here I was, kissing her on the very object of my treachery.

I told her I was sorry for it, but I wasn't. Lying was the kindest thing I could do for her at this point.

When I finally felt my self-control return, I followed her out, grateful for the space. Milla was already peering through the slit of the door, her backside covered in black dust from the inside of the box.

I looked down at myself, found my hands smeared with the same soot, realizing those stains around her waist weren't from the box,

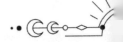

they were my markings. Everywhere I grabbed her. A map of my exploration.

I wanted to blur those lines until I had touched every inch of her, until she was covered in darkness. My darkness.

"Do you see anything?" I asked. While the train's width forced our proximity, I maintained as much distance between us as possible. Ever since she could walk on her own again, it was a feeble goal I made every morning, to avoid all contact, and yet somehow broke before the sun set each evening. She shoved me deeper into Oblivion with each day that passed, but if I was already pegged for damnation, I might as well do it right.

"I can't see what they're unloading very well, but it appears to be heavy machinery. Like the kind we build the locomotive engines with, but on a *much* larger scale."

"Let me take a look." I crossed the car to peer out into the slice of space overlooking the bay. "Do you notice anything strange about that ship, Milla?"

"Besides the fact it's still floating? Not really."

"Look at the sails."

She gasped, understanding. There weren't any, which meant this ship had an engine, and I'd bet money it ran on steam.

"The storms . . ." she murmured. "That's how to get past them. The turbulent winds can't sink a ship if there aren't sails to bring it down. But who is supplying these parts? And why have I never heard of this supply run if I'm to own this company?"

She pushed away from the door, pacing the length of the car. I would've once believed she lied about her ignorance, but Camilla was a terrible fibber. Her voice always changed a pitch too high and her hands gestured obnoxiously. She appeared genuinely troubled by this, being shoved in the dark by the same family she'd sacrificed her future to save.

"Here's a better question," I said. "Is your family even in debt, or did your brother lie about that to get money to build this ship?"

Her steps paused, turning slowly to face me. "I beg your pardon, Nico, but I know you aren't suggesting that my brothers sold me off to fund a new project."

"The evidence is difficult to deny, Milla." I waved a hand in the direction of the ship.

She shook her head, but I knew from the way she shifted her gaze away from my view, my words had snapped something fragile inside her, rubbed a raw spot of insecurity. She said, "I've seen our accounts. After Father died and your family blew up half our tracks, we drained our savings to repair it all. I just need to speak with Aramis about this. I'll give him the benefit of the doubt until I assume the worst."

Irritation tightened my fists. "He doesn't deserve it."

Her eyes narrowed. "Everyone deserves a chance to explain. I'm certain there is a reasonable explanation why he'd keep this from me."

I scoffed, unconvinced of her sureness. "Why are you letting him treat you like this?"

"He's my family, Nico. What do you expect me to do?" Her hands fanned at her sides, lithe figure shrinking smaller by the second. "Aramis, Giles, the twins, they're all I have. I can't just cut them out of my life."

"They use you," I growled.

Even in the faint light seeping through the cracks on the car, I could see her jaw trembling, her fists blanching. "They're allowed to. We're blood—"

"That's not what makes you family, Milla."

"Well, that's what makes mine." She turned to wipe her face, hiding the way this conversation tortured her. "I know we aren't *perfect* like the Attanos, but we have a reason for it. Gio Marchese was a hard man, but he was our father, and I'm the reason we lost him. I'll do anything to make it right for them. I can't go back to that house and be treated like a traitor again."

That soft heart of hers made her dangerous. Desperate people made biased decisions. If she prioritized earning her family's love over all else, she'd turn on me in a second. No kiss would change that. If I knew what was good for me, I'd let her run back to her brothers and take them all down together. But lately, I enjoyed playing her fool.

"My family isn't perfect, Milla," I said. "My father committed suicide, my uncle gave up on all of us, and I'm pretty sure my Nonna is paying the haelen to make sure we don't find out she's dying and throw her in a Hael House." Her mouth twitched at the mention of the old woman. An almost smile. I approached her slowly, like nearing a threatened viper, hoping I could charm the fight out of her.

"Would you like me to air more of the Attano dirty laundry?" I asked. She glanced at me. Wet lines over her cheeks caught the light, but she nodded. I happily continued if it meant easing the weight off her slumped shoulders. "Luther is permanently damaged because I brought him on a hopeless quest. Esme has barely left the house since Anna died, and yet she left for *you*, Milla, when she thought you were in trouble. My cousin is obsessed with my wife—"

"Oh *saints*, Gideon is not obsessed with me." Her words blended with a giggle, and the sound sucked me closer to her orbit, a ring around a star. The train began to hit full speed, stirring the empty car with more cold wind.

"And my wife," I drawled, "where do I even begin with her?" She faced me, the lift of a brow the only warning I'd get. From this close, I noticed the chill bumps littering her neck. The crimson coat she wore did wonders for her figure and nothing to keep her warm. I shimmied off my own and draped it over her shoulders.

"What about your wife?" she asked, pulling the edges of my coat tighter around her body. My hand went for her throat, the only section of bare skin available, and slid around the curve of her neck to thread my fingers into her hair. With a gentle pull, I canted her chin, made those hazel eyes focus where I wanted them.

"I think I've slept a whole three hours since she took the title of Mrs. Attano. Chaos every damn day, almost started another war with the queen of bleeders, has nearly died under my protection *twice*."

Milla rolled her eyes. "At least I'm not afraid of a box."

I smiled, continuing. "Yet she has managed to charm my evil grandmother, befriend those who were once her enemy, wear the color of my family with the grace of a princess." My fingers squeezed her neck gently, sucking a gasp from her parted lips. Her pulse was a feathery stroke across my thumb. "They are not all you have, Milla. You have me, and there is no time limit for my friendship. No contract to negotiate those terms. It is freely given for as long as you'll take it."

"Nico," she breathed. Never had my name sounded so sensual. I wanted to kiss her again just to know what it would taste like.

"I see you, Milla. I see all of you. The good, the better, and the best because there is no bad in you. You are *enough*. Stop letting those Marcheses make you think you need to do something to earn their approval. There is a house full of Attanos who think you're wonderful, just the way you are."

Her eyes squeezed shut, severing that connection between our gazes. I almost didn't hear her over the sounds of the train when she said, "I wish I could stay."

She looked to me for agreement, but I couldn't give her that false assurance. Hating myself for it. "Get some rest, Milla. You need to go see your brothers as soon as we get back to the city."

Lie to her, lie to myself, that's all I had to do to keep the both of us in check, to soften the crash of this fall. Forcing myself to let her go, I reclused to a corner of the car, fighting her pull one step at a time until I was far enough it felt more bearable to withstand.

There seemed to be an understanding between us, as she slipped into the shadows of the opposite corner. We rode the rest of the ride back to Lynchaven in a silence too heavy. Too encumbered with *what ifs* and *why nots.*

But she was enough, and I hoped in our short time together, she'd at least take that away from this shameful union.

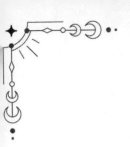
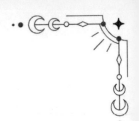

CHAPTER 27
CAMILLA

The Attanos already occupied the formal dining room as I came down for breakfast. It'd been two days since we were jumped in broad daylight, two days since that kiss, and still I felt the remnant of both wearing on my body. Nico didn't tell his family about the ship or the incident, and I maintained our secret, even though Nonna had come up with her own explanation for our absence—and I learned then she had quite the imagination, and obviously thought Nico admired his bride far more than he did.

"What's going on in here?" I asked, finding them all huddled around a set of pictures. Nico wasn't part of the group, nor were his cousins. Which meant something was up if all the muscle in the family were out together.

"Good morning, Milla." Solomon, who arranged the pictures out for the whole family to view, glanced up at me. "Nico followed up on those discrepancies you caught. Turns out, he hired an assistant very recently, around the same time they began. Fran and Lucinda followed her from work, gathered some information about

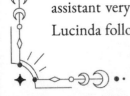

her from her neighbors and the bank she has accounts with. It turns out she applied for the job at the factory under a false identity."

I took the seat across from him, analyzing the black and white pictures for myself. The focus was off, taken in a rush, but the subject in each of them was clear. "Is that her?"

Fran placed her hands on Solomon's shoulders and nodded. "The picture on the left is the woman Nico hired a few months ago. The others were borrowed from an ex-Crown."

"There's no such thing," Solomon murmured.

She swatted him lightly. "He joined when he was very young, when the remnants moved to the Isle. Overtime, he saw the group for what it really is—a cult. Now he only attends the annual parties to keep up with their affairs, and I asked him if he had any pictures from the last one."

Solomon slid two specific pictures across the table for my comparison. One was of a woman on the street, completely unaware her photograph was being captured. The other, a group shot. The same woman sat poised between four men on a velvet chaise. I didn't recognize the subjects of either picture, but something—someone— caught my attention in the background of the second.

"Would you mind if I held onto this picture? I think I recognize some of the other faces. Maybe I could be of some further use to you by recalling their names and business."

He gestured vaguely to them both. "Be my guest. Nico's already seen enough to pass her judgment."

"Which is?" I asked.

Nonna giggled darkly at the end of the table. "She'll join the bones of all the others who have lied to the Attanos at the bottom of the Ada."

I swallowed back a nauseous swell creeping up my throat, realizing I'd killed this woman just by exposing her. Pocketing the picture, I stood to leave.

"Will Nico return soon? I was supposed to visit my brothers this morning. I can take a carriage if he's too busy—"

"That won't be necessary, princess."

I plastered a forced smile across my face to mask my grimace. "Oh, good," I said, turning to face Nico and the cousins entering the room. "You're back just in time."

Gone were the crimson coats; instead, the group dressed in matte black from their caps to their boots. Nico's sleeves were rolled up over his thick forearms and false hand, but his skin and contraption were clean. As were the vest and tailored pants that were too flattering for such a dirty business. He lingered in the doorway while Luther and Adler sat themselves in front of the fruit spread laid out for breakfast.

"Now, you boys know the rules: no guns on the table!" Nonna snapped.

Luther spoke through a mouthful of toast, "We won't be staying long, Nonna. It's empty anyway."

"Took care of everything, then?" Solomon asked, looking at Nico. He nodded once. "Did she say anything?"

"She didn't talk, but they never do. I didn't feel like wasting time on someone who's just a pawn on the power game board. Besides"— his eyes shifted to me—"I have plans this morning with my wife."

As if my stomach wasn't already in knots with the idea of confronting Aramis, I'd have the shadow of my angsty husband following closely behind. This was bound to go over as smooth as gravel.

Instead of showing my nerves, I approached him in the doorway, where his scent met me first. Whatever fabric he used for his suits hid the sight of blood, but not the smell. I swallowed back the metallic coating it left in my throat. "You smell like a bleeder. Change into something decent and meet me in the driveway when you're ready." I looked back at the cousins rising from their seats. "That goes for the rest of you."

"Any preference?"

I arched my brow. Since when did he care what I thought about his outfits? "Wear your black tweed with the silver pocket square. It matches your stupid eyes."

"I love it when you talk dirty to me," Nico murmured beneath his breath.

"Are you always in this good of a mood after dealing with your enemies?"

His grin was infectious. "Nothing like a little torture over your morning coffee to get the blood pumping. Perhaps I should indulge my enemies more often if it pleases you."

I rolled my eyes and shoved past him. "I prefer my moody gentleman. He smells better. Make sure he's in the carriage in ten minutes."

We left at the same time, parting in the hall without another word.

THE MARCHESE MANOR seemed so much smaller now that I was standing outside of it. It'd been almost a month since I left through the side entrance, stood in this courtyard, and signed my name over to the bender at my side. His presence was now unnervingly more endurable, even if he still maintained his argumentative behavior.

"I don't feel comfortable letting you go in there alone," he muttered as we strode into the courtyard.

"It's an old Marchese rule. No one is allowed inside unless you're paid staff or family." I paused in front of the fountain, gesturing to a bench he could sit at while he waited since he refused to wait in the carriage like his cousins. "I'll be fine, Nico. They're my brothers. What's the worst that could happen?"

His grey eyes dimmed, doubtful. "I've learned to plan for the worst when it comes to you, Milla. Just make this quick, before Luther and the rest get restless in the car and decide to join me. We might get a little loud for the likes of your neighbors."

"I still don't see why it was necessary to bring them," I said.

"If I can't use my remnant, I'd rather have the security of extra guns."

I rubbed my temples, feeling the beginnings of a headache. "I thought we agreed no fighting. *Giver and Greed*, since when did you get so protective?"

He slowly sat on the metal bench, propping his boot over his knee to make himself comfortable. "Since I promised Nonna I'd keep you out of trouble. She almost busted my balls after the Pit incident. Now, I'll be watching the window. When you're ready, just send me the signal like we practiced, agreed?"

I rolled my eyes. "Yes, *Daddy*. Can I go now?"

The moment his right dimple deepened with a smirk, I knew I'd made a mistake. He planted both feet flat on the pavers, slipped his fingers through my belt loops to yank me forcefully between his legs. The momentum threw me forward, and I braced my hands on his broad shoulders to keep from tripping into his lap.

"I'd be very careful about calling me that again." His voice was soft against the damp breeze, but his fingers spoke a more aggressive language. A carnal hunger in his eyes made my knees buckle, sending my weight into my palms, feeding the tension locked in his shoulders.

"My brothers are watching," I said. The curtain moved aside on the third floor as soon as we stepped inside the courtyard. I could feel

Aramis's stare burning through my deep-red overcoat, attempting to decode the conversation of our bodies. But he'd have an impossible time, seeing as I couldn't decipher it myself.

"I hope so." Gloved knuckles slipped down the front of my thighs. The cold metal of his false hand pierced straight through the fabric of my pants, skating my skin. "Don't keep me waiting, princess. Be a good girl and make it quick."

I shoved the front of his cap down low over his face, hiding his growing grin. A frigid wind nipped at the blush flaming my neck, cooling the rising heat beginning to settle beneath my skin.

"I was teasing, Milla," he called out behind me.

That was the problem. He didn't tease me like this when we first made this arrangement. His touch wasn't as gentle as it was now. His smile that treacherous. Our threats now held less promise. Something changed between us, precariously discreet, like the slow fade of fall as it feeds into winter.

This bargain we made to be free of each other began to lose its appeal as the hourglass ran out of sand. My heart had joined the stakes. Something told me his had too. And here I was, about to conspire against him as he sat in my courtyard. Forget the bottom of the Ada, if he knew my true motivations, he'd shred me into fish bait for betraying both his family and his friendship.

Our footman, Hector, saw me coming and held the side door open, gesturing up the stairs as I entered the west wing. The floorboards groaned louder than I remembered, the glass windows a duller shade of green. Everything in this place seemed a half-shade less enchanting than it had a few weeks ago. Or perhaps living in a truly magical world had only revealed how mundane my old life was all along.

By the time I reached the third floor, Giles was already there, meeting me at the top of the landing. "There's my favorite sister," he said with a smile warm enough to banish the lingering chill.

"You mean your *only* sister," I said, just as he swept me in an embrace. I smiled into his mane of blonde hair.

He pushed me away, looking me up and down, noting the color of my coat. "Red looks good on you, Milla." He winked. "How has your new husband been treating you?"

"He's not so bad," I said quietly, taking care not to let my voice drift down the hall.

"Oh. My. Saints," he said, blue eyes widening. "You've kissed him."

I shrugged, and Giles gasped like I'd just shared something scandalous. "Babe, I want the details. Was he good? Have you gone further? Does that metal hand of his have any toys?"

"Giles!" I slapped him lightly on the shoulder, but my reaction only made his grin stretch.

"Hells, I'm so jealous. Has he got any brothers?" He threw his arm around my shoulders, where I seemed to fit perfectly since he was a head taller. Technically, they all were, but none of them were as tactile with their greetings as Giles.

"No, but he has cousins. You're always welcome to come visit, you know." I glanced up at him to assess his reaction. "The Attanos would be more than welcoming for a brother of mine."

He frowned. "I doubt that very much."

"It's the truth. I'd make them."

"Showing them who's boss over there?"

I laughed at the irony. "Something like that."

We passed my old bedroom door, where my father had kept me across the hall from his own room. A careful arrangement to always keep me under his watch. The office door was already open at the end of the hall. The twins sat in a pair of armchairs near the fireplace, offering me odd smiles. Aramis hardly turned to greet me, still staring down at the courtyard, watching my husband with an unreadable look on his face.

"Oh, Camilla," Aramis sighed. "What have you done to that poor man?"

Shrugging off my coat, it took me a moment to work through his question. "What do you mean?"

He turned to face me at last, a sneer slathered across his thin face. "That bender has got it fucking bad for you. His eyes haven't left this window."

"He's protective of his investments, Aramis," I said. "Nothing more."

"It sure doesn't look like you're an investment." He strode behind the desk—my desk—and sat with his feet propped on the top. An obvious show of how seamless his transition into my seat had been. "It looks like he's very fond of you, sister."

"Wasn't that the goal, *brother*?" I asked, crossing my arms. I'd hardly taken three steps into the office and suddenly felt like I stood on a completely different side of the river. "Weren't you the one who told me to get close to him?"

"Oh, I am very pleased to see him panting after you like a lost puppy. The fact he risked crossing the river to accompany you proves you've become very valuable to him." Aramis shifted, planting his feet on the floor then. "The problem, little sister, is how *you* looked at the Attano."

The room fell into a breathless silence, waiting for me to respond. But I didn't know what to tell them, had no idea how I looked at Nico or what it meant. "It's a game. How am I to gain his trust if I don't make him feel desirable?"

Perhaps if I told him what he wanted to hear, he would share his own secrets. Maybe, for once, he'd respect me enough to tell me the truth.

"I thought you didn't like playing mouse?" Aramis said with a half-smile.

"I can do anything for money, Aramis," I quoted him back.

He shrugged one shoulder, slicked back his pale hair with a hand before replying, "How about we just get to the point of our visit, seeing as your new husband is waiting eagerly for your return?"

I found a seat in a chair facing the desk, where he used to sit in front of me when I claimed Father's old chair—the Marchese throne. Before he had the chance to be disappointed, I said, "Let me just preface this conversation by saying I don't have much. Not enough to get out of this deal yet. The Attanos have only recently opened up to me. Gaining their faith has been hard-earned."

"Then why did you arrange to meet with us before you had sufficient blackmail?" he replied, his voice dipping low. "Have you done anything in the last month besides flirt?"

My hands squeezed into fists in my lap. "I've done more in the last four weeks across the river than I have here in the last four years. I told you, I'm getting close, and I'll have the information before my birthday. Don't you think I want out of this more than anyone? This is my home, Aramis!"

"Which is why I'd have thought you would have been more motivated to get the intel, so you could return. But perhaps you have forgotten who you are." His words could cut steel, the way they lanced me.

"What are you suggesting?" I asked, thankful my voice remained steady. That the rage in my chest didn't filter through.

He braced his elbows on the desk and stared at me, an amateur attempt to look like Father, the man he could never be. He finally shook his head, rerouting the conversation. "Never mind. What can you tell us, then?"

Giles came to sit beside me. A silent support in his proximity, enough I could lift my chin again and look my older brother in his cold eyes. "I know Nicolai Attano is a mercenary. He gets summoned at random moments, and his subjects are never clear, but one of them was—"

"Silas Durnham and General Branwick," Aramis finished. "Sera told us."

I nodded. "I don't know who he's working for, but if it is someone like the Overseer, someone important, then I'd be inclined to believe that's where he gets his big paychecks."

My brother sucked his cheek in thought. "What about the bombs?"

"That's factory stuff. I've asked to go on a tour, but I don't think they make them in-house. The workers there are various singular benders. Some have the affinity to fire like Nico has for air. The Bane remnants make loads of stuff with their gifts, but the only weapons I've seen are the ones they carry."

Giles spoke then, "Whatever happens these next few weeks, we need to make sure we have those explosives in *our* hands. Before we hit them with that final piece of blackmail."

"*If* she gets it, Giles," he replied, his tone bored. "Until then, we'll have to work on our Plan B."

"What do you mean?" I asked, snatching the easiest opportunity to pry about the ship. Aramis poured himself a double from the decanter on the desk. Swirled it twice in his glass before answering.

"The Firenzes are still willing to bargain with us should you fail with the Attano."

My jaw hung open for a moment, unable to command myself to

shut it in my shock. "You'd still have me wed Felix? Have I not done enough?"

He shot back a sip, slammed the glass back on the desk with a wincing sound. "You haven't done anything. I still don't have the next hundred I was promised by your husband, and I'll be damned before I see an Attano take my shares. He forgets I still have your marriage license, and it hasn't been filed yet. Even after you turn twenty-one and inherit the company, he won't own anything. He's not even legally bound to you yet."

The news should have been a comfort. After all, it had been my idea to wait to file, to give myself and my family a chance to get out of this. But my head had a hard time convincing my heart, which only felt dirty shame for being so deceitful.

"I don't trust the Firenzes," I told him. "Didn't you receive any of Nico's messages? They've sent bleeders after me *twice* to kidnap me from the Attanos."

"Bleeders?" Giles said quietly. "What's this about bleeders, Aramis?"

My eldest brother's face flashed an irritated grimace. "The Firenzes are our allies. They wouldn't do anything I wouldn't do. I trust them explicitly."

"You trust them over my word? Your own sister? You truly underestimate me, brother, if you've gone to such extremes in case I fail." I reached inside the velvet inner lining of my coat, where a covered pocket contained an envelope. Nico sent with me the next payment he'd promised Aramis, honoring his side of the deal even after witnessing what his own blood money could be funding.

"Can you blame me?" He smiled, but there was no kindness composing his demeanor. "This is the future of our family, Camilla. I can't leave something so important up to you. Especially when it's preceded by the claims of an Attano."

His words started a silent battle inside me, chipped away at the fragile bones of confidence I'd grown during my time away. How easy it was to slip back into my old skin, let him push me down a peg and let those bones break.

They've tamed you well, princess.

I swallowed the bitter pill of realization.

"In light of your need of motivation," he drawled, picking up a file that had been thrown across his desk. "I've also decided to donate your shareholder earnings back to the railway."

"You *what?*" I hissed. My fingers let go of the marks in my pocket, fell back into my lap.

"You married into the wealthiest remnant family on the Isle. Why would you need more money?"

"Because it's mine!" I shrieked, standing in a tight-fist fury. He might be able to cut me out of this house, but he wouldn't cut me off the payroll. Whatever schemes he manipulated behind my back had officially reached my pockets. "Father made each of us equal share-holders, so we'd all be taken care of."

He stood from his seat as well, meeting my anger. "Whatever Father did wasn't *equal*. Just ask the rest of your brothers how they feel about being cut off from the railway. That's our biggest source of income and you're taking the whole pot. Yet, you still want to have your portion of the shares. That's quite selfish of you, if you ask me."

It was a punch to the gut, that word. As if I hadn't bent to their demands enough over the years, as if I still deserved to be punished for all that had gone wrong in our lives.

"Selfish?" I scoffed, shaking my head with little else to say. I wasn't worried about the money; I was concerned about my seniority in this enterprise. Being estranged was a slippery slope, and Aramis waved so many red flags, he might as well have been wearing my Attano jacket.

He sat again, his temper dissolving after winning the closing argument. "Don't worry, sister. You'll get your shares as soon as you get your last name back, and since you're so confident you'll do so, it shouldn't be a problem."

A challenge. One I desperately wanted to win so he wouldn't have another excuse in his arsenal to treat me like a child. Aramis wasn't happy with what I'd given him, but he was satisfied—for now. Like a greedy god staring over his altar, my information was mere scraps of an offering, but it had appeased him enough to leash his wrath.

"I'll get your information, Aramis. I've got that Attano wrapped around my finger."

I wanted to wipe away the bitter taste those words left in my mouth but crossed my arms tight in front of my chest instead, pushing down the guilt. I knew I'd have to double-cross Nico eventually, and the time to do so was coming soon. Nothing about my circumstances had changed that fact, just the way my heart felt about it.

My brother smiled. "Prove it."

Thank the saints—a dare. "Fine." I dug into my pocket and pulled out a long cigarillo, rolled thinner for my little hands than my husband's usuals. From my other pocket, a flint box. I strode to the nearest window, where the curtain was still pulled back to stream a glaring light across the dusty floors.

"One question for you, Aramis." I spoke to my brother while staring down at the bender, sitting where I'd left him, still staring at this window. He wiggled his metal hand in a mechanical wave. "Have you ever seen a ship without a sail?"

The room went still, the only sound a clock on the wall ticking by each unnerving second. That was it then. He knew. *He knew something,* and he deliberately kept it from me. I didn't dare look at

Aramis and let my face betray my thoughts. Instead, I flipped open the top of the lighter and held the flame against the tip of the cigarillo, letting it hang at my side until ribbons of grey smoke curled in front of my face.

"I have," I murmured into the condensation covering the windowpane. I glanced down at the courtyard, which was already empty. Nico was already on the move, which meant I should be going as well.

Turning to face the room again, I had all four of their attention. Giles was the only one who seemed remorseful for what our dynamic had become. My family only lacked three things: love, faith, and money. If he wanted confirmation that the Attanos called me one of their own, I'd make the evidence so damning, he'd never question me again.

"Be careful what you ask of me, brother. If you want proof, you'll pay for it." When I reached the hall, I looked back once more with a small grin afflicting my cheeks. "I'd cover your ears now, boys."

I shut the door just as an explosion shook the house. The sound of breaking glass and the destructive force of air shook the door as the wall of arched windows shattered. Nico promised he wouldn't cause too much damage, just enough to distract my family long enough I could make it outside in case they tried to threaten me or keep me from leaving for some reason—his imagination knew no bounds when it came to my safety.

My hand hardly skimmed the railing as I descended the stairs, returning to the main floor. Giles was a floor behind me, calling for me to stop.

"Milla, wait! Are you insane?"

"Why are you in this picture, Giles?" I dug the photograph out of my pocket and slapped it into his chest when he made it to me. He took it into his palms and looked it over.

271

His brows pinched. "Where did you get this?"

"Does it matter?" I asked. "Why are you with the Nine Crowns? Tell me you're not a part of that awful organization."

His jaw hovered before speaking. "Milla, you don't understand . . ."

"Yes, everyone keeps saying that," I hissed. "Surely you can tell me in a few words why your face is in the background of this picture. My husband is hunting people associated with the Niners. If my family is part of it, I need to know."

Giles stuffed the photograph in his pocket. The look on his face was eerily calm. "I promise, babe, he won't be coming after us. The Marcheses were one of the original nine families who created the organization fifty years ago, but we've split—"

"Is she still down there, Giles?" Aramis's angry voice echoed from the top of the stairs. My heart thundered against my ribs. I wanted to leave before he had the opportunity to scold me.

"Would you do something for me?" I asked quietly, glancing up the stairs to see if he was coming down yet.

"Of course, Milla. Anything."

I whispered the favor into his ear, careful to keep my words shielded from a stray servant.

"I . . . Are you sure?" He looked at me like he didn't recognize my face, straining to see some fragment of his sister left behind in the girl in front of him.

"Yes, please. Trust goes both ways. If Aramis won't listen to me, then I'm taking my safety, and my future, into my own hands."

He scrubbed his face. "Alright then. I'll get it done."

My shoulders sagged in relief. "Thank you. Please, don't tell Aramis. I promise I'll set all of this straight. Goodbye, Giles. And please, stay away from that group."

He muttered a goodbye just as Aramis appeared at the top of the stairs. I didn't wait for the footman, slamming the door in poor Hector's face on my way out.

Nico waited at the gate, leaning casually against the metal post with his arms crossed and watching me approach. He wore the smallest of smiles. One that touched not his lips but his eyes. The kind that sent all the heat in my body converging and left the rest of my flesh covered in chills.

"Everything alright, princess? We almost stormed the castle to come get you."

"I'm not the princess here anymore, Attano. I'm the fucking dragon. Now, let's go before my brother decides to shoot you." He considered me carefully, and I looked away from his inspection to hide the glaze over my eyes.

"You heard the boss. Back to the Row," he called to the men parked in the street. Just as I passed him, he snuck a hand around my waist and pulled me close, stopping me in my tracks. "And just for the record, Milla," he purred into the crown of my head, "you're still my princess."

He loosened his hold without letting me go, keeping his hand on the small of my back all the way to the car.

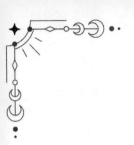
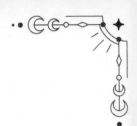

CHAPTER 28
NICOLAI

What the hells was she doing here?

The Summoner made her presence known at the bar just as the waitress served our meal. The aunts demanded lunch with their sons, meeting us on our way back across the river. Milla had perked up as the hour passed, snapping out of whatever mood her brothers had put her in.

I'd seen my wife shift through emotions like she changed her gloves, but only today had I watched her wear one this quietly. She was simmering, her thoughts braising a plan. Whatever went on in that pretty head of hers had forced her focus far away. Thankfully, Esme's arrival had provided enough distraction to pull a smile out of her, even when my own efforts failed.

But now, I was the one in a foul mood.

"I'll be right back," I announced. The rest of the table hadn't even looked over their plates, while Milla's head snapped away from her conversation with my cousin.

"Where are you going?"

My jaw locked, grinding my teeth. She hadn't bothered to look my way all morning and suddenly now I was all interesting. Figured. "To take a piss. Must I ask for your permission first?" I asked.

She rolled her golden eyes. "I only asked to see if you would bring me back a drink. The waitress forgot mine."

The Summoner caught my gaze and stood from her seat, and I watched her turn down the hall beside the bar. I pushed my glass towards Milla. "Take mine. I'll get another."

"But I don't want that."

I tossed my wallet in front of her to appease her request, before following the Summoner down the long hall that led to the kitchens. I caught the wisp of her cloak as she turned a corner, the slightest move of a door as she slipped inside the single stall bathroom. I trailed behind her and shut the door. The lock, unfortunately, was little more than a busted chain.

"What are you doing here? I thought we agreed you'd only summon me in private. Not in front of my family and for the world to see!" I hissed as quietly as my rage would allow.

She pulled her hood back, revealing short red hair and the green of emeralds in her eyes. "It's an emergency. Trust me, I've had to follow you all day just to corner you here." She dug into her purse, a black clutch on a beaded chain, and handed me a folded paper with the inspector's seal.

I cracked it open and read the name. All the moisture in my mouth, the blood in my face, drained like someone had pulled a plug. "Now?" I asked.

She only nodded.

The name blurred itself before my eyes; my jaw opened and shut. "Is this the right time?"

"It's the only time," she whispered. "And it must be done soon. A week from tonight."

"*Shitting saints*," I growled. "That's the same night as the Salt Ball."

"Exactly. It's perfect. Every descendant will be at the ball, which will give the OIC a harder time of blaming a remnant on his death." Her eyes flickered to the paper in my hand. "This is it, Attano. After this, it's just the train, and you obviously have that under control."

I could have laughed. Control could never be used next to Milla's name. "And if I fail?" I had to ask. After my last screwup, I wasn't feeling particularly confident about this one.

"You either get caught or you don't. If you do, you'll go down alone. There is no evidence to tie the inspector to these deaths. And you already know what happens if you refuse."

I nodded. Back to Hightower. My mouth dried at the thought. The walls in this small bathroom began to close in.

"We'll get you a double. He'll switch out with you at the party, that way you have a solid alibi. Make sure as many people see you as possible."

Why did that make me feel even worse? I bit back a refusal, knowing it was my best chance of being successful at this last job. "Did you get the records I asked for?"

She shook her head. "No. They don't exist."

"What do you mean? I'm married to the person those records belong to. They must exist if she does!"

She shrugged. "There are recordings of Camilla Marchese from schools and the biannual census. But no birth records."

I bit the inside of my cheek, wondering what that meant. Had they been lost? Stolen? Had her father sealed them so well that not even a top-ranking government official could get his hands on them?

"We'll keep looking," she said when I fell silent for too long. "Until then, try to keep a lower profile. You're a hitman, not a spy."

I wanted to tell her the two were synonymous at this point, but stopped when I heard my name being called from the hallway. The Summoner cursed and said, "Someone's coming."

Soft footsteps were approaching, closing in on the only door on this side hall. "Nico?" And spoken by the very last voice I wanted to hear at this moment. I panicked, glanced around the small bathroom, but nothing could hide either of us.

"Nico, are you alright?" she asked, the knob on the door turned.

The Summoner slammed her lips onto mine, shoving me against the wall so that her back was to the door, and I had a perfect view of Milla's face as she discovered this woman forcing her kiss on me. From her reaction, the Summoner's ruse worked well. Milla slammed her eyes shut in mortification. She ducked her head, muttered an apology, and quickly shut the door without another word.

I shoved the woman off my face. A new fury pumping my heart into a frenzy. "What the hells was that for?"

"I was covering for the both of us," she said, wiping her mouth. "Doubt she'll be asking questions now."

"You have no idea who you're dealing with," I groaned, scrubbing my face. "Make sure my money is in my account the next day. I have an investment I'll need to put down a payment for." Shoving the Summoner aside, I spat at her before opening the door, "And don't ever summon me in front of my family—or my wife—ever again."

MILLA WASN'T at the table when I returned, but judging by my family's awkward glances, she'd made a fine show on her way out. Her chair was empty, her coat and gloves gone with her. I asked the lot of them, "Where did she go?"

No one answered, each looking at each other in a quiet show of unity. I snatched my cousin's shoulders from behind and asked him directly, "Where did she go, Luther?"

"She asked us not to tell."

"And we're on her side, so don't expect us to spill," Esme snapped.

I took a long, steadying breath. "It's not safe for a Marchese to be out in the Row alone, Esme. For her safety, tell me where she went!"

My cousin smiled. "That's why Gideon went with her. He knew you'd say that, so she let him tag along."

"*Giver and Greed*," I muttered. A thousand and one curses hanging on the tip of my tongue.

Fran spoke up then. "It's best if you leave her alone for a while, Nico. She seemed pretty upset. I think the whole day has just been hard on her. A little retail therapy can do wonders for a girl."

Shopping? That's where Milla decided to take my cousin for an escort? I gripped Luther's shoulders so tight he squirmed. The thought of them together, picking out her clothes, letting him assess her new outfits, helping her in the changing rooms—the unwanted visuals sent me spiraling. I patted down my pants, realizing something else that made my blood hot.

She took my wallet.

Just when my frustration had reached its peak, she shoved me over the edge. There was still so much undecided about these next few days, but I knew one thing for certain.

Camilla Marchese was going to be the death of me.

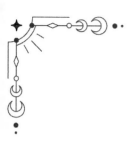
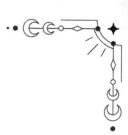

CHAPTER 29

CAMILLA

"Look who finally came home." Nico's voice was hollow as I unlocked my door. I turned to find him leaning against the doorframe leading into his bedroom. His eyes fell to the bags in my hand, taking stock of his unwilling purchases.

"Were you waiting for me?" I asked. It was late. I'd used some of the reoles leftover from shopping to buy me and Gideon some dinner. My reluctant accomplice for the evening suddenly lost his conscience with the promise of a free meal.

"No," he drawled. "I just happened to open the door as you walked up."

"Remarkable timing, as always."

"One of my many gifts."

I dropped my bags by the door and crossed the width of the hall to stand in front of him. His eyes were glossy as they stared down at me. His shirt was unbuttoned halfway, matching the disheveled mess of his hair. The smell of hard liquor and smoke hit me as I came close; obviously he'd been drinking.

"I see you had fun," he muttered.

I crossed my arms, showing off a row of gold bangle bracelets. His eyes widened at the jewelry. "I did. Would you like to see what you bought me?"

"Yes," he drawled, wincing as his gaze fell to my new shoes. "And no."

I smiled and handed him back the wallet I'd been using as a handbag all afternoon. A small groan left him when he felt how much lighter it was. After catching him with his mouth on another woman, I decided to hurt him back the only way I could—by emptying his pockets.

I'd be lying to myself by pretending it didn't hurt. We'd shared a moment on the train only days ago, and I still remembered that kiss like it was a brand on my lips, seared into memory. Apparently, it had meant nothing to him. As did his promise that he'd never be with someone else while we were still tied to this union.

An understanding settled between us, a wordless surrender on his part as he tucked the empty wallet into his back pocket.

"When was the last time you got a haircut?" I asked, noticing the way it curled a bit at his nape.

He shrugged. "I've been too busy jumping on trains and running from Collectors. Haven't had the luxury of time to think about my hair." The shoulder he leaned against slipped off the threshold, and he turned his back to me, retreating into the darkened bedroom. The gas lamps were turned off, the only light summoned by the fire in the hearth.

I took the liberty to step inside his room for the first time, since he so often let himself into my space without asking. The place was spotless. Not a pillow was out of place on a bed tightly made. The only unclean place in the room was the table in front of the fire, which was a catch all for bottles of various brandy, partially burned cigarillos leaning against an ashtray, and a book with the title hidden beneath a half-filled amber glass.

"I can cut it for you," I offered.

"I'm drunk," he scoffed, "but I'm not *that* drunk."

I rolled my eyes. "I'm not going to the Salt Ball with you looking like you spent the last five weeks braving the Wilds." He muttered something about the wilderness being preferable at this point, to which I ignored. "I'm assuming you own trimmers."

"Milla..."

Before he could deny me further, I was already in his bathroom, flicking on the lights to illuminate the vanity on the far wall. He didn't have a tub like I did, but a spacious shower to fill the space. The content of his drawers revealed him to be incredibly organized as well. While my own belongings were thrown together in an organized chaos, Nico grouped his products based on purpose and size.

"Second drawer, on the left," he grumbled behind me.

Smiling now, I placed a pair of trimmers, a thin comb, and a blade on the marble counter, counting each one into my arsenal.

Nico slumped onto a stool he pulled up in front of the mirror, drink in hand and a towel draped over his shoulders. "I swear, if you fuck up my hair, I'll fuck up your dress for the Salt Ball."

I frowned at his reflection. "It's a trim, Nicolai, stop being so dramatic. And who said you were choosing my dress?"

"I'm taking care of it." He took a long swig from his glass. "If you're making me go to a stupid party, you'll wear what I want."

I opened my mouth to disagree, but the look he gave me said his terms were nonnegotiable. My fingers combed through his dark hair, enjoying the feel of the feather-soft strands as they slipped through my hands. If I didn't know better, I would have thought he leaned into my palms, might have caught the way his eyes fluttered as I wet the length with a bit of warm water from the sink.

We fell quiet as I started to cut. He watched me through the mirror as I trimmed and combed, making sure to line up the edges of each strand to appease his high expectations. It wasn't as good of a job as his usual barber, but by the end he looked as dashing as the day we'd met. So handsome it made my heart a little hurt to look at him.

"There," I said, finishing. I combed the top length back with my fingers in the style he usually wore to assess my work. "Now you at least look like a gentleman, even if you act like a beast."

I used the edge of the towel around his shoulders to clean off his neck, dusting off the tiny hairs that had accumulated below his hairline. Without thinking, I blew softly into the shell of his ear, drawing a little jump from his shoulders.

"Saints, Milla." He sighed. "Why does everything you do have to be so . . ."

I arched my brow. "So . . . what?"

His chest rose with another despaired breath. "So *sexy*."

My hands fell from his hair to his shoulders, finding a tension there that hadn't been before. I tried to swallow, but my throat was suddenly bone-dry, parched from the heat in the gaze of his reflection.

No, he didn't get to do this. He didn't get to flirt and make my heart flutter. He didn't get to make me feel things only to crush them later. I cleared my throat and took a step back. "Why does everything *you* do have to be so irritating?"

"Because I'm an idiot."

"At last, we agree on something."

His shoulders fell an inch, his stare to his glass. "I'm sorry about today. That . . . wasn't supposed to happen." He was being sincere. I'd known Nico long enough to know his apologies were rare and that pitiful look he wore like a sad puppy was almost nonexistent.

"Well, I'm sorry I spent all your money." I wasn't, but it was better than saying I forgave him.

A dimple appeared with the start of a smirk. "I'm going to have to start giving you an allowance."

I feigned appall. "Careful, Attano. I know where you keep your trimmers now." I chopped his ear with my middle and forefinger, mimicking the motion of scissors. He reached back to snatch my arm, but I twisted away, slipping through his grasp. Nico's chair let out a harsh sound as I escaped the bathroom, his steps chased me out.

"What are you doing *now*?" he asked, sounding exasperated.

"Why is your bed so much larger than mine?" I asked, ripping the black sheets from their tuck beneath the mattress.

"Why are you being such a menace to my room?" he asked, picking up the pillows that had fallen.

I kicked off my heels and dove between his sheets, enjoying the way it made him cringe. "It's more comfortable, too!"

"You're more than welcome to spend the night," he chimed, watching me from the bench.

I ignored his offer, leaving it as an open invitation, and found a book beneath the pillow under my head. "What's this?"

"Nothing," he said too quickly.

My smile spread wide. "I thought you didn't read."

"I'm not good at it, I never said I didn't read," he corrected. "Sometimes I can't sleep at night. It helps take my mind off things. I found it on my mother's bookshelf a few years ago."

My smile softened, and he climbed in bed, lounging next to me on top of the sheets. "What's it about?" I asked. *The Revenge of Dacre Discanio* was written in gold foil on a purple cloth binding, the corners worn and frayed. The pages themselves were yellow from time.

"Dacre is an arrogant man who got rich off of taking advantage of people in his village. His deeds eventually catch up to him, and the night before he is to wed his beloved, he's kidnapped, beaten, and sold into servitude by the same people he swindled. The rest of the story tells about his adventures, the masters he serves, and the way they challenge him. Eventually he buys his freedom, goes back to his village, and finds that his bride married someone else."

"That's how it ends?" I asked.

He shook his head. "He realizes he never actually loved her, just what she could do for him. Only once he lost everything did he realize where true happiness came from. He went back to his original master's house and married the first person who ever showed him kindness, a fellow servant he worked with."

I hummed a thoughtful sound. "I do enjoy a good redemption story."

He nodded. "Me too. It's always good to remember that even villains can have happy endings."

I traced the gilded letters with my thumb. "It sounds like a lovely story. Your mother must've had good taste."

His lips tipped in a small smile. "She did."

I rolled to my side to look at him, inhaling the smell of him knitted in his pillowcase. He sat against the wooden headboard, a cushion shoved behind his back. "Do you think she would have liked me?"

When his smile fell, I thought I might have wandered somewhere forbidden. But he sighed. A gentle breeze roused the curls laying over my shoulders, followed by the icy kiss of his remnant across my skin.

"She would have adored you, Milla. Just like the rest of my family does."

I smiled and couldn't help the satisfaction that smothered the breath in my chest. Clearing my throat, I handed the book to him. "Will you read some of it to me?"

He looked surprised I asked. "Are you sure? Listening to me stumble over words can be quite tedious."

I nodded. "I really want to hear you read it, Nico."

His throat convulsed with a swallow, and with a wave of his hand, the light in the room brightened as he opened the book. "I really need to learn how to say no to you."

He started reading from a dog-eared page, in the middle of Dacre professing his love for a woman named Evangeline. Nico was an excellent storyteller. Despite his impairment, he hardly missed a beat, and I wondered just how many times he'd read these scenes to narrate them so seamlessly. He changed his voice for each character, deepening in pitch for Dacre while hitting a higher note for Evangeline.

"You sound like your Nonna," I said, holding back a bubble of laughter.

"*It's rude to interrupt, Belladonna,*" he spoke in a nasally voice, mocking his grandmother with a sly smile. A giggle burst from the seam of my lips. Only once I fell quiet again did he continue, serious as ever and wholly invested in the words on the page.

A weight fell over my eyes, the draw of sleep pulled them shut. Wrapped in Nico's scent, warm in his bed, listening to his deep voice tell the story of a villain's heart of redemption, I fell asleep. The last words lingered on the edge of my dreamland.

"*Why do you look at me like that, Dacre?*" *said Evangeline.*

"*Because you are the most beautiful thing in this land, Eva. And I am an admirer of beautiful things.*"

I thought, perhaps, I had heard this story before.

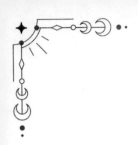

CHAPTER 30

CAMILLA

The next morning, I awoke still in Nico's bed, though the bender was long gone. He hadn't even unsettled the sheets on his side, and I wondered if he'd even slept beside me or taken the couch. I wondered why the latter made me feel disappointed.

He spent his days at the factory, the steel business taking up much of his time. The Collector's trail had gone cold without a recent disappearance combined with the lack of witnesses to give us anything to follow. Before I knew it, the day had come for Sabina's ball, and I was anxiously preparing for the party of the year.

"For the love of the lost saints," I muttered. "What in the void is that?"

Sera tracked my gaze to the scrap of fabric lying across the bed. "It's your dress for tonight."

"Where's the rest of it?" I shrieked.

She pinched her lips into a tight line to hide her smile. "It is a gift from Mr. Attano. He had his own personal seamstress make it

special. Asked me last week for your measurements and your preferences."

"Did you tell him my favorite color was *skin*?"

"Oh, stop being so dramatic," she snapped at me, her smile on full display now. Sera had grown more comfortable scolding me when I was being ridiculous, but I didn't find this to be one of those instances. "It's actually quite stunning. I think it will look perfect on you once you get over how much cleavage you'll be showing."

I hadn't even noticed the neckline until she pointed it out. Plunging—just like my morals. "I don't have anything else?" I moaned, inching towards the gown while still wearing my towel. Sera had curled my hair with her hot iron, pinning one side half up and against my head while the rest flowed in long curls over my shoulders. My makeup was darker than I'd ever done it, with smokey powders over my eyes to make them look large and mysterious and a red lipstick that exaggerated the fullness of my lips. I hardly recognized myself, and perhaps that was a good thing if I were to wear this dress —a garment I'd never choose for myself.

"Milla," she said slowly, "this is a very nice gift. You don't own anything nearly as exquisite. Just try it on at least."

"Fine," I said, fingering the velvet bodice. *Saints*, it was soft. I had a bad feeling about this, but Sera ignored my reluctant sighs and laced me inside the crimson gown, pushing me in front of the mirror when she was finished.

I didn't know the woman in the mirror. She was too beautiful to be the same person who usually stood in place of my reflection. Staring back at me was a version of myself I could get used to. Not the excess makeup or perfect hair, not even the revealing gown which—to my admittance—fit me perfectly. But a woman who was taken care of for the first time in her life. This dress and all its gaps, my hair and the attention given to it, each detail was a reminder I was no longer alone in a world where I once had to fend for myself.

And it was nice, even in its fleetness.

"It's . . . not as bad as I thought," I admitted. Black-velvet constructed straps dove over my shoulders and down each breast, meeting at my navel. The fabric hugged my curves like a second skin, forbidding any indecent views. The skirt was more embellished, constructed of a silky, crimson underlay beneath a sheer top layer. The outermost fabric was beaded with hundreds of iridescent black stones, all sewn in a damask pattern that popped against the red underlining.

"See?" she said, crossing her arms all smug. "Perfect. I'll get your gloves."

"Are you sure you don't want to come?" I asked. "I'm sure we could find you something—"

"Definitely not," she said. "I'm taking my night off to visit a friend."

Three knocks tapped quickly against the bedroom door. Sera went to unlock it, smiled at whoever was on the other side. "Evening, Mr. Attano."

"Is she ready, Sera? Esme and the boys are waiting in the carriages."

I stepped around the door, quickly slipping on my last glove when our eyes met. Nicolai always dressed immaculately, but tonight he was the definition of elegance and class. His suit jacket was the typical Attano red, a raised design in the velvet matched the kind covering my skirt. He studied me, smoothing his hands over the glossy finish of the lapels, adjusting the tailored fit over his broad shoulders.

"You look . . ." he started, but seemed to lose his place, falling silent.

"Different." I finished for him. He nodded, grey eyes continued to roam over my body.

Sera cleared her throat, looking between us. "Good saints, look at the time. I should be going." She grabbed her bag and muttered a personal farewell to me. When she was gone, Nico approached, taking in the details of the gown from a closer angle.

I swallowed, feeling suddenly exposed under his attention. "Thank you for the dress, by the way. When you said you took care of it, I didn't expect something custom."

He blinked, as if snapping out of a trance. "Of course," he finally said, taking a step toward me. "This is our first appearance as a couple. What kind of husband would I be if I let you show up in something another descendant was wearing?"

"A normal one," I replied.

He scoffed. "Our situation is far from normal." He stood in front of me, curling a lock of brown hair that had caught his interest. "Milla, you need to know something about tonight."

My hands wrung together. "What is it?"

His gaze slid up to mine. "When the Attanos rose to power over the Row, we stepped on a lot of toes. There are descendants who are bitter toward us, who would like nothing better than to knock me from my throne. There are also descendants who hate the Marcheses, as I'm sure you're well aware. If tonight is to go smoothly, we need to be convincing."

"Convincing?" I asked. "I don't follow."

He took a stalling breath, tucking his hands into his pockets. "We need to make sure everyone truly believes we married for each other, not for business. If other families find out we're doing this for money, it might provoke them to use you to manipulate themselves into our deal. Especially Sabina. Do you understand what I'm saying?"

"I'm not only in danger because I'm a Marchese, but because I'm an Attano as well?"

"Exactly."

I shrugged and began looking for the tabs of glint I snagged the other day while we were visiting the Steam District. "I'm used to the danger part. As for convincing everyone I like you, that will be more challenging." I popped a blue capsule down my throat, feeling more confident to have a level of protection in a den of descendants. "But if it gets me free champagne, I'm down to try."

"It has to be more than like, Milla." He came behind me, calloused fingers swept the curls off the back of my neck. "You've got to love me tonight."

His perusal sent a rash of chills down my spine, and with the low backing of the bodice, he probably noticed. I'd never understand how the warmth of his fingers could chill me to the bone, how I could be both flushed and fevered and yet shudder from his touch.

"Won't it be worse if people believe we're in love?" I asked. The words sounded strange together. "Will it not put a bigger target on my back if people see me as a weapon to wield against you?"

"Perhaps, but two powerful families uniting for business purposes—everyone will see that as a threat," he said quietly. Two fingertips bladed down my spine, skimming over the velvet where the mark of the voidwalker was hidden beneath. "Lovers have nothing to hide."

I turned to face him, feeling his hands skim my waist as I spun. "Will any of your other lovers be attending the ball tonight? I would like to know just in case I run into you being devoured again."

His right dimple flashed with the briefest smirk. "Only you get to devour me tonight, princess."

"How generous of you," I said dryly. "I think I'll pass."

"The night is still young." He reached behind me and plucked a dagger from the top of my dresser. "Have you dipped your knives?"

"A few. Just need to slip my sheath on and I'll be ready." Grabbing the leather brace, I pushed my skirts aside to attach it around the leg that didn't have a slit all the way to my hip, but it was complicated to finagle the straps while holding so much fabric.

"Here," Nico said, watching me struggle in my balancing act. "Before you break your ankle on those ridiculous heels you call shoes."

Without letting me refuse him, he knelt. I braced a hand on the dresser to keep my knees from giving out as he slipped his hands around the thickest part of my thigh. Even his calculated touch raised the hair on my skin. The last time we had been in this situation, I couldn't feel it, a small mercy compared to the trouble building between my legs where his head hovered.

He laced the sheath meticulously, running his finger beneath the straps to test the tightness, before reaching up for my blades. I handed him three, each coated in a special glint mixture that would render a remnant powerless should they need humbling.

"All set," he said, starting to stand. I shoved him back down with a heel to his chest.

"While you're down there," I said, "would you mind fixing the strap?"

Nico's eyes traced the length of my leg, looking up at me slowly. He smirked, taking the beaded straps too loose around my ankle and tightening them until they were just right. His hand smoothed up the back of my calf to ease my foot off his chest.

"Anything else I can do for you, princess?" He reached the bend of my knee, cupping the slope of my thigh. "While I'm down here."

My traitorous mind flashed images of being devoured, of those hands spreading my legs while I clung to the dresser behind me. The mental image had me clinging to the top of the furniture a little tighter, if only to ground me back to this reality. Remind me I was supposed to be planning his demise, not my own.

"Nope. All set," I blurted.

The loss of him was too noticeable as he let my leg slip through his fingers. I might have imagined the flush in his cheeks when he stood, meeting my gaze again, but he turned away too quickly to study. Nico was already at the door by the time I settled my skirts— and my heartbeat.

He adjusted his coat and held out an arm to me. "Ready to do this?"

As I'd ever be.

* * *

WE ARRIVED FASHIONABLY LATE, nearly an hour after the party had been set to start. Empty cars filled the circle drive in front of the abandoned meat factory, a four-level building that had been hollowed out to make room for Sabina's lavish parties.

The windows were frosted over from the winter night, golden light refracted in the ice glazing the glass.

"You look lovely tonight, boss," Gideon said as Nico and I spilled out of the carriage. His cousins stared at me with their hands in their coat pockets, looking suddenly bashful. Luther whistled, muttered the same. Adler was too busy escorting Esme up the front steps, who was eager to leave us behind and join the party.

"Thank you," I said, feeling Nico tense beside me. I nudged him in the side with the arm that connected with his. "See? That's how you compliment a girl."

I could practically feel him roll his eyes. "Let's just get this over with, shall we?" I noticed him jut his chin towards Adler. "Remind those two that just because this is a party, doesn't mean we let our guards down. Don't drink too much, don't take anyone home, and above all"—he dipped his head to look at me directly—"don't cause trouble."

"Unfortunately for you, Nicolai," I said, pulling him along, "I have already made a bet with Esme to see how many more years I can shave off your life."

"Sometimes I wish you'd just kill me and get it over with."

My laugh burst past the barrier of my lips, unrestrained from the night sky watching over us. I glanced sideways at Nico and found him grinning. That genuine smile was a rare wonder, and it made my heart swell. Thankfully, he still wore his gloves and couldn't feel the racing pulse in my wrist as his arm intertwined with mine.

We passed through the shadows of the pillars standing guard in front of the building. A cold breeze rolled off the Ada, flowing just behind the building. A distant rumble from the sky insisted on an incoming storm, filling the air with petrichor. The footman tried to take Nico's coat, but he refused, hardly glancing at the man as he escorted me inside, just as the rain began to fall.

My senses were slammed the moment we entered the main hall. More open space in a building than I'd ever seen before, chandeliers dropped from a tiled ceiling across the room, draping the room in low light. Hundreds of tables hosting centerpieces with spilling floral arrangements lined the edges of the room, spaced around a dance floor with a ten-piece band.

Remnant entertainment lined the alcoves on the second floor. Benders balancing fire in their hands, dancing with the flames as they spun the evidence of their magic on the edges of the balconies. Twin bars lined the foyer, where barmaids mixed tonics with the flick of their hands, cups barely touching the bar made of solid ice, keeping the drinks cold as patrons conversed between each other.

A shirtless man dressed in pink tights ran up to me, and Nico shifted himself between us. But the eccentric player of Sabina's ball games spun around him, throwing sand up from his palm. In three quick seconds the grains fell into the form of a rose, glowed red and orange until crystal clear. He handed me the glass flower, the details unbelievably thorough right down to the textured stem and the curled lip of the blooming petals.

"That's amazing," I breathed. "Thank you."

He nodded with a low dip of his head and danced away, on to another maiden. Nico snorted, taking my gift and slipping it inside his coat pocket. It was a revelry of magic. Everywhere one looked, a remnant was on display. I ate it up, my hungry eyes hardly settling on one place too long.

"I have an alcove in the center reserved for us." He had to bend to speak in my ear.

"Right in the middle of everything?" I asked, feeling my nerves buzz with excitement.

"Best seats in the house."

I wanted to ask how he managed such a reservation, since it had been my idea less than a week ago to attend. But before I could utter a word, he pulled me along again, the cousins who normally trailed us disappearing to their own fun.

Nico's alcove sat on a raised platform behind the line of tables on the right side of the building. Instead of chairs, the circular cutout was lined with a bench that followed the bend of the nook. The flooring, seating, and walls were all pressed with a soft, blue velvet. Gold and emerald silk pillows were tossed throughout, and a bucket of full champagne bottles sat on ice. We had a full view of the entire room.

And the entire room had a full view of us.

I saw eyes. Hundreds of them. Watching us step up to our alcove, stare as Nico poured me a drink in a crystal flute and sat on the upper part of the bench. He operated like no one else existed, like this was another day having a drink at the Attano estate. Meanwhile, I felt the weight of the world and their judgment, felt the coldness of cruel thoughts freeze me into place.

"Milla?" Nico asked, arching his brow.

"They're all looking at us," I murmured, hardly breathing.

He looked out into the crowd, offered a two-finger wave before looking back at me. "It would seem they are. Do you remember what I told you?"

I had to act like I was in love with him. This man whom everyone thought was my husband, that I married by choice. I took a long sip of my drink, my hands shaking the whole way to my lips. I swallowed. "You were right. This was a bad idea."

"Saints, it feels good to hear you admit that." Nico smiled and removed the glass flower from his jacket, placing it on the seat beside him before extending his hand to me. "Come here."

I made myself accept his offering, and he pulled me closer with a gentle tug, spreading his legs to fit me between them. His hands slipped around my waist, cold metal and warm skin sunk into the bend of my spine. With his elbows on his knees, he was inches from my face. My own hands trembled around my glass with nothing else to fill them.

"All they want is a good show. Give them what they want—something to talk about—and they'll move onto something more interesting." He took my glass and set it aside, next to the rose. "Sit down, Milla. I'll do the rest."

I glanced down at the seat he propped his feet on, where he wanted me to sit between his legs. Taking a steadying breath, I turned slowly, facing the crowd again, before bracing my hands on his knees and lowered until my arms were resting on his thighs like my personal throne.

"Better?" he asked.

"Not at all. I can see everyone again."

Nico's fingers skated around the column of my throat, shoved me back against his chest. "Fuck all of them. Just focus on me."

"How are you doing this so easily?" I asked him. The way he gripped my neck, stroked my shoulder with the back of his false hand, how it traced the edge of my arm—it felt adoring, like he'd done this a thousand times.

His words came out silky and slow. "Wanting you isn't hard, princess. It's all the rest that makes it difficult."

I understood that better than he knew.

Gradually, his touch stole the world around us piece by piece. And inch by inch his hand slipped lower, until the pads of his fingers swept the valley of my breast, coaxing the wind from my chest without even using his remnant. His lips brushed the shell of my ear. "This okay?"

I could only nod. The air was suddenly too thin to breathe now that Nico's scent wrapped me in tobacco and gin. He smelled of all the forbidden pleasures, and the placement of his touch only deepened that carnal desire to indulge in the wrong and the wonderfully tempting. His calloused fingers bladed a place that had never been touched by another, and my grip snatched his thighs, digging my fingers into his thick muscles.

He hissed into my hair, and my face flooded with heat. Suddenly the lights in this room burned me alive, the gas lights in the alcove too bright. The drums from the band challenged my heart to a battle of beats. I turned my face to where he dipped his head. "Are you alright? You made a strange sound."

"It was a good sound. Trust me." His voice was breathy, words brushing all the bare skin exposed to his view. "I should have told you before . . . you look beautiful tonight. I like your hair like this."

For the first time since we stepped in this alcove, I was thankful my face was to the audience so he couldn't see me bite my lip or witness the flush crawling up my neck at his confession. "Thank you," I tried to say. But it sounded more like a sigh, my words too rushed.

"All I've been able to think about since I first saw you tonight is how good it would look wrapped around my fist."

"*Nicolai* . . ."

"Forgive me for this, Milla."

Before I could argue, his fingers combed the length of my curls, catching the ends in his palm. He looped the strands twice around his fists before gently yanking my head to the side, exposing my throat. It didn't hurt, not in a bad way at least, but it was forceful enough to pull a squeak of surprise from me.

Nico *hummed* a low sound, full of delicious satisfaction. The sharp tip of his nose traced the hollow of my neck all the way to my ear. Teeth scraped the soft skin behind my jaw where my pulse danced for him, and it wasn't enough. I wanted more, communicated that need by smoothing my palms down his inner thighs. My body could finally relax against him, and I felt the full size of his desire press against my back.

We might be putting on a show, but neither of us were acting. The sounds he made were too ravenous, the heat in my lower belly too smoldering to be anything but real.

"Maybe you should . . . kiss me. If we're trying to convince everyone."

A snide laugh cooled the heat flaming my back. "Kissing would be most convincing. We should definitely try, for everyone's sake."

Metal cusped the curve of my throat. "How would you like it, Milla? Soft and sweet like a lover or . . . something else."

I turned my head to look up at him, to trace his eyes for the first time since we started this little show and found a hunger there. "I want you to kiss me like you mean it, Nico. Does that answer your question?"

His mouth was on mine immediately, so fast it knocked the wind from my chest, leaving me no time to be anxious or nervous. This kiss was so unlike the one in the train car, this one on display for the world to watch. He pulled the hair at my nape to angle my head back into an unnatural position. I couldn't move from beneath him, wedged between his legs, his grip around my throat. It was everything I imagined it would feel like and *more*.

My hands smoothed up and down his thighs, enjoying how his body tensed beneath my touch. His tongue speared my mouth with an appealing sweep, inciting his desire with every stroke, sending me into a passion-drenched fever pitch. I was swiftly drowning in this connection, submerged in a pool of unyielding desires.

All my life, I had been too cautious, too afraid of the consequences of giving myself to someone physically. But with Nico, there were no surprises. I knew where we stood, where this would lead. I could be whomever I wanted and know it wouldn't change how this would end. My heart was safe with him because he would never try to steal it. He didn't want it.

And for that reason, I took his free hand in mine and guided it beneath my bodice, letting his fingers trace the swell of my breast. The coarse sound of surprise he made was enough reward, his encapsulating heat a pleasure too addicting to be anything but a drug.

"Camilla Mercy Marchese," he murmured, eyes hooded. "Are you trying to torture me?"

"Is it so horrible to feel me?" I asked.

He made a strangled sound, thumbs swirling higher with every stroke. "I have no right to touch you like this."

I turned my head, kissed the inner part of his forearm. "You have the only right, the one I've given you."

He burrowed his face into the curve of my shoulder the same time my head fell back against this chest. It turned out we fit together perfectly. I reached up for him, slipping my fingers behind his taut neck. People still watched, but there was a shift in power granted to me when I suddenly stopped worrying about what they thought. I was too bewitched by his hand to focus on anything else.

The rough pads of his fingers sent my back arching, filling his palm. He pinched a sensitive peak between two fingers, and I bit my lip to hold back the cry building in my chest. This was a terrible idea, getting a taste of his touch. I knew I'd never stop wondering what his calloused fingers would feel like between my legs, stroking my wet center, slipping inside . . .

"Sorry. My hand is a little rough," he said, mistaking my writhing for discomfort.

"I like your hands," I breathed. "Both your hands."

He cursed, his breath heavy and building speed across my neck. "*Saints*, Milla, if you don't stop talking like that, this is going to get very *out* of hand."

I flashed a smirk, but there was a disappointment that leashed my full smile. "We can stop. It looks like everyone has moved on."

"Do you want me to stop?"

Hells, no. But I couldn't admit that. This was supposed to be an act, but I'd found myself enjoying it far too much. Thankfully, I didn't have to answer. A man in black robes and a red sash approached our alcove, disturbing our exchange. Nico sighed. Those unmerciful fingers slipped from my dress, leaving a trail where they dragged long after he let me go.

"Can I help you?" Nico asked, his voice hard.

"Sabina is requesting a meeting, sir."

"Now?" He looked at his watch and cursed again. "Fine. Tell her I'll be there in a moment."

He nodded and hurried off back in the direction he came. I stood to let him step down off the bench. Before he left, he grabbed my hand and said, "I'll just be gone a moment. I'll go find a cousin so you won't be here alone, but do not leave the alcove."

His overbearing orders made me roll my eyes. "I'm perfectly fine being on my own, Nico. You've made your territory quite known to the descendants here tonight."

He shook his head, dismissing my claim. "About that, you don't need to worry about keeping up appearances any longer. I think we've gone quite far enough, and everyone has more or less moved on."

Disappointment welled in my chest. "Well, if that's how you feel, then alright. I thought maybe . . . I thought you were enjoying it."

He squeezed my hand. "Milla, of course it was fun."

I scoffed, masking the hurt with indifference, but it was far less convincing than my performance a moment ago. I unraveled my fingers from his and snatched my hand away.

"Fun? Is that what I am to you?"

His face softened, realizing the backhanded blow of that word. He used it once to describe another woman just a few weeks ago, and it was a sobering slap to the heart. I was angry at Nico for saying such a thing, for putting me in the same category as someone that should have meant far less to him, but mostly at myself for giving him the chance to make me feel this way.

I cleared my throat, feeling it start to close. "Good. That's just fine. Job well done, Nico. You almost convinced me you were being genuine for a few minutes."

"Milla, I didn't mean—"

"I'm going to get something to eat. And really, don't bother sending anyone. I'd rather sit here alone than share a space with another Attano."

I spun too sharply, feeling the beginnings of the alcohol start to mess with my head. Perhaps I could blame it on the drink I downed, that I would feel this way for anyone if they touched me like he had now that my inhibitions were dulled. I decided not to indulge in the stuff ever again, both the drink and the man.

"Milla!" he called after me, but I refused to acknowledge him. Sabina was obviously too important to refuse, because when I looked back a moment later, he was gone. The alcove was empty, like this pit in my chest.

He didn't want my heart—he wouldn't take it. But there was a hollowness where the vessel once beat, as if it had already been stolen.

Or given away.

I pushed through bodies, crossing the width of the ballroom floor on the shortest path to the meat displays on the opposite side of the room. There were roasted beasts of every kind from the Wilds where Sabina's hunters scourged, but my stomach churned at the salivating smells, my appetite soured by my shame.

My cheeks were still hot, my body left on fire with need. I sought out a side door, a back entrance, a way out of this room and its *audience*. A worker finally pointed me down a hall obscured by an ice sculpture. I squeezed through the floating figure and the remnant keeping it chilled and ran to the end of the darkened hall.

Moments later, I was outside, bursting through the last door. The quiet hit me immediately, the cold tamed the flames in my marrow. I took a few steadying breaths with my eyes shut, sucking down the shame and letting it accumulate with the rest. The sky was in the middle of a downpour beyond the narrow overhang that extended from the building, rendering the already frigid air almost numbing.

I let it sting me deep, soak through the layer of my skin to deaden the clash of wants inside me. I wanted to make my family proud, wanted to find a way out of this contract. I wanted my freedom from the Firenzes, from the government, from being force-fed my wrong-doings on the Marchese silver platters.

And I wanted from Nicolai. I wanted . . . but I couldn't name the desire. All I knew was that each day that passed, that want was starting to overtake the others, and I couldn't afford for that desire to win out.

I wiped my forehead free of wetness, coated by the mist. Collecting my nerves, I turned to go back inside...and found I wasn't alone out here.

"Camilla Marchese," he said my name in greeting. My reply came out as a shaken whisper.

"Inspector Gavriel."

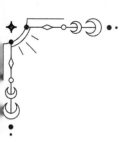
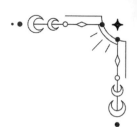

CHAPTER 31
NICOLAI

Life has a cruel way of reminding me every day, that no matter how hard I tried, no matter how many sacrifices I made, no matter the path of pain I'd taken to claim it, I'd never have it all.

Try as I might, the world was a slippery thing. I could hold on to my family, my freedom, the legacy my father started. I could fit the Row and the city of Lynchaven in the palm of my hand and still have room for the fame and fortune that came with the life I led.

But Camilla Marchese was a falling star, and if I wanted to catch her, I'd have to let go of the rest.

I'd told her the purpose for being so flashy with our affection was for her safety, which was partly true, but it was mostly for myself. I needed to make sure every man, woman, and monster in this room saw my face and would remember me clearly. And after watching an Attano bury his hand beneath a Marchese's bodice, I'm sure none of them would forget. I certainly wouldn't.

Saints, she was stunning. She was always attractive, but tonight,

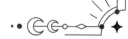

she was incomparable. The way she curled her fingers around my neck, arched her chest into my hand. That smile she had, knowing she was the most beautiful woman in the room—it had the power to undo me. Which was why I didn't chase after her. I let her go. Because I was so fucking ashamed of myself for using her to strengthen my alibi, and for enjoying myself while I did so.

I maintained a short distance behind the robed man. He was dressed like a Blood remnant working for Sabina tonight, but I'd seen him before. We were employed by the same man, covering me once before when I needed a double.

A Mirth remnant, a shapeshifter. All the unsavory types came from Mirth.

I had to admit, he was a professional at his craft. By the time I followed him to the second floor and into a blocked-off section of the building, he had already morphed into my character. He quickly began to strip his robes, turning so I could do the same. We swapped clothes before discussing the next business.

"I don't know when I'll be back tonight, so you'll have to think of a reason to leave the estate. Say you need to check on a pipe that busted from the freeze at the factory and leave as soon as you get home. Try not to let my cousins overhear." I threw the hood of the cloak over my face. Beneath the draping of the robes, he'd concealed leather armor to aid my stealth tonight.

"I can handle your family, Nicolai. They'll most likely be too drunk to tell the difference," he replied. *Saints*, did I sound that condescending all the time?

He slipped long leather gloves over his bare hands. While he was able to recreate the look of the false arm, he couldn't make it operate like the one I owned. It moved too naturally, like it was flesh instead of metal, so we agreed to cover it just in case.

"One more thing, shifter," I said, taking a step toward him and jutting a finger in his face. I looked at my reflection, like I was scolding myself instead. "I left things tense with Milla on purpose. When you go back to that alcove, you will not touch her. I don't care how much of an asshole you have to be. Keep your hands *off*."

My double smirked. "You just worry about your mission, Mr. Attano. Let me worry about our wife."

I snapped. My false hand went for his throat. I watched his eyes bulge as my hand compressed tighter each second that ticked by, minded him with apathy as he gasped for air, made those desperate gurgling sounds I knew all too well. The strength in my metal hand was limitless, a perk of science and gold and magic.

"Do not touch her," I repeated slower this time, so he'd comprehend my threat. "And if I find out you skimmed a bead on her skirt, I don't care what face you wear, I'll never stop hunting you until I take the air from your chest for good."

I released him when his skin turned pallid, and he collapsed to the moth-eaten carpet lining the unused room. Without waiting for him to catch his breath, I left him to regain his coloring, certain we'd come to an understanding.

As if the night couldn't be any worse, the rain was freezing as I slipped through a fire exit and made my way to the abandoned stables a block away from the old market. The dull sounds of the band followed me on the way out, the wild drums a pulse, beating the heart of the party to life. I stole one last glance at the glowing windows, envying the warmth they contained, and found the horse my double had left for me.

It was going to be a long, wet, freezing ride to the Overseer's mansion, but the misery found in the rain was nothing compared to what I was leaving behind.

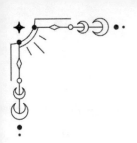

CHAPTER 32

CAMILLA

"Inspector," I repeated. "What are you doing here?"

It seemed he hadn't shaved since I saw him last. A short auburn beard lined the edge of his jaw, slightly lighter than the locks he tied back behind the base of his head. Gone was the usual grey uniform he wore, replaced with an expensive suit the color of the Ada in a thunderstorm.

He smiled politely. "The Society requires Sabina to host officers throughout the venue—undercover of course. I always attend her parties. I can't afford to let the opportunity for such good gossip slip by."

I swallowed. He must have seen my own bit of gossip that I incited. "Heard anything scandalous yet?"

His grin widened, though something about it was off—appearing maniacal. "Plenty. I've actually heard quite a few stories about you."

"Me?" A breeze rolled off the river and slammed into the side of the building, slipping beneath my skirt to chill me all over. I was

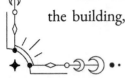

trembling then, from fear or nerves or the cold. My breath came out shaky in a white fog.

The inspector pretended not to notice, only adjusted the lapels of his jacket. "Yes. You have quite the creative approach trying to break things off with the Attano. Between jumping into a pit to free him of Sabina's charges to that little display you put on tonight, one would begin to assume you care about him."

I swallowed against the rawness in my throat, recalling his warning from the derby. "Why are you so worried about the Attanos sharing my company?" I asked. "You were fine with the Firenzes. What difference does it make as long as the debt is paid?"

"The difference is where your loyalties lie, Camilla," he said slowly. Lightning flashed behind him. The wind picked up and threw the rain sideways against the building, rendering the overhang useless. "Which side will you be on when this is over?"

"When what is over?" I asked, clutching my arms together.

His glare worsened without a smile to soften it. "You could have broken things off with Nicolai much easier than this, Camilla. Now he will suffer."

The spray of the rain was no longer cold. Numbness spread across my skin at his threat. "What are you talking about, Inspector?"

He looked out over the Ada, ignoring my question. "We received a tip tonight. Someone is going to try to assassinate the Overseer."

My eyes widened. "Who would attempt such a thing?"

He shrugged. "Whoever they are, I am eager to lock them down once and for all. It has been only one of many attempts on the lives of my comrades. Someone is eager to cut down the leadership of this city." Gavriel's gaze clutched me like an unwanted embrace, staring unashamedly where the gown exposed my curves.

"Just as the Collector has raised paranoia throughout the remnant community and undermined the reputation of descendants

307

in the streets. It seems you have more important things to concern yourself over than my little affairs. Wouldn't you agree, Inspector?"

"I would agree to disagree, Camilla. Especially from what I saw at the registrar the other day. What *was* Giles turning over to the House of Records?"

My throat nearly shut as I swallowed back the burn of bile. If Gavriel found out about the favor I asked of my brother, I had put us all in grave danger. I lied through my teeth. "I don't know what you're talking about."

"Of course not. You're just the heiress, not the boss." He turned to the side to let me pass, gesturing toward the door. "I'm sure your *husband* must be wondering where you are, Camilla. Don't let me keep you."

Without hesitating, I took advantage of his dismissal and darted towards the side door, eager to reunite with the warmth of the party and escape his interrogation. Every encounter with the inspector left me feeling less like an associate and more like a suspect.

The alcove was still empty when I returned to the main room, losing the inspector somewhere in the crowd when he followed me inside. The brass band played a jovial song, upbeat and loud, drawing a heavy crowd across the dance floor. I pushed through the horde of dancers, ignoring the bumps and hands that *accidentally* brushed my backside as I slipped past. Just as I made it halfway across the floor, someone knocked into me, nearly sending me sprawling on the floor. If my heels had been any higher, I might have.

"Watch where you're—" the voice snapped, then softened. "Oh, it's just you."

Of all the bleeders in the room, I had knocked into the queen of them all, the host of this revelry. Sabina wore a white gown that hugged her thick thighs and hourglass hips. Two other women danced beside her, their sleeves stained red from a bite gash on their upper arms.

"Where did Nico go?" I asked her, seeing as their meeting was over.

She looked at me strangely. "How should I know?"

"Because you just met with him."

"No, I didn't," she said. "I've been out here all night. No business with pleasure." She winked and promptly returned to grinding between her two companions.

Her interruption left me confused. Why would a man come retrieve Nico to visit Sabina if she wasn't seeing anyone tonight? And where did he truly go? When I looked up at the alcove, I discovered he'd returned. Relief and rage battled senseless in my heart.

"Where have you been?" I asked Nico as I stepped up into our nook.

He filled the right curve of the wall, arms wide and legs crossed, as if to take up as much space as possible. "I told you where I went, love."

"Sabina?"

He only nodded.

"What did she want?"

Nico had barely looked me in the eye since I arrived, his attention fixed on the dancers wrapped around the ribbons dangling from the ceiling. "Just wanted to make sure we were on good terms again. After what happened in the Pits that night, we've been the talk of the Row."

He was a good liar, a trait I could both admire and despise, mostly due to the fact he had so many secrets to keep. I wouldn't call him out on his falsehoods just yet, however. I'd wait until he dug himself a hole so deep, it would conveniently meet the standards for a proper grave. I settled on the bench opposite of him and reached for a water, my annoyance killing all delirium the alcohol had initiated.

An awkward silence stretched. It was odd to me how Nico could change performances so quickly. The bender that sat across from me felt like a completely different man than the one I kissed only half an hour ago. The distance between us only worsened the tension set by his lies. The night had started promising, but it was quickly falling apart.

I looked out into the scene, shielding my eyes from the glare of candlelight in search of a familiar face. Luther drank at one of the bars with some man with powder blue hair. Gideon had a conversation with three women who all seemed very interested in whatever he talked about. Esme hadn't even left the dance floor since we arrived. Which left the only other face I knew to be the one across the alcove, who suddenly had no concern for me now that my purpose had been served.

My stubbornness conceded my desperation for a good time, and I stood to my feet to approach him. He finally looked up at me. "What do you want?"

"A dance."

He sneered. "Definitely not. I don't dance, and I already got my fill of you earlier."

The aftertaste of his rejection burned as I swallowed it. "I understand you're done touching me, Nicolai." My hands were clammy beneath the velvet lining of my gloves, even as I flexed and curled my fingers in a nervous fidget. "But I never got a turn."

His eyes widened slightly, so small was the movement, I thought I imagined it. He canted his head and shrugged his shoulders. "Well, I'd hate to be unfair."

"I was hoping you'd say that." With the pull of a sash, a pair of curtains fell across the face of the alcove, shrouding us in privacy. The double gas lamps on the wall were burning low, darkening his grey gaze into an abysmal depth.

"A private dance?" he asked, sitting up straighter. "You should have led with that, love."

I smiled. "Close your eyes."

He did as I requested without hesitation. I quickly kicked off my heels and climbed behind him, sitting on top of the bench as he did before, our positions reversed. "Take this off," I mumbled in his ear, taking the initiative to slip my hands beneath the edges of his lapels in encouragement.

He eagerly shirked off the fitted jacket and tossed it on the bench beside him, and I used his distraction to swipe a knife from my thigh. I noticed he put his gloves back on, wondered if he had gone outside to warrant their requirement.

As he settled back between my legs, I feathered my fingers down the slope of his shoulders, felt the tension laced in his neck and throughout his body, the type of tautness only hardened by long experienced stress. Even as he relaxed, his heart raced beneath my palm as I slid it down his chest, feeling every crevasse lining hard muscle, enjoying the feel of Nico's body without Nico ever knowing.

Because this wasn't him. I didn't know how, what remnant had the power to steal faces and bodies, but there was another power at work here. I'd spent almost every waking second with the bender for the last month. I knew the rhythm of his breath, the notes of his scent, the way his smile always curled on the right side before lifting on the other. I knew he didn't drink anything besides double malt whiskey with three cubes of ice. But most of all, I knew all his names for me, and none of them had ever been *love*.

I let the dagger slip from my palm and into my fingers, pressing the blade lightly against his pulse. He stiffened again, feeling the cold sting. "Who are you?" I asked.

The man sucked a breath, held it for a second before replying. "Camilla, what are you talking about? I'm your husband."

"Good," I replied, letting the dagger fall a little, giving it slack. "Then you'll forgive me when I do this—"

I sliced a line across his throat just deep enough to break skin, exposing his bloodstream to the glint on my blade. His hands went for his throat, clutching the sight in surprise. I shoved him off the seat and to the floor, watching from a king's perspective as the man wearing my husband's face began to transform.

His skin, normally a dark tan, lightened several shades. His piercing glare angled into almond shaped eyes, grey bled into brown. The bones of his face jumbled like a pot of boiling water, before smoothing out to reveal a stranger in Nico's clothes.

"I'll ask you once more." I took out another dagger, this one gleamed violet in the light. This one would burn. "Who are you?"

"My name is Regulus," he hissed, still holding his hand to his neck. A drop of blood beaded down the center of his chest.

"I don't care about your *name*. Who are you? What remnant do you hold? What are you doing with Nico's face?"

"I'm a shifter, a remnant of Mirth." He stumbled to his feet, retreating to the opposite side of the space. "And that's not my business to tell. He hires me to be his double, and that's all I know."

"Liar," I spat, but Regulus only crossed his arms. Determined to keep his lips sealed. My heart hammered in my chest, recalling the information the inspector slipped like a threat. I hadn't worried about it then, believing Nico was here with me. But if he had left, if this was more than just coincidence that he had required a body double the same night the Overseer was supposed to be assassinated . . .

No. Nothing was a coincidence with Nico. He was going to the

Capital to kill the highest-ranking official on the Isle—and he was going to get caught.

"You listen to me," I said quietly. Stepping off the bench, I approached him, daggers in both hands. "The inspector knows there is going to be an attempt on the Overseer's life tonight. Now, I am not a stupid woman, so do not lie to me and claim ignorance for the man you claim to work for. If Nico's agenda is to do just that, then he is in trouble, and we need to warn him."

He hesitated to answer, but his eyes widened, realizing something terrible. "Fucking saints, it's a trap."

"What was that?" I asked.

"We need to leave now, then. How long will this glint take effect?"

"A few minutes. I barely pricked you. I'll go get the carriage ready. Meet me outside when you're Nico again." I snatched the coat from the bench and threw it at him. "Try to make it fast. He already has a considerable lead on us."

"Doing the best I can," he drawled while holding a hand against his throat.

As soon as I stepped out of the alcove, I noticed Luther pacing casually around the steps. When he saw me, his eyes lit up. "Milla! I was just hanging about. I saw the curtains shut and I . . . Well, I didn't want to *disturb* anything." He tried to wink but ended up pinching both eyes shut at the same time.

"Luther, are you drunk already?" I asked.

He held a finger to his lips. "Don't tell boss."

Well, this was just perfect. Nico was in danger, and I was literally the only person who could help him, assuming his other cousins were similarly inebriated. "Nico is about to step out, so you might want to make yourself scarce. We're about to leave, actually."

"Oh, you are? And where are you going?" He grinned, brows rising.

Giver and Greed . . . Luther was usually so quiet and reserved, kept to himself. Alcohol made him meddlesome. "Not sure, probably East End. We'll see you in the morning."

I pushed by him toward the front doors, but Luther called out after me. "You kids have fun tonight! See you in the morning, lady boss."

I faked a smile and prayed he was right.

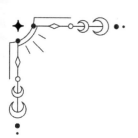
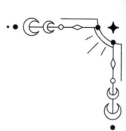

CHAPTER 33
CAMILLA

The quiet in the carriage was interrupted by the downpour of rain. Heavy taps against the hard top pulled me out of my thoughts—which were all of Nico. Where was he now? How would I explain how I knew about the tip? Would I even get to him in time to tell him? I tapped the glass to the driver on the other side and called for him to go faster. Wheels skidded on the wet cobbles, the carriage tipped occasionally, but I urged him to challenge the horses and the make of the car. Every second counted at this point when Nico already had nearly a thirty-minute head start.

I said, "The High Overseer's Mansion is deep in the Steam District. Behind rows of guardhouses, it's the most secure area in Lynchaven. Probably the whole Isle. How is Nico going to break in without getting caught?"

He nodded. "The mansion is heavily guarded, though it won't be so bad tonight since most of the Watch are in the Row. While the Districts are separated by gates, the mansion is isolated by a wall separating it from both Districts. Behind it is an embankment so large, it

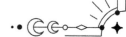

could hold the town square. There's no way around the back where the wall cuts off."

A weight of uncertainty burdened my shoulders as he described where we were to follow Nico. From his descriptions, I didn't understand how even a descendant as powerful as Nico could slip through such a highly monitored area. "How are we to get to him then?" I asked. "It sounds impossible to get close to the Overseer by your standards."

"That's because it is," Regulus said, "but Nico won't be taking the obvious route. Tell your driver to take us to 1435 Hollow Street in the Third Sector."

"But that's nowhere near the Capital!"

"Trust me."

I bit my cheek in debate. If he was wrong, I'd lose my chance to get to Nico in time. If he was right and I chose not to listen to him, the same ending played out. Either way, I'd put Nico's life into this stranger's hands who appeared indifferent about this entire situation.

I slid the grate and gave our driver the new address.

Regulus gave me a half smile. "You know, for two people who claim to have married for ambition, you both seem to care an awful lot about the other's well-being."

"How do you know about our deal?"

He licked his thin lips. "Who do you think Nicolai works for? Who do we all work for?"

I shook my head. "I don't know. I wager it must be someone of substantial rank. Someone like the Overseer or . . ." My heart sank behind my ribs. "The inspector."

"Ding, ding," Regulus smiled, but it was fake.

"Why?" I couldn't think of a single reason he'd work for a man he hates. Gavriel must have had something over his head to control him into committing such crimes.

"He got Nico and his cousin out of prison, and in exchange, he does his dirty work. I might have avoided Hightower under similar circumstances." His dark eyes shifted to the window.

The inspector was the one who was targeting the Overseer in the first place, and yet, he had arranged for Nico to be caught. He was going to tie up all his loose ends right before he took the high seat.

"Why would he keep this from me? Why didn't he trust me?" I didn't realize I had spoken out loud until the shifter in front of me sighed.

"I think he cares too much about what you think of him to tell you the truth."

"That doesn't make sense."

Regulus loosened the collar of his shirt and tugged it down low enough to show me a red mark already starting to bruise around his throat. "That is what Nico did to me when I made a joke about touching you."

"*Saints,*" I murmured. My own hand flew to my throat absent-mindedly. "Well, to be honest, you ended up better than the bleeder who threatened me a few weeks ago. That still looks like it was an unpleasant experience."

"Yeah," he said with raised brows. "I thought *this is it*. This is the day my mouth finally gets me killed. Thankfully, he still needed me as an alibi."

An alibi.

I shut my eyes; the realization sunk in my chest like a stone in deep water. Nico wanted everyone to look at him tonight because he needed a strong cover—not because it aided their perception of us. *Hells,* he was good at fooling me, and yet here I was still trying to save the conniving bastard.

Perhaps the shifter had a point. Perhaps I had taken an irrevocable step forward in our relationship without considering where it would lead. It would've been all too easy to let him go, get caught for a crime he *should* face the consequences for, and take his money to the bank while he was shipped back to prison. It would've been the easiest way out of our arrangement, the simplest plan to buy back my freedom—and the hardest decision I'd ever have to live with for the rest of my life.

My head rested against the cold window of the carriage. Maybe it wasn't a question of what I wanted when this was over, but what I couldn't live *without*. If I didn't get to Nico in time, I supposed I'd learn the answer to both those questions tonight.

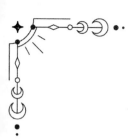
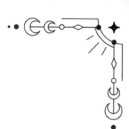

CHAPTER 34
NICOLAI

The apartment on Hollow was exactly as I'd left it a few weeks ago, and yet so much had changed since the General's assassination. I needed to be quick tonight. There was no room for error or mistresses. Just one last job, one last kill, and I was free. The quicker I completed this task, the sooner I could return, go back to a life of legitimate business and being honest with my family.

Not to mention that sleazy Mirth remnant was probably already taking advantage of my identity. Hopefully, I'd left Milla in a foul enough mood she wouldn't talk to my double for the rest of the night, though looking back, I could have been crueler. I *should* have been crueler. Even if she hated me for it, I should've made sure she was too hurt to let that man wearing my face touch her. Holding back had done her no favors.

I needed to be quick tonight—if only to get back to her.

A velvet drape concealed the mirror pushed in the corner of the bedroom. To anyone else, it was an insignificant oval-shaped mirror with opulent edges. Far more dated than the rest of the decorum, it stood out on its own. That, and the fact that the image reflected upon its surface was not of the one that stood on the other side, but of one beyond it.

Long before the overseers had been elected to govern the shared powers of the Inner Courts, the Isle was controlled by the three governors, each head of a third. Before the industrial advances of the train, they required a means of communication versus the slow route of a horse and messenger.

The mirrors had been a gift from the old kings of the Continent when the boats still ran between the lands, said to have been formed from shadows stolen from the void itself during Magrahel, the one day of the year when the veil between realms was the thinnest. Created by master darkthieves with old magic neglected over the years, the legend of the mirrors had been similarly forgotten.

Three mirrors from three vales to each governor over their Third. The Lowland mirror had been broken during transportation when a gale storm blew away part of the south coast. The Mez still had theirs stored away in an attic in the Overseer's mansion. The Upper Notch had lost their mirror years ago. The Watch, the Society, and the Inspector had searched high and low for the relic, but it was never found—because it was stolen.

The silver frame was inscribed with black lettering of an old language connected to the ancient practice of spinning shadows into portals.. It flickered awake at my presence, glowing an unnatural green as the face of the mirror rippled from the old magic thrumming like a heart beating somewhere beneath the surface.

Like it was a living being, alive and reactive to the life appearing before it. I hadn't used the mirror yet, had only been given vague instructions to use the portal like any other open doorway.

I reached out tentatively, touched the shadows, let them curl around my arm like they were clawing at my arm, begging for me to join them.

The mirror thrust me forward into darkness, spun from a place beyond death, where the pitch-black world was darker than a starless sky. I was both weightless and yet my bones were made of lead, still and yet passing swiftly through space, until this traveling realm inside the mirror finally settled into the shape of a long hallway, the edges of the world oddly bordered with walls and a ceiling and a tangible floor.

There was a circular space that stood in the center of three branching corridors—an intersection. One led to a dead end, the Lowland mirror. The other to an entrance at the end of another long hall. It occurred to me then that these mirrors weren't mirrors at all —but actual doorways. Connecting portals. A celestial road paved from the same stuff composing the void—the dead realm beyond this life that held every hell for every creature. The conception of this place intrigued me, but I had no time to study the shadows constructing this place and how they provided a traveling loophole through my own world.

I crossed the length of the corridor, the echo of my footfalls unclear and distant as if disconnected from my strides. Glancing back at the way I came, the mirror was a speck in the distance; somehow I'd walked a quarter of a league in a few steps. The idea rolled an uneasy chill down my spine, and I pressed through the second mirror, hoping the only time I'd ever return to this place was after I finalized this last mark.

There was no dusty attic.

The mirror had been moved, if the Summoner had truly believed its location to be stored away. I stood in the middle of a darkened sitting area. The fire in the hearth long gone cold, the only sound a distant ticking of a clock in the next room. A door separated the two.

But the moment I realized I stood out in the open, I ducked behind a settee, listening for any sound that would suggest company.

Nothing stirred, not even in the room beyond. I glanced around the area to gain a clue of where I had just landed. Worry stripped my armored confidence. If the mirror had been given away, if someone else had taken it from the Overseer, this would all be for nothing. I would not get another chance past this night to kill the man, nor would my foreman give me one.

It was his life or mine, and I'd learned with Milla that I was a selfish bastard.

The portraits on the wall settled my nerves some. The past four generations of High Overseers lined the wall. The current, Valentino, posed in a large, wooden frame hung above the hearth. The mirror was still in the mansion, but it had been moved. How recently was a question I wish could be answered.

It was the dead of night, mere hours from dawn. I stayed low, crouched on all fours, and shifted between shadows, passing through slices of moonlight that spilled through the open drapes. The door to the next room was wide-open. An odd discovery since most preferred to shut their doors in the winter to preserve the heat in the bedrooms.

But studying the peculiar wasn't part of my schedule, I had no downtime to assess the situation and react. The deep desire to get this done quickly pushed me onward, into the dark hanging like a shroud over the bedroom.

The only light came from the open entry, beaming like a spotlight over the four-poster bed on the opposite side of the room. My remnant was active here, no way to punish my power. It was almost too easy, like the Overseer invited me to kill him.

"I wondered when he'd send you."

My strides came to a stop. The gas lamps flickered alive to reveal the High Overseer, Vito Valentino, sitting on a tufted chair on the far right of the room wearing a night robe and velvet slippers. If he'd expected me, he didn't dress for a meeting with death, but at least I knew he wasn't hiding any weapons.

He slowly stood, groaning as his joints complained at the movement. "When the inspector pulled my usual guards for the night and sent them to that bleeder ball, I knew he was up to something."

I said nothing, only watched the Overseer slowly walk to a bar cart pushed against the wall and pour himself a double. He gestured with the glass to the chair nearest my position. "Sit with me a moment, before you kill me. Allow an old man one last drink." Eyeing his suggestion warily, he added, "I promise, I won't give you any resistance when it comes time."

"You won't fight me?" Slipping a dagger into my palm, I sat where his outstretched arm suggested. I wondered if the tremors shaking his hand were from fear or age, but the way he held himself implied he wasn't afraid at all. Instead, he seemed accepting of my presence here tonight.

He laughed and gestured to his thin frame. "Do I look like I'm in the shape to fight someone like you, the bloody hand that has killed a line of men leading straight to me? I knew Gavriel was coming for my position after Branwick's murder. His death was brushed under the rug too swiftly for him not to have been involved."

"And you did nothing to protect yourself?" I asked.

He swatted at the air, like the idea was nonsense. "I'm eighty years old. There's not much loyalty left for me these days. Everyone is always looking to have an influence in the rise of a younger, more ambitious leader. Can I ask you a question before you proceed?"

I shrugged. "Why not?"

He smiled and drained the rest of his drink. Before he could stand to his frail feet, I was at the bar cart, grabbing the dram to pour him another.

"Thank you," he said with a soft smile. "I wondered what the inspector has over you to make you do his dirty work?"

From the inner pocket of the lightweight stealth leathers, I took out the pictures. Flipped them open a final time for a final mark, to see if their familiarity meant anything to them. Valentino took them from my hands and laid them out in his palms, studying the faces of my mother and sister thoughtfully.

"Do you know who killed them?"

He looked up at me, as if comparing the features in my face to the ones in his hand, before handing them back to me. "The Attano murders over a decade ago. I remember them well."

His admittance was startling. I never thought the High Overseer nor anyone in a position of power cared about two less remnants in the city. "They were killed by Niners, an organization known to support you."

He shook his head. "They were not killed by Niners. Former Niners, perhaps, but after the killings, they were immediately kicked out."

The news sunk my heart beneath my ribs. "What do you mean?"

He leaned back and took another long sip. "The Clemontes were one of the Nine families who started the group. Three families from each of the three divisions of the Isle represent their territories. Can you think of the other two bloodlines powerful enough to run this city with influence alone?"

"The Marcheses and the Firenzes."

He nodded. "The Clemontes were removed, but since there was no evidence at the scene of the crime, we couldn't convict them. They denied involvement, and a vendetta wasn't enough to throw them in prison. Merely enough to run them out of the city."

"Where are they now?" My palms began to sweat inside the wrappings of my leather gloves.

"Some went north into the mining communities. Others never left," he slurred. "They changed their names since their reputation was ruined and they lost their steel empire to your fam—the Attanos." His eyes rolled lazily, locking on mine. "You should be looking for Hawthorn, not Clemonte."

The air in the room fell heavy, the realization crushing, pushing resistance against the beat of my heart as I came to terms with what the High Overseer insinuated. "Are you saying that Gavriel Hawthorn is really Gavriel Clemonte?"

His smile was sad. "The very same. I think you've been working for the very man you've been hunting."

Fire in the gas lamps flickered as my remnant primed in anger, the breeze flipped a book open on the coffee table between us, tossing aside the pages one by one. The inspector had been using me then, knowing I held a grudge against the Niners when it was *his* vengeance I claimed, not my own. Not that it would've mattered, anyway. I was too far gone into the inspector's plans to stop now. He had my future in his hands, could send me back to prison tomorrow if I defied him.

"You know something?" the Overseer murmured, swirling the amber drink around the glass. "I'd be worried if I were you."

"Why do you say that?"

"If Gavriel gets my seat . . . well, he won't need you anymore"—his gaze slid to me—"and you know far too much now to be that unnecessary to him. I know from experience."

The old man was right, no matter how much I hated to inwardly admit that. My throat was dry, words raspy as I asked him, "If I let you live, would you help me take him down?"

His face twisted in a grimace. "It's far too late to stop him now, Mr. Attano. You'd need an army."

"Maybe I'll get one," I said quietly. The glass rolled from his hands, cracking as it hit the rug with a dull thud. "Valentino?"

He didn't answer. His eyes were wide in an unfocused stare, lips parted and unmoving. The rest of him went just as still, from his shoulders to his fingertips, every inch between falling limp. I stood and lunged to the decanter on the cart, sniffing it, confirming my suspicions.

"Poison," I spat, returning the crystal to the cart. The clock on the wall struck the midnight hour, and—almost as if it were timed—the bedroom doors burst open. Members of the Watch filled the room, their guns aimed at my chest.

There were very few individuals who knew I'd be here tonight. The shifter, the Summoner, and most incriminating of all, the inspector. Valentino's suspicions had been spot-on. I'd fulfilled my purpose, and men in business this dark and cruel cared little for honoring their word or their bargains. Gavriel Clemonte Hawthorn had double crossed me, led me straight into a trap.

"*Fuck,*" I hissed through gnashed teeth.

"Put your hands where we can see them," one of the watchmen ordered. I didn't comply, and instead watched the group circle like vultures ready to pick apart a dead man.

"We got you now, Attano." The voice came from behind me just as a metal barrel was shoved into the small of my back. "And you better take a good look at that moon in the sky, cause it'll be the last time you see it for the rest of your saints-forsaken life."

There were at least seven guns pointed at me, from what I could see in my peripheral. "I'm not going back to Hightower," I muttered. I'd see Oblivion before I went back to that place.

"Oh yeah?" the man behind me mocked. "I'd say you're gonna go where we tell you."

I chuckled, flipped the blade in my left hand around my middle finger, which only made him press the gun deeper into the bend of my spine. "You and what remnant, officer?"

"Don't even think—"

Before he could finish his warning, the room spun with the wind of a turbulent thunderstorm. Rage primed my power, explosive in its form. Violent and disorienting, throwing furniture and grown men. I moved before the officer behind me was tossed into the wall. I organized the bedlam, forcing the air to push the broken furniture in front of me, forming a barricade around a corner.

It wouldn't hold them for long. Their bullets ripped through the upholstery even as I shoved the dressers, bed fragments, anything loose that I could manipulate to thicken this blockade. I needed time, I needed these men to run out of bullets, and—*saints*—I needed to get back to that mirror. I lay almost flat on the floor as they continued to unleash their ammo.

The shots ceased. I almost forgot my own gun, too preoccupied with holding them off to fire back. I slipped it from the holster, held it against my chest as I slowly rose to my feet even if I hadn't planned on using it. One more burst from the angry core thrumming inside my chest and these watchmen would be skewered on the coffee tables.

My remnant stroked the power in my bones like the air to a flame, each steady breath escaping my lips added to the pressure building between my fingertips. I gathered that energy, converging all I had into a ball in the center of my chest, leaving my hands trembling and my feet cold. My head ached from the shunting of my blood.

I was just about to release my wrath upon the room when the sound of shots had me hitting the floor again.

But these didn't come from the watchmen, obvious in their surprise and the shouts of conversation following.

"He's got backup! Shoot to kill."

"But it's a woman—"

My heart fell into my stomach. There was only one woman who would be insane enough to follow me here. The men outside my barricade focused their shots on the other side of the room, evident by the sound of bullets tearing apart the wall furthest from me.

"Milla!" I shouted for her, couldn't let go of the air in the room until I knew it was her.

"Nicolai, you are in so much trouble!"

Another shot fired from the watchmen, and Milla's foul mouth screamed a curse. I almost panicked, realizing she must be hurt, possibly hit by a bullet. My hands shook as the force of what I contained burned fire down my arms, across my back. But I couldn't let go of it now, or I'd risk impaling her as well.

"Nico!" she cried out for me. My remnant had never left my body so fast.

Wind sliced through the barricade like a falling knife, shoving the pile of broken furniture to either side where they splintered against the wainscoting. Two men were already on either side of the doorway leading out to the foyer, guns in hand, ready to infiltrate while she was hurt.

I burned through my remnant like a flame eating away at a wick, the explosive nature of my actions had only served to drain me fast, but I had enough for one last burst—something strong enough to use the rest of my remnant, something powerful enough to get us out of here.

But first, the witnesses needed to be removed. They had our names and our faces, would go straight to the inspector with them both and send the Watch on a hunt for Milla—and she couldn't be sent to Hightower. Not even with her heart of teeth and talons, her courage she wore like a chest piece of armor. That place would ruin her like it ruined me.

For that reason, I used every last ounce of power in my marrow, bending the air to snatch the sharp debris lining the floor and shooting it with a force that speared the wood straight through their backs and out their chests. The simple move had taken out four of them, one turned to face me, shooting off his gun. I raised a hand, stealing and holding the second until time stopped completely.

My bones began to pulse with pain, reaching the bottom of my remnant. I quickly pulled the man from the center of the room and stood him in front of his own bullet, letting go of the second to let the shot rip through his chest. A rush of relief eased the burden in my flesh as I let go of the power.

The last two watchmen were in the parlor with Milla, but their guns were silent.

I lunged through the doorway. One of them held Milla, his arm wrapped around her throat in a suffocating vice, the other sent a fist into her stomach, speeding up the process. The sight made the scraps left of my magic gather into a vengeful wrath, enough of it left to steal the very breath from both their chests.

"Release her," I hissed. The watchman that bound her with his body quickly let her go to reach for his own throat, which collapsed as if crushed by an invisible fist. Both staggered to the floor, but Milla charged for me as soon as she was free, her eyes wide.

"Milla, what—"

"Get down!"

I ducked, trusting her too much now to second guess her orders. There was a blur of satin and beaded skirt, the skim of the fabric over my shoulders as she leapt over me, colliding with a weight behind me. I looked back to see she had tackled a watchman to the ground.

A red blade—a Niner blade—in his grip.

Milla had both arms around his forearms, pushing the hilt of the blade into his chest. I lunged for them, but the watchman rolled out of my reach until they'd swapped positions. Milla laid on her back, the tip of the blade dug into the center of her chest where the neckline of her dress fell low.

"Milla!" I screamed as if it could do something. She might not have a remnant to be turned against her, but the piercing knife could still kill her.

The serpent around her arm slithered to life, diving between her breasts where the tip of the blade pierced her skin.

She screamed in agony. The sound moved something in my chest —my heart—shattering it until I was a heartless, soulless thing. It shed any humanity in my body, left me with nothing but anger and retaliation, no purpose beyond destroying whatever caused her pain.

I had no weapons left in my hands. I didn't need them. I lunged, my false hand finding the watchman's face, digging each metal digit into an orifice of his face until his screams replaced hers. My remnant was dangerously drained, but it didn't take much to extend the daggers built within my false hand and let them slip into his head. My arm shook, using what little strength I had left to rip them out and leave him faceless.

Blood soaked the carpet where it leaked from him, dripping from the metal tubes of my false hand, from my gloved one. My breath returned in gasps, filling my chest with the slow return of reality. I'd shifted into someone I'd never met before, a thoughtless reaction to the pain of the person I cared more about than anything in this world.

"Milla," I gasped. The dagger was in her hand, as if she had pulled it from her chest, but there was no blood from the insertion site. Instead, black liquid bubbled from the spot, seeped into the velvet bodice. Her familiar was gone.

"Nico," she whimpered. I was there, picking her head off the tile and propping her up into my lap. She was burning up. Sweat beaded on her forehead and upper lip. Tremors quaked her fingers, gradually spreading up her arms until her entire body was afflicted with violent shivers.

"Milla, what's going on?" The fear returned. This shouldn't be happening. She said she had no remnant, had said so under the Vex Veritas. The poison from the blade shouldn't be affecting her at all. Unless . . . unless she didn't know.

"My hands," she said weakly. I pulled off her gloves and couldn't help the curse that left my lips. They were solid black, the veins in her arms filled with ink, filling her fingers and hands. I followed the lines, tracking them to the spot on her back that had been given to her by the voidwalker.

"Does it hurt, Milla?" I asked, feeling helpless. "Are you in pain?" I remembered my mother's wails as the cursed blade poisoned her remnant. Anna had been small, so the blade's power had taken her blessedly quicker. It hadn't affected either of them like this, however.

"Not pain," she mumbled, eyes fluttering open to look at me. There was still color to them, golden brown and beautiful, despite the terror filling them.

Her voice fell into a whisper. "Not pain. *Power.*" Her eyes slammed shut, and her mouth opened to rip a cry into the world that blew the windows out. Glass shattered, the fire died in the gas lamps as they broke and were exposed to a turbulent breeze as my own remnant pulsed with panic. The mirror had been destroyed in the disarray.

A group of watchmen appeared in the doorway, checking on the trap that had ultimately backfired against them. They took one look at Milla's hands, the room, their disfigured colleagues, their eyes

ALEXIS L. MENARD

widening with every detail before turning on their heels and retreating back down the stairs.

"You need to go," she said. "I . . . I can't control it. It's too much."

"I'm not leaving you."

"I don't want to hurt you." Tears leaked down her cheeks.

"And I don't care. I won't leave you like this. I'm going to help you." It was a lie, one I didn't know if I could make true. If she was coming into a great load of power, I might not be able to stop anything priming in her spirit now.

I pulled her close anyway, hoping to stroke it down, calm her and her remnant until it was small enough to handle on her own. My fingers skimmed the sheath around her thigh, and I cursed myself for not thinking of it sooner.

I might not be able to stop her, but a bit of science could.

"Milla," I warned her, "this might hurt for a second."

"What are you—*ahh!*"

I sunk a blue tinged blade into the meaty side of her thigh, where the glint would have the quickest effect. Almost immediately, her body relaxed against mine, her head sunk into the curve of my shoulder as the ink in her hands receded into her veins and back into the mark on her spine. Her chest heaved with gasping breaths, body still shaking, but not nearly as fierce as before.

"I . . . I feel better," she said, though her eyes were still shut.

"Good." Relief eased my heart of the anxious squeeze around it, but we were far from safe yet. I needed to get us both out of here before the Watch returned. Worse, they had seen our faces, knew exactly who was responsible for this scene and the death of the Overseer still slumped somewhere in the bedroom. The inspector had his evidence. He'd come for us sooner or later.

Her warm fingers slipped around my neck as she buried her face into the cowl around my throat. "What's happening to me?"

"Well, for starters," I said, standing with her still in my arms, "you're a descendant. That kind of power could only come from a remnant."

She shook her head. "Descendant of what?"

I didn't answer her because I couldn't.

Getting home through the mirror was out of the question. The obvious way was too full of people who wanted to arrest us—or worse. I strode to the wall of broken windows, discovering we were on the third floor with nothing but a stone ledge and a courtyard below us, overlooking the back of the manor. The yard was built on a small embankment. A canal, one of the hundred or so that ran through the city, lined the opposite side and carried the sewage of the Basin all the way to the tunnels beneath the city—out into the Ada.

"The pipes," I spoke my plan out loud as it developed. "You can go through the sewage pipes and follow them home. If you follow the streets, you'll come out right near the river. A carriage will be waiting at the end of the bridge."

"Nico—"

"The ground is soft enough from last night's rain that it shouldn't hurt jumping from this high."

"Nico, look at me." She pulled my chin to look at her face, and I was locked out of my thoughts for a moment when her gaze stole mine. "I hope you don't expect me to go without you. We're a package deal now. Where you go, I go. Till death parts us."

Part of me had hoped she'd say that. The more prevailing half cursed her for being so stubborn. I set her back on her feet, feeling the strength return in her body, but kept her close. The morning draft tore at the stray hairs that had pulled from her pins, catching the dew on the breeze.

"They'll be looking for the both of us. If they find me here, that might appease the Watch enough to forget you. I'm giving you a way out of this, Milla."

She shook her head and smiled. "You won't get rid of me that easily, Attano. You have successfully corrupted me."

In the span of a single second, I realized three things: I should've told her about the inspector a long time ago. I would do anything to keep her out of his hands. And, most dominant of all those developments, I was hopelessly falling for my wife.

But could an act of valiance now erase a multitude of deceitful ones? I supposed we'd find out together.

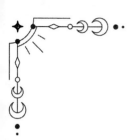
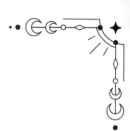

CHAPTER 35
CAMILLA

Ten bloody minutes.

That was all the hot water the pipes offered in East End. I stood in the bathroom doorway, holding the spare clothes I had left in my trunk when we never returned weeks ago. Nico had already stripped down to his pants, leaving his soiled clothes at the back door and far from sniffing range.

He glanced at me from where he leaned over the sink, guns and blades laid out across the vanity. "You're tracking mud everywhere, Milla. For saint's sake, just take off the dress."

"I can't," I mumbled. "I'm not wearing anything underneath." His grip tightened around the porcelain edge, and I shrugged in defense. "I mean look at this bodice. The neckline on this dress is ridiculous."

"I thought it flattered you well last night."

"So much you were trying to get me out of it."

"Still a top priority." He smirked, eyes traveling the length of my

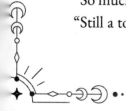

bare skin as if he could see straight through the fabric, anyway. "How are you feeling without your familiar?"

My hand fell to the spot the crimson blade stabbed me, destroying the serpent with its strange science. "I can feel the glint beginning to wear off, but my remnant isn't as loud as it was before. Before it was overwhelming, like I'd plunged myself into a pool of power. Now it just feels like . . . like a whisper instead of a shout. It's still there, but not consuming."

It was uncomfortable even discussing the reality of having a remnant myself and highly disturbing since neither of us knew what I was descended from. Thankfully, my birthday was just around the corner, and my records would be officially available for my review. Perhaps then I could finally get some answers for the both of us.

He nodded like I had somehow made sense. "Good. That's how you're supposed to feel. Though I might keep your blades nearby until we can get you more glint tabs."

I crossed my arms, uselessly trying to keep face and pretend like none of this bothered me. "Whatever, just hurry up and take your bath first. We can split the time."

He scoffed and pushed off the sink, making his way to the free-standing tub shoved between the narrow walls. "I think I deserve a full ten minutes after carrying you for an hour through the sewers under the Capital backstreets. If you want to cut your time, go for it. We can either share, or you can freeze, but I'm utilizing all the hot water I can."

Of course, he was. It was impossible to argue against his claim, and I was already on the verge of doing anything for that bath. Desperate times called for desperate exceptions. "You promise you won't look?"

"Do you promise *you* won't look?"

I frowned. "Your modesty is unconvincing."

336

"On the contrary. I'm very shy." With his back turned to me, he ripped his belt from his waist with one hand and dropped his pants. I silently sucked a breath in awe of him, appreciating and absorbing the details of his backside before my shame forced me to avert my gaze. He was perfect, as the fit of his custom suits had already hinted. From his broad shoulders, the lines that corded his back with lean muscle, the smooth slope of his back that tapered to a thin waist, tempting me to drag my gaze lower . . .

"Fuck me," I muttered beneath a breath.

He looked over his shoulder, still wearing that despicable grin. "What was that?"

"Nothing," I sighed. "Before you start the water, could you at least unlace the back of my bodice?"

"Absolutely."

He sounded delighted I'd even asked. I turned before I could see the front of his naked body, something telling me I'd have a much harder time fighting my gaze which disobeyed my determination.

He fumbled with the straps for a few seconds, huffing a breath in frustration when he realized the sophistication of such a gown. In the corner of my eye, he snatched a blade from the vanity, the only warning I received before he slashed through the ties.

"Nico!" I shrieked, slamming my arms around the loose bodice before it fell to the floor from the weight of my skirts.

He leaned forward to murmur in my ear, voice coarse as sand between my fingers. "I'll buy you another one. Drop the dress, Milla. I won't look until you beg me to."

I didn't beg. I'd never do such a thing for a man's attention, but Nico had a way of bringing me out of my comfort zone, pushing me beyond my boundaries to try all the things I *didn't* do. Showed me all the ways I could change and grow while still committing to my true self.

When the sound of water rushing through the pipes in the walls groaned, I dropped the filthy dress and stepped out of the pile, feeling lighter than I had with the caking mud weighing me down. He was already in the tub, his back to me as he faced the shower head, soaking up the first drops of hot water, tan skin glistening in the light from the single candle on the vanity.

He had removed his false hand as well, and it laid idle for him in a chair next to the bath. It was the first time I'd seen him without it, and yet was no less the man I'd come to befriend.

I followed him less reluctantly than I'd been a moment ago. Steam quickly filled the room with a cloud of heat. Nico was quick with the soap, handing me the bar as he lubricated his chest. He sucked a breath behind me and released it with a groan, a sound of suppressed pain.

"Are you alright?" I asked, looking over my shoulder slightly to find him holding his side. Nico nodded, but tension knotted his shoulders as the hot water burned a grazing wound on his side. Blood from various men dripped from the stains on his hand, coloring the bottom of the white tub a pinkish red.

"I can dress it for you when you're done. Just until you can see a proper healer."

"I'd appreciate that, Milla." His breath hitched. "You can have the water now. I'll get out."

He passed a hand through the length of his hair, squeezing out the water, about to step over the rim when I touched his arm.

"Wait." *Please, don't leave yet.* The rest of the command on the tip of my tongue, waiting to be released if a single word wasn't enough to convince him.

Nico went utterly still, chin shifting an inch as if fighting the impulse to look at me. I draped my hand over the curve of his shoulder, hiding behind his stature. "You missed your back," I told him.

Without waiting for a denial or an excuse, I rubbed the bar between my fingers, using my bare hands to slather his skin, reach the places he couldn't with long, explorative ministrations.

His muscles bunched beneath my perusal at first, and I noted the way his breath filled his chest differently. The way it shifted from sharp breaths to lengthy, bliss-filled exhales. Each one shuddered beneath my fingertips as I cruised each crest and valley composing his broad back. It took a second to realize some of them weren't muscle, but scars.

"How did you . . ." I started. They felt so similar to my own. Thick, raised flesh swathed over the back of his shoulder, spreading down his left arm. I'd never noticed them because of the ink painted across his skin, but now the evidence was plain to my touch.

"No," I murmured, touching my own where the flames had licked me seven years ago. "No, that's not possible."

He said nothing; the only sound was the screech of the feeble shower head as it sputtered the last warm drops. His lack of reassurance sent my thoughts spiraling. My fingers trailed to the end of his arm, where it had been sliced at the elbow. It was so small a chance . . . so impossibly coincidental.

"But it was you," I whispered out loud. "You pulled me out of the burning car."

"Milla, I can explain," he rasped.

My hands fell from his back. "Why didn't you tell me?"

He turned slowly, inch by inch as if waiting for me to stop him. I didn't. Not until I could see every gloriously perfect part of him. Steam curled off his skin, drops of water falling from his unkempt hair, tracing the edges of his sharp jaw to join the sheen across his chest, falling from the slope of his nose.

"I didn't want you to think you owed me," he said quietly. "You already compared me to your family once, I didn't want you to feel like you had to right a wrong that was never yours."

He thought I would have blamed myself. If there hadn't been a reason for me to be on that train, his family wouldn't have bombed it, wouldn't have given him a reason to save me. There would've been no opportunity for him to be sent to Hightower.

I dropped the soap and left him in the shower, grabbing a thick white towel and wrapping it around my chest before fleeing the bathroom.

"Milla, wait!" he called behind me, but I was already at the stairs, running toward the only bedroom in the flat. I slammed the door shut just as he made it to the landing, thankful to gain some space, some privacy to let my heart catch up with my thoughts.

I leaned against the thin door, felt a thud shudder the hollow wood as Nico did the same. "Milla, don't do this. Let me in."

"I need a moment." More than that, though, I needed an explanation. Aramis never said anything about the person who saved me. It was always a random, brave civilian who dove into the flames and pulled me out. Never had he mentioned a bender, an *Attano*. Never had he admitted he had the same man who saved me thrown into Hightower for being guilty of nothing but showing compassion.

Saints, no wonder he hated my brothers so much. They knew the truth and looked the other way. They condemned a man—a boy for retaliation over something that had never been Nico's fault. A rivalry that had nothing to do with any of us.

I flung the door open, and Nico nearly toppled into the room from the loss of its support.

"Do you regret it?" I asked. It was an understandable sentiment. He had lost his father, been sent to a prison worse than Oblivion, wasted away for a handful of years for a split-second decision.

"Regret it?" he spat, like the word defiled his mouth.

He took a step into the room, cornering me against the wooden dresser. In his rush to chase after me, he'd thrown a towel around his waist, but his body still dripped bathwater all over the threadbare rug. "You think I regret saving you?"

"Don't you?" I whispered. "You're reminded every day of what came from it." My hand took his false one and threaded my fingers between the air-filled tubes.

"I am reminded every day what happens when we let the past determine our decisions," he said more gently. "The only thing that gave me this hand, Milla, was my father's blind vengeance. He bombed that car trying to get back at your family for a crime they didn't commit, and I had to suffer for his choices. I don't blame my father for what he did. I understand, and I probably shouldn't have been on that train in the first place, but I'll be damned before I let you think you had anything to do with my misfortunes."

Nico pressed our joined hands to his chest. "Milla, when I pulled you out, I didn't even know if you had survived. You inhaled so much smoke, you were already unconscious by the time I got to you, and your brother dragged me away too quickly to see for myself."

He rested my palm against his chest as he reached for my neck, wrapped it softly around my nape while nestling his thumb into the column of my throat. I was painfully aware of each digit, the coarseness of his fingertips. "Every day I sat in Hightower, I prayed to whatever divine wove the fates of our lives. I hoped that the girl in the train car hadn't perished. Your name was the first I thought of when I walked out of that prison."

His grip around my neck tightened, just enough to make my heart lurch. "I was satisfied, learning you had lived—at peace even, with my choice to have saved you at the expense of my freedom. I was fine with the fact that the spoiled little Marchese heiress was safe in her tower over the Steam District. So imagine my frustration when a beautiful woman comes into my pub and hikes up her dress to reveal she's the same girl I've been trying to forget about every day for the last seven years of my life."

I could hardly breathe. Perhaps it was the steam still rising from his skin or the heat in his eyes—the way they followed his hand as it smoothed over my wet skin as my chest filled with a suck of air, desperate and hungry. I covered his hand with my own, guiding him to the edge of my towel, shattering my thoughts word for word.

Nico continued without missing a beat. "And not only did she turn out to be a fucking Marchese, a name I once hated more than anything else on this Isle, she had to make it worse by being so unbelievably perfect. The object of all my frustrations and desires, the one I can't go an hour without thinking about. Tell me, Milla, am I supposed to regret you now? After all we've been through, tell me none of it was worth finding each other."

My mouth sealed shut, unable to find the words.

"I would do it all again," he said in the absence of my denial. "I would run through fire and burn for you. I would lose arm and leg and limb. I'd do it all over, knowing what would happen to me, if it meant eventually having you as I do now. Milla, I don't regret anything about you but this," he spoke in a strained voice, as if holding back a river of temptation, "that now that I finally have you, I must give you up."

"Why?" The question claimed a hundred different forms. Why did he have to give me up? Why did he regret it? Why did this feel so good if it had to end?

The confusion was plain on his face as his brows kissed. "I thought you wanted to get out of this?"

On the contrary, I *never* wanted to get out of this. Not his arms, not his touch, not this room. But I had done something unforgivable without asking him first, and I had no idea how he'd react, learning that I'd taken the security of my future into my own hands at the risk of his own. "Nico, I need to tell you something."

His forehead pressed against my hairline while his hand blessedly gave the rest of my body more attention. "What is it?"

A palm gripped my backside, squeezing it through the towel and stirring a heat between my legs as his body towered over me. "I . . ." Couldn't think of the rest of the sentence. My mind liquified with my limbs as he stepped closer, caging me against the empty dresser until I bent. My grip on the towel faltered and the cover slipped an inch, drawing his gaze.

Grey eyes widened. "You haven't said you wanted me the entire six weeks we've been together. Not a single compliment, needy touch, wandering eye, nothing. You've proven through your actions that you care, otherwise you wouldn't have negotiated with Sabina or followed me into the home of a mark. But Milla, you don't have to earn my affection. If you want me, then say so."

"I don't know how," I admitted. Could he not see the way I looked at him, the way my breath quickened, how my skin peppered with chills as his eyes took in my wet body? Did my touch not trace the letters of longing across his skin, betray the password to the heart I kept locked away?

"It's just three words. Just say them, and I'm yours." His false hand lifted my own to his cheek, and he kissed the inside of my forearm. "Hells, I already am."

"What if those words aren't enough?"

His stare lifted to meet mine, peering through drops of bathwater that dripped in the shriveling space between us. "Then tell me I'm enough, Milla."

"Of course, you are." My voice firm and certain as steel. "You're more than that, though. You're . . ."

I struggled to articulate the rest. How could I possibly tell him I wanted him more than what my actions spoke for me tonight? There was nothing I wouldn't do for him now. I knew that. I just didn't know how to put everything I *felt* into mere *words*. There were very few that could articulate just what he'd come to mean to me. Language itself seemed inadequate for the task.

"I'm what?"

My gaze fell to his bare chest as it rose and fell in a frantic rhythm, to that symbol inked above his heart. Heat flooded my cheeks, but I didn't look away or hide the way my truth left me exposed and vulnerable, giving him the ability to reject and hurt or laugh at me.

There was risk in all business, even that of the heart.

"You once asked me why I let my brothers treat me so terribly when I had no problem putting you in your place. It's because you make me feel safe enough to do so. I know that with you, I can say exactly how I feel, what's on my mind, and you won't ever hold it against me. With you I can speak my mind, I can be myself no matter how ugly that is and even if you get angry, you don't stay that way. I can trust you'll still be there for me, that you won't shut me away. You have made me feel safe for the first time in my life."

"Milla—"

"I'm not done." I slid my fingers over his lips to shut him up. "Your safety has expanded the boundaries that used to contain me. A safe house, a freezing train car, beneath the city in a tunnel of sewage, no matter where we are, I'm always home when I am with you. Now, I'm navigating this new freedom you've given me, and I'm bound to get it wrong more often than right. But I will work at it if you are willing to wait for me. Because I want to feel like this every day. I want you, Nico."

The knuckles of his false hand skimmed the line of my collarbone, resting beneath it. He took my hand and pressed it over those interwoven circles, where his skin was warm and silky over solid muscle. It shook a bit as he spoke. "I've spent nearly a decade now trying to fix the past, but for the first time since I lost my family, I think about the future—a future with *you*. I thought my heart and my head were too broken to care for anyone, that this hole in my existence could only be filled with retribution and power.

"Now there is a weight there, and it gets heavy when you are gone. You are what I want every morning when I wake, every need of my flesh, every dream when I close my eyes."

"What about the contract?" I asked, breathless from his confession.

"Fuck it. I've fallen hard for you Camilla Mercy Marchese-Attano. I don't need a piece of paper to tell me or anyone else you have my name and my heart and the rest of my life. You are mine, and I am wholly and irrevocably yours."

My heart began to beat erratically from a mix of excitement, lust, and an unfamiliar fear. The kind that suddenly has something to lose, something the world can take that I cannot replace. It makes this moment, the feel of his hard body beneath my palms, the smile tipping his lips even sweeter—more valuable.

I found the rest of my words much easier this time. "I'll have you tonight, Nico. In this bed"—I tugged the top of his towel still tucked around his waist until it fell to the floor—"without this."

"Resorting back to those evil plans of yours?" His voice was strained.

"The most wicked,"

His lips crashed onto mine with startling pressure, his tongue spearing and claiming. Wanting and reverence behind every stroke of his touch as he ripped the towel from my body and clamped his hands around my waist. My arms wrapped around his neck, pulled him close to rub my breasts against his chest.

His tight grip dove low and lifted me, gently placing my backside

345

on top of the dresser to wrap my legs around his waist. He broke from my mouth for a breath to rake his gaze over my body, lingering where his erection pressed against my center, already collecting the wetness pooling between my legs at the sight of us together.

"Beautiful," he whispered into the bend of my throat. "May I touch you?"

"You're already touching me." I pushed my hips along his length, drawing a low sound from his chest. Nico braced a metal hand on the mirror behind me, and I thought I heard it shatter. Every muscle in his back bunched, straining as if holding back the accumulating force of all his wants.

"I mean *really* touch you." His opposite hand pinched my waist before skating down my hip, getting closer to the apex of all my furious desires. My knees fell wider in silent consent, my cooperation all the approval he needed before his warm fingers slipped between us.

His thumb pressed a pleasure point that sent my back arching, my hands grasping for his shoulders. The smallest ministrations over my sex drew a cry from my lips, a long groan of approval from his chest.

"You're about to find out what it truly means to be mine, Milla. I'm going to claim you first with my fingers, then with my cock. And when I'm finished with you, a contract won't mean shit. You'll belong to me the only way that matters."

"And what way is that?" I asked between hungry breaths.

A finger plunged inside me, and my thoughts gave way to delirium. My head fell back, hitting the mirror just as he pushed in a second. His false hand gripped a fistful of wet hair and snapped my head back in front of his, so I stared into stormy, violent eyes.

"Your heart."

"It's yours," I murmured through the haze of pleasure. His

dexterity was thoroughly impressive. The curl of his fingers inside me as his thumb continued to make lazy circles freed every confession I kept locked away. He kissed me hard again, his tongue incessant as it curled into my mouth. It rolled to the motion of his fingers, and I realized I wanted that talented tongue elsewhere. Downward, deeper, and desperately.

I pulled him back by his hair, gasping for breath. "Nico, I'm not . . . I don't know how to put some desires into words."

"Your experience doesn't matter, Milla. It's very simple. Tell me where you want my hands, my mouth, or my cock." His fingers curled inside me, hitting a spot I didn't know existed, and my vocabulary was reduced to his name and a handful of foul words. My hips lifted, grinding deeper into his hand.

"*Ah*," he smiled, "that's where you like it."

His mouth went to my throat, nipping my skin between his teeth as he made a line of marks with his mouth down my body until he reached my hips. He knelt in front of the dresser, one hand gripping the underside of my thigh as his other remained stroking my center, never missing a beat, never pausing his worshipful touch.

Nico stared at me until I squirmed at the vulnerable position. "Every inch of you is so saints-damned desirable, Milla." His wicked mouth stopped talking enough to *lick*, practically splitting me in half with his tongue.

I nearly broke as he pressed his lips along my center and sucked. It took what little control I had left to squeeze my inner walls, to remain on the edge of this cliff only moments away from falling and breaking apart. Sensation beat me down like a high tide, drowning all my nerves in a hot pool of pleasure.

"*Fuck*, you taste even better."

"Such a versatile word," I gasped, my fingers still threaded into his hair. "You've yet to use it the right way."

The work of his mouth finally stopped just long enough to ask, "How is that?"

I pulled his head back by his hair, canting his face to look up at me. "I want you to fuck me, Nico."

He stood quickly, lips wet with my desire. I ached from the loss of him, more desperate than ever to feel him inside me. His fingers dug into my backside and pulled me close around his waist. I thought he'd take me right there and then. But he only guided my arms around his neck, kissed me until we were sealed together.

"Let me take you to bed then, if you're sure."

"I'm sure," I said with no hesitation. I'd never been so adamant about anything in my life. I wanted Nicolai Attano in every way. His body, his name, his heart, I wanted from him. I wanted *everything*. Far more than I deserved, and yet no less than he was willing to give. We fell on the bed, a tangle of limbs and fevered kisses atop the wrinkled sheets.

He shoved me to my back, hips pinning me to the bed to stroke his erection between my legs in a question. I reached between us, taking his thick cock between my fingers. He was a delicious contradiction, soft skin over a growing hardness. A nervous shudder ran down my spine, worried I might not be able to take him—anxious to find out.

He remained utterly still as I stroked his length, leaving him tense all over and his breath a shaken exhale. Nico let me explore him, and I was an eager witness, learning the right movements of my fingers over his cock to pull the addictingly savage sounds from his chest.

"How does this feel?" I asked. His eyes glazed over, leaving me little reaction to assess my performance.

"You're perfect," he rasped, hips thrusting against the motion of my hands, pushing me deeper into the sheets. His head dipped to swirl a hot tongue around the peak of my breast, sucking the bud into his mouth.

He was oblivious to the way his praise made me feel, like I was something holy to be revered. The way his mouth adored my body like his own personal idol, devoted to worshiping every inch of my skin. He had successfully wound me up, coiled a tension in my core so tight it was moments from springing. The foreplay had been too much, and I was desperate for relief. The way his cock twitched in my hands, the way it swelled with every stroke, I knew he felt similarly.

"Milla," he growled. The muscles in his neck were taut as a bowstring. "If you don't put my cock inside you soon, I'm going to spill all over you."

If he meant that as a threat, it wasn't received as one. The problem was, I didn't know *where* I wanted him. My mouth so I could taste him, or between my legs so I could ride him. I wanted to please him as much as he wanted to please me. I wanted that praise, his heavy breaths, those deep moans that my body pulled from him.

I guided the tip of his shaft between my legs and gently stroked myself, chasing the trouble he started. "Will you do something for me?" I asked, my voice suddenly small and unsure.

"Anything," he breathed.

I let go, but he kept himself pressed against my entrance while I grabbed his false hand and brought it to my throat. His eyes widened when he realized what I wanted. "You trust me, Milla?"

I nodded, arched into the cool metal wrapping my neck. "Please."

His grip tightened, and my heart was giddy with anticipation. "We'll go easy the first time. If it gets too much, just tap my arm. Alright?"

"I'm not made of glass, Nico," I said with a grin. "You said you'd give me what I—" My words were stolen with the breath he took. His remnant alive inside me, pushing the last bit of air from my lungs, sucked between my lips with a driving kiss. When he pulled back, he thrust his cock inside me at last.

"Spoiled little heiress," he hissed above me. My view of him already started to blur as tears welled in my eyes. "Whatever you want, princess. The heart in your chest, the air in your lungs, I'll take whatever you offer me, and I won't regret it. I never do."

My jaw worked as I tried to cry out from the bullets of pleasure ripping through me. My chest burned and tightened, and I could only watch as Nico pushed into me, staring at the place we connected. Softly at first, tenderly, as if stretching me out, feeling the boundaries of my inner walls and pushing them further. After a few moments he gave me some air, and I gulped it down like I'd just come up from drowning.

"Seven hells, Milla. You feel so good," he groaned. A thumb stroked the hollow edge of my throat. He pulled out and left me empty, almost hurting from his absence. "Are you alright? Was that too much?"

I writhed against the sheets, wrapping my legs around his waist to settle back onto his cock. "Don't stop," I pleaded while arching my neck into his hand. "Don't hold back."

He didn't hesitate this time, slamming into me over and over again, gripping my throat with the kind of pressure I demanded. I reached for purchase, clawing the sheets, his hair, settling on his back, his matching scars. The air waned in my chest and left me dizzy in the head, pushing me further toward an unrelenting climax. Nico's pace turned frenzied and much harder this time, as if knowing by the pulse against his metal thumb that I was so close. And with his hand around my throat, I couldn't see anything beyond those eyes of liquid smoke.

350

"That's right. Eyes on me, princess."

I couldn't look away, even if I wanted to. He was my ruler and world and wicked purpose all in one.

Just as the borders of his face started to blacken, he pushed me over the edge with one last thrust. My walls clamped down around him, and a gulp of sweet air rushed to meet the fire filling the hollow of my bones, shaking my ribs with an anguished moan. I gasped, catching my breath to slow my heart, which was beating so fast I thought it might burst. I couldn't move, completely unraveled beneath him and yet more whole than I'd ever felt in my life.

Nico's hand fell to my breast, dragging a calloused palm over a highly sensitive peak and squeezed. His mouth took in the other, rolling a hot tongue over my nipple. A metal hand latched on my thigh, holding me down as he drove deeper than ever, impossibly more. My climax still shuddered through my hips as I felt him pulse inside me, his curses muffled as he moaned into my hair.

He pumped into me a few more times, whispering my name as he spilled into me. Our bodies contracted together; our breaths fell along with the race between our hearts. We slowed until the immersive waves of pleasure were smaller swells, and when Nico looked at me without the haze of lust, there was only unyielding adoration left.

From this close, in the light of the gas lamps, I realized his eyes weren't grey at all, but the palest of blues.

"And to think," I said between breaths, "we could've been doing that for six weeks."

A deep hum shook his chest as he dipped his head to rest in the curve of my shoulder. "To be fair, I tried."

"You might need to work on your pitch, then, because I don't remember you *ever* trying to do that." I sighed as he slipped out of me and rested his hips on mine. With his length pressing against my stomach, the heat returned to my core. I had just recovered from a trip over the edge, and I was ready to fall all over again.

"Camilla," he whispered again. "Whatever you want, and I'll give it to you. I'll lay this world at your feet if you ask it of me." He pushed off, gone for a moment, reaching to grab a towel off the floor to clean the mess he made between my legs.

I smiled and curled into his side when he finished, stealing a fraction of his warmth. My list of wants were now suddenly very small. "I want to sleep," I told him. "Then, I want to find out what I am."

"Sleep," he yawned, eyes fluttering shut. "Then chaos."

Chaos.

The word was a whisper spoken in a fever dream as I fell into the void of sleep.

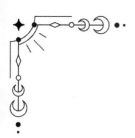
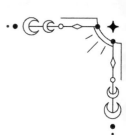

CHAPTER 36
CAMILLA

G rey light spilled through the canvas curtains, rousing us awake. The night had tempered our troubles, hid them away in the darkness behind the stars. Now day had come, and the hour to face the consequences of the night's events approached with the rising dawn. We lingered in bed long after the sunrise, holding onto this perfect moment as long as possible, until the day would finally drag us out.

What do these mean?" I traced the three woven circles tattooed on his chest with my finger.

He took a bliss-filled breath, stroking the curve of my hip as I filled the space beside him. "One circle represents what I want. The second is for what I need—safety, security, my family, things like that. The third"—he pinched my side—"is for my dreams. All my aspirations, my wildest fantasies. Some of the circles overlap; some things fit in multiple categories. But the center circle, where they all converge, that is where my purpose lies."

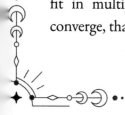

My hands swept over the symbol as I peered up at him. "And which circle do I belong in, Nico?"

His smile revealed both dimples. "You've moved around a bit. At first, you were a want. Saints, I wanted you so badly after our first dance, I wanted to take you upstairs and make you mine that night. I've wanted you every day since."

Heat pooled in my belly, and I swallowed down a flame. "You said you didn't on the Veritas, but I heard you throwing up."

He nodded. "I lied. I lied to you and to myself because you called us a mistake, and I wanted to believe it." He shifted to lay on his side, facing me. "After I learned your name, you were a way I could protect my family, something I needed, and you shifted into that overlap. But as I've gotten to learn everything about you, Milla, you've moved once again."

"Where am I now?" I asked.

"You're my dream." He grabbed my perusing hand in his. "You're the center of all my circles."

Tears burned my eyes. He was perfect. So absolutely right, I could never imagine calling him a mistake ever again. "You're in the center of mine too."

He pulled me in and kissed me, lingered in the shared space to speak against my lips. "I wish we could stay here all morning. I wish I could be inside you, from dusk till dawn."

Damn these wishes and wants. "What's stopping you?"

He sat up slowly, the blankets pooling around his waist. "I've got to get ahead of the trouble I've gotten us both into." Nico rolled on top of me, the sheets separating us improperly, before he leaned down and placed a whisper kiss to my lips. "I'm going to take back this city, Milla, so that we can both walk the streets again without looking behind us."

"You'll always have an enemy if you have something worth taking, Nico."

He grinned. "Then I suppose I'll be fighting the rest of my life."

"You want me to stay?" The question hung unspoken between us for weeks, it seemed. Only after hours of letting Nico worship my body did I summon the courage to speak the words out loud.

"Have I not made it obvious enough?" he breathed into the column of my throat, ran the tip of his nose across my skin. "You don't have to file our contract tomorrow. We don't have to remain married. You can keep your company within the family, but I'd like to keep you around, as long as you'll have me."

"I think we could come to another agreement." I sucked a breath as he pulled the covers down my chest, exposing my breast to the cold air beyond the warm cage of his body. He made a sound of appreciation before kissing the valley between them.

"Whatever you want, princess."

I smiled, enjoying the way he explored my body with his mouth. "Is that your new motto?"

"Fucking right, it is."

A pounding knock startled us apart.

"The cousins?" I asked between breaths.

Nico reached for a gun and his pants, dressing as he barked orders. "No, they know where the key is. Stay here until I find out who it is. If you hear shots, get to the roof and go down the neighbor's fire escape. The back door will most likely already be compromised."

He left quickly, and I threw on a change of clothes that I had still stuffed in a dresser from a few weeks ago—an emerald silk dress and some leggings to shield my feet from the cold tile. Standing near the top of the stairs, I heard Nico open the door.

"Sera? What are you doing here?"

Sweet relief loosened the breath I held in anticipation. From the landing, I watched her duck beneath his arm and let herself inside, getting off the street. "Where's Milla?" she asked, looking around.

My steps down the hollow hardwood stairs prompted her attention. "Is everything alright? How did you know we were here?" I asked her.

She shook her head, waving her hands flippantly. "There's no time to explain." She turned to Nico to address him. "The Society came to the house early this morning. Luther was arrested."

"Nico . . ." I looked at him, discovering his coloring had paled slightly.

"Shit." He paced the hall, tearing his hand through his disheveled hair. "Did they say anything when they detained him?"

"There wasn't an official charge, only that it was under the order of the inspector himself, who has now been temporarily given the seat as High Overseer since Valentino was found dead last night." Her gaze slipped between both of us, insinuating suspicion. "The inspector sent a message along with them."

Nico stopped his nervous pacing to stare at her. "Well?"

Sera licked her lips. "He said you are to meet him at the bridge if you'd like to discuss your cousins—" But Nico was already darting back to the bathroom where we left the rest of our clothes. He reappeared twenty seconds later in his usual suit and Attano coat.

"Your family said they'd meet you there and sent me, assuming you'd be here since neither of you came home last night."

My cheeks heated, wondering what they had assumed to reach such a conclusion. I looked at Nico. "Wait for me, I'll just be a second."

Nico answered, "Absolutely not." At the same time, Sera said, "Milla, you can't."

I whirled to look at both of them. "I think I proved last night how capable I am of protecting you, Nicolai." Besides the part where I nearly ripped apart the world with my remnant, but how could anyone have possibly prepared for *that*?

He closed the distance between us with slow steps, and I knew from the way he approached it wasn't good news for me. "Milla, don't get this confused. You are the strongest, most capable person I have ever met, but there's no way in any hell I'd let you go near that bridge."

"Why not?"

"Because," he drawled, "you are too precious to me. I need to keep everything I care about as far away from the inspector as possible, so he cannot use you against me like he's using my cousin."

"So what am I supposed to do, let you go alone? Wonder if you'll give yourself up or get yourself killed?" My voice shook from all the hypotheticals piling on top of one another. That bridge was no-man's-land. Rules and remnants didn't matter there. Shaking my head, I told him, "No, you can't just leave me here to worry about you."

"Milla," he said my name in that deep, commanding tone of his that made all the bones in my body still. He sucked a breath in a sigh. "I know you're not pleased, but you have to trust me. I promise I'll come back to you."

The logical side of my brain doubted how that could be possible and yet my heart believed every damn word. He cupped my face, fingers settling beneath my chin. "Do not leave this house. That is an order. Do you understand?"

"Yes, *Daddy*," I teased, hoping to break the solemnness of the situation.

He scoffed, but the barest hint of a smile tugged at his lips. "When I get back, I will make you regret calling me that, Camilla."

"Good. If it means you come back, you can punish me all night."

My chin tipped, begging to feel him on my mouth. "I already want you again."

His head canted, slowly dragging his mouth over mine to speak into my lips. "It feels good to hear you say that when I'm not naked."

"You thought your body coaxed that confession?"

"Didn't it?"

Sera coughed uncomfortably down the hall. I pushed him away lightly, trying to hide my smile. "Arrogant ass."

His hand snatched the back of my neck and pulled me back to his face, kissing me like I was the last gulp of air before plunging under-water. "Stay here. I won't be long."

He slipped out of my arms. Nico spared one last look at me before leaving out the front door, where a windowless carriage waited in front of the steps.

"*Saints,* I thought he'd never leave," Sera said quietly, watching him through the split in the curtains. "Now that I've finally got you alone . . ." Her gaze returned to me, looking me up and down. "We need to talk."

"About?"

"About recent developments." She jutted a thumb toward the door.

My whole face flamed with heat, unsure how I was supposed to tell my tailor I'd just slept with the family rival. Judging by the way her brows raised an inch, I didn't have to. She read my mind just by assessing my half-dressed state and the nature of that farewell kiss.

"Camilla . . ." Sera scrubbed her face. "This wasn't supposed to happen."

"*What?*"

"Nothing. Just thank the saints I gave you those contraceptives before this happened," she sighed. "Your brothers will not be pleased, but I'll leave that for you to tell them. Get your coat."

I stepped back as if in retreat. "I'm not going anywhere. You just heard me promise Nico."

"Your birthday is tomorrow, Milla. Time is up." She shook her head in confusion. "Don't tell me you're having second thoughts about getting out of your union. Just because he shared his bed doesn't mean you have to share your company."

"What I do with my company and my heart is my business," I drawled. "I—"

"No!" She squeezed her eyes shut. "Don't say it out loud. I don't want to hear it. Damnit, Milla!"

"What is going on with you, Sera?" She acted so strange, pressing her hands to her temples as if the silence between our words was too loud.

"With *me?*" she balked. "What happened last night is spreading all over the city. What the Watch saw . . . they couldn't even classify the kind of power they witnessed from you. Everyone now knows that the Princess of Steam is actually a descendant of an unknown remnant! And instead of running to where you are safe—with your family—you choose to hide out with a bender."

I scoffed, as if they had ever cared for my safety before this. "My family? What can my family do to keep me safe, Sera?"

"There's no time to explain. I told your brothers I'd get you out of here, and I will do so by any means necessary."

I arched my brow. "What is that supposed to mean?"

Her eyes narrowed on me, squinting slightly as if concentrating on a detail of my face. Then something snapped, a connection in my head severed as the distinct feeling of remnant magic shoved me into the back of my mind, so that I was no longer in control of my body.

"*You* have a remnant," I whispered. That's what I deserved, believing someone I paid to be around me was a true friend.

359

"My family has worked for yours since descendants came to this Isle, but that doesn't mean I'm not your friend, Milla."

So she could read minds as well. Sera nodded even as the thought occurred to me. "You're a poly then," I said.

Her lips tightened into a line, almost like she felt guilty for betraying my trust. "Ask me again how my father died. Please."

I snorted. "How did he die?"

"He was tortured by the Society," she murmured.

My blood turned cold. She wasn't suggesting . . . could she? "Why?"

She chewed her lip before replying. "Your father needed your memories erased after your incident, but using a remnant on another is highly illegal." Sera grimaced. "Someone who found out slipped it to the Society. They questioned him to find out what he took from you, but he promised your father he would never tell, and he stuck to that vow."

I shook my head, the feeling in my body draining into numbness. That was . . . heartbreaking. How could she stand to be around me knowing I was the reason her father was tortured and killed? "Does . . . Aramis know all this?"

"Yes, your brothers know about your remnant, but we were the only ones until last night when it was unleashed." She cocked her head in curiosity. "What happened?"

"I was stabbed with a Niner blade and my familiar protected me." I held up my arm, bare of ink. "It must have drained the magic in the serpent before it could reach my remnant." My fingers fell to the place in my chest, where the dagger tip had sunk beneath my breastbone. Had Nico not been there, it would have killed me, regardless.

"That's why it's so important to get you out of here, Milla. Your remnant in the hands of the Collector . . ." She refused to finish the thought.

My heart waged a silent battle. Nico on one side and my family on the other. Why did they always have to be on opposing sides? I didn't know if Sera told the full truth, but she had no reason to lie. She could force me out of this flat if she wished, and I'd have no control of what she demanded of me.

"And I will if you don't move in the next five seconds," she said, her hands on her hips.

I didn't want to concede, but I didn't want to lose control either. "Will you at least let me leave him a note, something to explain where I've gone?"

"Haven't you been listening to a word I said? People have *died* to protect your secret, Milla. My father, your father, we're all putting ourselves on the line to make sure those who hunt you stay off the trail. Do you want to put Nico on their path as well?" She shoved me toward the door with a wordless command. "If you care about him like I know you do, you will let him go."

Let him go.

Those three bullets ripped through my heart, but Sera didn't care about the holes her words left in me. Before I could open my mouth to defy her, she had read my intentions and settled on shoving me out the door herself. I was pushed into the back of my mind, aware of my body moving but no longer in the driver's seat.

A car waited in the back alley. Sera had taken the family carriage to retrieve me. She passed me to open the car door, pushing me along with her control over my mind. Never had I wished for a laced dagger of glint more in my life.

"Wait," I pleaded, voice straining against her compulsion. Her hold on me weakened slightly, and I was able to turn to look up at the flat one last time. My thoughts, though controlled by Sera, remained wholly dedicated to Nicolai.

After spending six weeks with him, I couldn't imagine not seeing him again. Not waking up to the smell of spiked coffee and a dimpled smirk. To never feel cold metal sweep my skin or his calloused finger-tips tug at my lips. To leave him with so much unsaid, so much unan-swered, and so many potentials unexplored.

I'd grieved for those who left me through death, but I had yet to know the pain of missing someone still alive. The distance of having something I couldn't have when it was so close. The family found in strangers. The friendship formed in a rival. Nico had given me more than just his money, he'd shown me the opposite side of every coin and what waited for me when I dared to flip my perspective.

"Please, Sera," I whispered. My throat closed to hold back a gasping weep.

Her power slipped into my mind with a gentleness she didn't use before, nudging me through the open door and into the carriage. Tears welled in my eyes, but before I could blink them away, Sera commanded me once more.

"Sleep, Milla."

I shut my eyes and slept.

———— ✤ ————

WHEN I AWOKE, the carriage was still rolling, but as I blinked away the compulsion of Sera's remnant, I realized we were in a different car. The velvet lining of the bench beneath my cheek was now soft leather. Dark green curtains lined with silver brocade hung over the frosted panes of windows with their shades rolled half shut.

I pushed off the seat to sit up, finding myself in the private passenger car on the Iron Saint. The twins were in isolated armchairs at the end of the car, Sera sat next to me, while Aramis sat at a desk pushed off center against the right wall. Giles relaxed on a chaise across from him, his boots flat on an emerald-colored runner lining the narrow aisle, all the way to the gangway connection.

Giles offered me a sad smile as he watched realization wash over me, one detail at a time, crushing any hope to get out of this. "I'm sorry, Milla," he said.

"I trusted you," I told him. My glare shot to Aramis, who looked up from his work now that I was awake. "And how dare you use Sera to force me to do what you want? We're supposed to be family, but you're treating me like a tool to use and put away at your convenience!"

"So you'd rather be used by the Attanos?" he asked. "You'd rather be with them over your own family?"

"Nico never used me," I spat. "We can trust the Attanos. Sera, you can search his thoughts. You'll see he's on my side." I pleaded with them to let me go back, but Aramis's mind was much less vulnerable than mine.

"I *have* searched him, Milla. I read his thoughts every day we were in that house. The only reason we let you remain in his keeping was because he was also looking for the Collector, and as we hoped, he led us to him. But unfortunately, it also led the Collector to you. If the inspector is extorting him, he could ask for you next. Are you willing to make Nico choose between you and his own freedom? His cousin's freedom?" Sera sighed when she saw the way her words damaged me. "It's better this way, to leave before you can be used against him. You're doing the right thing."

Her argument was rooted in sound truth. There was nothing stopping the inspector from giving my name to Nico next. I still hated the thought of deceiving him. "If I cannot return, then where will I go? There's nothing for me outside of Lynchaven."

She folded her gloved hands in her lap and borrowed a look from Aramis. "Your brothers have taken care of it, thanks to your union with the Attano and the money it has procured."

"That's not an answer."

"You'll understand soon enough."

I crossed my arms, hands balling into fists. Empathetic was never a word I would use to describe Aramis, but I'd have to convince him somehow to let me stay. We were one of the most powerful families in Lynchaven—the entire Isle. With the help of the Attanos, what force could defy us?

If we eliminated the threat, if we cut down the Collector, then I'd have no reason to leave.

"Don't waste your breath trying to argue with your brother," Sera murmured beside me.

"Get out of my head!"

"Stop thinking such obnoxious thoughts," she snapped.

"*Ugh.*" I rolled my eyes and attempted to empty my head of any and all ideas, staring at a small tear in the tufted bench instead. "Where are we going?"

"We're going to the Continent," Aramis replied. His blatant honesty shocked me, so much I didn't even believe him. "I'm assuming Sera filled you in on the ride here?"

"Vaguely."

"I'm sure it was good enough. Tell the engineer we're ready." He nodded to Jeremiah.

I stood then, having had enough of being spoken over, disregarded, treated like a nonentity. "I'm not going anywhere until you explain why you're ripping everything away from me. I did what you asked. I paid back our family debt and even secured a true alliance with what were once our rivals. Why do you care about anything beyond that now?"

Aramis was out of his chair as well, lowering his face to bring us nose to nose. "Did you ever stop and think that perhaps not everything revolves around you and your happiness, little sister?"

The car fell silent. The only sound was the distant hiss of steam from the engine as the boiler ate the coals. Giles stood then and announced, "I'm going to see what's taking Jeremiah and the driver so long. We should have left by now."

Neither of us acknowledged him. "My happiness has never been a factor in your decisions." The words spilled out of every grudge I held hostage in my heart. "You've taken advantage of my guilt from the day Father died and manipulated me to do things I never wanted to do. But I'm done, Aramis. I am your sister, and more than that, I am a person with wants and dreams and goals. Stop treating my life like it is something to negotiate with."

He sucked a long breath, but he didn't roll his eyes as I expected. "We have all given up our lives in Lynchaven to keep you safe."

"Why?" I hissed.

"Because war is coming, Camilla. And we need stronger allies than the Attanos if we want to win the fight to come. The Continent has been building a resistance for decades, far longer than the Niners have been organized on the Isle."

I rolled my eyes, a laugh bubbling in my chest. "You sound like Nico."

But Aramis didn't find it funny. He pulled something from a locked compartment and handed it to me. A folded paper with yellowed edges from age. "Perhaps this will change your mind."

I eyed the paper before snatching it from his hand. "What is it?"

"Your birth certificate. Giles mentioned you were looking for it. Bad news, Father had it sealed. Good news, that one's fake, anyway.

This is the real one he had made should anything happen to him. He wanted you to know when the time was right."

"Why am I just now being shown this?"

Some of the stiffness in his shoulders went loose, and I'd never seen him look so small. I noticed then the dark circles shading his eyes, aging his face from stress and sleepless nights. "Because your remnant makes you dangerous, Camilla. Father warned me to never ask about it, to never find out who you truly were, so we could keep all our minds clear from people like Sera who could read them and steal our secrets. Only when he was gone did I look and find out for myself. I kept it from you to keep you safe until your ignorance put you at a bigger risk."

"What about the company?" I asked. "You were so stubborn about not letting it fall into bankruptcy and now we're leaving. Why did any of this matter?"

His eyes shifted to Sera, who looked away, clearly uncomfortable. "We had to make sure the OIC didn't assume the title. I filed the old contract between you and Felix this morning. He'll get the company and make sure the inspector doesn't take advantage of the people in Lynchaven. We knew from the start this is how it would end, but I'd never let the OIC have the benefit of the train. They'd take advantage of our friends and clients and saints know what else now that the Overseer is dead."

Now that Gavriel was next in line to the high seat, I was thankful as well he wouldn't have control of the Isle's most profitable system of shipping and transportation. If they had our train, they could control everyone. The company would fall into good hands . . . just not the hands of an alchemist like my brother had planned.

Aramis withheld the truth from me all these years, but I had my own secrets that I would share when the time was right. Preferably when we were too far away for him to do anything about it.

I slowly opened the folded document, my nerves too burnt-out from the past twenty-four hours to feel anxious about the information. Nico had been right. There was nothing on this page that would change who I was. My mother's name wouldn't fill the absence of her in my life. That kind of power wasn't found in the ink on a page.

My eyes scanned over all the bits I already knew. My full name. The date and time. My father's name was printed as expected.

Then I read *her* name.

Nadine Mercy Marchese.

"They were married?" I asked quietly. Father never married. The only reason he had sons was because he needed heirs to run the company after he passed, but he never settled down. My brothers had nonexistent relationships with their mothers as much as I did.

"I was only seven or so when they met, but yes. It was a quick thing. In the courtyard at the beginning of spring. No family or friends." He sat next to Sera on the bench, eyes falling to her knee as it peeked through the slit of her grey skirt. "That was the first time he brought her to the manor. She was around until she had you. The next day she was gone."

"So strange," I whispered. Clearly, she'd meant something to Gio if he agreed to marry her. Or maybe they were both in it for their own selfish reasons. Either way, my spinning thoughts would never come up with the truth myself.

I skimmed over the remaining information. The hospital. The city and district. The year of the Giver and the rest of the mundane details.

"What is this?" I pointed to a symbol drawn on the bottom. The ink and pen were different, insinuating it had been added after the original was written. A circle split into two sides by a single line. The same symbol the demon from the pits had pierced into my skin.

"Aramis?" I asked again. "What is this?"

"That symbol is the reason you're going to go to the Continent," he said. His hand cupped Sera's knee, as if for support, and the gesture would have shocked me had Giles not burst through the door. The worry in his face tore my attention from the paper in my hand.

"Our driver is dead."

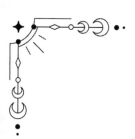
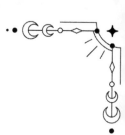

CHAPTER 37

NICOLAI

I took the back way, the longer, more discreet route behind the city between the residential part of the Row and the industrial. The clock tower chimed nine times, each one another hour from the moment that changed everything. The High Overseer's death would give the opportunity for new leadership, and I had rolled out a bloody carpet for Gavriel to take over, to ascend the ranks of the OIC.

And I had done it all for *money*. For *vengeance*. And yet the hollowness carved by the deaths of my parents and sister remained. Nothing could rectify their murders. My uncle tried to teach me that, but I had to find out for myself. The hard way. The more consequential way.

The bridge was barricaded for our meeting, members of the Society on guard in front of the blockades. Each one was armed to the teeth, rifles propped on their shoulders, handguns sheathed on their hips, daggers glowed blue in their sheaths from the utility belt

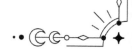

around their chests. A show of force completely unnecessary for the situation. He had my blood, and that should've been enough.

My family waited for me near the riverwalk, my cousins sat on the ledge that dropped into the river, Gideon took apart and assembled his gun while Adler counted magazines before slipping them inside the pockets of his coat. Esme paced in front of them while Uncle Sol murmured with one of our men, sending him off with the carriage I arrived in.

"You ready, Esme?" I asked her. She ceased her steps and nodded. "Good. I want you to stay far back, just close enough to hear our conversation, but distant enough they won't see you in the fog." I looked across the river, where the Districts were concealed by a thicker than usual mist. "Thankfully, the weather is exceptionally awful this morning."

"I don't like the thought of Esme joining you, Nico."

Of course not. Sol never agreed with anything I planned, had denied my ideas even after proving reliability repeatedly. "How truly shocking, Uncle."

"Nico . . ."

I pulled out a cigarillo and lit the tip with a flame from the thumb of my false hand, hoping he caught the wordless allusion the contraption suggested. "Just because you made a few terrible mistakes, doesn't mean I will do the same. I've had this moment planned for years."

He shook his head slowly. "More revenge, Nico? When will it end?"

"When everyone who has caused my family pain is dead."

"Your family?" he asked, taking a single step closer. "Or you?"

My patience had worn thin with my uncle. His council came from a good place, but he didn't understand the motivations of our enemies, how relentless they would become if they saw an opportunity to destroy us. My father had put us on top of this city at a cost, and I paid for it now with the very blood in my veins.

"The difference between you and me, Uncle," I said, gesturing between us with the burning cigarillo, "is that I will play until I lose. I have lost my parents, my sister, my very flesh and bone, but I haven't lost my fight. The day I have, you will need to carve the letters for my tomb. Because I will either die for what I love, or I will live forever."

He was quiet as I turned and approached the Society standing guard. "I need to get across."

One of them raised his brows, pulled at his belt to adjust his pants over his large belly. "That's too bad. The bridge is closed. Descendants stay in the Row, natives in the Districts."

"For how long?" I asked.

"Until the inspector deems it safe enough to allow remnants around the rest of us."

A wild laugh left my chest, and he flinched at the sound. "Yes, because we're the dangerous ones."

This was exactly what he'd wanted all along. The great divide between our kinds that had been drawn through the Continent generations ago was now gradually doing the same here. And I'd held the pen, sketched the first tracings of that line myself and was now forced to watch the ink bleed through the city.

"Well if that is the case," I said as I stepped toe to toe with him, looking down my nose, "then you should get the fuck out of my Row."

He gulped but made no move to step away. "You're the Attanos, I presume?"

"What gave it away?" My smile was not one of reassurance. "Now if you don't mind, watchman, and if you want to continue to work this bridge like a troll, I have business with your boss."

I pushed through him, shoving him aside with a directed wind.

He shouted a warning I did not heed, nor did the rest of my family as I heard their boots follow a few paces behind. The barricades were no more than half walls made with piles of debris, broken furniture, pieces of carriages, stones, and whatever else the natives in the Districts could haul to make staggered lines between one end of the bridge to the other.

The fog hid their figures until I was nearly halfway across. The inspector stood in the middle, Luther bound and gagged on his knees in front of him. Gavriel held a single revolver in his hand, the other hid inside his pocket.

"Nicolai," he said in a cheery greeting.

"Inspector."

More watchmen stepped forward behind him, forming three lines of security. "I wondered if you'd show yourself, considering I have witnesses that profiled you at the scene of the High Overseer's murder last night."

"Then why is my cousin at your feet?" I asked. If he had the evidence, why was I still free?

"Because I have one last job."

The bridge fell silent. Neither half of the city behind us made a sound. "I'm not doing anything else for you, Gavriel *Clemonte*. We're done."

His teeth flashed with a wicked smile. "I'm surprised it took you so long to figure it out." He stepped around Luther, who shivered violently without his coat—or they had scared him shitless by reminding him of his previous living conditions.

"You went to great lengths to make sure the world forgot your last name."

He pulled out a blade from its sheath on his belt, a dark red dagger the length of his forearm. Valentino's words came to life before my eyes as all the pieces fell into place. "When the Attanos took our company, we sought help from the Nine Crowns. They refused to support us, said they would rather one family fall then incite a civil dispute between the remnants and natives. They were afraid to use the power and following they had garnered over the last half century, since the remnants moved to this Isle. When me and my brother took matters into our own hands and sought revenge, they exiled us for what we did."

"You deserved worse," I spat, "for killing a child and her mother. They'd done nothing—"

Gavriel's face twisted with rage, spitting as he spoke, "Nothing? You call it nothing to watch your family fall apart, watch them lose everything. And why? Because people with abilities they did not earn, did not work for, came in and stole our livelihood. My family worked hard for generations to build that steel company. They sacrificed and gave their blood, sweat, and tears to give me and my brother generational success. And for what? So the *Attanos* could pull some strings and take it all out from underneath us. My brother became a worthless drunk, and I was forced to start from the bottom once again just to make a new name for myself."

I looked at the cigarillo in my hand and debated taking a drag. "So you got your vengeance, and you climbed your way up the ranks of the OIC. What now, Inspector? Where does all this lead?"

He smiled then. "Do you know why Hightower was created?"

"To hold people like me?"

He shook his head. "It was made by the first saint, Giver and Greed. The stone there is from the very void itself, wrought with magic. Only those who are gifted with a certain ability are able to manipulate it. The Remni and the descendants weren't the only recipients of powers beyond this world."

Gavriel began to pace the width of the bridge, and my heart pounded a triple beat for every lazy step he took. "When I was rejected, cast out by society and exiled from the city, I tried to go to the Continent and instead landed on an island. I quickly realized that it wasn't unclaimed land as I first assumed. It was a prison long before the OIC funded my efforts to use it for Hightower. A place for divine beings to be locked away."

"Why would a divine need to be imprisoned?" I asked, mildly curious.

His grin widened. "When Chaos came and destroyed the order of the world, it was written that she was sent into Oblivion and her demons destroyed, but they tried to imprison her first, to cut her off from her armies and her ability to create more monsters. But Giver and Greed lost their control, lost their order, and mankind has been corrupted ever since. An imbalance with the number of remnants running around and threatening the stability of the Continent, and now the Isle. My family wasn't the only victim of this disparity."

I rolled my shoulders back, taking liberty to move around the width of the bridge to keep my muscles warm. "Is that why the Firenzes came to fund your new Society? A fellow casualty in your perceived threat to the natives?"

He shrugged. "The Firenzes have similar ideals. You see, Nico, I'm only a collector of the rare and extraordinary, of remnants and their subclasses. I had the drive to change our city, but I needed the brains to do it. I needed an alchemist who dappled in the arcane science of remnants and their oppression. Who better to partner with than the creators of glint?"

It wasn't a surprise the alchemists worked for the inspector. They were known to be big donors to the OIC. What bothered me was that word. *Oppression.* The Firenzes had something worse than glint cooking in their alchemy beakers.

"It was you then. You are the Collector."

Gavriel smiled. "I have access to every record in this city. I know the poly's. I know where they live. It was quite easy, summoning them into a trap. People don't question authority like they should."

For once, I agreed with him. "Why are you collecting remnants? What does this have to do with the descendants?"

He held a finger to his lips. "I'm not giving away all my secrets, Nicolai. You'll just have to find out for yourself." Gavriel nudged Luther with the toe of his boot. "Though, you could just ask your cousin. He underwent several experiments while in Hightower. Unfortunately, he was one of our failures. Pity he lost his gift, but we'll find another like him, eventually."

The air beat the bridge, stirring the fog. I had kept my temper under control until my eyes locked with my cousin, whose silver eyes filled with shame before shutting, head falling between his shoulders. I ceased the wasted wind before it thinned the haze enough to reveal Esme.

Gavriel came to stand in front of him, stealing my attention. "You're a smart man, Nicolai. You knew a war was coming, but you could have never planned how big the scale would become when your little wife came into her power. Order will be reestablished when Chaos is destroyed."

"Do *not* bring Milla into this."

That anger returned, the same one that transformed me into a different man last night. Gavriel must have noticed him, because he smiled, held his gun with both hands instead of one. "It's far too late for that."

"What did you do?" My voice was laced with venom, my blood a liquid explosive in my chest.

"My last job before I claim this city," he spat. "I knew you wouldn't give her up, Nicolai. The Grey Hands that work for Felix, they came and sampled some blood for me at the scene of last night's massacre. They're hunting down Camilla as we stand here, and soon, she'll belong to the Collection." Gavriel spoke an order over his shoulder at his men to take Luther. "I'll be taking your cousin along, just to make sure you stay in line, Nicolai. I'm glad we got to clear the air this morning." He turned on a heel with a smug smile still sullying his face.

My voice trembled as I shouted the name, "Vanya Hartsong."

Gavriel stopped, turned slowly, grin fading. "What about her?"

"She provides you the names, correct? The ones for me to kill." It was my turn to smile now. If we were clearing the air, I'd need to be brutally honest with the inspector.

"What does she have to do with anything?"

I took a step forward, gaining a bit of confidence. "Her father was just recently promoted in the OIC. Chairman of Public Safety. Hartsong was an ex-member of the Nine Crowns, before the group became corrupted. Before your family split them into two sides: those who wanted to act on their hate for descendants, and those who preferred to keep matters handled in the voter's box."

His brows rose. "And?"

"You believed that Ms. Vanya could provide you a list with the party members of the latter side. That she knew the men and women who betrayed your family, and in exchange, you would promote her father to have full control over the safety of this Isle's citizens, both descendant and native once you took the position as High Overseer." I took another step, feeling reprisal within reach. "But she didn't give you a list of your enemies. She gave you a list of *mine*."

The inspector's face paled several shades as expected. I pushed the final nail in his coffin. "You unknowingly killed off the men that supported your efforts. The OIC has no one left who supports your cause, your ideals, or your methods. By order of Theodore Hartsong, the new Inspector of the OIC, you are under arrest for acts of treason against your city and conspiring the death of High Overseer Vito Valentino."

Two men behind him pulled out cuffs to bind him, but Gavriel jerked out their hands. "This is ridiculous. I am the inspector! You bastards work for me! That man killed the High Overseer!"

One of the watchmen shrugged before snatching Gavriel by his skinny arm. "The undertaker came out with an official report an hour ago. Valentino was poisoned."

"*Bullshit!*"

"He left a suicide note in his bedroom."

The inspector looked at me, eyes wide with rage. I shook my head, faking surprise. "He left a note. Saints bless him."

"This isn't over, Nicolai!" he seethed. "The Firenzes still have the upper hand *and* your girl."

"I haven't forgotten," I hissed, kneeling to free Luther from the ties that bound him.

"Nico," he gasped as I took out his gag. "They sent the bleeders after her. I overheard Gavriel say they tracked her—"

"Are you alright?" I held him by the shoulders. He nodded, and I pulled him to his feet, holding him until he could balance his weight. "Why didn't you tell me about the experiments? *Fuck*, Luther. I wouldn't have let you do this for me if I would have known."

"I don't know." His jaw locked, a lingering tremor shook his shoulders. "But I wouldn't have agreed if I doubted you."

"You have too much faith in me, cousin," I sighed. As pleased as I was to have taken care of a massive thorn in my side, I needed to make sure Milla was safe. I lifted him under the arm and escorted us both across the bridge, back to our side of the city. Esme appeared within a few steps, bracing her hands on her knees.

"Esme?"

"I'm fine," she gasped. "It's done."

"And the bridge?" I asked, realizing she was just breathless from using her remnant on a much larger scale than she was used to.

"It will fall with the right force. We can't let anyone use it until we know for certain what Hartsong will do. I'm afraid I might have weakened the metal foundations too much."

"We'll keep the borders up," I assured her. We returned to the Row, the rest of my family already unhooking the horse from the carriage to offer me a quick ride.

"We will not rest until Camilla is home. I'll go back to the flat in case they haven't tracked her yet, but I want every man scattered through the sectors. Get word out to the darkthieves in the Wet District. Tell the—"

My orders were cut off by the wail of a train. Two cries. A departure leaving the Row. A strange sound, only heard from this distance thanks to the solemn quiet hanging over this side of the city.

"Why is the train leaving the Row at this hour?" I wondered out loud. The sound called to something in my bones. These families in the Districts, the Marcheses and the Firenzes, left nothing to chance. Convenience wasn't in their vocabulary.

I needed to catch that train. Another whistle sighed another warning, that I might never see Camilla again if I didn't.

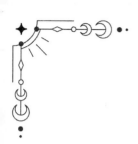
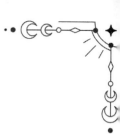

CHAPTER 38

CAMILLA

Aramis was on his feet without hesitation, replacing the paper in my hand with a gun he pulled from another drawer.

"What do you mean *dead*?" he asked, throwing Sera her own weapon.

"Shot in the neck," the twin answered. "Blood all over the fucking controls. It's a mess. Whoever did it is long gone."

"I don't give a damn about a mess. We need to get out of here now!"

"I'll go then," I said. They all looked at me like I was clinically deranged. I would have been offended if we had more time, which according to the tension in the car, we did not. "What? I'm the heiress of this train. Don't you think I learned how to drive the damn thing?"

Aramis winced, passing a hand through his silvery blonde hair. "Alright. Fine. I'll come help. Let me jump out first just in case the shooter is still out there." He looked back at Sera, and she smiled at some wordless exchange between them, nodding encouragingly.

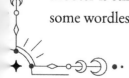

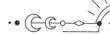

I followed him out, hopping between the adjacent doors where the coupler joined the cars, quickly darting up the length of the train to reach the engine just a few railcars ahead. The morning mist was thicker than usual from the steam curling between the wheels, insisting the engineer had begun the process to start up the train, but had clearly been interrupted.

Aramis gestured for me to climb in the engine first, pale eyes searching the fog for the return of any threat. Immediately upon stepping into the cab, my flats soaked up the warm blood slicking the floor of the cabin, the body of the engineer propped up against the hot boiler.

I found his position strange. Too poised for a shot to the throat. And it was surprising we didn't hear a gun go off with how quiet the morning was.

The ladder creaked as my brother followed me up into the compact space. I shrugged off my coat and draped it over the metal stool, one of the few unsoiled spots in the car.

"What are you doing?" he asked, watching as I squatted beside the engineer's body. His neck had been ripped open, right down the jugular vein—which explained the mess.

I swallowed back the rising sickness in my throat. "Bullets leave holes. His neck is mutilated. There's too much blood for this to have been from a gunshot wound."

"What are you suggesting?" But the look on his face implied he didn't need any further explanation.

"There's only one descendant that leaves a mark like this." Dread wrapped its icy fingers around my heart. "Aramis, are you *sure* Felix is on our side?" I've had minimal interactions with wearhs and both of them had been his fault. It was hard not to assume he had some influence in the death of this poor man.

My brother's stretching silence wasn't reassuring. Finally, he said, "Let's just start this train up and get the hells out of here."

I snatched the coal shovel and immediately started working on making more steam, heaping coal from the tender and into the boiler, feeling the sputters of rogue cinders nip at my bare shins, burn black marks into the satin material of the day dress I'd thrown on this morning. Sweat beaded my skin from the scalding heat as I tossed coal chunks in a flat pattern through the narrow opening. Soon my bare arms, my hands, even my cheeks were grimy with dust.

Aramis kept watch on the sides of the car, the mist curling around us, thick enough to conceal even the station. It didn't take long before enough steam had built up once more to start. Once ready, my brother abandoned his watch to man the controls, messing with the throttle and the control rod.

Neither of us took a full breath before the train began to move.

"Get back to the family car," Aramis gasped, clearly not acclimated to laborious work. "I'll get us the rest of the way until we reach the docks. We should be there before nightfall."

I wiped my face with the back of my hand, careful not to smear more black filth across my cheeks, and grabbed my coat. It was worth keeping, to have a piece of the Attanos to take with me. The red lining glistened in the lone hanging kerosine lamp light.

My brother followed my stare to the garment. "You really cared for him, didn't you?"

Care was too weak a word. I could only nod, unable to speak of Nico so soon. Not when we were leaving the city and everything else I loved within it.

"Hey," he said, coming to stand in front of me. "It'll get better. Once we cross the sea, we can be whoever we want. We'll keep your remnant suppressed, and no one will know what you are on the

Continent. We'll be safe." He cleared his throat and shrugged. "You don't even have to be our sister anymore, if that's what you wish."

His claim had me shaking my head. "Why would you think I'd want that?"

He dug dirty hands into his clean pockets, clearly uncomfortable with the tenderness between us. "I've been hard on you the last few years. Father loved you so much, it got him killed. I didn't want the same to happen to anyone else."

"I never asked for any of this—"

"I know," he nodded. "But it was because of you, nonetheless, and in my head that was damning enough to loathe you for so long. It was . . . unfair of me. Everything you said back there was true. I used you and it was wrong."

My head canted in consideration. "That's very insightful of you, brother."

"Sera has been helping me sort through my harsher judgements lately."

I smiled despite the awful ache in my chest. "Sera, huh?"

His lips tipped a sly grin. "Careful where you're about to tread, Camilla."

"I'm just surprised you'd go for someone who can read your mind." If hearts were made of metal, my brother's would've been steel. His stubbornness was renowned for being equally impenetrable.

He scoffed and stared at his boots. "I think that's why I'm drawn to her. There's nothing to hide. She sees me, all of me, and never flinches at a horrible thought. It's all genuine with her."

The ache in my chest tightened slightly. "I know what you mean." Glancing into the fog, I noted the train started to build momentum. I'd need to hop off now to get back to the car before we really gained speed. "And I'd never want to not be family, Aramis."

He sighed, his breath a stream of white vapor. "You might not always feel that way."

"Maybe not always, but no family is perfect. I've been the bane of your existence since the moment I was born, and yet despite all your loathing, you still looked out for me. Albeit in a few unorthodox ways, but they still count in my book."

He stared at me until the silence stretched longer than natural. "You should go back to the suite. I'll keep things going up here."

That was fine by me. The open cab was freezing, and I hadn't had time to layer properly before Sera had shoved me out the door with her remnant.

Dodging the streaks of blood that bled down the footplate, I climbed down the metal steps and into the cloud of mist surrounding the train as it rolled slowly down the tracks. The chug of the coupling rod as they circled the wheels in a powerful advance was loud enough to conceal any sound, the fog thick enough to hide anyone in its haze. It wasn't until I passed the tender until I saw a figure standing on the coupler between the railcars.

A wearh.

Crimson slathered his chin, forming a thick line from his lips and down his throat to the collar of his black shirt, which was damp with dew and what I assumed was the engineer's blood from the way it stuck to his body. Cursing, I slipped a hand beneath my coat to snatch the revolver Aramis had given me, but the bleeder was on me in an eye blink.

"Not so fast, love." His breath made me sick, copper and something foul. "You aren't leaving town just yet."

"What are you doing here?" I asked, hating the way my voice shook. The way it made him smile.

"Following orders. Mr. Firenze is not happy with your family, Camilla."

Of course, he wasn't. Aramis had made plans with him, and I'd ruined it. And neither knew it was me who spoiled their arrangement. But that also meant that if this wearh was a Grey Hand, he needed me alive. It was enough assurance to wrap my hand around the grip of my gun.

I shot once through my coat, not even bothering unsheathing the weapon and giving the bleeder time to react. His face twisted, confusion seamlessly shifting into rage as he realized my plan. But the damage was done. Even if he dragged me out of here half dead, I'd alerted everyone of trouble so they'd be on their guard in case this one had friends. The train abruptly came to a screeching halt, and I couldn't help but wince at the grating sound and the claws of the wearh as it latched a hand around my shooting arm.

"Bitch," he growled, throwing and pinning me against the rusted car. Stars lined my vision as my head hit solid metal. "Your family will pay for your mistakes."

"Don't fuck with my family, bleeder," I spat, tasting copper with every word. "It'll be the last thing you do."

"Threatening me will be the last thing *you* do. Our orders never said we had to bring you back alive."

He gripped my shoulders and shoved me again against the car, banging my head with the force of the whiplash. The world began to fray at the edges, darkness framing the bleeder before me until all I could focus on were dark red eyes and a vicious snarl. I fought to stay awake, wondering if this is what it felt like to cling to the last wisps of life, how death appeared as it consumed the soul until nothing was left but a vessel of a body.

There was a flash of crimson behind him, and the eyes of a killer suddenly widened with the fear of prey. Claws scraped down my arms, left tears in the sleeves of my coat as he crumbled to the ground. Aramis stood over him, a Niner blade in his hand.

"Milla!" He darted to my side just before I staggered into the bed of rocks lining the tracks. A scorching pain seared down my skull to the bottom of my spine, but I pushed away the lure of sleep, avoiding escape from the hurt that throbbed an echo throughout my body.

"I'm . . . okay," I muttered, blinking away the claws of sleep, allowing the world to return to its former vividness. I pointed to the blade in his hand. "How do you have one of those?"

My brother wiped the length of the blade clean across his thigh and handed the weapon to me. "Call it a family heirloom. Take it, Milla, in case another wearh comes for you." He pulled out his own gun and nodded toward the family car still concealed by fog. "We need to check on everyone before we move again."

"Aramis, there's something I should tell you," I spoke quietly.

"Can it wait till after we've gained some distance from the remnant of a literal hunter?" He pushed me through the mist, silencing any further conversation to listen to our surroundings. My hand shook around the hilt of the blade, as if the power inside the strange metal was repelling my touch, battling something that had long been dormant inside my bones.

"I can't hold this," I told him. Just the proximity was making me ache.

"Yes, you can. The blade won't harm you unless it pierces you."

The family car finally appeared, and we hopped off the track. I could sense my brother's impatience to check on the rest of our group from the way he nearly ran me over to get inside. The cabin was empty.

"*Shit,*" I whispered. "Where are they?" The place looked clean. Not a paper on the desk or a chair out of place.

"Search the coaches. I'll check the exterior for any signs."

"Aramis, wait!"

But he was gone before I could disagree with his plan. With a dagger in one hand and a revolver in the other, I took a calming breath and started towards the next railcar by attempting to open the gangway connection with my foot—but it didn't budge. The door was locked from the outside, somehow. Something blocked the way through. I dropped the dagger on the bench to pry it open, but it remained sealed shut.

The train then suddenly lurched into motion, and I ran to the window just in time to gain a glimpse of my brother running after the car at full sprint. Until the train shifted gears and pulled out fast, and he was swallowed by the fog.

My forehead remained pressed against the cold window, unable to take my eyes off the spot I saw him last or the landscape as the mist finally dissipated and revealed the rest of the city passing by, passing smokestacks and industrial yards. The gas lamps flickered out, veiling the cabin with a translucent darkness.

The shock eventually wore off, allowing me to move again, to process what was happening. I aimed the gun at the connecting door, shot three times to blow out the lock system and kick what remained of the exit off the hinges.

But the rest of the train was gone. Someone had separated the rest of the cars from this one, detaching the length of the train from this coupler. I was alone, speeding down the tracks into miles of uninhabited Wilds. If I jumped now, I'd die. And I realized then that this car was not a sanction from my hunters.

It was their cage.

"Going somewhere, Camilla?"

That voice. I remembered it from weeks ago when it had spoken in my courtyard. I turned from the exit to find Felix Firenze lounging in an armchair on the opposite end of the room. The same slippery smugness filled his smile.

"Got you now."

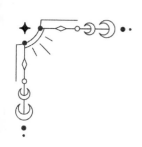

CHAPTER 39
NICOLAI

The station was empty besides a line of railcars stacked side by side near the boarding platform. There was only one depot on this side of the city, mostly used for industrial purposes due to its proximity to the factories in the Row. It hadn't been used for nearly a decade since our feud with the Marcheses, maintained instead as marshaling yard where the boxcars and passenger cars were sorted or parked when not in use.

Today, however, there was activity. That much was obvious by the steam curling against the brick, the heat and smoldering fumes of burning coal and grinding steel. The only thing missing was the actual train, which to my first assessment, was nowhere in sight within the boundaries of the fog.

A scream tore behind the row of passenger cars.

I quickly dismounted and ran toward the sound, sprinting around walls of stacked boxcars, whipping my head left and right to find the source of the sound. It didn't take long to come across two men, one limp in the other's arms. Both shared a face.

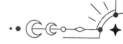

The Marchese twins.

Being identical, I didn't know which one was hurt and which screamed for his brother to wake up, but it didn't matter. If this was the aftermath of an attack, I'd arrived far too late.

"What happened? Where's Milla?" My gun was in my hand without thinking. The twin's glare rolled from his brother up to me, grief in his tears and the wrath of all the hells in his stare.

"My brothers are dead."

I swallowed, my fear manifesting as a bottomless well in my stomach, deep and consuming. "Where is everyone else then?"

He shook all over, and I noticed he didn't wear a coat or anything to shield him from the cold mist carried in the wind. I shrugged off my own and draped it over his shoulders, took the opportunity to check for signs of life in his brother. There weren't any.

"Giles is . . ." he choked on the rest, unable to finish. "Aramis is with Milla. They went to the engine before our car was attacked. Find him."

"Where did the train go?"

"Just follow the steam."

The steam. Of course, the bloody steam from the exhaust vent would lead straight to them. I made to stand, but the brother snatched my arm and muttered, "We shouldn't have screwed you over, Attano."

I shot him a questioning look. "What do you mean?"

He swallowed. "Aramis submitted the original license we contracted with the Firenzes to the registrar today. We thought they were on our side, but the bleeders who attacked us were with Felix. He lied to us and now we're all fucked."

No. The denial slammed through the shock. Milla was *mine.* She'd given me her heart, her hand, her body. If it took destroying the

Firenze family line to null that agreement, then so be it. "Not if he's dead before the day is over."

I sprinted back to the edge of the platform, where the rest of the passenger train sat idle and whistled for my horse. The black beast appeared from a layer of mist, and I mounted, kicking him off to race down the tracks where wisps of silver steam still trailed the air.

We hadn't been riding for more than a few minutes when a figure emerged on the track, diving out of the way as we approached.

"Aramis!" I shouted, catching a glimpse of pale blonde hair. His starched shirt was drenched with sweat or dew, clinging to his lanky frame.

He waved me on, eyes wide. "Go! Before they get to the ship!"

"How far ahead?" My voice was raspy as it returned on an echo.

"They drove off maybe three minutes ago. You might still have time if you—"

He didn't have to tell me twice. Slapping the reins, my horse took off down the tracks once more. I stood high in the saddle and let the fresh air from the foothills of the Wilds cool the sweat sheening my skin.

Time. A relative thing until every second mattered. Until every stroke of the hand on a clock was toward certain peril or reward. Thankfully, time was always on my side, a measure of it within my control.

I paused the second and stole a few back, and with the stop of the clock, made sure the hand of fate remained in my favor.

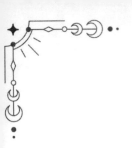
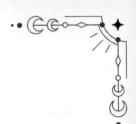

CHAPTER 40
CAMILLA

"What do you want, Felix?"

Dressed for traveling, he wore a simple suit, his coat thick for warmth in this wet winter. With a wave of a gloved hand, he gestured to the bench beside me, but I made no move away from the broken door. Wind sucked at my dress, my hair, tugging me away from his invitation.

"You know why I'm here."

On the surface, perhaps. But that didn't explain the wearhs, the weeks of hunts, the lengths he went to get me. "My brother turned in the contract this morning. You'll have your shares. There's no reason to do this."

He leaned forward, bracing his forearms across his knees. "Don't insult me by telling lies, Camilla. We both know that isn't true."

So he knew what I'd done. I didn't have an ounce of pity for him. "Sending a bunch of bleeders after a girl is a poor way to gain her heart, Felix."

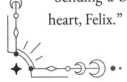
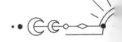

"I don't want your heart, Camilla," he hissed. "I want your remnant."

I stepped back as much as the drop off behind me would allow. "You know?"

"I'm an alchemist." He shrugged. "Your father gave us all the formulas from his previous one, when the last alchemist he employed died of *natural* causes." There was a gleam to his eyes that suggested otherwise. "He tied up all his loose ends, Camilla. All but one. What your father selfishly kept a secret will be used to create a better world, combining science and magic."

"I thought an alchemist used science to control magic," I said hesitantly.

He scoffed and stood from the chair. "They are two sides of the same coin. Alchemy is merely the study of their relationship, how to tap into the wells of the supernatural and combine it with the fundamental rules of our world. Our skeptics call us practitioners of dark magic, but those with an open mind just call it arcane science."

Now *that* wasn't what I expected him to say. He came closer, closing the distance between us in the short car until I could hardly take a breath, requiring all my focus to figure out a way around him. "You're taking the ship, I assume?" The only remarkable thing about the Upper Notch besides the mines.

He nodded. I kept him talking, if only to divide his attention from the hand slipping into my coat. "Why? Where are we going?"

"To Hightower."

"Because war is coming?"

Felix smiled. "You catch on quick, Camilla. We'll discuss it—" His eyes focused on something behind me, brows furrowed in focus. "What the fuck is that?"

Keeping my body in line with his in case it was a distraction, I turned my head slightly to assess what he was looking at. My knees almost gave out from the sight. A rider, barreling down the tracks as a favorable breeze pushed him along, the trees lining the railway indicating the shift in the air.

"Nico!" I might have whimpered his name, the relief stole too much of my breath. Felix shoved me to the side and over the bench, bracing his hands on either side of the doorway.

"Where the hells did he come from?" he asked no one. Without hesitating to consider my plan, I acted on pure hatred for the man, pushing off the bench to throw my weight at him.

Felix was solid as stacked stone, barely moving an inch as I tried to push him out of the car and into the tracks. Instead, he turned and grabbed me, shoving me in front of him. His opposite hand fisted my hair at the base of my skull.

"Is this what you came for, Attano?" Felix shouted at him. My toes barely clung to the edge. My eyes locked on Nico's, catching glimpses of him through my hair as it whipped in the wind slipping off the train. The alchemist threw me back into the car. He yelled back at Nico, "Come and get her."

Felix stepped over me and disappeared through the rear door. No sooner had the connection shut, the bench popped open, and Sera crawled out of the hidden compartment.

"Sera! What were you doing in there?" I helped her out just as the car groaned overhead. My captor was on the roof.

"Giles pushed me inside when the bleeders came," she gasped as she studied her surroundings. "What should we do? You can't go to Hightower, Milla. I've seen Luther's thoughts. They do . . . awful things to remnants there."

"First, we need to stop the train," I said, glancing at the door Felix just passed through. Shots rang out above us, and I ran to the opening to find Nico hugging the tree line to make himself a less obvious target, dodging the alchemist's poor aim as he pushed the horse as fast as the beast could tolerate.

"Let's get you to the engine then," she tore me back, pulling me toward the front of the train. Sera stopped just before the gangway. "I'll stay here and keep Felix distracted so he won't hurt Nico."

"Be careful, Sera," I murmured, having little time to say anything else. Fortunately, my thoughts and emotions were plain as print on a page for her to read.

She shook me hard by my shoulder, snapping me from my sentiments. "Go!"

There were two sleepers and two passenger cars in front of our family's private lounge, and I sprinted down each of them, bursting through each connection and past rows of seats covered in vibrant green upholstery. The details were a blur of emerald and brass and dark wood, my wild breath and fast steps the only sound alive in the coaches—until I entered the last passenger car.

Felix had more men. Natives, not bleeders, relaxing in the seats, smoking in a restricted area like they owned the locomotive. They noticed me as the door fell open, eyes widening on my figure draped in a bloody dress and equally sullied hands. I muttered a curse before slamming the door shut, watching through the stained-glass window as each of them jumped to their feet.

I retreated to the sleeper car, slipping into a booth and beneath one of the benches that fell open into a bed. There was nowhere else to run, so I was forced to hide. The limited length of the train made it quite difficult to avoid unwanted attention, but I grew up in these cars. I knew every nook and cranny, but more importantly, I knew how to lock the doors from the outside—to my youngest brother's annoyance. Giles hadn't appreciated my traps when we took the train as a family to the coastline, but I was grateful for the skills I'd accumulated whilst entertaining myself on the long rides south.

A herd of footsteps clattered down the corridor, the car so

hollow without passengers, I heard each man as they passed the booth. Once they had gone to the next carriage, I crawled out and ripped one of the curtains off the brass rod veiling the window.

Using a double knot, I tied the outside handle to a stationary metal rod reporting the short awning crowning the door. It wouldn't hold them long, but it would buy me time and enough distraction to get to the engine.

The final passenger car gave way to the postal cabin—which was inconveniently locked. No matter, I knew I'd have to climb to the roof at some point, as there were no walkways from the cab housing the engine and the passenger cars. I slipped my gun into the top band of my leggings and discarded my flats, ripping open the bottoms to have a better grip on the roof.

Satisfied I'd done all I could to improve my chances up top, I climbed the pole supporting part of the roof and clawed my way above.

The train traveled at a decent pace, and the winter air had teeth that gnawed at my knuckles as I pushed against its drag, crawling across the top of the car. I looked back for a moment, finding Felix was on his knees, messing with an ammo cartridge for his gun. The velocity of the train and the biting wind from its acceleration made it difficult to do anything up here, my limbs quickly numbed from the chill.

The landscape was a blur on either side of the train as I focused on the next carriage, one more until I reached the tender box. Dark grey smoke from the engine curled just above my head, roasting the air with a heady scent. My heart was ambushed with every kind of fear as my feet dug into the smooth metal doming slightly from the center of the roof, terrified of slipping to my death. If I could've felt anything besides the violent breeze, I would've probably found myself trembling, my fingers and hands blanched as I stretched them wide for balance.

A gap a few feet wide stood between the awnings of the next car. I'd have to jump, but I couldn't find the nerve. Couldn't dig into that determination that had driven me up here, feeling it freeze solid and unreachable like the blood in my hands.

"The roof!" a muffled voice shouted behind me. I looked back, discovered one of Felix's men had peeked above the line of rooftops and spotted me. I didn't think they would kill me, but not all bullets were aimed for such purposes. Some were to threaten, to manipulate, to hurt. The flash of silver melted my resolve, and I looked ahead. In the same instant, I forced my frozen limbs to jump.

Cold metal slapped my cheeks as I landed flat on the next roof, sprawling to grip anything I could to gain purchase. I barely let myself reorient before I stood on shaky legs and quickly toed across the final roof, just as shots whirred past my ankles.

Polished steel gave way to coarse rock as I leapt into the tender car on top of a pile of coal. It dug into my knees, tore the thin lining of my leggings until it ripped at my skin. By the time I reached the mouth of the tender box, where the edge dipped from the walls to allow one to shovel the contents, blood smeared my tights. If I hadn't been completely numb from the wind, I might've felt the sting of their bite.

A lone man in a fine suit sat on a stool in the cab, but he wasn't alone. My eyes scanned the rest of the engine, falling on another.

Giles.

He was impaled on the control lever. The rusted rod stuck out the left side of his back as the rest of his body was wedged into the small space between the engine itself and the side of the cab. The muscles of his back heaved with agonal breaths as the bar kept pressure inside his body to slowly bleed him out.

I could feel the shakes now. My stomach rolled at the sight of him, the air in my lungs rushing from its home in my chest. The man on the stool didn't even look at him, didn't care he was trapped in a slow agony.

From the pit of my core, a familiar urge coiled—*burned* against the cold fighting to suppress this new sensation. My racing heart ate away at any remaining glint in my bloodstream, purging it from my veins as this new feeling burnished me new inside. But unlike the night in the Overseer's chambers, I wasn't afraid.

I didn't understand this power or its limitations. I had no idea how it would manifest—the first time had been apparently erased from my memory. But there was a weight to it, like pulling back an arrow on a string, the tension building the more that string stretched. Watching my brother die slowly on a rusty lever threw it forward. The metal lip of the tender box began to erode away beneath my grip.

A wild sound tore from my chest, and I leapt from the bed of coal, falling on my knees in the cab just as Felix's man turned in his seat. My hand went to the gun sheathed in the band of my legging, watching as his lips formed a curse. The show of my revolver had him spring into action. By the time I lifted the weapon to aim at his chest, he kicked it from my hands. My fingers, frozen stiff, could barely curl around the grip much less find the trigger soon enough.

The gun skidded across the narrow cab before clamoring down the steps and falling off entirely. I stared up at him, my breaths shallow and quick, despising how he looked back at me. How he looked *down* at me. A sneer and a smugness that reminded me of his boss. Nico's voice replaced the familiarity, his words ringing truth into my heart.

I think they are afraid of you, Camilla. I think they know how capable you are, and they are making sure you never realize it for yourself.

He reached into his back pocket, pushing aside his overcoat. "Be a good girl now," he said, "and stay where you are until we get to the docks."

"You impaled my brother," I hissed.

"I didn't do anything. Only monsters have the strength to do that." His eyes glanced at Giles, who groaned a choked sound.

"You let him suffer!" I shouted against the racket of the engine burning through the coal, fueling the power to the pistons.

He pointed the gun he pulled from his waistband into my face. "I can't take him off until it's time to stop. Moving his body would require moving the lever—"

"Then I guess we're making an unexpected stop, Firenze."

I swiped a stealthy hand in front of my face, knocking his gun to the side. Using a maneuver Aramis once showed me when we were young, I ducked my head below the barrel while simultaneously throwing my hands up, a grip on his wrist and the other around the body of the gun. Holding his wrist firm, I twisted the weapon, breaking the finger still inside the trigger.

He cried out, crumpling slightly from the surprise of the pain. I ripped the weapon out of his hands and shoved it back in his direction. Pulled the trigger—only for the damn thing to be empty.

My frustration, my grief, my desperation to get through him, it sent me attacking this man as I'd never hurled myself at anyone else before. I hit him with the solid grip of the revolver, finding his skull through the defensive push of his hands. When he wrestled my arms down, the gun fell, and I was face-to-face with his bleeding glare.

He spat, "You'll pay for that, bitch. I hope you burn in Oblivion."

"I hope I see you there," I growled.

You are enough. You could do anything you want.

The tension in the center of my chest became overwhelming, desperate to be released, to fight back. As if I had an inner demon trying to claw its way from my soul and battle on my behalf. I dug into it, submerging a testing finger into a dark pool with an obscure bottom. And then, I let it out.

My hands found themselves around the man's forearms as he fought to pin my arms to my sides. I watched his face contort, glance where my touch worked that untapped remnant. A look of terror flashed through his eyes. He pushed me away, and from the short distance, I could see where my palms seared through his coat all the way to his skin. But his gaze wasn't on the holes in his coat, but on my hands. I followed his stare and gasped.

Solid black. From my nails to the veins of my forearm feeding the stain-soaked skin. Like I had dipped my hands into a bucket of ink and lifted them high to let the rest trickle down my arms. I set my focus back on Felix's man—and launched myself.

One hand found his face, the other his throat. In a rush it spilled out of me, this power unbidden, untapped, and unfamiliar. It was a high I didn't think I'd ever come down from. A feeling of total loss of self until the shock of its exhibition slammed into me hard enough to knock me back into reality.

Like fire from Oblivion.

Black tendrils of heatless flames engulfed his body in the blink of an eye. Nothing left of him remained. Red vapor clung to every surface in the engine, to my bare skin and dress. It was as if I'd destroyed the vessel of his body so quickly, the blood inside him had nowhere to go but bursting from its cavities.

The remnant stored in my chest waned, falling quiet as the threat was eliminated, and I stared down at the ashen remains of what was once a wiry man in a black coat. The color filming my hands gradually receded until they were once again a cold, pallid pale.

But there was little time to wonder over what I'd done when Giles was still stuck. I shakily made my way to him and tried to squeeze between his side and the wall of the cab, my hands smoothed down his shoulders.

"Giles?" I dropped my head to whisper into his ear. "It's Milla. I'm going to get you off of this, alright?"

He groaned. I didn't know if that was a refusal or permission, but he couldn't remain this way. And if I wanted to stop this train, I'd have to move the lever back. I'd have to get him off. An act that would likely kill him.

I knew with certainty it had to be done. That every second he was thrust upon this metal rod was another he was tortured with. But it didn't ease the guilt, the dread of delivering the merciful end—the beginning of what I knew would be a different life. A world without him didn't seem fathomable.

"I love you," I told him. "I didn't say it enough. We never said the word enough, but I love you, Giles. I'm so sorry this happened. I'll never stop being sorry."

A shudder ripped through his flesh in a silent response, and I took a steadying breath, resolving myself to finish this. For Giles. For Nico. For Sera. For all who fought with me and for me, on this day and the ones before.

It was a tedious process, lifting him straight off the lever. Finding the path of least resistance meant taking on most of his weight. I was able to wiggle myself beneath him and push him off that way, thankful the sounds of the engine were loud enough to mostly cover the guttural sound of the lever sliding through his chest.

Once he was off, I staggered with his weight and laid him on the cab floor as gently as I could. My arms were deadened, the adrenaline quickly burning out, leaving me weak and shaky. It took all the rest of my strength to dance the throttle and pull back the control rod. As soon as the train began to slow, I threw on the air brakes and fell beside my brother.

His chest bled profusely, but he was somehow still alive as I curled into his side, listened to the wheezing gasps of breath he sucked, searched his bright blue eyes for some awareness. They caught on mine, and I discovered a peace in them.

"I'm sorry, Giles," I cried. "I'm sorry they did this to you, but they'll pay for it. I swear."

He tried to speak, choked on a throat full of blood before raspy words left his lips. "Love you, babe."

Thin tears fell from the corners of his eyes, the blood that had drained down his temple dyed them red. He looked back at the silver sky, at the line of steam that had followed us our entire lives, and died with a small, blissful smile on his face.

My anguished cry was muffled by the slap of a thick fist over my mouth.

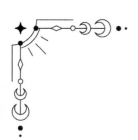
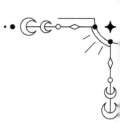

CHAPTER 41
NICOLAI

Felix wasn't a stupid man. He crawled to the top of the train car and laid flat, shooting at me while I rode the horse hard and fast. The supply of my remnant was fickle, using most of it to stall time to catch up to the Iron Saint. Even now, we could barely keep up, and the only plan I had left was to kill anyone who slowed me down from reaching Milla before she was taken.

Even if I wanted to use a bit of wind to knock the alchemist from the speeding locomotive, he was too flush with the roof to hit accurately, too far to steal the wind in his chest. I relied on my own bullets instead, using his head as a target.

Milla appeared in the doorway at the end of the last car, her eyes wide and desperate as if trying to think of a way to get to me that didn't include jumping to her death. She disappeared a moment later, and the loss of her worsened the aching worry hollowing my chest.

Pain licked my deltoid as a bullet skimmed my shoulder, forgetting Felix in my distraction. He stood now, I only needed to throw

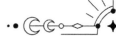

him off-balance and send him tumbling—until another joined him on the roof.

"Milla, stop! Go back!" I shouted commands at her, but she ignored me. Though, I knew my voice traveled far enough against the wind, as it alerted the alchemist of her approach. I might've damned her by not trusting whatever insane plan she had come up with. Might have damned us both.

He lunged for her, turning his attention from me for a moment to grab Milla and pull her against his chest. Now I couldn't shoot or push him. And he knew it. The way he smiled when he faced me again, Milla writhing against his hold, had me backing off. His grin widened.

Sparks flew from the wheels, spooking my horse so that he jolted to the side, nearly tossing me off. Someone had thrown on the brakes, bringing the short entirety of the locomotive to a slowing stop. Sharp screeches of metal against resistance had me recoiling from the wheels, the sudden opposition to the train's momentum sent a tremor of force through the railcars, knocking Milla and Felix off-balance.

Losing sight of them, I stood in the saddle, led the beast as close as possible to the side of the car now that it ran slow enough to match pace. Using one of my last bullets, I shot through a window and dove inside the railcar. My momentum sent the desktop I landed on crashing sideways, sending us both to the floor.

By the time I made it through the gangway and up the makeshift ladder Milla had used to get on the roof, Felix was underneath her. Her hands were around his throat, speaking something over him that stilled his body straight as a steel beam. I didn't dare distract her. She knew I was here, the way her eyes darted to the side in my direction.

"You will not hurt him." Her words were barely audible in the wind blowing at my back. She leaned in close, whispering something in his ear that was impossible to read from her lips alone. Whatever she told him had his eyes go wide.

Before I could take a step toward them, Milla sat up higher, looming over him. No longer pinning him to the roof, his hands were free to reach for the gun he'd tucked in his waistband when he grabbed her before. Whatever happened between them during my ascent up here, I'd never know, but it was something crucial enough to let her lower her guard so significantly. There was no reaction from either of them as he put the gun between them and shot her through the stomach.

He might as well have shot me instead, the way it gutted me.

"Milla!" The only sound in the world was my voice and a ringing noise caught between my ears from the proximity of the gunshot. She fell back, sprawled across the roof as Felix slipped from beneath her and rolled off the car. The train skidded to a complete stop. My legs finally moved, taking wobbling steps that ate the distance between her body and mine.

"*Milla*," I groaned. Driven to my knees before her, I scooped her body in my arms—a stubborn part of me refusing to acknowledge the bleeding wound in her stomach.

She'd given up, and Milla never surrendered so easily. Not the upper hand, certainly not her life. It didn't make sense, and yet the evidence was plain as the stagnant pulse beneath her skin.

"Nicolai." My name was coarse as unrefined stone from her lips and sunk just as heavy in my chest.

"Milla, *why*?" I dragged her face to mine, brushed my thumb over the crest of her cheekbone. All the edges of her were already losing an appeal of warmth. "Why did you do that?

"To keep her safe." Her chest convulsed with a wet cough. "Your family is proud of you, Nicolai," she murmured. A crimson stain sprawled from her middle, soaking her grey dress. "You should have told her."

"What do you mean?"

"You love her," she said weakly. "You should tell her, before it's too late."

"Milla, I don't love anyone else, I promise. I love—"

"No! Don't waste those words on me," she said, grimacing.

I shook my head just as her eyes rolled back, fluttering shut. "Milla, wait! Don't leave me yet." She obeyed, forcing them open, looking straight at me once more.

"Bring my body back," she sighed. "Show them all what was done today."

"Whatever you want." The pad of my thumb traced her bottom lip, and I kissed them one last time. The drag of her mouth on mine tore a fresh hole in my chest until I felt nothing but the loss of her, even as I still held a fraction of her life in my arms. "Just please, grant me more time with you. Saints, I needed more time."

It wasn't enough. I hadn't been enough. All the days I tried to convince her of the word, and it all fell short in the end.

"Nicolai, I . . ." She shuddered, the words caught in her throat.

Those gilded eyes lost some of their focus. Lost their gleam. When I was sure her soul had left the vessel of her body, I let the anguish shake me to my core. Let the sharp edge of grief slice away the soft edges Milla had exposed in me until I returned to the same vengeful, hateful creature she found me as—but this time I would be worse. This time I had a reason for it.

I set her body down and aimed my gun at the lone rider who stole my horse and shot Felix Firenze in the back of the head just as he entered the border of fog.

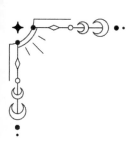
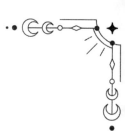

CHAPTER 42
NICOLAI

Time did not heal all wounds. Instead, I found it made some fester.

A week had passed since I carried Milla's body back home. Two days since I buried her in the Attano graveyard next to my parents and little sister. No point between then and now did the grief in my chest wane. Not even a flicker of relief at any moment. My sorrow hung like a cloud over the city, something I was just going to have to learn to live with, as there was no getting rid of it.

A knock at my bedroom door had me putting down my drinking glass for the first time today, and it was nearly noon. "It's open," I called to the visitor.

My Aunt Fran pushed the door open slowly before slipping inside. A pause followed her entry, as she must've been taking in the state of my bedroom. I hadn't found it necessary to leave since the funeral. My work piled high on the desk before me, and I ignored the entire stack like the rest of the clutter building on every surface in the room.

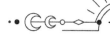

She said, "There's a solicitor in the parlor. He says he has some documents for you to sign."

I snuffed out the cigarillo I'd been burning and stared into the fire in the hearth that had dwindled too low for warmth. "I'll be down in a moment."

Hartsong must have sent him. Things were changing in the city, and I wasn't sure if he was good for the Row or not. He claimed to be interested in helping me free the remnants locked away in Hightower after I provided evidence of a wrongful accusation on more than one occasion. But most politicians agreed to whatever the collective desired in order to get the extra push they needed into a seat of power. Whether he followed through was something else completely. If there was one thing I trusted less than bleeders, Mirth remnants, and Firenzes, it was a politician.

"Nicky," she drawled. I sighed, sensing an unwanted pep talk on the cusp of my name. "I know you are no stranger to this kind of loss, but you've got to get out. You're starting to stink."

I didn't have anything to say. Instead, I replaced the old cigarillo with a fresh one, letting the smoke permeate the room like incense. Fran's footsteps came up behind my chair and snuffed it out.

"She wouldn't have wanted this for you." My aunt ran her fingers through my outgrown hair. My lips twitched in an almost smile as she cringed, wiping the grease off her hand on her robe.

"I shouldn't have left her."

There was nothing to justify my choices that morning. I'd left her open and unguarded just to catch the inspector and steal a piece of vengeance for myself. Sol warned me , but I stopped listening to anyone a long time ago, stubborn against learning my lessons in a bad way.

"Would you have let Luther be taken then?"

Fran liked to ask hard questions. Unfortunately, his arrest hadn't been necessary since I already had the upper hand with the inspector. One step forward, one massive leap back. What was left of the Firenzes now controlled the railway. The city was literally split in two with a new Overseer, and she was gone. I lost everything I wanted just for a good show.

"I'll be down in a minute," I repeated.

She dragged a long sigh before leaving, as if stalling to try to think of something else to convince me it wasn't as bad as I thought it was. She must have thought better of it because there were no excuses left that would convince me.

I strapped on my false hand and left my room, ignoring the empty one that sat across the hall, and met the solicitor in the parlor.

He sat at a desk near the window, a folder opened to reveal blank ledgers. "What's all this for?" I asked.

"The OIC needs you to sign the title for the railway, Mr. Attano." He pulled out a pot of ink and a pen.

I shook my head. That wasn't possible. The Marchese son said they had filed Felix's contract earlier that day instead of mine. "I think you're mistaken, sir. I don't own the Iron Saint."

His brows furrowed, and he opened the briefcase next to his chair to pull out a second set of documents. He fumbled through the pages briefly before handing me a stack. "You are the Nicolai Roman Attano listed on this license, are you not?"

"Nico?" Uncle Sol stepped into the parlor. "What's going on?"

I blinked several times at the page, wondering how such a thing could exist, and handed my uncle the license. Couldn't bring myself to say it out loud as my throat closed with a hard swallow. He snatched it from my hand and read it out loud. "A marriage license?"

"You were married to the late Camilla Mercy Marchese-Attano, heiress to the entire railway corporation. Due to her untimely passing and the disappearance of the rest of the Marcheses, who have now been presumed dead as well by our inspector and his subordinates, you are now the sole owner of the Iron Saint, Mr. Attano."

I reached for a chair near the hearth and slowly lowered myself into the seat. Aunt Fran, Luther, Esme, Adler, and Nonna had been waiting outside the parlor and had pushed themselves behind Sol to read the contract themselves.

"When?" I asked, still in disbelief. "When was that filed?"

Luther murmured a date as he squinted over Sol's shoulder. We had been legally married for over a week before she died, and she never said anything. But that also meant the contract the Marcheses had filed was null and void since they turned it in afterwards. Felix couldn't wed someone who was already married. Had that been why he turned on the brothers and sent the bleeders to slaughter them?

"Nico," Esme breathed. "Do you know what this means?"

I nodded, my chest crushing for the weight of multiple realizations slamming into me at once. "Camilla has given us a gift." But no, it was more than that. "She has given us control of Lynchaven." The OIC would have to outsource all imports through us now that we had the main transportation to both sides of the city. We had reign over the minerals from the mines up north, the crops in the farmlands in the south, and every saints-damned thing in between.

Camilla had given us protection, control, and freedom. Everything her family had passed down through generations, everything my own had to fight for since we came to this wretched Isle.

"Mr. Attano," the solicitor snatched my attention back to the blank title. "If you'd please sign these quickly, I'd appreciate it. I need to get this filed as soon as possible."

With a couple quick signatures, the Attanos owned the Iron Saint, and I was no less stunned at the turn of events when he left. My aunts were crying, Nonna was too, and I'd never seen the mad dog shed a single tear. But to know her family was finally taken care of, after crossing the Sea and planting us here fifty years ago, it must've been an incomparable joy.

Gideon came to my side, separating from the rest talking jovially over each other. "You alright, boss?"

"No," I sighed. I was still in the gutter of grief, but seeing my family truly happy was a lifeline I didn't know I needed. "But I think I'd like to get an ale if the rest of you are up to it."

He slapped me on the back and shouted an order at the rest of them.

<hr />

THREE CARRIAGES and a short trip to the First Sector, my family filled in the House of Bane and made Dom earn his tips. I watched them from a barstool not far from the one I first noticed Milla. She'd been so sure of herself even then, even without her strange remnant in a dangerous side of the city.

Saints, I missed her.

"Mr. Attano?" Dom placed a tall ale in front of me. I shot him a look. He knew my drink of choice, and it wasn't that. "Someone came in the other day and bought you a drink. Asked me to give you this as well."

He handed me a folded piece of glossy paper. A train ticket.

"Who the hells asked you to do this?" I asked.

He shrugged. "Said he was a friend of the family. I'm glad you came in, the timestamp is for this afternoon. I almost ran it to your place, but the pub got packed."

The ticket was indeed printed for today at the sixteenth hour. The Industrial Station. That would mean the train waited in the Row.

I took a few sips of ale before slipping off my barstool. Mentioning to Luther that I'd be back soon, I escaped without the rest of the family noticing, too busy drinking themselves bloated to realize I'd left, and took a carriage to the station just in time.

The Iron Saint was a beautiful piece of machinery. A solid black engine, silver steam already starting to pour from the chimney spout. The cars behind it were painted a dark green with brass framing to the windows. For some, it was a means of travel, others for trade. For me, it was now a weapon to use against anyone who defied my family's control.

"Ticket, sir?" A worker approached. The platform was empty besides the two of us. I handed him the ticket, and he gestured to one of the private coaches behind the general passenger cars. He opened the door for me and stepped aside to allow me through.

But as I entered, I realized I wasn't alone.

Aramis Marchese sat on a bench at the end of the private car donned in a three-piece suit with a silver chain draping from his vest button to a tweed pocket. Not dead. Not like his sister. He looked very well from the last time I saw him.

"We need to talk, Attano."

My mind jumped to the possible conversation topics, but nothing made sense. If he was alive and well, why was he hiding on this train—my train.

"What do you want?"

He pulled out a cigarillo from the inside of his jacket and lit the tip. "Do you smoke?"

"No."

He nodded. "Pour yourself a drink, then. You'll need it for what I'm about to tell you."

I lazily stepped toward the desk where a decanter was half

emptied of a dark brandy and poured myself a double. Only once I took a sip did Aramis speak again.

"Sit down, Nico."

I tossed the rest down my throat and slammed the glass on the top of the polished wood. "I'm not your fucking dog, Aramis. What do you want?"

He had the audacity to laugh. He'd lost his own sister and still found a way to make the sound. If I wasn't intensely curious about why he arranged this meeting, I'd have crushed him for it.

He blew a line of smoke into the air. "Don't look at me like that. Whatever you think about me, I think far worse about myself." His glare swept over me, something I couldn't define hardened the sharp lines of his face. They might have been siblings, but Milla had looked nothing like her brothers. "I can see why Camilla likes you so much."

"She—" My words faltered on what had to be a mistake on his part. "What do you mean *likes*? Camilla is dead—"

"Camilla Marchese is not dead." Aramis took a long breath, smoothed his hands down the pinstripes of his trousers. "My sister, Milla, is very much alive."

I sat down on the chaise across from the bench. It was impossible. "Are you fucking with me, Aramis?"

His brows jumped. "I lost two brothers a few days ago, Attano. I wouldn't joke about something like this."

"I saw her die! I was there when Felix shot her! I held her in my arms and watched the light fade from her eyes."

"What was she wearing?" His eyes slitted. It was a ridiculous question. Why would her dress matter in a time like this?

I thought back to the memory that replayed every time I shut my eyes. "She wore . . ." My voice trailed, recalling a detail I'd been too distressed to note in the moment. "She wore grey. A grey, simple dress."

Aramis offered a small nod, something rising with his breath, pushing back his shoulders. "And have you ever seen my sister wear grey?"

Never. She wore jewel tones and expensive fabrics of silk and satin—the spoiled little heiress she was. "I carried Milla's body back four miles through the foothills of the Wilds. I laid her in the ground and buried her myself next to my family."

"You buried our tailor, Sera." His voice cracked on the name. "She was a poly remnant of Mirth, one of her abilities being shifting. When we were trying to flee the city, the Firenzes attacked us with their hired hunters. Sera hid in this bench"—he tapped the seat below him—"and waited until Camilla could get away so she could take her identity and die wearing her face. It was always a . . . last resort."

"So Felix would think she was dead," I murmured.

Aramis nodded. "Camilla found out about the ship, which I'm sure she shared with you." When I nodded, he continued, "We've been working on a steam vessel for years. It was a project my father started when the storms first made passage to the Continent impossible. The union with the Firenzes promised a local investor, whom we were already on good terms with, and the opportunity to keep the company in friendly hands, or rather, away from the OIC. But they betrayed us in the end."

He started to make me nervous. If Milla was alive, why wasn't she here? "What is so important about her that you'd have to fake her death and ship her off? Is it her remnant?"

Aramis clenched his teeth, tapped the burning cigarillo in the ashtray as he stared at something far away. "You have to understand," he said, "that when my father died, it was my responsibility to protect Camilla. No matter how much she hated me, I had to keep her secret safe."

"I would never do anything that would threaten Milla's life," I said quickly, without hesitation. "Look, I understand you dislike me. I know you believe my family is to blame for the hardships yours has faced over the years. But you threw me in prison, Aramis, for a crime I didn't commit. You charged me with manslaughter after I pulled your sister's body from a burning car and scalded my arm in the process."

He paled a shade, recalling the day. "I was young and afraid once as well, Attano. Some choices we can't take back."

"But we can learn from them," I said. "Our families have made many mistakes concerning each other. It has cost us countless lives: fathers, uncles, and sisters. How many more will we lose before we learn our lesson? You can trust me, Aramis."

He nodded stiffly before standing from his seat and handed me a piece of paper. "Consider this, Nicolai. You have cared for my sister for six weeks. I have cared for her for twenty-one years. You'd be hesitant to trust anyone as well."

Unfolding the note, I read the contents at least twice before looking up at him again. It had to be a joke, but there was no mirth in his solemn stare. "A descendant of Chaos?"

He shook his head slowly. "Not a descendant. Camilla is an original. She's a Remni."

I stared at the words written in black ink on the ripped parchment. Chaos. Milla was a *Remni* of Chaos. Hells, it all made sense now.

"Aramis?" I spoke quietly, feeling as though my voice would break if I spoke too loud. "Where is my wife?"

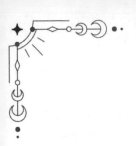
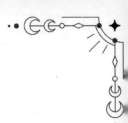

EPILOGUE
CAMILLA

Something slid just outside my door. No, not something, but someone. The sound of a still body being dragged across an unfinished floor. It was so unlike the other sounds in this place. The grinding of stone on stone, the wailing of a woman who'd been screaming for hours, the sharp split of salty wind as it snuck through the cracks in the walls.

And there wasn't a door at all, just four walls of solid obsidian and the darkness between them. The woman's screams had stopped shortly before the sliding sound. I would've worried for her if I wasn't so relieved not to hear her wailing anymore. This place was already icing my heart, and I couldn't fathom how Nico had lasted five years in this place and still had a sense of compassion.

"Who are you?" A voice from the darkness spoke. I jumped, pushing my back flush against the wall, realizing for the first time since they threw me in here that I wasn't alone.

"Milla," I said.

A considerable quiet followed before she replied, "I'm Vesper.

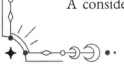

414

Callow is in here somewhere."

"Over here," a deep voice returned.

I pulled my knees tighter into my chest, even though my bareness was concealed by the lack of light. "What is this place?"

"We're in the tower. Congratulations, you just became interesting enough to become a specimen to the watchmen. What's your remnant control?"

"What does it matter?" I countered. I didn't care for Vesper's interrogation style.

Someone shifted in the room, a brush of skin against the coarse floor. "They only take the ones they don't have."

"What does that mean?" I asked to clarify.

"The remnants. They're collecting every kind from every saint and class. That's why I was wondering what remnant you wielded."

"You know a lot for being locked in here with me."

A snort came from the opposite side of the room. "The watchmen talk outside. We've been here long enough to piece together their conversations."

"How long exactly?"

He grunted. "Dunno. Days, maybe? Time is relative in the dark."

"Days?" The panic pitched my voice higher. I couldn't take another hour here, much less an entire day. The darkness was consuming, the kind that matched the back of my eyes, so I didn't know if I was awake or asleep. If this was a bad dream or a real-life nightmare.

The wall I leaned against began to shake, and I pushed away to the other end of the holding room just as the block of stone slid aside into a pocket in the wall. Three watchmen stood on the other side, two of them holding kerosene lamps to fill the hall behind them with beautiful, golden light.

Now that the holding room was dimly lit, I looked to each side to catch a glimpse of my companions . . . but I was alone.

I didn't have time to wonder where the voices came from when the officer in front threw something at my feet—a grey smock of a uniform.

"Am I supposed to wear that?"

The light of the kerosine outlined his silhouette, but I could feel the perversion in his words when he said, "You don't have to wear anything."

I snatched the wilted material and quickly tossed it over my body, grateful for a bit of modesty from their stares as the watchmen forced me to walk between them all. One of them had to wield a remnant, the way the floor and walls shifted for us as we ventured up a spiraling staircase built into the curved walls.

"Where are we going?" I asked the man's back. He said nothing as anticipated, but just as my legs began to ache in protest from the climb, the wall shifted before us to reveal a laboratory.

An oculus rounded the ceiling, revealing the first clear night sky of winter. It was the only pleasant view in the room, as crudely bent metal tubes and glass beakers lined the furthest curve of the wall. Sharp instruments, stained from recent use, cluttered a table nearby. The center of the floor was empty besides a pair of chains and dark stains glistening against the cobbled floor and an apparatus that hung from the metal framework doming the oculus.

From here, there was a perfect view of the prison beyond the tower. A multifaceted building composed of a large main tower that jutted from the black rock face of the island and dove deep into its heart. It was surrounded by a square base and eight corridors sprawling from the center building, each leading into a tower topped with a spire.

Beyond all of that, however, was the wall of storms that hovered over the Narrow Sea. In the distance, a veil of darkness briefly illumined by flashes of dry lightning veining inside an ominous cloud wall. The waves slapped the island as if they sought their own retribution from this place.

A woman stood from a desk shoved in the curve of the tower near the start of the windows. It took me a few minutes to register who I was looking at.

"You," I murmured. "I remember you."

The alchemist smiled. The last time she looked at me like that, she'd given me my familiar. "Hello, Camilla."

My heart shuddered. "I thought you were dead?"

"You aren't the only one who can fake their death." She pulled out a syringe from her apron pocket, twisting a long needle into the flange.

Fake my death? The question must've written itself in the expression on my face because the alchemist approached me with long, unhurried strides. "Everyone thinks you were killed, Camilla. There was a nice funeral and everything. My cousins in the Wet District sent word this morning, not realizing our men grabbed you at the last minute and snuck you here. I might wait to share with them the good news."

My racing heart sunk beneath my ribs. If they thought I was dead, then Nico must have thought so as well. Even my family—what was left of them—might not know the truth. Which meant no one was looking for me.

No one was coming for me.

Before I could step back, she lunged, thrusting the short needle into the base of my neck. "Don't worry, love," she hissed. "We're going to take good care of you."

The flames in my soul were doused before I could even ignite the wick of my power. Instead of becoming the fire from Oblivion, I was consumed by it.

ACKNOWLEDGMENTS

Thank you to my husband, first and foremost, for supporting my dream in every way possible. From forcing me out of the house to write away from the kids, picking up overtime at work to pay for my very pretty character art, and just making things happen every day so that I have the time and mental space to write books every day, I will always be most appreciative of how much you believe in me.

I started writing House of Bane only four weeks postpartum and having a creative outlet during such an emotionally stressful time was so therapeutic for me. Presley, one day you'll get to read the book I wrote as I held you when you were only months old. I hope it makes you proud, and for the love of our relationship, please skip Chapter 35. To my oldest child, Nash, thank you for being the coolest kid. I love working while you "read" your books next me in the office. Thank you for reminding me how much I love being a mom first and motivating me to chase my goals.

Thank you to my family. To my mom, you never fail to hide your pride in me when I talk to you about my latest achievement, no matter how big or small it may be. And my sister, Britni, thank you for reading every single book I write. It means so much to me, and I probably wouldn't be here if you hadn't of suggested I read a certain SJM series all those years ago.

Thank you to my editor, Brittany Corely! I'm so lucky to get to work with you, book after book. Your enthusiasm for my words and my story has made this a book I am proud of and excited to share. I'm not sure where I would be right now if I hadn't of had you in my corner at the very beginning of my indie journey, but I will always be grateful to you and your friendship.

Thank you to my Beta readers, Devon and Tori, who combed through the rough version of this book and helped me make it shine! Thank you to all my ARC readers for helping me share this story with the world, for all the hype you helped create, and the dream you supported with every friend you shared it with, every post you made on social media, and every rating you left online.

Thank you to my readers! Thank you, thank you, thank you for taking a chance on me. I am so humbled to have my story in your hands, and it means the world to this girl in the middle of Small Town, USA that you chose to spend your time in my world when I know you have endless TBRs to get to. I appreciate you more than you will ever know!